New York Times bestselling author **Maisey Yates** lives in rural Oregon with her three children and her husband, whose chiseled jaw and arresting features continue to make her swoon. She feels the epic trek she takes several times a day from her office to her coffee maker is a true example of her pioneer spirit.

USA TODAY bestselling and RITA® Award–nominated author **Caitlin Crews** loves writing romance. She teaches her favorite romance novels in creative-writing classes at places like UCLA Extension's prestigious Writers' Program, where she finally gets to utilize the MA and PhD in English literature she received from the University of York in England. She currently lives in the Pacific Northwest with her very own hero and too many pets. Visit her at caitlincrews.com.

Nicole Helm grew up with her nose in a book and the dream of one day becoming a writer. Luckily, after a few failed career choices, she gets to follow that dream—writing down-to-earth contemporary romance and romantic suspense. From farmers to cowboys, Midwest to *the* West, Nicole writes stories about people finding themselves and finding love in the process. She lives in Missouri with her husband and two sons and dreams of someday owning a barn.

Jackie Ashenden writes dark, emotional stories with alpha heroes who've just gotten the world to their liking only to have it blown apart by their kick-ass heroines. She lives in Auckland, New Zealand, with her husband, the inimitable Dr. Jax, two kids and two rats. When she's not torturing alpha males and their gutsy heroines, she can be found drinking chocolate martinis, reading anything she can lay her hands on, wasting time on social media or being forced to go mountain biking with her husband. To keep up-to-date with Jackie's new releases and other news, sign up to her newsletter at jackieashenden.com.

A Cowboy for All Seasons

MAISEY YATES

CAITLIN CREWS
NICOLE HELM · JACKIE ASHENDEN

HQN

H
HQN®

PLEASE RECYCLE
THIS PRODUCT IS RECYCLABLE

Recycling programs
for this product may
not exist in your area.

ISBN-13: 978-1-335-01409-2

A Cowboy for All Seasons

Copyright © 2020 by Harlequin Books S.A.

Spring
Copyright © 2020 by Caitlin Crews

Summer
Copyright © 2020 by Nicole Helm

Fall
Copyright © 2020 by Maisey Yates

Winter
Copyright © 2020 by Jackie Ashenden
Copyright © 2020 by Jeff Johnson, interior illustrations

All rights reserved. No part of this book may be used or reproduced in any manner whatsoever without written permission except in the case of brief quotations embodied in critical articles and reviews.

This is a work of fiction. Names, characters, places and incidents are either the product of the author's imagination or are used fictitiously. Any resemblance to actual persons, living or dead, businesses, companies, events or locales is entirely coincidental.

This edition published by arrangement with Harlequin Books S.A.

For questions and comments about the quality of this book,
please contact us at CustomerService@Harlequin.com.

HQN
22 Adelaide St. West, 40th Floor
Toronto, Ontario M5H 4E3, Canada
www.Harlequin.com

Printed in U.S.A.

CONTENTS

SPRING   7
Caitlin Crews

SUMMER   139
Nicole Helm

FALL   279
Maisey Yates

WINTER   421
Jackie Ashenden

Spring

Caitlin Crews

To Nicole, Maisey and Jackie
for making this so magical.

To Flo for believing in the magic.

And for Grandma Junes everywhere, who loved
so hard and so true it stays long after they go.
I love you, Gram and Nana. Still and always.

SPRING

Dearest Keira,

It's a very strange thing to get old, to know that eventually the world will go on without you. To see clearly your successes, and your mistakes, and still not know what you could have done about either.

You, my poised girl, so full of elegance and surety in yourself, have filled my life with happiness since the day you were born. Summers with you always reminded me how much the world had to offer my four wonderful, vibrant, different girls.

I've missed you, and though I know you won't admit it to yourself, you've missed your heart, as well. It's all good and well to see what the world has to offer, but sometimes only home can bring you true change.

I have many things to ask of you this spring, and I doubt you'll be surprised I've asked you to spend this particular season at home, tending to the land and the cattle. I know you'll appreciate watching the season bloom around you, and find a way to do that yourself.

First, you'll need to face your past and make

peace with your choices—past ones, and the ones that await you in the future.

Let my spirit guide you in all that you do and let this house take care of you as it has always cared for me.

Love always,
Grandma June

CHAPTER ONE

KEIRA LONG WAS finally ready to face her ghosts.

That was what she told herself as she climbed out of the car she'd driven down from Seattle, packed full of all her worldly possessions—which told a sad, small tale about her past five years—and faced the house that had stood for over a hundred years and been the only safe space in her life for what felt like much longer than that.

Grandma June's farmhouse. Keira's favorite place on earth.

And for the first time in her life, without Grandma June, whom they'd lost just over three weeks ago.

Keira had promised herself she wouldn't cry, so she looked at the old farmhouse instead. It stood stout and settled against the moody March afternoon, no matter its weathered paint and signs of age and care. Keira chose to take that as a sign. She'd left Seattle before dawn and driven all the way down the interstate, then over the familiar rolling hills on autopilot, skirting her hometown of Jasper Creek, Oregon, and taking the country roads she knew so well.

A wave of sadness washed over her, but she concentrated fiercely on the dogwood tree that stood in front of the house. In a matter of weeks the buds she saw fighting for purchase on its branches would burst into color—a glorious pink that made Keira feel light and happy every time she saw it. It didn't matter that it wasn't in bloom yet. It would be.

Keira breathed past the sadness and tried to let it go. That was what the funeral had been for. Grief and ghosts and trying to hold on to the past when it was already gone.

She'd flown down three weeks ago to stand in the pretty little church in town and say her goodbyes to her grandmother. She'd stood in a pew with two of her three cousins, JJ and Lila, and wished that they were all still as close as they'd been when they were kids. She could have used the sort of easy intimacy they'd all taken for granted back then: leaning on each other's shoulders, crowding together in a closet in Grandma's house, giggling through a game of sardines. That kind of closeness had seemed far away to her then, wearing stiff black clothes that fit wrong and that she knew she would hate forever and never wear again.

Still, it had been good that they were there, if sad that no one had seen their youngest cousin, Bella, in far too long. Keira was the only child of problematic parents so she'd always viewed her cousins as her sisters. They knew things about her no one else did, or ever would. And at the funeral, no matter how they'd all grown apart, JJ and Lila had been the only members of her family she'd wanted to see…as well as providing an excellent buffer.

There were ghosts Keira hadn't particularly wanted to face. Worse, there were her parents. Keira had spent the last five years trying her best to get over them as she forged her way through her very own adult life. Wasn't that the project of any woman in her twenties? It was certainly Keira's.

And it was a project that a season spent in Grandma June's beloved old farmhouse could only accelerate.

Keira had parked her car where she always had, hating that she was the only one here now. All she could hear was the sound of the wind blustering about over the hills and around the eaves of the house. The air was still cold, holding on to winter and the snowcapped mountains in the distance, but there was a softness in it that Keira chose to think was hope.

She breathed in deep, then let it out slow, imagining that could clean her—clear her—from the inside out.

She was ready to be new. She was ready to take on her grandmother's challenge and spend her season here. Each of her cousins—assuming anyone could find Bella—would do the same.

Keira liked the symmetry of it. Four cousins. Four seasons. Four chances to...

Well. Keira didn't really know what her cousins might get out of their time here. She only knew that for her, it was time to come home. She couldn't go to any of the houses she'd grown up in because they'd changed hands so quickly, in line with her parents' roller-coaster fortunes. And she certainly wouldn't use the word *home* to describe life with her parents. She'd spent as much time as she could with Grandma growing up, had left for college at eighteen and had never slept under her parents' roof—assuming they even had a roof this week—again.

Maybe it was better to say that Keira was ready to make her own home, at last. And this farmhouse was the closest thing she'd ever had.

Keira tucked her hands in her jean pockets, glad she'd worn a warmer outer layer to ward off the chill as she started across the cold, muddy ground toward the front porch. She knew this walk, from the crunch of gravel beneath her feet, to the creak of the gate in the picket fence that surrounded the house. She knew the uneven plank on the porch that caught at her bare feet every summer. She loved the enduring charm of every inch of the place—a little bit ramshackle and a little bit worn, but always welcoming.

She found the key where it was always hidden under the mat. Grandma June had liked keys that looked like keys, and the one that opened the door looked like a proper antique. There was scrollwork and a compass, and Keira liked the weight of it in her palm.

She fit the key in the lock, jiggling it to get the door open.

Do not cry, she ordered herself as she opened the door to step inside.

Because she was forced to confront the fact that no matter how perfect and welcoming the house looked to her, no matter how familiar it smelled as she stood in the hall, her grandmother wasn't going to be here.

There was no scent of anything baking in the kitchen, the way there had been every time she'd come to visit. There wasn't the light Grandma June had brought to the place, even when she wasn't in the same room. The windows were shut up tight, when Keira knew Grandma June would have opened them all up on a moody spring day like today.

Keira squeezed her eyes shut against a new prick of tears, and could almost feel her grandmother again. As if she was standing there, just around the corner out of sight, waiting for Keira to come in and say hello.

So she did.

"Hi, Grandma June," Keira said out loud, into the deep stillness. "I'm here."

She instantly felt foolish, and flushed.

But it was as if a weight had lifted. As if the house had been waiting for a proper greeting, and now Keira's grief could subside a little.

She set about unpacking her car and moving herself in to her favorite bedroom upstairs, the way she would have any of the summers she'd stayed here. Her parents had always dropped her off as soon as they could reasonably get away with it. One year it had been April, which hardly made it a summer vacation, but neither Keira nor Grandma June had been all that interested in twelve-year-old Keira accompanying her parents to their latest couldn't-fail, get-rich-quick scheme in Vegas.

Michael and Katy Long had accomplished nothing on that trip, of course. Because all of their schemes ended in pain, tears and humiliation. Like the year Dad had claimed they were going to go on a big adventure, which involved moving from their trailer into a tent in one of the campgrounds on the outskirts of Jasper Creek. *Adventure* was one way of putting it. *Terrifying* and *scarring* were the words that leaped to Keira's mind.

Keira had hated every second of the out-of-control roller-coaster ride that was her entire childhood. She'd learned early on that the kids around her in their happy, stable houses, where things made sense, couldn't understand what she went through. And she was never, ever to tattle. To anyone.

Keira had always been perfectly happy not to talk about her parents, to keep her head down and to dream about turning eighteen and finally being free.

She'd always preferred it here in this farmhouse,

where she knew there was a bed for her and food in the fridge. She might have to do chores, but the reward was feeling like she belonged. Like she was safe. Like the house would be here in the morning no matter what.

When she was done emptying her car and arranging her things the way she liked them, she found herself walking down the hall, with its creaky floorboards, to Grandma's room. She sat there on the end of her bed the way she had in those later summers when she was older, too conscious of the kind of future she had before her if she wasn't careful, and so in love she couldn't see straight.

She ran her hand over the quilt her grandmother had made by hand, then looked out the windows to where the trees were starting to look as if they might snap out of their winter slumber and make a run at spring. Keira felt much the same.

The end of this bed was where she'd sat and poured her heart out to the only person who she'd known would, if not always understand her, support her. No matter what. The only cousin she'd confided in back then had been JJ, as they were so close in age, but she hadn't even told JJ all the details—afraid that that would be exactly the sort of tattling her father had always warned her against. She'd saved her darkest truths for Grandma June. Sitting here again felt like completing a very long circle.

Grandma June was how Keira had gotten up the nerve to apply for college. Then to actually go, when her parents had only laughed at the notion. They'd pressured Keira to stay in Jasper Creek, marry the man who happened to be a member of the prominent West family, who hated her father, and settle down right out of high school despite her scholarship—because it would benefit them. Because her parents were always thinking about themselves. And as for the rest of the small town of Jasper Creek, the undercurrent to every conversation back then had always seemed to be that the daughter of known liar Michael Long certainly couldn't expect to do *better* than marrying a West, could she?

Grandma June had shrugged her shoulders and told Keira that she wasn't aware love was a Black Friday sale, available only one day and gone forever the next.

If it's love, Grandma said, *it will find its way.*

And four years later Grandma June had sat next to her and gathered her in a hug when Keira had broken her own heart into pieces because she knew it was the right thing to do—no matter how much it hurt.

"You'd be proud of me," Keira said out loud now, and it was already easier than the first time. It felt perfectly normal to talk to quiet rooms filled with her grandmother's things. "I saw him at the funeral. And you were right all along. I built it up in my head and I felt some stuff, but it was fine."

Grandma had always told Keira that there was no need to avoid her past. That pasts had a way of catching up to a person the harder they tried to run. And that Remy West, who had been Keira's first love— her first everything, from kiss to marriage proposal to heartbreak—was no reason to avoid coming home to Jasper Creek.

And maybe Keira had been using him as an excuse, at first. She'd graduated from college and turned Remy down in the same weekend, and she knew that no one in this town was ever likely to understand that decision.

But she'd done it. And the past five years hadn't been easy, but they'd been rewarding. She'd carved out a life in Seattle. She had her own savings now. A retirement plan. She had no debt. She had quit her job so she could live in her grandmother's farmhouse for a whole spring without risking anything.

For a girl who'd been raised by a con-man father and a mother whose entire life was about indulging his every whim and scheme, it was nothing short of a miracle.

Keira pressed her palm against the faded quilt, and let the emotion roll over her. It was still so hard to believe she was never going to hear her grandmother's voice again. The particular way Grandma June said her name. The magic of her chortle when she was trying not to laugh. The cards she sent on every birthday, without fail, that had Keira smiling the moment she saw the distinctive handwriting on the envelope.

Not to mention her full name. *Miss Keira Catharine Long*, the envelope always read.

A deep sob clenched her in its fist as it hit her, truly hit her, that this would be the first year that card wouldn't appear.

Keira stood up with a sigh. She wiped her eyes, happy to see all the photographs on the dresser, right where they belonged, including the one of all four cousins taken that last, sweet summer they'd all been together here. Then she headed back downstairs.

The sun was already heading toward the mountains outside, sending cooler air gusting through the farmhouse as the sky darkened. Keira loved it. She'd picked up a few staples from the big supermarket out on the freeway—the better to avoid the actual town of Jasper Creek and all the people she didn't want to see—and found herself moving around the kitchen as if it was hers.

This kitchen was more familiar to her than the tiny, efficient apartment she'd lived in for the past five years. She pulled out what Grandma June had called *the fancy plates* and made herself an indulgent dinner of cheese and crackers, and a big glass of wine. She took it all out to the front porch, and sat there wrapped in the blanket Grandma June had knitted one winter. She could feel the weather changing, the dampness moving in, and what was left of winter rustling around in the fields. The forecast hadn't said there would be rain for a day or so, but this was rural Oregon, where the land did as it pleased.

And the longer she sat there, the deeper she seemed to sink into her own bones.

As if it wasn't the comfortable old house that was settling behind her, but Keira who was settling back into place at last.

She finished the cheese and the crackers and tipped her head back to watch the stars come out, remembering all the summer nights she'd sat right here on the wide top step wondering what would become of her if she didn't get away from her parents. What she would do to make sure she could leave at eighteen and never go back.

And above all, what she should—what she *could*—do about Remy.

Thinking his name didn't hurt the way it used to, but she'd worked hard to achieve that. So hard she'd almost convinced herself she wouldn't react to seeing him at all.

Then she'd walked into her grandmother's funeral, and there he was.

Ouch.

When they were younger, the age gap between them

had been only one of the reasons they were a community scandal. But these days, the handful of years seemed like nothing. Remy had looked as if each one of those years had weathered him—but that only made him look better.

Which should have been impossible.

She and Remy had stared at each other, there in the foyer of the church. Keira had planned it all out in her head on the flight down. She'd be mature, obviously. Gracious. Quietly *aware* of their past without being *nostalgic*—especially with the whole town looking on, and no doubt muttering about the uppity Long girl who thought she was better than that steady, hardworking West boy who'd so foolishly defied his family for her.

But there had been no need for any of that.

Remy had gazed back at her, unsmiling. The eyes she remembered as hazel streaked with gold had looked dark and distinctly unfriendly. He'd nodded his head, acknowledging her, and she'd been…paralyzed. She hadn't been able to smile. Hadn't been able to say anything, and certainly nothing *gracious*. She hadn't even been able to offer her own polite nod in return. She'd only stared back at him, frozen, while her stomach flipped over and took its time sinking down into the floor.

She really hadn't expected it to affect her so much, all these years later. She hadn't expected him to cause that same wallop she remembered so well. Surely everyone had moved on, she'd told herself on the plane. That was what happened when people broke up. They moved on. They grew and changed. And they left behind…all of that.

Keira hadn't expected Remy to greet her with a wide

smile and a big old hug, the way he would have back in the day, but she hadn't been prepared for the extent of his, well… She couldn't really call it coldness. He simply hadn't been the Remy she knew.

He'd looked like an older, harder man.

And out in the dark, on the front porch of the farmhouse on a spring night that was turning downright cold a little too fast, Keira found herself rubbing at her heart as if she could make all those jangly old feelings dissipate.

That was the thing with hard choices. Keira had made hers and she couldn't regret them. Not when she'd done things she knew she couldn't—and wouldn't—have done if she'd stayed here to be with Remy.

But that didn't mean it didn't hurt.

Especially when she was back in Jasper Creek and the road not taken wasn't theoretical anymore, but looked a whole lot like the dirt road that wound up to the West family ranch in the far hills. She knew, down to the second, how long it would take her to jump in her car and drive out that way, how fast to take the wicked curves that cut through the forest, and—

"That is not helpful information to remember," she told herself.

Maybe a little too fiercely.

Keira went back in the house and set about cleaning up after herself the way she knew Grandma June would have expected. She climbed the stairs, testing her weight on the creaky boards that Grandma had called her insurance policy against any amorous teen boys—they'd all groaned in pretend horror at the idea—and found her bed. She considered showering in the weak upstairs shower, but couldn't face it until she investi-

gated it for any unwelcome spiders in the cold light of
day. Instead, she piled the old rusted iron-frame bed
high with all the blankets and quilts she could find and
snuggled down deep into the embrace of it, letting the
sound of the breeze through the still-bare trees outside
lull her to sleep.

And when she woke up again, it was with a jolt as
the light snapped on in the small bedroom.

Keira shot straight up in bed, then scrambled back
against the iron rails of the headboard as she saw the
figure of a man—

But in the next second, she recognized him.

She suspected she would always recognize him.
Anytime, anywhere.

Remy.

She was plastered against the head of the bed, her
pulse galloping around inside her. She blinked, trying
to make sense of the fact that Remy West—the man
who'd cast his shadow over most of her life—was now
casting that same shadow here in an upstairs bedroom
at Grandma June's house. At—and Keira had to glance
at the clock on her bedside table twice to make sure
she wasn't hallucinating—four thirteen in the morning.

He was dressed like the cowboy he was. He'd worked
his father's ranch since before he could walk, and now
he walked low and loose, like he was not only prepared
for any eventuality the land could throw at him, but was
more than capable of handling it.

And if she thought he'd looked grim at Grandma
June's funeral, it was worse closer up.

Or better, a sly part of her suggested.

He looked carved from implacable stone, and yet
that did very little to take away from the fact that Rem-

ington Eli West was the most beautiful man Keira had ever seen. When she was a teenager, or anytime since.

He was tall and folks were always tempted to call him lanky, but he had too much rangy muscle for that. He was standing in the glare of the overhead light dressed in a cowboy hat, a flannel shirt, jeans and boots—and he was mouthwatering.

When they were younger, he'd had a focus and intensity that Keira had found as overwhelming as it was thrilling. He'd brought that into everything he did. *That boy isn't dating just to date*, Grandma had told Keira at the beginning of it all. He'd been in his early twenties then, and there'd been absolutely no doubt in anyone's mind that he was already a man.

All these years later, there was even less doubt in Keira's.

"What are you doing here?" she asked while her heart was still performing calisthenics in her chest.

From the fear and shock, she told herself. That was all.

His eyes glittered with something that looked—and felt—a lot like temper. His jaw might as well have been granite.

"Are you wearing my T-shirt?" he demanded.

Keira was definitely not prepared for his voice. That *voice*.

Low, raspy, dark and nothing short of delicious. And she could feel herself responding, the way he'd taught her all those years ago, readying herself, flushing, melting—

She yanked the nearest quilt up to her chin.

"I have no idea," she said. "It's just the shirt I sleep in."

That was a lie. The green-and-gold duck that had once been bright on the black background was fading now, but she knew it was there. She knew exactly whose T-shirt it was. And she could tell from the way a muscle tensed in that hard jaw of his that Remy did, too.

"It's great to see you again, Remy," she said, the way she'd practiced before the funeral. Three weeks ago she'd been half-sick with grief. Weak. But having gotten the first sighting out of the way, there was no need to wallow in it any further. "I mean that, though I think I would mean it more if it weren't the middle of the night."

He stared at her for so long she almost started squirming. Almost. She could certainly feel her cheeks get hot.

Remy kept studying her as if she was some kind of science experiment. Possibly one that had gone horribly awry.

"This isn't the middle of the night," he said after what felt like a very uncomfortable lifetime. "It's the beginning of the working day. Why are you still in bed?"

"The working day?"

Keira was slightly more awake now, thanks to the minor heart attack. Her hair was probably matted to the side of her head, which was certainly not how she'd envisioned running into her ex again. She told herself not to be so shallow, but when she rubbed her hands over her face in an attempt to wake herself up, she smoothed down her hair, too.

"I got a letter from your grandmother," Remy told her shortly. "She told me you were coming to deal with the cattle. Guess what, princess? We deal with the cattle in the middle of the night. Every night."

Keira managed not to flinch. Remy had sometimes called her *princess*, back when. He'd called her *prin-*

cess because she wasn't one. He'd called her *princess*, with a laugh, as he'd taught her how to handle the herd the way they did on his father's ranch. He'd called her *princess* because she was his.

And she didn't have to know a single thing that had happened to him over the past five years to understand that he was not using the word as an endearment tonight.

"I also got a letter, but it didn't mention that we would be…" She cleared her throat. "Mine said I was supposed to handle the cows."

"Yeah? You remember how?"

Keira waved a vague hand. She'd decided to dive straight in to what she was called to do here, the same way she'd jumped into her new life in Seattle—a comparison she thought better of making out loud. "Grandma June always hired hands to help her out as needed. And I've been doing a lot of research."

"Research."

The flat line of his mouth curved a little, but she was pretty sure it was derision, not amusement. And coming from him, it left her breathless. Hollow.

"Good thing you have that college degree, then. You can read all those books. Or—" Remy jerked his chin toward the door, his dark eyes glittering like he hated her, a possibility Keira really hadn't allowed herself to consider "—you can get on up out of that bed, come outside and do some real work for a change. Your choice."

CHAPTER TWO

THE DEVIL WAS back in town.

And wearing his favorite long-lost Oregon Ducks T-shirt.

Remy West glared at the woman who'd ripped out his heart, stomped on it until it was dust beneath her shoes and then kicked it off to the side of the road on her way out of town. He congratulated himself on behaving like a gentleman.

Or as close to a gentleman as he could, given the circumstances.

Though if he had this to do over, he would rethink the part where he busted into her bedroom and found her…in a bed.

That had been nothing but dumb.

Because the last thing he needed to do was fill up his head with images of Keira Long, soft and sleepy and warm, and wearing nothing *but* his T-shirt.

He'd be better off pounding his own head into the nearest wall.

"But—" she began, then stopped herself.

By biting down on her lower lip.

And this was the trouble with Keira, right here.

She never *looked* evil. Right now, for example, his old T-shirt clung to her entirely too lovingly. And made him remember…too much. Her soft brown eyes were still sleepy and her mouth was as wide and full as he remembered it, and her nibbling on it didn't exactly help. Her hair was lighter, falling around her shoulders with a lot more gold mixed in to the usual mess of different browns and reds. It hung around her in a tangle that reminded him of more things he ought to forget already, but he'd cut off his own hands before he let himself touch it.

Or her.

"Okay," she said, her voice much too even. The Keira he remembered would have blown up at him for calling her *princess* like that, to say nothing of the college crack. "I bet that dig made you feel good. I don't blame you. But I really don't know—"

"There's no argument here," he said, cutting her off. "Grandma June hired me to take care of her herd years ago and that's what I've been doing. I'm guessing you're here to decide what to do with them now that she's gone. I'm not going to sit around and research with you, Keira. If you want to know about the cattle, you're going to have to come on out and take a look at them yourself."

Grandma June had always treated him like family instead of a hired hand, but it had occurred to Remy that the woman who'd had no trouble refusing his ring might take a different view of the situation. Grandma June had been so sure the two of them could work together, and Remy hadn't had it in him to tell her that the likelihood was that Keira would show up, make a big gesture toward handling her grandmother's herd and then vanish the minute her season here was up.

He was so sure that was how it would go that he hadn't bothered to put out feelers for other work.

Another potentially bad idea, he admitted.

"Wait a minute." Keira frowned at him. "Why do you work on my grandmother's land? Why don't you work on your own?"

It was funny how a man could have wanted a particular conversation for years, and then when it started, want nothing to do with it at all.

"Funny you should ask that," he said. Maybe a little darkly.

She tied her hair into a knot on the back of her head the way she had years ago, and he wanted to punch himself because he still found it effortless and elegant and—

Focus.

"Is it funny?" Keira asked, and the fact she sounded good-humored made it worse. "You don't look like you think it's funny."

He didn't want to consider the things he liked about her, such as the fact she was the only person alive who didn't take him too seriously, and yet took him very seriously at the same time. Most people usually fell into whichever camp irritated him more in a given moment. But not Keira.

Who he'd once imagined had seen all those jagged parts of him and loved him, anyway.

Sometimes the amount of things he'd been wrong about when it came to her threatened to take him down like a vicious March storm, sweeping over the hills and lashing the fields with its fury.

But not today.

He could feel the smile on his face then, and it wasn't nice. "It turns out that once you turn your back on your family and decide you're going to marry the daughter of their sworn enemy, but then don't, it makes it all a little too complicated to carry on ranching the family land together. Your grandmother offered me an opportunity and I took it."

"Really? And then what? You go on back home to your father's land and pretend that everything's—"

"I don't live on my father's land. I live here." He glared at her, because he didn't want to say this next part. "In the cabin."

She blinked. And Remy told himself he didn't care that he could no longer read every single thought that moved over her pretty face. He clearly hadn't been all that good at it in the first place, or he would have seen it coming. He would have known that she was going to throw his love—and his ring—in his face. And Lord knew he hadn't had the faintest clue.

"The cabin?" She said it very carefully, as if the word might hurt her. "You don't mean…?"

She didn't say *our cabin*, the way she would have years ago. He figured her sense of self-preservation must have kicked in.

"Yes, Keira," he said, and he wished he sounded angry. Cold. Something other than rough and still too dark. "The same cabin."

It was a cabin tucked into the woods on the edge of one of the higher pastures, that Grandma June—who had insisted that everyone in the younger generation call her that, even if she wasn't their actual grandmother—claimed was the first place her own parents had lived as newlyweds way back when.

It was the cabin where Keira had found him when she was seventeen, where she had kissed him, both sweet and bold all at once. Then blushed, bright and hot and cute when she'd told him she'd never done that before. The cabin where, the following summer, she'd cried when she'd told him she loved him, but that she wanted to go to college because she didn't want to turn into her mother.

He hadn't known what that meant. Keira had never talked much about her parents and she'd gone out of her way to keep them all from spending any time together back then. *His* parents had been pretty clear that Keira's parents were awful, Keira was too needy and fragile to be a rancher's woman, and as the future owner of one fifth of the West ranch, he needed to be careful about such things.

All red flags, in retrospect.

But the cabin was where Remy had ignored those red flags. It was where he'd promised himself to her. He'd promised her he'd wait for her to go off and get her degree, if that was what she wanted. And then he'd accepted the gift of her innocence, the most precious thing he'd ever been given, with a reverence that could still shake him now if he let the memory sneak up on him.

He obviously worked hard to make sure it didn't. But then, usually, she wasn't right in front of him.

The cabin was where they'd spent time together when she'd come home from college, away from red flags and family members alike. It was where they'd told each other stories of the future they'd have, together. It was where they'd dreamed. Laughed. And loved each other with such intensity, Remy was surprised the building still stood.

And it was the cabin where, after Keira graduated with honors at the top of her class, Remy had gone down on one knee and offered her the quietly elegant ring he'd bought because it suited her so perfectly. He'd been imagining it on her finger for years.

He'd been completely blindsided when she'd said no. *Blindsided* was a mild way to put it.

"I had no idea anyone was living there," she said now. Quietly. "Especially not you."

"I've been living there for five years."

She frowned. "And your family is really okay with you—"

"Keira." He belted out her name as if it was a curse. Because as it happened, it was his favorite one. "You don't get to ask me these questions."

Her face looked pale. But he told himself he didn't care.

"You have three minutes," he told her. "Get dressed and come outside. This is already taking too much time out of my schedule."

He turned to go, but her voice stopped him.

"I'm sorry," she said, low and soft. "I didn't mean to be…too familiar."

"You're not too anything," he said without turning back around. "Except late."

He pushed his way out of the bedroom and made his way out of the darkened farmhouse, annoying himself by leaving a trail of light behind him so Keira wouldn't fall down the stairs and break her neck. He wasn't sure he breathed again until he was out on that porch. A porch that should have been sagging from the weight of all the memories he had of sitting out here with Keira, keeping his hands to himself while Grandma June was there to supervise.

But the only thing that felt structurally unsound around here was him.

"You have no idea what you're doing, old lady," he muttered to the hint of dawn in the sky up over the hills.

He used to call June Gable that. *Watch yourself, old lady*, he'd say when he'd find her storming around the wet, muddy fields in rubber boots with a raincoat wrapped around her, as if she thought she could intimidate the herd into obeying her commands.

Watch yourself right back, she would reply with a little cackle at the end. *You're too young to be this curmudgeonly.*

I'm old in my soul, Grandma June, he'd told her once.

That time, she hadn't cackled. *Everyone thinks that, young man*, she'd told him. *Right up until the morning they wake up and discover that arthritis hurts a lot worse than their emotional baggage ever could.*

Remy had adored her. His father, well-known rancher Flint West, was a hard man who'd had only sons and had expected each and every one of them to grow up as tough as he was. Remy was the third of five, all named after guns of one sort or another, because why not stay on brand? And Remy's mother, Annette, was not exactly the nurturing kind. She'd always preferred the cattle to her boys, and had often joked that she should have branded the kids right along with the calves. His parents had been kind enough, but never coddling.

Grandma June had always been a revelation to Remy. He'd never worried about being tough enough for her, or whether he was living up to *her* expectations of what it meant to be a West and the kind of commitment *she* expected him to make to the land. Every moment he spent in Grandma June's presence, it was because she thought the world of him. It had been that simple. He couldn't seem to get out from under the weight of his grief at losing her.

And the footsteps he heard on the porch behind him didn't help any.

He glanced over when she got there, and hated himself for the way his whole body tightened at the sight of her. Keira had thrown on jeans, boots and a long-sleeved plaid shirt, and put her hair in a loose braid over one shoulder. She looked like every dream he still had of her—gorgeous in that down-to-earth way of hers and happy to see him again.

Because she had the nerve to smile at him.

That damn smile of hers that outdid the rising sun.

"Let's go," she said.

As if this was the life they'd dreamed about together all those years ago, when she'd been the one to walk away from it.

Remy ground his teeth together, swallowed down something mean that he'd regret later once he got a grip on himself and stalked toward his truck. He knew she was following him when he heard the creak of the gate. Then her boots on the gravel drive behind him.

The driver's-side window was down despite the kick of the March morning because Remy liked the country air in his face. It reminded him who he was. And at the moment, that window was filled with the black-and-white face of his seven-year-old border collie, Waylon.

The dog froze, and Remy knew why.

Just like he knew why Keira stopped walking behind him.

"Is that...?" she breathed into the still morning.

Remy scowled at Waylon, who usually responded to that particular expression with instant and abject obedience.

But not today. He ducked his head, looked from

Remy to Keira and then enacted his inevitable betrayal by barking joyously and leaping out of the window to get to her.

Remy turned around and watched the dog who until this moment had been his best friend on this earth—who Keira had helped pick out from a litter over in Gold Valley when he was only weeks old—bark and lick and basically make a fool of himself over her.

No more bacon for you, buddy, Remy promised him silently. *Ever.*

But no matter how he glared, his traitor of a dog continued to shower Keira with love and delight, even though she'd left them both.

Keira was crouched down, rubbing Waylon's belly and making those sweet little noises she used to croon at him when he was a puppy. Reducing Waylon, a well-trained herding dog who did the bulk of the work some days and was renowned across Jasper Creek for his abilities, into nothing more than a squirming, silly puppy.

The sky was getting lighter, and there was no disguising the amused, knowing look on Keira's face when she looked up at him again. "I'm surprised you didn't teach him to bite me on sight."

Remy couldn't help himself. He felt the corner of his mouth kick up. "I did. This is outright treachery."

She laughed and continued rubbing Waylon's belly as he gazed up at her in adoration. "But such cute treachery. How can you be mad?"

And for a moment, there in the yard outside Grandma June's house, Remy couldn't think of a reason. Everything felt easy. The way it used to.

The way it hadn't in a long time.

But then that was all part of the same betrayal, wasn't

it? Did it matter how cute treachery was? It was still treacherous. She might be back now, but she'd still left. And she was only here because of her grandmother's letter-writing campaign, not because she wanted to be here. Or wanted Remy back, for that matter. An enthusiastic welcome on Waylon's part didn't change that.

Remy lost his smile. He let out the sharp whistle that even Waylon didn't dare ignore. The dog bounded up, then jumped into the truck when Remy opened the door. Keira followed, too, sliding into the passenger side with that same ease of hers, graceful and smooth, that had always made him a little crazy when they were younger.

And it was betrayal piled on betrayal this morning, because it made him a little crazy now, too.

Remy drove out into Grandma June's property, through fields that upstart developers from places like Portland or San Francisco were always trying to turn into vineyards, claiming Jasper Creek was the next Napa Valley. He wasn't opposed to wine, but he didn't see how turning unspoiled pastureland into clogged country highways packed full of drunken tourists pouring themselves in and out of wineries was anything to aspire to.

He took Keira on a chore-laden tour of what he supposed now belonged to her and her cousins, if the rumor around town was right. He wouldn't have wanted to be the one who had to tell Katy Long that her mother hadn't left her a thing. Not Katy or her two sisters, who everyone knew had been nothing but disappointments to their mother and father.

Remy had always accepted the local narrative about Keira's mother and her sisters without comment. Grandma June was a delight and her daughters had broken her heart, anyway. That was the story people told.

Though it felt a little more complicated these days, now that Remy was the West brother who'd gone his own way against his parents' wishes.

Not that anyone dared talk about Annette West's heart. Not in her hearing.

None of which he shared with Keira as he reintroduced her to the land.

"I always forget how beautiful it is here," she said with a sigh when they were up in the high pasture, both of them going out of their way not to look in the direction of the cabin. "Seattle's gorgeous, of course. I loved my walk to work. And the fact that work itself was in marketing and branding coffee, which was almost like not working at all, which made the walk even better. On a perfect, crisp day, when the mountain was out and the water sparkled blue in every direction, you might be forgiven if you thought Seattle was the prettiest place in the world. But I don't think so. I think it's right here in this valley. Moody, green and rich, inviting—"

"Are you writing an essay?" he asked, feeling bad-tempered and surly.

Or more than usual, that was.

Everything about her was getting to him. The small talk, for one thing. On and on, merrily, as if she didn't notice that he was responding in as few syllables as possible. As if he was any guy she might have found herself with for a day out in the fields. She'd good-naturedly done her share of the chores. He knew perfectly well she could repair a fence, having taught her himself when they were kids, so he shouldn't have been so irritated when that was what she did. She'd even brought her own work gloves.

As if everything was *fine*.

She was driving him crazy.

Her rich brown gaze found his, and held. "Oh, I see," she murmured. "Was I supposed to come out on this early-morning tour of yours in sackcloth and ashes? With a scarlet letter stamped on my forehead? You should have been more specific with your instructions when you woke me up."

"No sackcloth and ashes required, princess. This is your land, not mine. But I don't know what you're trying to prove. We're not friends. I don't *want* to be friends."

He thought maybe that got to her, and instantly felt bad about it. But then again, he couldn't read her the way he once had.

"Grandma June wanted me to handle the cattle," Keira said after a moment. "That's what I'm trying to do. If you're already handling them, I'm guessing that means we're going to have to work together."

"We can work together. I have no problem with that."

"Are you sure? Because you can see how this looks like it might be a problem, right?"

Something in him liked that she didn't back down the way she would have when she was younger and more fragile. That she folded her arms over her chest, cocked her hip and gazed back at him, cool and unfazed. His Keira hadn't been quite so armored. She'd had an attitude sometimes, but she'd been much softer. More malleable, maybe.

Needy, his mother had pronounced after the first time they'd met her. *And* needy *doesn't get the cows fed.*

I get the cows fed, he'd retorted. Then.

Here, now, he didn't understand how he could like this new version of Keira and mourn the lost one at the same time.

"You can't pretend nothing happened between us," he told her instead of mining his feelings for answers he knew weren't there. "I mean, you can pretend anything you want, but I'm not going to."

"Was I pretending? Or was I attempting to have a perfectly polite conversation with someone I'm stuck with for hours?"

"I know what you're doing, Keira. I don't like it."

"Of course you don't like it. Because if you actually talk to me like a person, I can't be the monster who broke up with you five hundred years ago. And then what?"

Remy rubbed a hand over his jaw, his eyes on the land and on the cows grazing contentedly before him. "It was five years, not five hundred."

"You do know that I didn't break up with you just to hurt your feelings, don't you? Or are you still not able to hear why I had to do it?"

"You've got to be kidding me."

But if she heard the way he muttered that, she gave no sign. "You know what my parents are like."

"I think I met your parents twice. If that."

"This is Jasper Creek," Keira scoffed. "You know the story. You know my mother got mixed up with my father when she was sixteen years old. And he's been manipulating her ever since. She chose him over her family. Over her friends. Over every single thing she had in her life, and then she had a child. Me. So she could carry on choosing him over yet another person who should have been important to her."

"Is this the part where you compare me to your con-man loser of a father?" Remy growled at her. "The one who stole a prize steer from my father and thought he could get away with it? But only after he pretended they were best friends first, to really stick that knife in? Are you doing that again?"

"It wasn't about you." Her voice was flat, her gaze direct. And she wasn't crying this time. She wasn't sobbing the way she had five years ago, as if she was ripping her own heart out of her body—and his, too. "I needed to make sure that no matter what, I would never end up like my mother. And you couldn't do that for me, Remy. Or with me."

"You told me all this back then," he gritted out. "You said you couldn't be your mother. I said I'm not your father, so how would it matter? That argument didn't work. I wanted to marry you, Keira, and you didn't want to marry me. That's the beginning and the end of it."

"Everything is not as black-and-white as you'd like it to be." And it was like time crumpled in on itself. They might as well have been right back where they were five years ago. Or any other time in their relationship. Remy almost felt dizzy. "There are such things as shades of gray."

"You either love someone or you don't," Remy said flatly. "You made your choice."

"That sounds even more ridiculous five years out—"

But Remy didn't want to air old fights and go a few new rounds. He didn't want to revisit terrible scenes from their shared past. He didn't want any of this. If it had been up to him, he never would have laid eyes on Keira again.

Because it was better not to have her at all than to have a little of her, but not enough. Never enough.

"I'm not doing this," he said, cutting her off.

"Yet here we are. Doing it. As always."

"You're not understanding me, Keira. I'm not going to do this with you. Whatever you think is happening…isn't."

"You think I don't know that I hurt you?"

And she didn't ask the question angrily. It would have been easy to brush off if she'd been angry. But instead, there was something imploring in her expression. Her voice. And the way she looked at him, as if she could see straight through him—

That was the last straw.

"You don't know," he hurled at her. "You knew the man I was then. You don't know the man I've become. You don't know how I feel. You don't know what I had to do to survive you, and you have no idea what my life is like now. Don't pretend you do."

She rocked back on her heels and bent her head. But when she raised her face to his again, he couldn't read her expression at all.

He was ready for that to stop making his chest hurt. Any minute now.

"Noted," she said coolly.

And he felt like an ass. Instantly.

Because he knew how to be angry at her. He'd been practicing it for years. But there was nothing in him that was okay with hurting her. Even now.

She moved away from him, across the muddy field, as if she didn't notice it was dirty, as if she didn't care that spring was coming in, and that messed with the image of her he'd been carrying around all this time. Sophisticated, wannabe-city-girl Keira. The one who needed bright lights, big cities—anything but this. Anything but the land, and the home they could have built here.

She was here again, and Remy hated the way she fit.

As if she was a part of the landscape. She was tall for a girl, lithe and graceful no matter what she was doing, and she stood with that cowgirl practicality that called to things in him he wouldn't have known how to name.

But that was a lot of thinking around the fact that she still felt like his.

That looking at her, planted in the land with her eyes on the cattle that were his present and future all wrapped up in one herd, felt right. She was as much a part of his own personal landscape as that big tree he'd climbed when he was a kid. Or those hiking trails that wound up into the mountains, where he and his brothers had hunted and camped when they were boys and the starry nights had felt like freedom.

He preferred to think of Keira in high heels and fancy dresses, off glittering brightly somewhere. Unreachable. And unsuited for grassy fields, lowing cattle and spring mud.

Having her back here was sheer torture.

But he comforted himself with the knowledge that it was only for a season.

Just one season, Grandma June had told him in her letter.

And if Remy knew anything about Keira, it was that the more she felt like home to him, the less likely she was to stay here and build one.

The more she felt like his, the sooner she would leave him.

It was true five years ago. It was true now.

The only difference was that this time, he knew better.

CHAPTER THREE

KEIRA LOVED LIVING in the farmhouse again. And for longer than a too-quick summer vacation this time.

She loved feeling her grandmother all around her. And she loved getting to wake up in a house that she knew so well. She had never thought about that before this unexpected spring—that living in a beloved place could feel like its own intimacy.

There had been nothing like that in the parade of living spaces she'd inhabited with her parents. From fancy houses to trailers, to much worse and occasionally better. All those temporary places had ever had in common was the sure knowledge that they wouldn't last. That Michael Long would make another bad bet and ruin it.

Keira had never let herself get attached.

After years spent in college dorms, she'd settled into her cute, if tiny, apartment in Seattle, but they were just…places she lived.

Grandma's farmhouse was a home. And as the days rolled on, while green things began to poke through the winter brown in the fields and the buds on the dogwood tree out front grew bigger, she almost felt as if it was hers.

Almost.

Remy came by every morning, and Keira was ready for him. After that first morning, she decided it was in everyone's best interest that she not give him the opportunity to storm her bedroom again. The second day he picked her up she was waiting on the porch with a big travel mug filled with hot coffee, which she sipped serenely in the passenger seat while ignoring the dark looks he sent her way as they bounced along a muddy road out into the pastures.

The next morning she brought him his own travel mug. She set it down in one of the cup holders, crooned her hello to Waylon and then carried on sipping her own coffee with tremendous serenity. And neither one of them acknowledged it when he picked up the mug she'd prepared for him and drank from it.

It became something of a routine. And it wasn't the routine she remembered having with him when they were younger, that was for sure. But there was something peaceful in it. The early mornings, so quiet before dawn. Making coffee in the ancient coffee maker she dug out from the depths of the kitchen cupboards. Filling up the two travel mugs and then making sure she was out there on the porch, appropriately dressed for the changeable weather, by the time his truck started up the drive.

What it felt like was a sweet little life, all land and lazy evenings to herself.

The kind of life she'd imagined she would have with Remy once she was finally free of her parents. When they'd been young and doing this, she used to fantasize about what it would be like if this was their land, their herd. Their life, together.

But she hadn't dared gamble on the possibility they could build that life between them back then, because if there was anything Michael Long's daughter didn't want to do, it was gamble. She was taking her spring season here as an opportunity for a second chance at an old dream. It didn't have to be a second chance with Remy. She wasn't pretending that was on offer, but she'd worked so hard to forget how much she loved it here. How much it had felt as if she'd hacked off her limbs when she left. Being back out in the fields, surrounded by cattle and mud and the Oregon mountains, did something to her. Sometimes, growing up, getting outside into this valley with the deep green trees and the enduring hills was the only thing that had kept her going. It stitched her back together. It made her feel like herself again.

Whole, something whispered inside her. *Loved.*

And whether or not she was holding out for a second chance with him, she knew being around Remy had a lot to do with that. Since he was a big part of the reason she knew what *whole* and *loved* felt like in the first place.

Keira was feeling so freaking *whole,* in fact, that after she'd been back at Grandma June's for a couple of weeks and had let herself relax into it a little, she figured she might as well venture out into the town she'd been avoiding since her arrival.

Jasper Creek not only looked exactly as she remembered it, but also as if she was looking back in time. The sweet, postcard-ready Western buildings on either side of the main street stood tall and proud in the sudden sunlight peeking through the clouds. Everything was just where she'd left it.

It was a little town in the middle of a pretty bit of nowhere, but the Jasper Creek shops seemed to be doing a fairly brisk business for an early April afternoon. Relatively speaking. There were boutiques, a handful of restaurants and a new bookstore with a black sign featuring a woman with an arrow. There was an antiques store that actually appeared to be filled with antiques rather than the junk Keira remembered. A glance at the license plates parked along the street suggested people had driven up from California and down from Portland—or, as in her case, from Washington.

With a sudden burst of inspiration, it occurred to Keira that Jasper Creek was the perfect place for the start-up coffee cart she'd spent at least the last three years daydreaming about while she toiled away in her corporate coffee job. She'd been thinking in terms of food trucks in urban areas, but that was always a crowded market these days. Why hadn't she considered Jasper Creek?

Because you were afraid that when you broke up with Remy, you ruined all the good things you found and felt here, too, a voice inside her that sounded a lot like Grandma June replied. Too quickly. As if this was something she had known all along.

As she sat and helped herself to a late lunch at one of the new restaurants, she sketched out a few of her ideas on a napkin, one coming almost on top of the next as if all it had taken was coming back to Jasper Creek to get *really* inspired. She took her coffee very seriously, of course, like any born-and-bred Oregonian, and planned to serve it in all the time-honored ways. But there was no reason she couldn't offer other hot drinks, too. Like her grandmother's famous hot chocolate, for example. The very thought of it made Keira smile. She drew herself a little picture of the perfect trailer she'd love to convert into a traveling coffee dream, and found herself sketching out the sign that would go on the side, too.

June's.

She was still smiling, maybe too brightly, as she folded up the napkin and tucked it away in her pocket. And sure, maybe her eyes were a little damp. But she felt more than whole as she walked back outside. She felt like everything made sense, finally.

That she'd come back here for a purpose that had nothing to do with her past or any ghosts she might encounter along the way.

So she wasn't at all prepared to step off the restaurant's wooden stair and come face-to-face with her mother.

Keira had spent more hours than she cared to recall coming up with strategies for moments like this one. And she would click into them any second now, surely. But first there was the way her stomach sank. There was the instant surge of frustrated love, and the helplessness that always followed in its wake.

Because she only had one mother. And she kept wishing and praying that Katy would be a better one, despite all evidence that that was unlikely to occur. Ever.

Keira made herself smile. She'd seen her parents at the funeral, of course. There had been so many people there that it had been easy enough to keep her distance without appearing to do so. She'd given each one of them a hug. She hadn't run to the opposite side of the church or anything. But she also hadn't stuck too close to them, because she'd been determined to avoid any of the usual unpleasantness.

But now she was standing on a street on a random Thursday with no funeral niceties to observe.

"Hi, Mom," she said, calmly enough.

She'd practiced that, too.

Her mother looked back at her, and Keira felt that same sense of hollow recognition she always did. Because they looked so much alike. The same oval-shaped face. The same cheekbones and nose.

Except Katy Long was a bitter, beaten-down woman, and looked it. Her hair was streaked with gray now, and pulled back in a joyless bun on the back of her head. Her face was creased, but not from the sun or any laughter. There were brackets around her mouth, from trouble and cigarettes. And the look she leveled on her only child wasn't exactly loving.

"How do you think it looks that my only daughter comes back to town without so much as dropping by to say hello?" Katy asked, sounding the way she always did. Wounded and victimized, and a little bit mean with it.

"I'm sorry, Mom," Keira said, because there was no point defending herself. She'd accepted that there were fights she was never going to win, and was better off not even trying. The only thing her mother recognized was her own pain. So she went with that. "I didn't mean to hurt your feelings. I got a letter from Grandma. She wanted me to stay in the farmhouse for a few months, so I am. That's all."

"That's just like her," Katy said, frowning. "Trying to manage things that aren't her business from beyond the grave."

Keira felt her stomach twist at that, but she didn't touch it. *Change the conversation*, she lectured herself. *Don't act as if you're trapped in whatever fight she wants to have.*

"How are you?" she asked instead. "And Dad?"

"I don't understand the fascination with that farmhouse," her mother said instead of answering Keira's question. "It's nothing but a dumb old house surrounded by cows. I couldn't wait to get out of that place. Stranded out there in the middle of nowhere." She shook her head, her frown creasing her forehead into folds that seemed more permanent than they used to. "But your grandmother indulged you a lot more than she ever did her own daughters, let me tell you."

"Isn't that what grandmothers are supposed to do?" Keira asked lightly.

Katy sniffed. And Keira thought, the way she often did, that her mother was trying too hard. Too much eye makeup, always. All that spiky mascara that clumped in the corners and made her look harder, not sultrier.

Keira knew better than to offer her opinion.

"Your father and I want you to come over for dinner tonight." Keira's heart sank. "And don't give me that look. He has a business proposition to run by you."

Of course he did. There was always—*always*—a business proposition. There was always a great new idea and an unmissable opportunity. Keira's father lived for the sales patter. He loved nothing more than a captive audience, because Michael Long was utterly convinced he was smarter than everyone he'd ever met or ever would.

You gotta stay two steps ahead, he'd always proudly declared. *You need to keep dancing just out of reach.*

If Keira had ever dared complain about things like that summer in the tent, her father would always reply the same way. He would accuse her of focusing on the negative. And forgetting the good parts, like the year or so they'd lived in that sprawling ranch house, with stables and horses, and he'd swanned around like he was landed gentry.

Until the deputies had come and run them off, and Keira had been forced to drag out her few possessions in a garbage bag.

"That sounds great," she said now. "But I'm afraid I can't tonight."

"What are you doing instead?" Katy demanded. "Don't tell me you started up again with that West boy. I know your grandmother was fooled by him, but you want to be smarter than that."

"I don't know what that means," Keira said, fighting to keep her voice steady. "But I don't—"

"Your Grandma June lived to spite me," Katy told her, shaking with affront and victimization, as usual. "That's the long and the short of it. She never approved of your father and you better believe she took every opportunity to make sure I knew it." Another dramatic sniff, in case Keira had missed her suffering. "Maybe Michael and I would have liked the chance to live rent-free in a cabin on the family property. But, no, of course not. She went and handed the cabin over to Remy West. When she knew the way his father treated us, and still treats us. She *knew*."

A cloud traced over the sun, casting the street in shadow. But there was still sunlight down at the far edge of town.

Keira should have shut her mouth and tried to look sympathetic.

But she didn't.

"In fairness, Mom," Keira said instead, "Dad did try to steal a prizewinning steer from Remy's father. I don't think anyone takes kindly to cattle rustling around here, or anywhere, last I checked. And what with the steal-ing of cattle and everything, I can see how Grandma might not have felt like Dad was the best choice to watch over her herd."

She regretted it the minute she said it. Because ev-erything she'd said was true, but what did that matter? Her mother twisted every fact she encountered to suit herself. And it definitely did not suit Katy Long to be confronted with the fact she'd picked the wrong side a long, long time ago.

She had all of Grandma June's stubbornness and none of her sense. If there was a family curse, Keira was fairly sure that might be it.

"Well, well, well," Katy drawled theatrically. "I see you've come on back to town as high and mighty as when you left it. And why am I surprised? You always did chase after that boy like a lovesick puppy. And let your grandmother fill your head with poison about your parents all the while."

Keira had already jumped into the deep end. It was sink or swim.

"I didn't leave town high and mighty, I went to col-lege. And Remy and I were together for years and very seriously. But I think you know that, Mom."

"I'm sure he'll take kindly to you defending him," her mother sneered at her. "But only after you decided you were too good for the likes of him, anyway."

If Keira couldn't have that conversation with Remy, she certainly wasn't going to have it with her mother.

"And as for Grandma poisoning me," Keira contin-ued softly, evenly. The way she wished she could have done when she was younger and no one else was around to stand up for her. "She didn't have to. You and Dad did that all by yourselves."

"Here we go. Another list of all the ways you were so mistreated." Katy rolled her eyes. "You look just fine to me, Keira. More than fine. Maybe it's time you stop blaming everyone else in the world for your troubles, and take a little responsibility for yourself."

"All I have ever done is take responsibility for myself," Keira retorted, stung into responding emotionally when she knew better.

She knew better, yet here she was. Standing on a street in full view of all of Jasper Creek, arguing with her mother.

This was exactly what Katy wanted. This was what her mother *did*. She dragged Keira down to her level and then accused her of being the one who lived there in the first place. It was maddening. But it worked.

It always worked.

"Everything I have in this life I had to make myself," Keira said, aware she was revealing too much by responding. "And I did, with no help from you or Dad. That's not something you can say, Mom. You like to talk about how terrible Grandma was to you, but that didn't prevent you from running to her with your hand out anytime things went bad, did it?"

"Oh, yes, your perfect saint of a grandmother." Katy let out a very fake, very staged yawn. "The things I could tell you about that woman would curl your hair."

"I don't want my hair curled. I don't care what Grandma June did in her spare time." Keira lifted a hand and started counting off her fingers. Maybe also with a little bit of that Long family theatrical flair, since it was going around. "I don't want to hear about one

of Dad's business opportunities, I'm not going to give
you any money and it's not an accident that I haven't
stopped by since I've been back in town. And I know
that this will never happen in a million years, but it
would be great if just this once you would go back
home—assuming that's the right word to call wherever you're crashing—and think for a minute about
why that might be."

Then she did what she should have done from the
beginning. She didn't wait for her mother to answer or
throw something else in her face. She stepped around
Katy and charged down the street, heading for her car.

But she wasn't all that happy with herself as she went.

She'd been so proud of herself, up there in Seattle.
She'd read so many books, so sure that having taken
the time to try to understand her parents, she would no
longer be affected by them.

Surprise, surprise. It had taken Katy, what, five seconds to dig her fingers deep beneath Keira's skin?

She hurried down the street a lot faster than she'd
walked it the first time. There was a group of people
blocking a portion of the sidewalk outside the bookstore,
so she moved around them, stepping into the street and
around a lamppost—only to collide with a wall.

Except it wasn't a wall. It was Remy.

She made a little *oof* sound. He didn't.

He caught her by the upper arms, and she tipped her
head back, looking up. And then up farther, because he
was so much taller and bigger than she remembered.

"Ouch," she said flatly.

And, she could admit, a little aggressively.

His dark eyes glittered. "I think what you meant to
say was 'Excuse me, Remy, I didn't mean to mow you

down while paying absolutely no attention to my surroundings.'"

"You know what?" A wave of emotion was cresting inside her and though she should have fought it back, she didn't. "There is no denying I love it here. I love everything about Jasper Creek, I always have, and no, this is not an essay. It's beautiful here. But really…it's home."

Later, maybe, she would think more closely about the hitch in her voice and what that told him. Or the fact that when she said the word *home*, their eyes met and something jolted in her, hard and deep, something she was sure she could see spark in him, too. To say nothing about what it felt like to have his hands on her, hard and weathered, and yet so gentle. It made her want to cry.

But that was later. Right now, staring up at Remy, she kept going. "But I always underestimate how deeply unpleasant it is to be here when I'm surrounded by people who go out of their way to be as awful as possible."

His gaze searched her face, and it made her feel warm again, when she hadn't realized she was cold.

He let go of her, but he didn't step back. "What happened?"

He wasn't her friend. He'd made that clear. He wasn't her friend, and he wasn't the man in her life because she'd walked away from him of her own volition. None of her cousins were here, and yes, of course she could call them, but what was the point? She didn't know where Bella was. Lila would say something bouncy and seemingly unrelated in a bid to cheer her up. JJ would ask her what she'd expected would come out of a conversation with her mother.

She'd made the decision years ago not to talk about her parents to anyone she wasn't related to by blood.

Not even to Remy.

"I miss my grandmother," she said, and to her horror, she felt her eyes fill with tears. "I just miss her, that's all. And it's one thing to be in her house without her, because I can feel her everywhere and I can pretend. But she's not here. And it hurts. And I would give anything to have another day with her. Anything at all."

Keira felt her tears spill over. She couldn't believe she was doing this. Giving the entirety of Jasper Creek a show, from her mother to these tears, right here on the street. She was horrified at herself. But all she could seem to do was cover her face with her hands, and wait for the earth to swallow her whole.

It didn't.

But after a moment, to her shock, she felt Remy's arms go around her. He pulled her close, tucking her against his chest in a way that felt like another bittersweet slap. A key into a lock, the way it had always been. And she knew he felt it, too.

Because they had always fit perfectly.

They had danced like this. Held each other like this. There had been a time in her life when Keira had imagined that this particular circle, strong and warm, would always be her safety net.

She didn't dare sneak her arms around him, too. Or press herself against his chest the way everything in her longed to do. That would be far too familiar.

She made herself step away as she wiped her face, and then she made herself look at him straight on, because she was her grandmother's daughter. And she, by God, wasn't going to hide from the bed she'd made.

"I'm sorry," she made herself say, though her throat was so tight it hurt, and not touching him made her fingers cramp. "It's a lot harder than I thought it would be to go a little ways down the road not taken. Even if all I'm doing is taking a look."

She expected him to say something cutting. Maybe she wanted him to. Something that would remind her where she was. Which version of herself she was supposed to be. Maybe it would even make her hurt less, because she could focus on how dark and bitter he'd become, and stop wondering what he would have been like if she hadn't left him.

But Remy had never fit neatly into any boxes, especially the ones she wanted him to. He only looked down at her, his mouth in that straight line that she found almost more fascinating than those smiles of his she'd once loved so much. And the hint of gold in his eyes gleamed so bright she forgot to miss the spring sun when it moved behind more Oregon clouds.

"You're back in the country now, Keira," he said in a low voice that she could feel inside her like a shudder. "Did you forget? If the road doesn't go where you want it to, you go on ahead and make your own."

CHAPTER FOUR

SPRING ROLLED ON.

Stormy gray days gave way to sparkling green, bright blue and so much giddy sunshine it made a man almost forget about winter. And then the rain swept in again, making everything smell clean and new.

It was tempting to do as much of nothing as he could, and just enjoy it. But that wasn't who Remy was. And besides, spring meant something very specific to a man with a cow-calf operation. Work. The cows moved from feed to grass once the grass came in up in the pastures. And there was the enduring project of calving, which Remy liked to do in both spring and fall, because he'd never been one for habit and conventional wisdom over innovation.

Handling calves meant everything from births to vaccinations to branding, and Remy couldn't do it all alone. Or even only with Keira. He usually hired hands from the surrounding area, or exchanged labor with other ranchers he knew. Tonight he'd listened to the rain while he'd made a dent in his usual pile of paperwork, then had started thinking about who he needed to call to help him out.

Keira hadn't asserted her authority over her grandmother's herd the way Remy had half expected her to, which meant that he planned to go ahead and do what he'd been doing for the past five years. He kept telling himself he should force the conversation. Or go see about buying that land over in Logan County he'd heard about, because maybe it was high time he owned what he worked. But he never quite got around to it. He figured he'd keep on doing what he was doing here until Keira decided what she was going to do with her grandmother's cattle. Or with him.

Or until spring turned into summer and she took off again.

Because he knew she was going to leave. He knew it.

Remy tensed at that. Then he made himself breathe. There was no sense anticipating trouble that might never arrive. And there was no point in worrying about something as inevitable as Keira Long leaving.

Remy counted himself lucky that at least this time it wouldn't surprise him.

He'd hated it when she'd cried in his arms in the middle of town, because he couldn't stand to see her cry. Yet he'd wished that she would keep on crying, because he still loved her in his arms.

He still loved the way she fit.

Remy tensed. Again. But this time, for a different reason altogether.

"Get a grip," he muttered to himself, and then returned his attention to the stacks of paper before him that always seemed to multiply of their own accord every time he looked away.

Waylon was sleeping by the fire, herding cattle in his sleep, but a while later he rolled himself awake and alert. He cocked his head, then whined out an alarm. He padded over to hover at Remy's side.

A moment or so later, Remy heard a pickup making its way along the dirt road that led to his cabin.

Remy braced himself. Waylon barked out a sharper warning.

Which told Remy that it wasn't Keira. If it was Keira, Waylon would have forgotten himself entirely and gone for the door like an excitable Chihuahua, wiggling and carrying on and embarrassing himself.

Maybe Remy would have, too.

He was already irritated when he got up and went to look out the window. But when he saw the truck outside, he felt no particular urge to wiggle or carry on. He scowled.

He tossed open the front door and stood in the doorway, hoping he looked as unwelcoming as he felt.

And watched his oldest brother, Colt, unfold himself from his pickup, then take his time looking around the wide clearing, from Remy's barn back to the cabin, as if he expected the forest might have changed since the last time he'd come up here to perform this song and dance.

"Interesting strategy to come alone," Remy drawled into the quiet, while he could still pretend things between them were the way they used to be. "I think I prefer it when all four of you roll up here together, like my very own redneck revival."

"Now, Remy," came his older brother's mild, irritating drawl, which he knew Colt was drawing out for effect. "You know your mother prefers *country* to *redneck*."

"That's because your mother is a redneck with money. It's called putting on airs, I believe, no matter how many acres she likes to call her own."

Colt let out a laugh. "I didn't live this long by talking back to that woman, thank you. And I notice you're only this bold while you're living on the opposite side of the valley and know full well she can't hear your blasphemy."

Remy was tempted to smile at his brother, which only made his temper kick at him all the more.

"We don't need to have this argument again," he said as Colt sauntered around the front of his truck, then leaned against it, as if he was prepared to have a battle to see who could look the most languid.

Colt would probably win, too. He usually did.

"I'm glad to hear it," Colt said, an edgy grin on his face that meant he was 100 percent going to have the argument, anyway. "It's only taken you five years to see sense. No need to go around hiring hands when your brothers will help you for free."

"I don't want your help."

"And there it is. The patented Remington West stupidity, rearing its ugly head."

"What I do with my head has nothing to do with you. Any of you."

"I'm not Dad, Remy," Colt said mildly. "You've spent so long sitting out here by yourself that you've mashed your whole family together in your head. I'm your older brother. I never cared who you were dating, and believe me, I never will."

Remy stared him down, but Colt only grinned wider.

"Though, rumor has it Keira Long is alive and well and living in her grandmother's farmhouse when she's not fighting with her mother in the street. I'm sure you meant to tell us."

"Yeah. I can't wait to talk about Keira with Mom

and Dad again. That's pretty much my whole bucket list right there."

Colt sighed. He was three years older than Remy, but all the West brothers had grown up close. Maybe too close. They'd been roughhousing, wrestling, camping, hunting and working cattle together on and around the West ranch their whole lives. And also getting up in each others' business with alarming regularity. Remy was the only one who had walked away from that, after the friction and bad feelings his relationship with Keira had caused. Because Flint and Annette West could hold grudges like it was their job, and they hated Michael Long. Flint especially. As far as they were concerned, once Keira had dumped their son, she was no better than her father and just as unwelcome.

Remy had taken exception to that attitude. While he and Keira had been together, he'd stayed on the ranch because he'd thought he could turn his parents around on her. After all, while they hadn't loved her at first, they hadn't *hated* her.

They'd thought Keira was too clingy, too needy, at seventeen. They'd wavered between thinking she was smart to go to college and lamenting the way Remy put his life on hold to wait for a college girl who might not come back. They'd never welcomed her with open arms, but he'd thought—or maybe he'd wished—that his parents would thaw over time.

And he'd thought his brothers could have had his back more instead of asking him what his hurry was to settle down in the first place.

When Keira had left him, Remy had gone ahead and done what he should have done years before: he'd moved off West land and refused to let his family into his life again. They could have supported him when he'd asked. They hadn't.

It was his hill and Remy was prepared to die on it.

"We're your family, whether you like it or not." Colt only shook his head when Remy, perhaps predictably, started to say how much he didn't like it. "You made your point. You holed yourself away out here like a hermit and you've kept it up for five years. Congratulations, you couldn't have given Dad a more effective middle finger if you tried. You actually outstubborned the old man. But where does it end?"

Remy only stared back at him, his face wooden.

"Are you back together with Keira? Is that what this is? Are you…protecting her honor?"

"Are we in seventh grade, Colt?"

"You sure seem to be," Colt replied with a laugh. "Rumor is she was crying on the street like something out of a *Twilight* movie."

"Because you know from *Twilight* movies."

"I have a daughter," Colt said loftily.

"Maybe you should go back home and ask her to braid your hair then."

They stared at each other a moment. Remy hated this part. Because he forgot the reasons he was keeping his distance. The reasons that seemed so clear to him when he was alone.

"Remy." Colt wasn't grinning anymore. "I think you've taken the martyr thing about as far as it can go, but that's between you and your thirst for suffering. You've been punishing us all for *five years*. Do you think that's going to get her back?"

"I'm not a martyr, jackass," Remy retorted, and for the sake of the adulthood they should have reached by now, he ignored Colt's last question. Because if he acknowledged it, there was likely to be a scuffle.

But on nights like tonight he wondered if the person he was really punishing was himself.

"You don't want help. Fine. It's your call if you want to be an idiot." Colt shrugged, but his gaze was hard. "But at a certain point, you're not sticking it to Dad. You *are* Dad."

And long after the sound of Colt's truck faded away into the sweet sounds of the damp woods, Remy found he couldn't get that parting shot out of his head.

Because he was willing and able to be a lot of things in this life—including lonely and bullheaded, apparently—but he was not his hard-assed, unyielding father.

He was *not*.

Remy sat in the cabin that was stuffed full of ghosts he pretended not to notice and listened to what was left of the rain. Those loud, off-tempo drops seemed to hit particularly hard out there in the stillness.

It felt like his heart.

Beating hard and insistent, whether he wanted it to or not.

Maybe he shouldn't have been surprised that he found himself up on his feet, then heading for the door again.

The night was close and cool and smelled fresh. Dark and green, and spring straight through.

He opened the door to his truck, and Waylon jumped in before him. Remy slid in after, and wasn't particularly surprised to find his dog giving him the eye.

"Mind your own business," he muttered.

Waylon made a funny little sniffing sound, which Remy opted to ignore.

He told himself he didn't know where he was going. That he was out for a drive, that was all. Minding his business in the Oregon countryside. Enjoying the aftermath of a spring storm, where the clouds hung close to the mountains and the fields rolled out in all directions.

Still, there wasn't a single part of him that was surprised when he found himself pulling up to Grandma June's farmhouse.

Something about this place got to him. The lights were on inside the house tonight, cheery and bright against the thick darkness, and it made his chest feel tight. He had always felt this way, he knew.

Outside, looking in.

Flint and Annette weren't bad parents, necessarily. Remy didn't hate them. He felt certain they'd done their best, but it was a hard sort of best. There had never been any place to land. It was his parents' way, or no way, with no special treatment and no deviation, no matter what.

He was nothing like either one of them, he assured himself, no matter what Colt said.

Meanwhile, everything at Grandma June's was soft. Accessible. Sweet, despite how salty the old woman used to get when she'd had a mind to speak her piece.

And Remy knew that it was something special about this house, because he hadn't only felt that way growing up and then falling in love with Keira. He'd felt this way all throughout the last five years, too, when missing Keira had been wrapped up in everything—and this had still felt like the only safe space in Jasper Creek.

He found himself standing on the other side of the

white picket fence that ran around the house, and he hardly remembered how he'd gotten there.

But he wasn't surprised when the front door swung open and Keira stood there before him.

Not surprised, maybe. But he felt the kick of something deep and fierce at the sight of her.

It felt like joy.

And it roared in him like a new kind of flame, a far better fire.

Or that same old one that he'd never quite managed to extinguish.

The light spilled all around her. She had her hair piled on top of her head, messy and cute. She was wearing a cozy-looking white sweater that was too big for her, but still somehow managed to look perfect as it slid off one sweet shoulder.

He wished he knew why that about killed him.

"The porch light is on," he said, and his voice sounded odd. He told himself it was the thickness of the weather and the way it muffled and distorted things, and not…something else. "Expecting someone?"

"I didn't leave the porch light on." Keira tucked her hands in her back pockets, and there was the strangest expression on her face as she peered up at the light in question. "In fact, I deliberately turned it off earlier. But sometimes I think this house has a mind of its own."

"Makes sense," Remy said, and somehow it did.

Keira didn't ask him what he was doing here tonight. She only stood there, the door wide-open and the light all around her.

And a heat in her eyes that Remy knew all too well. Because he'd put it there himself a long time ago.

"Did your mom give you any more trouble?" he

asked, because it was the kind of thing he would have asked. The kind of thing he would have wanted to know, back when they'd been together.

Though it occurred to him then that Keira had never really answered questions like that. She'd dodged around them. Maybe that was why she'd told him she didn't want to be like her mother, but he hadn't understood what she meant until it was too late.

And here he was now, standing outside her house, like he'd learned nothing from the past five years except how to wait for this exact moment.

That notion should have sent him storming back to his cabin. But instead, Remy stayed where he was.

"No," Keira said softly. "No more trouble just yet. But it will come. It's inevitable."

Answering him without really telling him a thing. "Funny you should use that word."

Remy opened the gate before him, the squeak of the old hinge loud in the stillness of the soft spring night.

"Which word?" she asked.

"Inevitable." He walked toward her, aware of Waylon zigzagging behind him, as if he thought he needed to herd Remy straight to her. "The thing is, princess. You're going to go. That's what you do."

He expected that to scrape at her, but she only smiled. A little sadly.

"It's what I did once," she said. "Just once."

"No. First you went to college. Then you went for good." He made himself smile, too, and that was when he felt the scrape of it. In him. "But I know that now. That has to count for something, doesn't it?"

"You need it to count? Are you keeping score?"

"I don't know what I need."

"You say that, Remy," Keira said quietly. "But here you are. It's coming up on ten o'clock at night, and I know you have an early morning."

"So do you."

"Remy." He'd never gotten over that, he could admit. The way she said his name. As if it was precious to her. As if tasted to her the way she did to him. "I never stopped—"

But by then he was on the porch. And he didn't want to hear her finish that sentence.

"I try to stay away from you," he told her, something dark and urgent in his voice, telling her things he would have preferred to keep to himself. "Even when we're together these days, I try to keep my distance. But I can't do it."

This close, he could see the sheen in her eyes that let him know she had all the same emotions he did.

But he didn't want that to be true, either. He didn't want to accept it.

"No one's asking you to stay away from me," Keira said, her gaze steady on him. "You can stop that anytime you like."

Remy moved closer. He reached up to catch the door frame on either side of her, because that seemed a lot safer than touching her. He thought she might step back and put some more distance between them, but she didn't. She just tipped up her face and met his gaze head-on.

"I knew you were bad news when you started looking at me when you were seventeen," he said in a low voice. "I knew you were going to get me in trouble, and you did."

"Some people are very young at seventeen," Keira

replied. "But I wasn't." He looked down between them as she reached out, and slowly—almost carefully—ran her fingers over the hollow in the center of his chest. "That's what happens when you have to parent your parents from a very young age."

It was the kind of thing she'd always said. Offhand. Almost like an aside. Why hadn't he realized she was telling him the most crucial things of all that way?

"I've been trying to get over you for a decade," Remy gritted out. "It never seems to work."

She smiled, as if it hurt a little. "Maybe you should stop trying so hard."

Remy traced a pattern over her face. Her pretty face that had been haunting him for so long now he hardly knew who he was without Keira in his head, cluttering him up and making him crazy, whether she was right in front of him or ten hours away in Seattle living her own life.

And she felt the way she always did.

As if she had been specially crafted to fit him perfectly.

Remy didn't know how to make that feeling go away.

And here, now, with a soft night all around them, the light spilling from inside the house, and that smile on her face as if she'd never stopped loving him and never would, Remy couldn't think of a good reason to stop.

"This isn't why you came back," he said. "You came back for your grandmother, not for this."

Not for me, he thought. But somehow managed not to say.

Keira leaned her cheek into his palm. Her smile was brighter than the lights from inside this cozy old farmhouse, sweeter than the spring night spread out behind them, and wound around and around and around him, as if she would never let him go.

He'd believed that once. God, how he'd believed that.

"You know what they say about those country roads," she said softly, as if she could see inside him the way she had, once. The way he wanted her to, still. "Sooner or later, they get you where you need to go."

Remy didn't know if he bent down or she rose up. He didn't know which one of them started it, or if both of them did.

But in the next second, his mouth was on hers. And she was pressed up against him, kissing him back as if she'd never stopped.

As if she never would, when he knew that was a lie. A dream.

But he didn't care, because she was heat and yearning, need and belonging. She was Keira. She was his.

And Remy threw himself, head over heels, into all that perfect fire.

The way he always did.

CHAPTER FIVE

IT WAS LIKE dying and being reborn.

Maybe that was melodramatic, but Keira couldn't think of another way to describe what was happening to her. In her.

Remy was kissing her, she was kissing him and it was as perfect as it had ever been. Better than she remembered, if that was possible.

He was her first. Her best.

Her only.

And there were so many things she didn't know how to talk about with him, so she poured it into her kiss. She wound herself around him, leaning into it when he angled his head and took the kiss deeper.

He moved them inside the farmhouse, the door slamming shut behind him as if of its own accord. And then he was lifting her up, hauling her into his arms as he kissed her again and again. As if he couldn't get enough. As if he would never get enough.

And a glorious wildfire burst into life between them, consuming them both where they half stood and half leaned against the wall at the bottom of the stairs. Until Keira couldn't tell where Remy ended and she began. She didn't want to. She wanted to stay like this forever—all sensation, all delight, hot and bright and *together*.

He helped her off with her sweater, then she stripped his shirt from his mouthwateringly wide shoulders. And then his hands were on her skin, finally.

Finally.

Keira moaned and pressed herself against him as he traced his way over her belly, then around to her back to flick open the catch to her bra with the skill and ease that had always made her shiver.

It did again today, and they both laughed a little as goose bumps prickled into being all up and down her arms.

This felt new and beautiful.

And so familiar, she ached.

And Keira didn't care that they were in the front hall of Grandma June's house. She didn't care they couldn't seem to keep their hands off each other, right there within sight of all those family photos on the fireplace mantel and her grandmother's paperweight collection.

All she cared about was Remy. And this.

God, how she'd missed this.

His hands were greedy, yet reverent, but so were hers. And it was as if she couldn't touch him *enough.* As if she couldn't quite forget what she hadn't known five years ago—that this could end. That there could come a great many days when she couldn't touch him like this.

That she would have to let him go.

But not right now, she told herself fiercely.

And when he picked her up, she wrapped herself around him, hooking her legs around his waist because she wasn't going to waste a single second worrying about what came next. Because she'd already lived through five years of what came next, and this was better.

This was so much better.

Remy only stopped kissing her as he carried her up the stairs, concentrating so that they didn't fall back down. Keira was completely unhelpful. She made the most of the way she slid down against him, cradling the hardest part of him right where she needed it most. She might have rocked herself against him a few times, just to make sure it still sent that spiral of heat and delight arrowing straight through her like a slippery ache.

"You're killing me," Remy growled at her as he made it to the top of the narrow stairs.

"You always say that." She raked her teeth down his neck. "And yet you live."

He carried her down the upstairs hall, and there was something about the familiarity of the sounds, feet against the loud wooden floorboards and the glorious familiarity of Remy's body against hers. It all fused together, like a different sort of homecoming, and by the time he laid her out on the full bed in her favorite bedroom, Keira hardly knew if she was about to cry, come apart at the seams or explode from sheer happiness.

His eyes locked to hers as he looked down at her, sprawled there before him with only her jeans on. And the more heated gold Keira saw in his eyes, the more her world narrowed in on him. The way it always did when he was around.

It was why she'd fallen so in love with him. It was also why she'd left.

How could anyone need someone as much as she needed him…and survive? How could this do anything but wreck them both? And when it did, would Keira be any better than her own mother, who'd lost herself completely in a man and depended on him to protect her from anything and everything, even the messes he made himself? Would Keira follow suit and stay lost the rest of her life, just like Katy?

Remy made her feel beautiful. Safe.

But the way she loved him was so huge she was afraid it would swallow her whole.

The corner of that hard mouth of his crooked up a little, and she shoved away those older, weightier concerns. And concentrated on the way he looked at her, as if he planned to eat her up. Every inch.

Keira flushed with heat at that image, bright red and hot enough that she wasn't surprised Remy could see it. They both laughed.

"I agree," Remy said.

And then it was a race to see who could get naked first and fastest.

A race that had no losers and only winners, as Remy kicked off his boots, then his jeans, and joined her on the bed.

And this part was even better than Keira remembered—and she remembered everything.

The heat between them, bigger and wilder. That delirious, impossible need that had terrified her when she was younger. Terrified her and tempted her in equal measure.

Now it was all temptation, no terror.

They rolled. Keira wasn't sure she had ever expected this to happen again, and she was bursting with need and delight that it was. It really was. And she was pretty sure Remy felt the same way.

And yet cutting through it was the sharpness of the very real possibility it would never happen again, either.

Keira hardly knew where to put her hands. She settled for everywhere. She wanted to touch every single part of him. Taste him. Learn him, all over again, because she knew every inch of the body he'd had before, but she wasn't sure he was still the man she'd known back then. There were five years' worth of changes that might very well be imprinted on his skin.

She wanted to drown herself in each and every one of them.

His mouth caught hers again, and the kiss changed, getting deeper and wilder. More impatient, more glorious.

He muttered something against her mouth, and then moved away from her, digging in his jeans.

The old Keira would have asked questions. Teased him, maybe, about carrying condoms around and what his expectations might have been—

You don't get to ask me these questions, he'd said.

And she figured that held steady here, too. The craziest part was, she didn't care. She wanted him more than she wanted to ask questions.

He rolled on the condom, then settled himself back on top of her. And they both grinned at each other, maybe a little fiercely. Maybe with a little too much emotion.

But that was nothing compared to how it felt when he slid his way home.

Perfect.

It was still perfect.

And something changed between them, then.

There had been heat and greed, but now it felt hushed.

Sacred.

Remy propped himself up on his elbows and cradled her face in his hands. And Keira wrapped herself around him, welcoming him inside her. Hoping her body could tell him all the things she didn't dare say out loud.

Slowly, Remy pulled out, making sure to drag his way along every last part of her so that she caught her breath. And shivered, more goose bumps rising all over her skin.

His smile was fierce as he slid back in.

And then he set about building a careful kind of rhythm, as if this was new. As if this was the first time, all over again.

She could remember that, too. He'd been so careful. So determined that there would be nothing but joy between them. And whatever else had happened, however they might have broken each other's hearts, this part had always been pure, wild joy.

Joy, she thought as the fire built, growing and growing the way it always did. *This man is joy.*

Joy, and love, and all the things she had put on hold in those years she'd spent finding herself.

Finding herself, finding her own feet, keeping herself safe because she couldn't trust anyone else to do it—

But always missing this.

Always missing him.

Missing a part of herself she could only get back when they were together. *Joy.*

There were too many words on the tip of her tongue that she knew she couldn't say.

So she whispered his name instead, again and again. Because it was as close as she could get. Because it was the best she could do.

Because really, it meant the same thing.

And when the fire burned too hot inside her, she surrendered, crying out his name even louder, holding him tight as he followed.

Afterward, they lay the way they always had. When their future was bright and sweet and filled with nothing but this particular glory. Keira settled her head on his chest with his big arms around her and cautioned herself not to get too comfortable. Not to forget this could only ever be temporary.

Because he'd said so. Because he was right, she had been the one to break them apart. So she could hardly turn up and expect everything to go back to the way it had been.

And there were so many things that she wanted to tell him. How hard it had been, these last lonely years. How was she supposed to know who she was when she wasn't with Remy?

She'd found the answer to that. She could make her own way and, unlike her mother, didn't need to lose herself in a man to find some kind of definition. She'd enjoyed the challenge of her job. She'd had a whole life.

But she'd lost out on all this joy. And she'd missed him the whole time.

She wasn't sure she'd admitted that to herself before. It swelled inside her, bright and sweet, prickling at the backs of her eyes, but she didn't let it burst free. She didn't say a word. Keira was pretty sure it wasn't something Remy would be open to hearing.

So she stayed quiet, drawing patterns on the ridges of his marvelous abdomen beneath her hands. She could feel his heart beat beneath her ear. This was a whole lot more than she'd had yesterday, so she took it. She basked in it. And she promised herself that she would enjoy whatever this was as long as she could.

Joy was joy, however she found it.

And she was still telling herself that, over and over, when Waylon began to bark downstairs.

"Someone's here," Remy said.

Keira looked at the clock beside the bed. It was coming up on midnight, and she couldn't think of a single person who would come all the way out here—

That wasn't entirely true, though. She could think of two.

She pulled in a sharp breath and rolled out of the bed, the joy and sweetness she'd been feeling minutes before becoming jangly and sharp, a hallmark of any interaction with her parents. She dressed as she went, pulling back on the jeans she'd thrown off not so long ago.

She shrugged into her favorite sweater downstairs, and secured her hair in a knot on top of her head that she hoped disguised what she'd been up to.

"Is that your parents?" Remy asked, coming down the stairs behind her and scowling out into the yard.

"Sure looks like it," Keira said tightly. "To be honest, I'm surprised it took them this long."

Even as she spoke, it was as if the house changed around her. As if the lights got a little brighter, the walls a little thicker. It was almost as good as having Grandma June here again, ready to tell her parents to leave Keira be. Then make them go away.

Keira could remember too many scenes just like that from her childhood. This house had always been her safe space, Grandma June had been her defender and Remy had been her heart. She hadn't forgotten all that, but feeling it surge through her again reminded her that she could do this. That she wasn't a little kid any longer.

And that she didn't have to hide this part of her life. From Remy or anyone else. She hadn't chosen her family, but she sure had chosen her shame and her secrets.

Keira had spent enough time with both. Here, tonight, she'd tasted joy again. And she wanted more.

Real joy wasn't euphoria, she understood now. It was layered and complicated. It was knowing her grandmother was gone, yet spending this season in her house to feel her presence. It was knowing she'd broken Remy's heart, but letting him heal hers.

It was the past and the present, with no fear of what might come next.

And as her hand wrapped around the doorknob, she felt stronger than she had a moment before.

You belong to you, Keira, Grandma June had always said in her steady, no-nonsense way. *Remember that.*

"Thank you, Grandma," she whispered, so low even Remy couldn't hear.

Then she threw open the front door, and there they were.

Her parents.

Like Keira was ten years old and they'd come to drag her home. Not because they wanted her. Just because they could.

CHAPTER SIX

IT HAD BEEN one thing to run into her mother in town. That had felt unexpected. Accidental.

But this could have been any scene from her childhood.

When Keira stepped out onto the porch, Michael and Katy stood just inside the gate, looking shifty at this strange hour. Because Michael believed that keeping people off balance was a fine way to get them to do what he wanted. It was a major tool in what he considered his arsenal.

"It's a little late to swing by, don't you think?" Keira asked, surprised that she didn't have to work too hard to sound calm.

As if the front porch was lifting her up and holding her steady.

Keira knew her parents couldn't see Remy, though his truck announced his presence. He had chosen to stay out of sight, which made her feel almost ridiculously warm. He was *right there*, but he was letting her handle this. He might not love her the way he had, but he wasn't the kind of man to stand by and let anything bad happen to her, either.

"If you wanted us to come by at a more convenient time, Keira, you should have issued an invitation," Michael said in his most friendly, reasonable, you're-being-irrational voice.

Keira tried to look for the good in this man, or at least something familiar. Something more than the basic biological things they shared, like a blood type and long arms.

Michael could be funny when it benefited him to be seen as funny. When he felt rich, he could even play at generosity, but only where people could see his largesse and compliment him on it.

At the end of the day, no matter how Keira looked, her father really was the man she saw before her tonight. Tall, with a dark beard and dark eyes, though there was more gray in the beard now and less hair on his head. His smile was mean, if you knew what to look for. And his eyes were flat, no matter how wide he smiled.

She could tell from the car he was driving and the edge to the way he looked at her that things were not going well for Michael Long.

When things were not going well for Michael, they tended to go badly for everyone around him, too. He was an expert at making them apologize, deeply shamed and confused, for the situations he'd caused.

And she understood now that no matter how much it had hurt, and no matter that Remy would never forgive her for it, she had been absolutely right to go away. To find her own path far away from these people. From her father, in particular.

Because there was a time when she would have felt racked with guilt and panic that she couldn't solve her father's problem, whatever it was. He always needed help, or money or something else Keira didn't want to give. Time. Energy. Labor. All of the above.

But she had spent five years learning how to be an adult on her own. Which meant she knew that her father was extraordinarily bad at it himself. And better still, she knew it wasn't her fault that he was such a failure of a grown-up. He didn't want to succeed. He wanted to win something or have it handed to him. Anything else and he considered himself a victim.

That wasn't Keira's fault, either. None of this was her fault.

"You should go," she told her father. "You shouldn't have come out here in the first place."

She tried to find her mother's gaze, but Katy...disappeared when Michael was there. She turned herself into his shadow. The woman who would happily start something with her daughter on the main street of town faded away when her husband was near.

Keira had watched her do it her whole life. It had terrified her.

She'd asked Grandma June about her mother's vanishing act all the time. Especially after she'd met Remy.

Did it happen all at once? she'd asked one time, when she'd been home from college and curled up there at the foot of Grandma June's bed. Her grandmother had been sorting through the fabric scraps she kept in a big canvas bag for the new quilt she planned to make one day to replace the one Keira was lying on. *Did my mother wake up one day completely under his thumb? Or was it more gradual?*

Some people are born with an unfillable hole inside of them, Grandma June had said, her gaze on the fabric swatches as if they were something more than bits and pieces of other better things. Discarded strips of stuff that actually mattered more. *And they're always looking for something to fill it. Between you and me, it's usually the worst thing they can find.*

Keira knew the story. Katy had met Michael when she was young. Too young. And everyone always claimed that he'd molded her. Changed her from what she could have become into what she was.

And Keira had followed right along in her footsteps, hadn't she? Michael had said that, too, when she and Remy had stopped keeping their relationship secret. *Like mother, like daughter*, he'd laughed.

Keira had wanted to argue that she was nothing like her mother, but that hadn't been precisely true, had it? She remembered those early days. She'd wanted to melt into Remy. If she was brutally honest with herself, the way she'd learned to be, she'd disappeared a bit herself when she'd been with him.

She remembered her grandmother's old, gnarled hands in all those brightly colored pieces of fabric. She remembered wondering if she was just another discarded thing Grandma June had collected because she didn't like waste. Maybe if she kept Keira the way she kept all her leftover swatches from this and that, she could keep her granddaughter from making her daughter's mistakes.

Love is supposed to be a good thing, Keira had said eventually. *Isn't it?*

Grandma June had lifted her head from her bag of fabric and leveled a look on her that had made Keira think she knew exactly what sort of dark nonsense was running around inside her.

Love is a wonderful thing, Grandma June had said. *It's the things that look like love, but aren't, that cause all the trouble.*

Keira had concentrated fiercely on the quilt before her. *How can you tell the difference?*

Love doesn't make you hurt other people, Grandma had said. *Or yourself. Love makes you better, not worse.*

Deep down, Keira had always been afraid that her parents sick, sad connection was no different from hers and Remy's. And if it was no different, how could Keira be sure that she wouldn't wake up one day and find she'd completely disappeared, right there in plain sight? How could she make certain she wouldn't treat a child she and Remy might have the way her mother had treated her—as if she was an irritating afterthought, a mistake and, sometimes, a competitor for her husband's wavering affections?

What if you don't know what love is? Keira had asked on that visit, pretending she couldn't hear her own voice crack.

You will, child, Grandma June had said, her gaze kind. *I promise you, you will.*

And that was what Keira had thought of when she'd broken up with Remy instead of accepting his ring.

She hadn't known the difference then, but she did now.

Remy hadn't liked it, but he'd let her go. He'd hated the choices she was making, but he hadn't kept her from making them. And he hadn't punished her when she'd come back. Instead, he'd made love to her as if she was more precious to him than ever.

There was nothing sick or sad about that man, or how he made her feel. There never had been.

And Keira wanted nothing more than to walk back inside, slam the door on her parents and focus on what actually mattered to her. But she knew she couldn't.

Not with the two of them seething out there in the dark while her father sized her up for weaknesses.

Because that was what he did.

And the only thing he knew how to do.

"Your mother and I don't want any trouble, Keira bear," Michael said soothingly, using that revolting nickname that he'd never actually called her when she was a child. He'd only ever used it in public, to convince other people that they were the sort of family who used endearments. It was all part of his act.

He probably couldn't remember which was which.

"Why would there be trouble?" she asked.

"This is a little embarrassing," Michael said with a chuckle. And it was the chuckle that clued her in. He knew Remy was here, of course. He knew whose truck that was, and that was why he was performing. "I'm not sure what made you think you can come back here after being away for so long and squat in your grandmother's house like this. People are beginning to talk."

"Even if they are talking, Dad, I doubt very much they're talking to you," Keira pointed out in the same calm voice.

Her father bristled, but he drifted up the path all the same. "Your grandmother wasn't a very nice woman."

Keira thought the house shuddered a little behind her at that. Or maybe that was just her.

"I know you won't agree with me, but that's called brainwashing," Michael said with all the confidence in the world, none of which he deserved. "She wasn't kind to her own daughter, you know. And that's what counts."

Keira shook her head. "I'm not the right audience for this. I'm really not."

Michael nodded as if he understood that completely.

As if he supported her fully in all things, despite the irony of him commenting on how parents treated their kids. What was funny was how little it hurt her now. She'd been away too long to let him get to her. Because once you could see his act, all you could see was his act.

But that particular freedom didn't feel like any kind of joy. It was just sad. That was the thing with her father. Deep down, beneath everything, he always made her sad.

"Your mom and I talked it over," he told her, his brow wrinkling in a convincing imitation of a concerned and kindly person. He must have seen one on TV. "Given that your mother is the only one of June's daughters who stayed in town, we think it's only fair that she gets the land and the cattle."

There was a faint sound from behind Keira that could have been a door slamming. Or it could have been Remy letting out a laugh at the sheer gall on display here tonight.

She kept her eyes on Michael.

"I knew you couldn't possibly be coming to visit me," she said softly. "It always has to be about money with you, doesn't it?"

"Lord knows your mother's sisters aren't worth a damn," Michael continued in the same cheerful sort of way, as if this was a real discussion in which he was being more than fair to Keira, who clearly didn't deserve that from him. Still, he soldiered on. "But that cattle operation makes a penny or two, I'd wager. And everyone knows what land prices are around here. So. It's only fair."

"It's not yours," Keira said, very distinctly. She shook her head at him, then cut her gaze to her mother. "It's not yours, either, Mom. Didn't you hear? Grandma June left a will. She was very specific. You're not in it and this kind of behavior is why."

And if they didn't know about the seasons of cousins, she wasn't going to clue them in. They could find out along with everyone else in Jasper Creek as the year wore on.

"You can't really think you can turn up here a few weeks after a funeral and take over where you're not wanted, can you?" Michael asked, and he didn't sound quite so kind or cheerful any longer. "Or maybe you think you can slide right back into a life you threw away once already? That's not how it works."

"If you and Mom are interested in my life, I'd be more than happy to share it with you," Keira said, and this time, emotion didn't get the better of her. She could still feel the way Remy had held her out there on the street after her first run-in with her mother, and it gave her courage. His silent presence behind her, just out of sight, made her feel strong enough to handle both her parents, no tears necessary. "But I don't think you are. You never have been before. I doubt very much that all of a sudden, a little before midnight tonight, you were seized with a powerful urge to find out what I've been up to all this time."

"Now, Keira bear, you know you're easily confused about reality sometimes," Michael said, and he sounded both exasperated and sorrowful at once.

There was a time when that would have hurt her. It would have made her wonder. Was she confused? Why would he say something like that if it wasn't true?

Even though she'd watched him do the exact same thing to her mother all her life.

Tonight Keira only shook her head. "You're trying to intimidate me, shake me down the way you do everyone else, but it's not going to work. Grandma June didn't leave you anything. This farmhouse isn't yours, the land isn't yours, and the cattle definitely aren't yours. You're going to have to make your way without leeching off her. Or me."

"You better watch your tone, young lady," Michael began, and he put his foot on the porch step.

And then straight through it.

He pitched forward, letting out a shout and catching himself on his hands.

Keira stared. She'd sat on that step every day, every single morning, while she waited for Remy to pick her up. She could have sworn it was solid.

"That seems like a real clear message to me," Remy said, coming out from behind the door.

And Keira could feel the heat of him as he came to a stop behind her and stood there like they were a unit. She knew they must look like one to her parents.

Her mother hurried over to help Michael up, but he was red-faced and furious, and slapped away her hands.

"None of this belongs to *you*," Katy threw at Keira as if she was a stranger who'd wandered in off the county highway. "It's not right."

"When's the last time you visited Grandma, Mom?" Keira asked softly. "And I don't mean asked her for money, I mean really visited her. Sat with her and asked about her life. Did you ever?"

Katy glared at the house as if she wanted to hurt it, then transferred that look to Keira.

"I'm the one who came and tended the flowers in the garden when your grandmother's arthritis got bad," she said almost sullenly. "And maybe things could have been better between us, but the years are made of regret. That's how it goes. Maybe you know your own life, Keira, but you don't know mine. You don't know me."

Keira shook her head, glad Remy was there behind her and all around her, like the sweet Oregon air and the quiet strength of the mountains.

"You're right," she said. "But whose fault is that?"

Katy looked away. Keira should have been used to feeling heartbroken around her mother. But this felt different, somehow.

Because clearly Katy was capable of love and affection. But there was only so much to go around, and never much for Keira.

For the first time in her life, Keira felt certain that wasn't her fault, either. She'd deserved better parents.

That felt like a revolution.

Katy swung her head back toward Keira and away from where Michael was aggressively brushing at his jeans like he could wipe away his fall that easily.

"I know you think your grandmother was perfect," Katy said, "but she wasn't."

"I didn't need her to be perfect," Keira replied. "I didn't need you to be perfect, either. I needed someone to love me, Mom, and Grandma June did. Always and without question. I don't think you can say the same."

And when her father started to respond, Katy shocked everyone—especially him—by shushing him.

"You have a lot of opinions about love for someone who didn't know a good thing when she had it," Katy said tightly, her gaze moving to Remy, then back. "I'm not going to apologize because I didn't make that same mistake myself."

"Of course not," Keira agreed. "After all, if you start apologizing, where would you stop?"

She expected it all to ratchet up into yelling. Screaming. Maybe Michael would break more of the front step to prove a point. But something was different tonight. She could see it on her mother's face. Something almost sad.

"Come on, Michael," Katy said. Her gaze held Keira's for an uncomfortably long moment, then dropped. "It's time to go."

As her mother and father went back to their car and climbed into it, Keira had the distinct sensation that was about as close to an apology as she was likely to get.

She stood there, Remy warm and solid at her back, and watched them drive away.

And then she hardly knew what to do. She'd always gone out of her way to keep Remy as far away from her parents as possible, so no matter what stories he heard about them, he would never see what they were like firsthand. She'd gone out of her way to shield him from it before.

But everything was different now.

"Family," she said ruefully, turning around and checking his face for pity. But there was none. "I guess they're always a whole thing, aren't they? No matter what."

Remy studied her face. He reached over and brushed back a stray piece of her hair, and Keira wanted nothing more than to curl herself up in his arms. Except maybe with kissing. And nudity.

You'd better not, she cautioned herself, though his glorious chest was right there in front of her. And he was looking at her the way he always did, as if she was the prettiest thing he'd ever beheld, so pretty nothing could ever tarnish her. Not even the choices she'd made that had hurt them both.

And suddenly she couldn't remember why she needed to caution herself around him at all. After what had happened between them tonight, why was she bothering to pretend that she didn't feel all the things she felt? All the things she'd always felt?

She knew better than to say them—

Or did she?

"Remy…" she began.

"I don't really know what family is or isn't, if I'm honest," Remy said then, something hard settling on his face again and making her think he hadn't heard her start to speak. Or knew what she had been about to say. He shrugged. "I haven't really talked much to mine in years. Five years, if you're counting."

CHAPTER SEVEN

REMY DIDN'T CARE for the look on Keira's face then.

She looked…dumbfounded. Something almost like betrayed, though that didn't make any sense.

He headed back into the house and heard her shut the door quietly and carefully, which he figured didn't exactly bode well.

He'd dressed in a hurry, thinking he might have to get out there and handle Michael himself. And now Remy wished he'd put his belt back on, since his jeans were riding low on his hips, reminding him with every step that he'd gone ahead and done it.

He'd gotten the taste of her all over again, and that was that.

He could tell himself all the lies he liked, but one taste was all it had ever taken.

Remy had it bad for Keira.

Distance hadn't lessened it any. Time hadn't cured it.

And he wasn't any happier about it now than he'd been back when she was too young and too bold and too focused on him.

Remy got a glass out of the cupboard and filled it with water from the tap, then drank it all down, as if the real issue here was that he might be dehydrated. Instead of just pissed and filled with a very old, very dark storm that had already about drowned him once. He didn't need to do it again.

Why was he doing it, anyway? Why was he here, doing this? Again?

He could see his reflection in the dark kitchen window, here in this farmhouse that had been everything to him even after Keira had left him. And now he'd gone and messed that up, too, when he could have played this a lot smarter and just waited for summer to come. Keira would leave again. Another one of Grandma June's granddaughters would come.

Life would go on the way it always did, and he wouldn't have to *feel* all this crap inside him. He wouldn't have to wonder, yet again, if he'd survive it, when he already knew the answer. He would. He had, and he would again.

But it would be lonely and long, bitter and cold, and the years would feel like nothing at all the next time she aimed that smile at him.

Damn her.

He might as well have loved spring itself. At least it came around every year.

"Why haven't you talked to your family in so long, Remy?"

She was using that cool, even voice on him. The same one she'd used on her father. The one that reminded him that she'd gone off and grown up out there, whether he liked it or not.

"And don't tell me it's not my business, or that I don't get to ask the question," she said before he could throw some version of that at her. "You're the one who brought it up."

Remy set down his glass. Then he ran his hand over his face.

"I didn't have much to say to them after you left," he said gruffly.

"What does that mean?"

"It means I didn't have much to say." He turned around to see she'd followed him to the door of the kitchen and stood there with her arms crossed, glaring at him. He didn't much feel like being glared at just then, so he returned the favor. "They didn't support me much when you were here, did they? The problem wasn't you. It wasn't me. It wasn't our relationship. It was them, and I wasn't about to pretend otherwise just because you were gone and the relationship was over."

Keira shook her head slowly, as if she was trying to clear it.

"I don't understand what you're saying to me."

"Not sure I can say it any clearer."

"I understand the words, Remy. Just not *why*. Is that why you're living in the cabin?"

"It turned out I didn't much want to work for my father, either. Since he threatened so many times to cut me off, if not in so many words, I figured, why not do it for him?"

Does you wanting to marry Michael Long's daughter mean I'll end up supporting Michael Long? Flint had asked, more than once, while Keira was in college and Remy had made his intentions clear enough to be seen all the way over at the coast in Copper Ridge. *Because Keira's sweet enough, but no way in hell am I giving that man a handout.*

That was when Remy had still worked on the ranch with the rest of his family. He'd had every intention of marrying Keira and continuing that work. When Keira had been around, no matter how frustrating it got to have her treated like she might spontaneously transform into her father at any moment, Remy had maintained a certain amount of optimism that he could make his father see his way, eventually.

But when she was gone, Remy had lost any shred of optimism.

You really want to cut off your nose to spite your face? his father had demanded when Remy had announced he was leaving. *We wanted to like the girl, Remy, even when all she seemed to do was cling to you. We did our best. Why are you defending her now?*

Your best needs work, Dad, Remy had retorted.

And while he might have regretted how complete that cut was at certain points over the years, he couldn't say he missed having to deal with his father's famous temper, his mother's hard-as-nails version of affection and the fact everything he did required a committee vote with each and every one of his brothers. Grandma June had let him do as he liked, and as long as he kept the operation running smoothly and in the black, she was happy.

"What about your brothers?" Keira asked now, staring at him like she didn't recognize him, which made him feel put together wrong. "I can't imagine they'd let you just…stop talking to them."

"It's not about what they *let* me do, Keira. And I talk to them when they hunt me down to get in my face. I ask them, real nicely, to leave me alone."

"There are more of them than you. Why didn't they hold you down and make you deal with them years ago?"

"They tried that. A couple years running."

He shrugged as if he could hardly remember any of it, anyway. As if he didn't care.

Keira stared at him.

"You know, it's funny," she said in a soft sort of way that felt like a blow. "Every time I think about what happened between us, I think about how it was my fault. What I did. All the ways in which I betrayed you. How I walked away from something wonderful, which is such a part of the story of us that my mother, of all people, threw it in my face earlier tonight."

"That's how I remember it."

"I bet you do." She did something with her hand, and he couldn't tell if she was pointing at him or trying not to. "But I always forget *this*."

He didn't want to ask the question. He didn't want to encourage whatever look was on her face. Much less that storm in him that wanted too badly to get out.

As if he *wanted* to drown.

But he couldn't seem to stop himself. *"This?"*

"No compromise, no give, and that's it," she said very distinctly. She slashed a hand across the air. "They're cut off forever. Believe me, I never thought I'd say this because I know they never liked me much, but I have sympathy for your family."

There was noise in his head and Remy knew it was that same old storm, pounding into him. Shaking him.

"You have a lot of gall saying something like that to me," he managed to get out.

"You gave me a ring and that was it," Keira replied, clearly unaware of the danger. More likely, she didn't care, not if she was prepared to stand there in front of him like this, no tears or *I'm so torn*. Just that fire in her gaze he found he admired a little less when it was aimed his way. "We had to get married immediately. On your schedule. Any deviation from that schedule, and that was the end, as far as you were concerned. Total betrayal."

"You gave me that ring back, Keira. I guess you could have picked up a knife and actually stabbed me in the back if you wanted to make yourself really clear."

"First I asked you to wait." She didn't sound calm or amused. She sounded…angry. At him. When he would have said he'd never seen more than a hint of Keira's temper, and only in passing. And never, ever aimed at him. "I wanted to get engaged. I had no problem whatsoever making that commitment. But I wasn't ready to walk down the aisle. I had things I needed to do first."

"Yeah, because everyone needs to run off to some city and pretend they're someone else for a while." He rolled his eyes. "Like doing that in college wasn't enough."

"I didn't ask you to do it. I told you it was what I needed."

"Who needs to do that, Keira?" he demanded, and he could hear the echo of the past in his words. In the sound of his voice.

Because he'd known, hadn't he? He'd known it when she was eighteen and she'd cried when she'd told him she wanted to go away to college. He'd known then that he wasn't enough for her, but he'd convinced himself that college would fill in that gap. That she would get what she needed there and come back. But it hadn't worked. And she might have said she would wear his ring while she tried on different lives that day in the cabin, but he knew she wasn't going to be satisfied with that.

She already hadn't been satisfied. And what if his parents were right?

Do you want a wife who has her eyes on the horizon instead of the land? his mother had asked when he'd shown her the ring he'd bought for Keira.

But what if Keira never turned that gaze of hers to him? What if she always wanted something out there—something Remy could never give her?

She said she needed a little more time, a little more space. Did that mean other men? Other hands on her perfect body? Did she really want time, or did she not know how to walk away from him? *She needs you a lot, Remy,* his mother had said. *Are you sure you can be* everything *she needs?*

He'd wanted to be. But whether she wore his ring or didn't, Remy knew how it was going to go if she took all her needs to a city where he couldn't follow. Where he didn't want to follow. Because sooner or later, wasn't that how it always went?

Remy had always wanted all of her.

"Who wants to do that? Maybe someone who was forced to live a hundred different lives before she turned ten," Keira said now, temper and something else all over her face. "You know who my father is, what he does. He tried to do it to your family, too. And I think you know your father isn't this angry all these years later because my dad tried to rob him. It's because he pretended they were friends and your father believed it."

"You refusing to marry me is my father's fault? Is that what you're saying?"

"Imagine what it was like to grow up with that," Keira invited him. "Your father is tough, but he's not slippery and awful, always trying to make you think maybe you're crazy. I needed to live somewhere no one knew him. Or me. So I could see, once and for all, how much of that man I inherited."

He thought of all the questions she hadn't answered. All the times he'd asked the right thing, but hadn't noticed how good she was at directing his attention elsewhere.

All the things he'd missed, and she'd hidden, that had led to her handing him back that ring.

"Maybe you should have said all this then."

"I didn't know how, Remy. And it wouldn't have mattered, anyway, because it's not as if you could come with me, could you? You belong here. You love the land. The hills, the fields, the woods. You would die in a city."

He'd died without her, Remy almost said.

Almost.

"You could have asked," he said instead.

"When?" Keira shook her head. "You told me it was everything or nothing. Because that's what you do, isn't it? That's what you did to your family. Why not me, too?"

The unfairness of that stung him, so hard Remy was forced to wonder if maybe there wasn't a little bit of unpleasant truth in it.

Not that he wanted to face that.

"You'd already made me wait for years for our life to begin," he reminded her. "It had already been forever, Keira. What point was there in waiting around to see what you'd *need* to do next?"

"Or we could have been engaged." And her voice was so quiet it made Remy almost *see* what that could have been like. All those dark, lonely years, brighter. Better. Still missing her, but not mourning her the way he had. "And we could have done all of this together. But you didn't want that. We had to have the future you imagined, the way you imagined it, or you didn't want it at all."

"I'm not going to have this what-if argument with you," Remy bit out. "That's not how it happened and you know it."

"That's exactly how it happened," Keira retorted, instead of backing down, as he'd half expected she would. "And if I had any doubt about that? If I wondered if maybe I was changing things around in my head because it made me feel better not to shoulder all the blame—"

"It's not about blame. At the end of the day, if you wanted to leave, it's a good thing you did."

He almost meant that.

"Remy." The way she said his name seemed to expand inside him, like another unpleasant truth he didn't want to face. "The fact that you cut your family off for half a decade proves it wasn't just me. You're a remarkably stubborn man. Maybe you're more like your dad than you want to admit."

She was the second one to say something like that to him in a single season, and the sheer injustice of that accusation just about ripped a hole straight through him.

"My father could teach hardheaded to a slab of granite," he thundered at Keira.

"You're making my point for me."

"He's unbendable, unforgiving and has never met a grudge he can't—" He stopped himself, because Keira was smiling.

"Look, I grew up here," she said. "I know tough men. I don't know anyone who gives their whole life over to the land who isn't hardheaded and stubborn as hell. How would you make it if you were any other way?"

"I appreciate the vote of confidence." He glared at her. "But I'm not my father."

"Okay, but is Flint a con man who loves nothing and no one but himself?"

"He loves two things. His land and his woman, and nothing else, as he'd be the first to tell you."

"He loves more than that." Keira rolled her eyes at Remy's expression. "Your father never had much use for me. And your mother never actually told me you could do better, but I know that's what she thought. And you know why? I was a silly girl who was dating their son. With five sons you'd think they'd come to a place of peace with silly girls, but no. You were serious about me and they didn't like it."

"They don't like anything."

"That's not true at all or they wouldn't have a single friend in this valley, and they're widely beloved. They weren't sure about me because they love you, Remy. A lot."

He stared at her as if her words didn't make any sense. Because he'd never thought about Flint and Annette West as being capable of love. Not like that.

He'd always thought they viewed their sons the way they did their cattle: useful. Especially as they grew older and could take on more of the work. His parents weren't emotional. Not the way Remy always was where Keira was concerned. He'd never imagined it was possible his parents could feel *that*.

Then again, the story they told about how they met boiled down to one look across a Christmas party and that was that. They'd been together ever since, working ranch land and raising boys, which couldn't have been easy. *And* they still preferred each other's company to anyone else's.

What was that if not love? And if they loved each other hard and tough, it wasn't a huge jump to think maybe they loved their sons the same way. Flint and Annette weren't going to gather Remy on their collective lap and ask him about his feelings.

But they'd sure as hell harbor serious reservations about a girl who they'd worried from the start would break his heart.

Why hadn't Remy seen this before?

He felt like the world had shifted beneath his feet. Like if he wasn't still standing there at the sink, he'd fall off it altogether.

"My parents loved *you*, of course," Keira said now. "They thought that they might have a connection to the West family again. So people would have to stop talking about that steer and what a backstabbing liar my father was."

"Keira."

But he had no idea what he was trying to say. What he could say.

"My parents love only themselves." He wished she was still looking at him with anger. Whatever this was, it was worse. It made that shifted-world feeling grow inside him. "Your parents wanted to save you from pain. And from my family, while they were at it."

Remy's head was swimming. He didn't understand what was happening inside him. He couldn't seem to get it under control. It was like something was cracking open. Or cracking into pieces.

And he couldn't understand why, when he knew this

was all Keira's fault. He had the strangest notion that if he could only cross the kitchen floor and put his hands on her, she could save him.

He tried to shake it off. "You're the last person in the world I would have thought would lecture me on the things you have to do to handle family."

"You actually have a family." And Keira didn't sound cool and controlled anymore.

She sounded as ragged as he felt, as if the world wasn't any steadier beneath her feet. Something in him wanted to see that as a victory. But all he felt was hollow. Raw.

Messed up, all over again.

"They don't try to steal things from you," Keira said, her voice tight. Almost harsh. "They don't demand you give them money and tell you it's your duty to provide it. They don't try to tarnish your grandmother's reputation or try to muscle in on the house she left her granddaughters. My God, Remy." And her voice broke then. "Do you know what I would do to have what you have? Why would you throw it away?"

There was no pretending that wasn't emotion in her voice, deep and painful. She scrubbed her hands over her face, shook her head as if she couldn't let herself think about this any longer and then turned away from him.

But she didn't walk away.

And he wanted that to mean things it didn't.

He felt as if he was pushed into moving, whether he wanted to or not. All he knew was that his feet started heading across the kitchen floor, seemingly of their own accord, and then he was behind her.

He wrapped his arms around her and dropped his head down next to hers.

Because he might feel hollow and scraped raw, and he might not know how to handle all these things storming around inside him. He might still be pissed. At everything. And she might never convince him that she hadn't betrayed him by refusing his ring, no matter what he might have done in return.

But she was Keira.

And he'd had a taste of her again.

He couldn't seem to keep himself from sampling her a little bit more. His mouth moved against her neck, in apology and in support, and because he had never stopped loving her just because she'd left. He tasted her until she made a broken sort of noise, and turned around in his arms.

"Remy..." she began.

"I'm tired of talking," he told her, gruff and certain.

And so he spoke to her in a different way altogether, right there on the kitchen table, until it smacked so hard into the wall it should have knocked the light fixture out of the ceiling. But it didn't.

In case that didn't quite get his point across, he picked her up afterward and carried her back upstairs to her bed.

Where he set about telling her all over again. And again.

How he loved her. How he missed her.

And how he didn't think he had it in him to let her go again, the way he knew he would have to.

But not tonight.

He told her these things over and over and over again.

But he never said a word.

CHAPTER EIGHT

MAY STARTED BLUSTERY, but only got prettier as the days passed.

Brighter. Warmer. Sweeter.

The buds on the dogwood tree out front grew bigger and hinted at pink, but didn't quite bloom.

"Not yet," Keira said, running her finger very carefully over a fragile bud one Sunday afternoon. "But soon."

And when a little shiver ran down her spine, as if her words were some kind of foreboding that changed the air around her, she only smiled and wished her grandmother was there on the porch, watching her go. The way she always had, so she could wave Keira off, as if that simple act would surround her in love as she went.

Maybe it had.

Keira had spent the morning digging around in Grandma June's closets until she'd found that big bag of scraps she remembered so clearly. Better still, it was stuffed full. She'd started sorting through the pieces down in the living room, where she could lay out the little swatches all over the rug and the sofa under the watchful eye of the family photographs on the mantel.

This little bit of pale pink was her prom dress from high school. This little bit of blue was from her graduation gown in college. Keira might not have known either of them by sight, but as usual, Grandma June had been prepared. She'd pinned a little note to each and every bit of fabric she'd collected, noting where it was from and who it had belonged to first.

Spreading out all the fabric and picking her way through each bright little bit of history was like listening to Grandma June's stories all over again. And this was the first day that thoughts like that hadn't made her sob her heart out.

Grief bloomed, too, it seemed. One season moved into the next. It didn't matter if Keira was ready.

Who gets to be ready? Grandma June had asked once.

It had been one of the earlier summers, when all four cousins had been together. She'd told the girls they all had to jump in the pickup because they were headed to town *right now* and fifteen-year-old Keira, with her outsize crush on the older Remy, who wouldn't notice she was alive for years yet, had wailed that she wasn't *ready* to go out in public.

Life isn't about ready, *child. It's happening whether you're ready or not.*

Keira took that with her as she drove into town.

Jasper Creek was sleepy today, as it often was on Sundays in the quiet season before summer road-trippers stopped here on their way from the coast to Crater Lake National Park. The brunch places that catered to the after-church crowd were open and bustling, but Keira didn't stop to sample their offerings, despite the scent of bacon in the air. She wandered in and out of the shops and boutiques, letting herself daydream about what it would be like to live here. Who she would be, if this was her town again. If she knew the women in the bookshop by name. If she picked up food from the farm kitchen for her lunch, or went to see local musicians play at open-mic nights at the bar.

What would it be like to live here as an adult? To choose this place? To settle in this pretty valley and build a life here, all on her terms? To make her living here? And she let her daydreams get away from her then, because it was all too easy to imagine working the land with Remy and maybe opening her coffee truck on the side, for afternoons like this one.

Careful there, she cautioned herself. That heart of hers was like the buds on the dogwood tree, swelling up ready to burst wide-open at the slightest provocation. *You don't get that life. You turned it down once already.*

She stopped for too long in the bookstore, gazing at the carefully selected books by local authors and about local areas, daydreams lapping at each other inside her head. Because her heart was ready to bloom whether she wanted it to or not. She and Remy could live in the cabin, the way they'd always imagined they would. They could have the life they'd always dreamed about, only a handful of years later than originally planned.

The past month had been a preview of that life, and Keira didn't have it in her to pretend it was anything but perfect.

Close enough to perfect, anyway.

Because she was in love with him and she didn't dare tell him. She felt certain it was information he didn't want to know.

Keira didn't want to have another fight. There was no point hashing over the past yet again. They'd said everything there was to say, and so she did her best to simply live in the moments they had together. To sink down into this season she'd been given, and for once in her life, not worry about the future. And while she was at it, not mount an endless and exhausting defense against the past.

She just lived. And let herself feel alive.

Her cousin JJ texted her often, wanting to know what it was like being back in Jasper Creek. To live there for more than a summer or school vacation. Keira thought what JJ really wanted to know was what it was like to be in the farmhouse without Grandma June, and she never knew how to answer that.

Because Grandma June wasn't here anymore, it was true.

Except when it wasn't true.

And in those moments, Keira didn't know how to text her extraordinarily practical cousin to talk about a farmhouse that had a mind of its own. Or those distinct feelings she had sometimes that Grandma June was right there in the room with her. That if Keira closed her eyes long enough, she would feel her grandmother's hand on her shoulder again. Or catch the scent of her on the breeze.

Keira could have told JJ all that, of course. She typed things out a thousand times, but always ended up deleting them. Because her cousin was due to spend the summer here, and Keira figured she was better off experiencing it for herself.

And in the meantime, Keira let herself free-fall into this sweet, full life with Remy that she'd been so terrified of five years ago.

Because this time, she loved every second of it.

They stayed in the farmhouse, which Keira liked, because it wasn't the cabin, which she'd once thought would be theirs. It didn't feel quite as much like the life she could have had—the one she had to make up for. Instead, it felt a whole lot better than that.

Like a honeymoon, she sometimes thought.

When that alarm went off well before dawn, they woke up together, wrapped around each other in the bed upstairs. And sometimes last night's dreams spilled over into the morning, making it necessary to handle all that excess heat there and then.

Remy showered while Keira fixed the coffee, then she went up to shower and get dressed while he checked in with the various hands who were helping him out that day. Then they drove out together, Waylon between them on the bench seat of Remy's pickup, to watch the sun rise up over the land.

Keira wasn't sure she'd ever known this kind of contentment before. It ran into her bones, like strength. It felt as much a part of her as the mountains were a part of the land. Enduring and tough, but sweet down deep.

It was a tidy little life. A sweet one. And as each day passed, Keira felt more and more of a sense of peace she'd never had when she'd been living in other places.

She took the farmhouse kitchen as both a gift and a challenge. Grandma's old cookbook—the one she'd made her own with her notes in the margin and pieces of paper stuck into the pages with her version of the recipes—still sat there next to the old stove. And Keira did her best to replicate all of her favorite dishes.

Because it was one more way to feel her grandmother's presence, right there with her in the cheerful green kitchen.

Remy came back in the evenings, Waylon barking ecstatically as he came running in to find her. They would eat whatever Keira had cooked that day, or they'd cook something together, and they would talk. The way they used to talk, when they hadn't had to catch each other up on their lives. When they could discuss a thought, the news, television programs or things that had happened in the course of the day, either to them or to the cattle, or just out there in the fields.

This is the good stuff, Keira would find herself thinking, sitting on the couch with her favorite cowboy beside her. They were always touching, somehow—a hand, or her feet tucked up on his lap—but they didn't talk about all the deep and heavy things that hung between them.

They both knew they were there. But there was no point clawing at them any longer and hurting each other in the process.

Sometimes they made it to the bed upstairs, sometimes not. And Keira could still recall the kind of love-making that had characterized their relationship when they were younger. Sweet. Careful. Reverent.

This was not that.

This was all the darkness, all the longing. Greed. Temper. Sweet, delicious fury and all those lost years. This was the words they couldn't say and the fights they would lose if they spoke—but both won, there in the dark.

They took it out on each other's bodies, crying out each other's names, and then collapsing into a heap of skin and limbs and ragged breaths.

Keira wasn't sure she'd ever been this happy. Maybe for a moment, once in a while, an hour here or a day there, but never like this. Never one week into the next as the world around her got greener and brighter and more colorful every time she looked out a window.

She felt deliciously, erotically battered from head to toe, and even now, standing in a bookstore surrounded by neighbors and friendly tourists, she couldn't keep herself from flushing a little bit in anticipation of the next round.

Keira had never felt so fully alive in all her life.

And she told herself she didn't care that May was winding along and her time here was running out. Because wasn't that the lesson? Time was always running out.

No one stayed forever. Whether they died like Grandma June, after a long and full life, or whether they broke up like she and Remy had. Life carried on. Seasons changed.

Keira could do nothing but love him here and now. So she did, as best she could.

Her parents hadn't come back to torture her further, as she half expected they would. Not while she was there, anyway, though someone did seem to keep turning up to weed the flower garden while Keira was out.

She was almost tempted to hope that she'd gotten through to her mother somehow. That things could be different—

"No more living in the future," Keira said to herself.

She bought a book about the history of Jasper Creek, because the stories inside sounded like ones her grandmother would have told. Then she headed back out to the town's main street, smiling at all the Western prettiness on display, the brick fronts of the old buildings bright with the green hills in the distance and the flowering trees everywhere she looked.

She decided she'd treat herself to that coffee, so she made her way toward the coffeehouse around the cor-

ner. And then stopped dead when an older couple came
out of one of the brunch places, and directly into her
path.

There was absolutely no possibility of escape. Or
even pretending that they somehow didn't see each
other, a favorite small-town method of avoiding confrontation.

Keira steeled herself. She made herself smile politely.

"Hello, Mr. and Mrs. West," she said to Flint and
Annette as they stared back at her, stone-faced. "You're
both looking well."

"Keira Long," Annette replied, which was far more
neutral a greeting than Keira had expected.

"I'm very well," Keira said, because maybe she was
neither as steely nor as adult as she wished she was.
"Thanks for asking."

"My condolences on your grandma's passing," Flint
muttered, glaring. Which Keira thought was his way of
saying he didn't want to have a conversation. "She'll
be missed."

Then he turned on his heel and headed down the
street toward the hardware store. Keira watched him
go. Looking at Flint West was like staring at Remy's
future. Still tall, still straight and with a kind of quiet
dignity stamped into his bones.

Even when he was being a jerk.

Keira took her time looking back at the woman who
had once reportedly said she would rather Remy marry
one of their cows than Michael Long's daughter. She
made herself smile again, because she didn't know if
Annette had really said that, or if her father had made
that up to hurt her.

Because if this was really the life she wanted, there

was no pretending Flint and Annette didn't exist. And there was only so much avoiding anyone in a town this size.

"Surely we don't have to keep doing this, do we?" Keira asked Annette. "What if we decided, here and now, that we were done with it?"

Annette West was the kind of woman who looked as if she might have personally taken on the Oregon Trail to claim the West family lands. She looked weathered and beautiful, with lines around her eyes, the kind of trim figure that only came from a lifetime of serious, daily horseback riding and pure steel in those hazel eyes she'd passed on to her son.

"Are you staying this time?" Annette asked, something in her drawl suggesting that Keira was as flighty as an easily spooked colt. "Or are you just passing through and planning to head back off to live whatever life it is you have out there that's more interesting than my son?"

The last time Annette had taken a swipe at her, the blow had been a lot less direct and Keira had been a whole lot younger. She hadn't been seasoned yet, with heartbreak and the kind of loneliness that came from doing the right thing—but wishing there was a way to do it differently. And this time, Keira had also faced down her own parents, which had made her heart hurt but hadn't kept her from doing what had to be done.

Because somewhere, deep inside her, she cared about her parents, and always would. For all their faults, they were still her parents. Keira suspected that it was an uneven kind of love that she would seesaw around for the rest of her life. Maybe that was the deal. Maybe all she could hope for from her mother was some stealth weeding.

But she didn't feel the same way about Annette and Flint. She didn't feel a seesaw of unwieldy love, based entirely on a few good memories of childhood.

Keira was prepared to tolerate a lot when it was her, but she didn't feel the same way when it came to Remy. Oh, sure, he might take himself off to the cabin and marinate up there like some kind of hermit in his own dark feelings, but Remy didn't complain. He wasn't aggressive or confrontational. She'd never seen him run from a fight, but he didn't go around starting them, either.

Keira had no such reservations.

"That's a pretty funny question for you to ask," she said to Annette, cool and even, staring the other woman full in the face. As if she'd been waiting for this moment all her life. "Given the way you treat him. Maybe you're no better at loving him than I am."

Annette blinked at that. And then let out a laugh.

"You have a lot of nerve," she drawled, temper flaring in her gaze.

"Am I mistaken? Or have you not been speaking to him for five years now?"

"And whose fault is that?" Annette snapped. "It wasn't bad enough you wrecked my boy—you ruined his relationship with his family, too. Does that make you proud?"

It was Keira's turn to laugh like something was funny when it wasn't.

"I must be awfully powerful to do all that while living in a different state."

"He hasn't been himself in years, and I know who's

to blame for that," Annette retorted. "Did you ever intend to do right by him? And now you're doing it all over again. Playing house, getting his hopes up... What do you think is going to happen to him when you leave?"

Keira had no intention of leaving. But as she hadn't told Remy that, she saw no reason Annette should know it before him.

"Maybe you should concentrate a little less on my plans and a little more on the son who's been right here this whole time," she suggested. And maybe leaned in a little as she said it. "The son you've let isolate himself up there in the woods. The son you've allowed to sink so deep into his own misery you're lucky he didn't drown himself in a whiskey bottle while he was at it."

Annette looked like maybe she was shaking, but she didn't back down.

"I appreciate the parenting advice, Keira," she said coldly. "But you'll forgive me if I don't put much stock in your take on family dynamics. Remy didn't take himself away from everyone who loves him because of *me*."

There was a time when that would have leveled Keira completely. It would have taken her to her knees. After all, this was a woman she'd fully expected would be her mother-in-law one day. The grandmother to her babies.

Keira wasn't that girl anymore.

"I can't believe how much of my life I wasted hoping I could get you to like me," she told Annette, aware that her hands had found her hips, but doing nothing at all to change that. She hoped everyone on the street was listening to this conversation. From her grandmother's friends—who pretended they were too old and riddled with glaucoma to pay attention to anything when the op-

posite was true, no matter the state of their glaucoma—
to the tourists who would no doubt chalk this up to a
little local color. "I think you know how little my own
mother was there for me, and there I was, foolishly imagining my boyfriend's mother could step in and fill that
gap. Which you could have done at any time. But you
chose a different path."

She thought Annette looked taken back, because the
older woman blinked a few times, and the look on her
face changed. But if Keira thought Annette might break
apart at that, or start making sweet protestations, she
was doomed to disappointment.

"I wouldn't know the first thing to do with a girl
child," Annette said after a moment.

And if Keira had been less fired up, she might have
chosen to view that as a kind of apology.

But this wasn't about her, or her teenaged feelings
that Annette had stomped all over—maybe without trying all that hard, given how easily wounded Keira had
been back then. This was about Remy.

Keira stepped closer to Annette, so she could be sure
to look the other woman straight in the eye.

"I was a lost, lonely kid who needed help," she said
calmly and quietly, no matter how much she wanted to
scream. "I was seventeen, and you knew what my father did to you. What do you think he did to me? And
then you threw away your own son because you didn't
like who he fell in love with and, sure enough, blamed
me for that, too."

Annette actually took a step back. But Keira wasn't
done.

"How does that make you any better than my parents?" Keira asked. "They don't pretend to be anything

but grifters. They just want money. You have money already, so what do you want? Obedience? Because I know you don't want simple pride in having raised your son into a good, decent man, because you've had that for years. And you're still not satisfied."

"You have no idea what you're talking about. What makes you think you can come back here and stir everything up—"

"Which is it, Mrs. West?" Keira asked quietly. "Am I the powerful Wizard of Oz, pulling my strings from Seattle? Or am I a needy, silly girl who has no idea what she's doing? I can't be both. And the fact that you want me to be tells me you need to look to yourself."

Annette made a ragged sound that Keira took to be a gasp. She knew perfectly well that Remy would not support what she was doing. He was a man who valued quiet respect and character, not carrying on in full view of all his friends and neighbors. But there was something kicking in her, urging her to keep going.

Because she loved him. And she doubted he would ever forgive her.

And that meant she had a very small window to say what needed saying, before Annette could dismiss it as the jealous rantings of an angry ex.

Life isn't about ready, Grandma June had said.

Keira would never be ready to lose Remy again. She would never be ready to move on. But she'd already done it once. She knew she would survive, little as she might enjoy it.

If this turned out to be what reminded Remy that she didn't deserve him, that was something she'd have to accept.

"If you don't like your relationship with your son,

fix it," she told Annette, not caring if her voice carried all the way down the street and up into the hills. "The way you should have done when you ruined it in the first place by not trusting him to handle his own choices. That has nothing to do with me and deep down I think you know it."

With that, Keira stepped around Annette West—who had never liked her and now certainly never would—held her head up high and resolved there and then that she was done paying for sins she couldn't fix. She was finished with the past.

And whether Remy loved her or didn't, whether he forgave her or couldn't quite get there, she was going to live happily ever after in this town. She was going to make her dreams come true, one after the next.

Right here in Jasper Creek, surrounded by people who'd known her all her life, for good or ill, because somehow that felt better to her than all the anonymity of a city like Seattle.

Keira was going to make sure she had the life she wanted. The life Grandma June had shown her this beautiful spring, in that house stuffed so full of memories it squeaked.

One way or another, Keira was going to be *alive*.

And filled with joy.

Whatever it took.

CHAPTER NINE

REMY WAS OUT fixing a fence.

Which was to say, it was any old Tuesday when a man worked with cattle.

When he heard a truck coming, he knew it couldn't be a good sign this far out on the property. He lifted his hat to wipe his brow and waited there, liking that it already felt like summer.

Well. He liked the warmer weather, but he didn't like that the closer summer came, the sooner it meant Keira was going to leave him.

He shoved that aside. There was no point wallowing in what was to come, because nothing he did was going to change it. He knew that. He'd accepted that.

Remy's hand ached, and he shook it out of the fist he'd made without realizing it.

Okay. Maybe he hadn't exactly accepted it, but he wanted to, if only because he knew it was inevitable this time.

The truck came over the ridge, and Remy sighed. It was his older brother Smith's pickup this time, but if he wasn't mistaken, he could see his younger brother Browning hanging out in the passenger side.

Terrific. More West brother nonsense when he had work to do. All that was missing was a visit from Parker, the brawny baby of the family.

Waylon whined softly at his side, and Remy dropped his hand to rest on the dog's head. But since he didn't relax, Waylon didn't, either.

"We have to stop meeting like this," Remy drawled when Smith pulled up next to him. "If only to keep me from charging you all with trespassing."

"I wish you would get me thrown in jail for a little trespassing charge." Browning flashed his usual wide, amiable grin that might have fooled most of the girls in three counties, but didn't do a whole lot for Remy. "I could use a little break right about now. Too much ranching, not enough fun."

"Did he come up here to talk to me about his social life?" Remy asked Smith.

But Smith, the second oldest of the West boys, wasn't much of a talker. He'd never said much before he'd gone off to fight for his country, and he said a lot less now. He lifted a shoulder in reply.

And once again, Remy felt that sense of dislocation. As if he wanted to mend things with his brothers. It was one more feeling he figured would go away again, once Keira did.

"I'm not here to talk about my social life." Browning wandered around the front of the pickup truck and propped himself against the hood while Remy stared back at him balefully. "I'm here to tell you a little story."

"I don't have to hear the story to know I don't want to hear it," Remy assured him. "Have I ever wanted to hear one of your stories?"

"This one, I think you'll like," Browning said cheerfully. "I sure did. It's a little tale I like to call 'When Remy's Girlfriend Took a Piece Out of Annette McAndrews West in the Middle of Town.'"

Remy blinked. "What?"

"Yes, sir. Last Sunday, your woman went toe to toe with your mother, read her the riot act and won, by all accounts." Browning lifted a hand. "Let's take a moment of silence to let that sink in."

Remy looked over at Smith, who was still sitting in the driver's seat of the truck. He expected a rolled eye. Or a shake of the head, to indicate that Browning was exaggerating, but Smith held Remy's gaze and nodded.

Remy had no idea how to feel about that.

Browning took his inability to speak as an invitation to fill him in on what had to be the biggest gossip to hit Jasper Creek in some time. Or at least since last fall's typically cutthroat Red Sled Holiday Bazaar over at Everett McCall's place.

"Why did you come out here to tell me this?" Remy asked when he was finished. "You want me to thank you?"

"Of course not," Browning said, and rolled his eyes with great drama. "Because why would you thank anybody when it's so much easier to storm around, growling at everything, and pretending you're all alone on an island somewhere instead of literally surrounded by one of the biggest families in this valley? You do you, Remy."

"Thank you," Remy said, holding his younger brother's gaze until he was pretty sure he'd conveyed each and every one of his aggressive thoughts. Browning smirked. "I appreciate you delivering the gossip to me, like you're old Mrs. Kim."

But after his brothers had left, with the usual threats of bodily harm and a few largely genial hand gestures that would have gotten them a smack from their mother, no matter how old they were, Remy found he couldn't quite throw himself back into his work.

His brothers kept coming after him, no matter how often or aggressively he told them to knock it off. And in between the odd lecture here and there about turning into a scary mountain-man hermit and/or their father, they mostly just laughed at him and acted like maybe the next time they showed up, he'd offer them a beer.

If asked, Remy would have told anyone that they were obnoxious. But they hadn't kept after him for five whole years because they were obnoxious. They'd done it because they cared about him.

He might not understand his parents, but clearly they loved him, or why would they care at all about whether or not Keira was back? Why would they bother to hold a grudge against her?

They wouldn't. His parents were busy people. So were his brothers, for that matter. And Remy had yet to meet a member of the West family who could be provoked into doing a single freaking thing they didn't want to do.

Why had he never understood this before?

He climbed into his truck, whistling Waylon in before him. Then he headed across the valley, turning onto a dirt road he hadn't driven up in a long, long time.

The West ranch was exactly as he remembered it. Beautiful.

The higher he climbed, the more he could see of the land his family had ranched for generations. The original farmhouse was still down at the foot of the hills, but his grandparents had built themselves a sprawling ranch house that his parents had added to as the years passed. The road meandered in and out of the deep, dark, mysteriously green Oregon woods, offering sweeping views across the valley toward the mountains in the distance, offshoots of the Rockies that had made the west what it was.

Some days, Remy felt that inside him like his own blood.

He turned the final corner and drove past the house where he'd spent so many years of his life; he skirted around the outbuildings where he knew his brothers lived, a couple in their own cabins, and the other two in the communal bunkhouse with the long-term hands. He headed for the barn complex and office Flint had built, and that was where Remy found his father, kicked back in his big leather chair with the phone to his ear.

Remy walked into the office without knocking and stood there, meeting his father's gaze full-on.

"Let me call you back," Flint said into the phone. "Something just came up."

He put down the phone, and for moment, father and son simply took the measure of each other.

"I'm surprised it took nearly two whole days for the gossip to reach you," Flint said in that same tough voice of his that echoed over the whole of Remy's childhood. And still echoed in him, hard.

But Remy wasn't a child any longer. Remy was a grown man, and it was time to act like it.

Flint lifted his chin. "What are you going to do? Continue giving us the silent treatment? Or is it going to be extra special silent treatment this time around?"

"I came to apologize, Dad. You can take that apology or not, but I want you to know, I understand it. You and Mom thought you were protecting me. And maybe I got carried away trying to protect Keira."

Remy blew out a breath. "I let my pride get the better of me. I didn't want you to say 'I told you so.' So. There it is."

"I wouldn't have said 'I told you so,'" Flint said gruffly.

Remy tilted his head to one side. His father made a low noise.

"I might have said it," he allowed. "But not to hurt you. That was never the goal."

"I can't say the same," Remy said. "I apologize for that, as well."

"I owe you an apology, too," Flint said, which were words Remy never thought he'd hear from his father. Not in this life. "Your mother and I only wanted what was best for you. It was never our intention to make things worse. Or run you off."

Even at the best of times, they weren't exactly huggers. So they nodded at each other, there on opposite sides of Flint's massive desk. And Remy felt like a huge weight was lifted off his shoulders—making him wonder why he hadn't done this sooner.

But he knew why. It was Keira.

He'd had to get over his pride to be with her this time. And he wasn't sure he ever would have done it if she hadn't come back.

If she hadn't forced him to face the fact that not only had he never stopped loving her, he didn't think he ever would.

"Keira said your mother and I couldn't see that we'd raised a good son to be a good man," Flint said, and his voice grew even gruffer. "I want you to know that's not true. I've seen what you've done with June Gable's land." His gaze was steady. "I'm proud of you, Remy. You should know that."

"Thank you, Dad," Remy replied, and something inside him cracked open at the praise from a man who Remy would have sworn could never—would never—praise anything or anyone. Maybe his father wasn't an unyielding block of granite after all. "I appreciate that."

They weren't a demonstrative family. And that wasn't going to change. But when Flint walked out of the office with Remy, he reached over and rested his hand on Remy's shoulder for a moment. Certainly not a hug. And not quite a pat.

But still, Remy felt the way he had when he was small, and Flint would pick him up and toss him so high into the sky that he was sure he could fly. He'd believed he was flying, just for a second, until Flint caught him again in those big, hard hands of his.

Remy was a grown man who didn't expect to be flying anytime soon, and knew his father couldn't lift him if he tried, but all the same, he found himself smiling as he got back in his truck.

He needed to talk to his mother, he knew. He needed to thank her for loving him even when he hadn't realized that was what she was doing. And he needed to buy his brothers a round or two of beers to thank them for looking out for him all this time, thankless as it had been. Maybe go a little overboard on the heartfelt discussion about *feelings*, to make them all squirm in horror, and get things back to normal.

The very notion made him grin.

Even as it made him realize that his brothers had loved him enough to let him go, knowing he'd come back.

Remy figured he could learn from that.

He drove off the West ranch feeling a whole lot lighter than he had in years.

Not only because he'd set things right, or set them in motion, anyway, with his family.

But because the other thing he'd realized about the story Browning had told him was that just as his parents wouldn't bother to go around disapproving of some girl if they didn't care about their son, the same held true for Keira.

He couldn't help thinking that she had to love him, at least a little, or why would she have rushed to his defense?

She had to love him, he told himself. *She had to.*

But even if she didn't, Remy figured it was high time he stopped pretending he had ever been anything but wildly, deeply, irrevocably in love with Keira Long.

Who was supposed to be his wife.

And if he had his way, still would be.

CHAPTER TEN

KEIRA SPREAD GRANDMA'S fabric swatches out on the dining room table and helped herself to Grandma's sewing machine, too. As the afternoon wore on, she started sewing together her favorite swatches, following the instructions Grandma June had given her so long ago now that it felt as if the knowledge was in her fingers. A part of her.

And she knew that the more pieces she put together, the closer she was to the sort of quilt that lay on the master bed upstairs, in the room Keira had barely touched. The room that still smelled like her grandmother's face cream and the bath salts she nestled in with what she'd called her *unmentionables*.

Keira didn't hear the truck pull up outside. Or the footsteps on the porch that Remy had fixed, good as new, weeks ago now, so no one would ever know her father had gone straight through it.

But when she glanced up and found Remy standing there before her, she only smiled.

And hoped he couldn't see the way her heart leaped inside her chest.

"I hear you had some things to say to my mother," Remy said with no preamble, his beautiful face stern and his mouth an unsmiling line.

Keira kept her hands flat on the swatches of fabric

before her, as if they could give her strength. As if they were Grandma June, holding on to her.

She kept her gaze steady on the big man standing there in her grandmother's sweetly fussy dining room, looking out of place and absolutely perfect all at once. "I was hoping you wouldn't hear about that."

"You know my brothers. Especially Browning. He's the biggest gossip I ever met."

"If you're going to be a hermit, Remy, you really ought to be one." Keira made a tsking sound. "That means no gossip sessions with your brothers."

"I'm trying to understand why you would rush to my defense like that."

Keira felt something shudder through her. Because obviously, Remy wasn't going to let her wave this away as something lighthearted. Or joke her way out of it.

"Is there a reason I shouldn't come to your defense?" she asked lightly, because that was safer, surely, than any conversation they tried to have about real things. Raw things.

"What made you think I need defending?" Remy asked.

Keira let her palm brush over the swatch directly in front of her. *Fred's old winter coat*, the note on the back read. *His favorite, despite the holes.*

It felt like her grandparents' entire relationship in one note, pinned to the back of an old scrap from a long-ago discarded wool coat.

"I take full responsibility," Keira said, which was as close as she planned to get to an apology—because she wasn't sorry. "I could have simply nodded my head, walked on and continued minding my own business."

"What I want to know is why."

There was something in his voice, then. Some edge that made her think of the way he drove into her when he was braced above her, when everything between them was tense and taut.

And much more raw and real than they ever talked about afterward.

"I don't know what you want me to say."

"I think you do."

Remy's voice was mesmerizing. Keira wanted to sink into it. He took his hat off his head and ran his fingers through his hair, but he didn't put down his hat. He held it to him, like his Stetson was a shield. Or a bouquet of flowers. He was a cowboy through and through, so really, it was both.

"I understand if this isn't what you signed up for, Keira. But I think it's time to clarify a few things."

She had half a mind to run upstairs and barricade herself in one of the bedrooms, the way she'd done when she was little and hadn't wanted to go home with her parents. Anything to keep him from saying the serious things she could see he wanted to say.

Anything to keep him from ending this.

Because as it turned out, she still wasn't ready, no matter what she'd told herself in town the other day.

But it was as if the house heard her, because the bedroom door upstairs slammed shut.

Okay, Grandma June, she said fiercely inside her head. *You want me to have this conversation? Then I will.*

She pushed herself up to her feet and met his gaze. She hadn't done that much the last time they'd broken up.

"I'm not sure clarification has ever led me anywhere

I wanted to go," she said softly when she was facing him. "Not with you."

"Tough." Remy belted the word out.

She blinked at that, but he didn't take it back.

Instead, he looked at her. Really looked at her, until she wished she'd done something with her hair after her shower, or had bothered to wear something other than her favorite old jeans. He looked at her like he was trying to memorize her. He made her feel…so many things at once she didn't think she could process them all. Or even name them.

It was all a single great and mighty storm, wild and intense.

It was all Remy.

He let out a breath, but she felt it like a blow. "The thing is, Keira, I can't stop loving you. I don't know how."

He sounded rough. Raw.

As if he was confessing something terrible.

And the look on his face was so intense, so beautiful, it made her eyes fill with tears.

She had never seen this man—this big, tough cowboy, who had always been like a mountain to her, made of granite and certainty even when she'd been that silly, needy girl his mother hadn't liked very much—vulnerable before. She'd seen him mad. She'd understood that he was hurt, that she'd hurt him.

But she'd never seen him look at her as if his heart was right there, wide-open and on his face.

And Keira wasn't sure she had ever felt more humbled.

"The truth is, it kills me that you left me," he told her. "I'm not over it. I'm never going to be over it."

"Remy—" she began.

But he wasn't finished. "And I know you will again.

You're going to leave me the same way you did five years ago. I keep telling myself it's fine. That I handled it once and I will again. But I'll be honest with you, Keira. It's going to kill me. All over again."

She shook where she stood, aware on some level that her tears were making tracks down her cheeks. And that she couldn't seem to speak, or move, or even breathe very well.

"I wanted to be your husband," Remy said. "In my whole life, I've never wanted anyone else. And it kills me that I'm just some guy you knew. Just your old boyfriend. Just—"

But Keira was moving then, rounding the table where so much of her family's past was laid out like a patchwork of memories, not fabric. And it was as if she could see, suddenly, every little swatch that made up her life with Remy.

That shy, first smile she'd sent him without looking away.

Their first kiss.

The way she'd looped her hands around his neck one afternoon as he'd slowly, haltingly taught her how to dance because he'd learned so she could dance with him at her senior prom.

The night she'd driven down from Eugene through the snow just to feel his arms around her. And the exquisite joy when she finally did.

A hundred memories and sensations that altogether added up to him. To Remy.

To this.

Them.

Then she was before him, reaching out to him, because how could she do anything but put her hands on him?

"No, Remy," she managed to say. "*No.* You're not 'some guy.' You're the only guy."

"You were away for five years," he ground out, looking down at her. "I accept reality. I want you to know that. I might feel however I feel about it, but I'm never going to mention it again."

She understood then that he would forgive her anything. That he already had. She felt light-headed.

"Remy…"

But he was pulling her closer to him, his eyes dark with emotion. With this storm that was only and ever theirs.

"I want what I've always wanted," he said, his voice like gravel. "You, Keira. I only want you."

He reached into the inside of his hat and pulled out something. She knew what it was before it gleamed in the afternoon light. She knew exactly what it was before he held it there in the palm of his hand.

The last time he'd offered her this ring, with the pretty solitaire that seemed to catch the sun and hold it, he'd done it on one knee.

"I want you to marry me," he said. "That hasn't changed. It's not going to change. I'm not going to fight with you if you need to leave. But I'll be here when you come back. I can wait. I will."

She could barely see. She wiped at her eyes, and then she surged up on her toes to hold his hard, square jaw in her hands.

"Listen to me," she said. "There has only ever been you."

His gaze darkened, but she kept going.

"I broke up with you because I was terrified that if I didn't, I would end up like my mother. You get offended when I say that, but I'm not comparing you to my father. I didn't know how to make sure *I* wouldn't disappear like my mother does whenever he's around."

He started to say something, but Keira shook her head.

"I thought I would go out there and do all the things my father refused to let my mother do. And I did. I got a degree. And a great job. I had a whole life, and it was fine. But it wasn't *this*. It wasn't *us*."

"I told you, I accept that you had to do that. I understand. I do."

"And that makes me love you even more," she whispered fiercely. "But there's nothing to accept but the years. And I can't regret them. Because I needed to figure out how to stand on my own two feet before I could stand here in front of you and say this. Say it and really, truly mean it, the way I couldn't when I was still so scared of what-ifs."

"You don't have to prove anything to me," Remy told her. "I didn't want to hear that I had anything to do with our breakup, but I know I did. You were right. I wanted it my way. I thought I'd waited long enough. I should have thought more about what you needed, and less about how it made me feel."

Every time she thought she already loved him too much, he made her love him more. Something in her told her that he always would. That this was what a lifetime with Remy would be like. Loving him more, letting it deepen and finding new ways to love him even more than that.

Keira was up to the challenge.

"This is what I need to say," she told him. "I love you. I've never loved anyone else. I've never touched anyone else. I didn't leave you because I wanted experiences with other men. I left you because I wanted to be the kind of woman who could stand tall on her own." She pulled in a breath. "Like your mother."

"My mother?" He sounded stunned. "The one you yelled at in the street?"

"Your mother is tough as nails," Keira said. "She's your father's partner in everything. Everyone knows she can ride any horse alive, drink any man under the table and, in her spare time, run a ranch and raise five boys. I wanted so desperately for her to like me when I was younger, but why would she? I was one more burden for you to carry. *Of course* she wanted better for her son."

Remy blinked. "I'm not sure I've ever thought about my mother that way."

"I love you, Remy," Keira told him. "And I didn't understand until now that I spent every moment of those five years away learning how to be not the seventeen-year-old girl who meant well, but a grown woman who can be your partner. Grandma June wanted you and me to work this land together. She didn't want her grand-daughter flailing around, crying and not knowing what she felt about anything. I thought she encouraged me to go because she knew this place was wrong for me. But now I think she knew I had to go because when I came back, it would be to stay."

She reached down to his other hand, the one he'd closed around the ring, and opened it.

She had the rest of her life to show him all the ways she'd trained to become his partner, never realizing that was what she'd been doing. The business courses she'd taken in college. The experience she'd had in her corporate job, learning how to sell, how to negotiate. All things that would serve her well on a ranch.

With a coffee truck on the side—because everyone needed a hobby away from the cows.

And together she and Remy would figure out how to be husband and wife, year after year, until they were finishing each other's sentences and doddering around in wool coats with holes in them.

"I love you," she said again. "I've always loved you and I always will. And I can't think of anything I'd rather be than your wife."

She went to pick up the ring, but Remy took it from her and sank down on his knees before her the way he had once before.

"Keira," he said, his voice a rumble and his eyes a great storm. "Princess. I love you. Marry me this time. Stay with me forever."

"Remy," she whispered, "it would be my very great honor to do both of those things."

And she couldn't help the sob that escaped her as he took her hand and finally slid that ring where it belonged.

Some people had to fight for their forever. And she and Remy would never forget those long, lonely years apart. But as the love of her life pulled her into his arms Keira caught a dizzy flash of color out of the corner of her eye.

"Look," she whispered.

Outside, the dogwood tree had finally burst into a riot of pink blossoms, so bright and happy that it made Keira tear up.

Spring's blessings came in blustery, hard and sometimes painful, but after the storm came the sunshine. The marvelous green.

Because everything bloomed in its time.

"Beautiful," Remy said, his mouth at Keira's ear. "But not as beautiful as you."

And Keira was sure she could hear Grandma June laughing in delight as Remy spun her around and around in the farmhouse's front rooms, dancing to the music they'd made across all these years.

Dancing for their future. Dancing for their past.

Dancing and dancing, the way he'd taught her long ago, because they'd finally found their way back home.

CHAPTER ELEVEN

KEIRA SUBJECTED HERSELF to an awkward initial dinner with Remy's family a few days after they got engaged.

His brothers were rowdy and irreverent, but that made the awkwardness feel almost funny, so she was okay with it. And the more they teased Remy at the table, the more she saw glimpses of the easygoing man he'd been years ago.

And would be again, she vowed.

"You called me out and you were right," Annette said when they were finally alone at the huge, rambling dinner table, Annette having sent her men off to make themselves useful. She smiled at Keira from her seat at one end. And maybe even winked. "Don't do it again."

And as Keira grinned back at her, she felt the first stirring of hope that Annette and she might actually get along, the way she'd dreamed they would years ago.

It was the same kind of hope she felt when she finished her first patchwork quilt, laughed at its flaws and spread it out on the bed she shared with Remy. It was the same hope she felt when she planted her own flower garden up at the cabin, and found that someone went up and weeded that little patch, too.

A flower garden wasn't the same as the mother she'd needed growing up. It wasn't the same as a heartfelt talk or an apology. But if she'd learned anything from her

spring in Grandma June's house, it was how to count
her blessings as they came.

And how to let things bloom as they would.

She and Remy spent the rest of May and most of
June in the farmhouse, but moved into the cabin when
it was time to make way for JJ. And summer. And the
rest of the seasons that would bring her cousins back
to Jasper Creek.

The day before JJ was due to arrive, Keira sat at
the kitchen table with a blank piece of paper, trying
to think of what she could tell her cousin. What she
should tell her.

She could smell the coming summer. She'd left all
the windows open, the better to pull in the sunshine.

If she closed her eyes, she could imagine Grandma
June was here with her, bustling around behind her and
humming something beneath her breath.

She crumpled up the paper and shoved it in her
pocket. Grandma June knew what to do. She always had.

Keira hefted up the big canvas bag of patchwork
pieces, tales of love in swatches. She was sure she'd
heard Remy close the door behind him when he'd gone
out a few moments ago, but it was open now, as if the
house was taking her by the hand and leading her out.
She went down the front steps and caught her foot on
that same old board, the way she always did. She smiled
at the last of the pink blossoms that clung to her favorite tree.

"I love you, too, Grandma June," she said.

And then she made her way to the truck, where Waylon grinned out the window and the man she'd loved her
entire life loved her back, hard and deep.

"Ready?" Remy asked when she slid inside.

"Always," Keira said.

Finally, she meant.

And they drove out into the fields together, heading straight on toward the rest of their lives and the whole of their big, bright future.

At last.

* * * * *

Summer

Nicole Helm

For my grandmas, who always gave me summer magic, love, and examples of strength and purpose.

And for the three best friends and writers I could have ever dreamed up to write a book with.

SUMMER

Dearest Jessamyn Joy,

It's a very strange thing to get old, to know that eventually the world will go on without you. To see clearly your successes, and your mistakes, and still not know what you could have done about either.

You, like the middle name your mother allowed me to pick for you, were one of my four greatest joys on this earth. Summers with you underfoot were never boring, and I've missed your straightforward and energetic need to do these past few summers without you while you've worked to prove yourself to your father at the greenhouse.

That'll make you sad, maybe even guilty, though you'll pretend it makes you mad. You'll pretend you just love your job, not that you've been trying to ensure your father's love and pride since you were a little girl.

But, whether I'm there or not, I know you, my earnestly determined JJ.

I have many things to ask of you this summer. First, to watch two little girls whose mother left them, while their hardworking daddy tries to provide for them. Your earnest determination is just

*what the two Mathewson girls need. They could
also use a woman's touch (I'm laughing imagining the way you'll sneer over that). When they go
back to school after Labor Day, you're free to go
wherever you please.*

*The second task is bigger, and it'll be harder.
I hope you'll remember your joy. I want you to
let yourself feel—for yourself, for your family and
for others.*

*Let my spirit guide you in all that you do, let
this house take care of you as it has always cared
for me, and I have the utmost confidence you'll
find that thing you've been searching for that you
never admit to yourself you're searching for. (And
don't roll your eyes at me, young lady.)*

Love always,
Grandma June

CHAPTER ONE

HER FIRST MORNING waking up in Grandma's creaky farmhouse, JJ Frost sat at the ancient, battered kitchen table and made a list on her phone.

Not a grocery list, or even a list of activities to do with two little girls whose clearly desperate father thought it'd be a good idea to unload on her.

She focused on the house, because it was here and so was she.

Buy new window screens
Replace old screens
Wash windows

It would be imperative to keep busy. Luckily there was plenty to do. During her cousin's spring here, Keira had busied herself with Remy West, who had been helping Grandma run the cattle operation these past few years. He'd also been Keira's first love.

And last love, apparently, as they were now engaged and Keira was staying in Jasper Creek, out at the cabin on the edge of Grandma's property.

The thought of Keira and her fiancé living together in that place made JJ's chest feel too tight, like the thought of Grandma not being here, and her sister being the next one of Grandma's granddaughters to move in.

The sharp stab of pain that lodged right below her breast would normally be passed off as heartburn, but she hadn't eaten yet.

It must be a hunger pain then, because she'd accepted long ago that Lila and their mother didn't understand her. Or want her. Which was fine. The break had been many years before, and there hadn't been any point in letting betrayal rule her life.

She'd had Dad. She'd had Frost Greenhouse. Most importantly, she'd always had Grandma. Grandma had never cared that she didn't want to play *imagine* with Lila, or join her for chicken tea parties.

Chickens could not consent to tea parties.

The burn spread lower, and JJ left her list and old hurts, and studied Grandma's kitchen.

The kitchen still looked exactly as it had through all those summers, and her less frequent trips recently. Keira hadn't changed anything during her spring. A large window above the sink looked out over the side yard, the cupboards were a faded green and the appliances were old and finicky.

But Grandma wasn't standing at the stove with her well-used cookbook at her elbow.

JJ could picture all four of them at the table during their last summer all together—her and Keira hotly debating the book they'd been reading together, Lila staring off through the window and Bella looking small and separate.

They'd been teenagers—Keira and JJ were older, at seventeen and sixteen, respectively, while Bella and Lila were just thirteen and fourteen—but Grandma's that summer had felt like the last grand hurrah of childhood.

JJ blinked at the stinging in her eyes. Allergies, surely.

Let yourself feel. Let my spirit guide you in all that you do, let this house take care of you as it has always cared for me.

JJ didn't believe in spirits, or houses magically taking any care, and she'd never let feelings rule her. The only way a person got through the world was with their feet firmly planted on the ground. Her father had taught her that, and nothing in life had ever proved that simple fact wrong.

A too-warm breeze wafted through the kitchen window over the sink, smelling like grass and clover. The perfume of her childhood summers.

Grief wasn't a new companion, but it was harder to mask and control here in the home of her happiest memories, and without the one woman who'd never made her feel like a mistake, or that she had to prove herself worthy of love.

JJ didn't have time for this…wallowing. There was so much to do.

She marched to the basement door. When she tried to open it, it stuck. She pulled harder on the ornate metal knob, but the wood bowed precariously, as if the knob might splinter off the door entirely. After another hearty tug, the door swung open.

The basement was dark, and had been the source of a few childhood nightmares for both her and Lila. But she was an adult now. No nightmares, and no little sister to share them with.

She flipped the switch, which only made a sputtering sound as a light flashed then went pitch-black.

Check wattage
Buy light bulbs
Check wiring to basement light

Once she'd added those things to her list, she opened the flashlight app on her phone and let the beam guide her down the rickety stairs. The array of fans she was looking for, most of them older than JJ herself, sat in the same place they always did out of season.

She set up her phone to shine on the stairs, then dutifully carried them all upstairs, arranging them in the places Grandma always had.

Sweaty, even with the fans now circulating fresh air from the open windows, JJ hauled one to the room she'd always stayed in as a girl.

With Lila.

Moving away from that thought, JJ took a quick shower. Then, after wrapping the towel around her, she picked up her phone and added more items to her list.

Call someone about the water heater
Buy all the bleach

She set down the phone and looked at herself in the foggy mirror. When she was a little girl she'd wished for Grandma's blue eyes, sharp nose or curly hair. Anything to look in the mirror and see a piece of Grandma in her reflection.

Her eyes had stayed resolutely brown, her nose a shade too close to pert and her hair wouldn't curl, a fact Mom had considered her greatest weakness. She looked like her father, through and through.

But JJ had Grandma's independence and work ethic,

because those were things she could control. So no use getting all emotional over what she couldn't.

Dressed for the day in sensible shorts and a plain navy T-shirt, she hoped against hope the temperatures didn't soar in the afternoon.

She would be watching the Mathewson girls from nine to four, with an hour-long lunch break.

The Mathewson girls. *Girls*. JJ had gone to the baby shower for one of them with Grandma, nine or ten years ago. Cade's wife, ex-wife now, had been one of those types who'd always looked perfect, like a model. Still, JJ had been surprised Melissa had ditched Cade and the girls since she'd always seemed happy, if aloof.

Now Cade was the single dad to a nine-year-old and a six-year-old. Though JJ had seen Cade now and again as an adult, it was still hard to think of him as a father of elementary-school-age kids.

In her mind's eye he was still a gangly teenager— the only neighboring boy who didn't get bent out of shape when she beat him in a footrace, or a contest to see who could climb the highest in a tree. He'd shake her hand and say "nice work," unlike his brothers or those West boys.

JJ had always liked Cade. Now she was going to be watching his girls. Day in and day out until school started again. Did he have any idea what he was getting himself into?

Do you?

Grandma had entrusted her with this task, so JJ would give it her all. A request from Grandma was the one and only thing that could have her doing something so outside her comfort zone. Or going against her father the way she had. He'd argued that Grandma June was gone, so why bother following her directives?

While JJ had been able to cancel trips to Grandma's at her father's request when Grandma had been alive, something about her being gone made it impossible. At first, JJ had been sure the hard work she'd put in to take a three-month sabbatical would appease Dad. She'd personally trained her assistant manager to take over all her tasks and to keep Dad's calendar, and she'd spent extra hours making schedules and notes and programming reminders.

Dad hadn't spoken to her for the three days leading up to her departure from Plainview. JJ had almost given in—she'd considered asking Keira or Lila to take her summer for her.

Every time she decided that, she was reminded of Grandma's funeral. She'd stood with Keira and Lila, Dad keeping close so he wouldn't have to speak to Mom. It hadn't felt finished. It hadn't felt right.

Maybe losing Grandma never would, but thanks to that letter, JJ believed this summer could give her… something. Grandma's death made this whole summer necessary. Watching two little girls and all.

Besides, Grandma had put together all sorts of instructions on what to do with Ellie and Lora. JJ could handle this task, because Grandma had asked her to.

She went into the kitchen and made herself some toast, brewed some tea and then gathered up the notebook of information on her babysitting job for the summer.

She settled back into the creaking wooden chair at the kitchen table and flipped through Grandma's notebook while she ate and drank. Inside, Grandma hadn't

just written notes, she'd drawn little illustrations—
flowers and fairies.

Ellie loves unicorns, anything that glitters and
picking wildflowers. I keep jelly glasses of her
bouquets on the windowsill just like I did with
you girls.

JJ let her finger linger on the words *you girls*. Her
grandmother's beautiful handwriting softened the blow
of having to deal with unicorns and glitter.

Lora has been in her princess fad (even you had
one of those—don't try to deny it!)

"She-Ra was a princess of *power*, Grandma," JJ muttered, but she kept reading.

Since she'd already read it a few times, she skimmed
the rest of the likes and dislikes and fanciful games
Grandma played with the girls—most of which she'd
played with JJ and Lila and their cousins.

JJ didn't realize she'd been lost in memories of Mo-
nopoly on rainy days with the roof leaking in the kitchen
until a knock sounded at the door.

A quick glance at the clock left JJ surprised at how
much time had passed and how little of her breakfast
she'd eaten, and how much the kitchen smelled like rain
despite the insistent sunshine outside.

The smell was just…imagination. She supposed she
still had one of those, no matter how she tried to ignore it.

She hurried to the front door and opened it, know-

ing Cade Mathewson and his two daughters would be
on the other side.

No matter that she'd seen him occasionally on her
rare visits, she still had that picture of a teenager with
unruly hair, a ratty cowboy hat two sizes too big and
a pair of jeans one size too small—the curse of being
the youngest of six boys and living in constant hand-
me-downs.

His smile was still crooked, but now his nose was,
as well. He'd filled out, and was no longer all limbs and
height. He was packed with muscle that his T-shirt and
jeans showed off rather invitingly.

His hat was still a size too big, though.

Her stomach flipped. Obviously because she hadn't
finished her breakfast.

"Cade," she greeted. "Good to see you." Belatedly,
she remembered to smile at him and the two girls, who
stood pressed to either side of his legs.

He made an odd noise, then cleared his throat. "Uh.
I haven't seen you in a while, I guess. You don't look
quite like I remember, JJ."

She nodded. "You were down with the chicken pox
for the funeral, if I recall."

Cade shuddered. "Please, don't remind me. I'd take
a hoof to the head before two girls with chicken pox
again."

She honestly couldn't imagine. Now, the girls in
question were going to be her responsibility. She looked
down at them standing on the porch. They both eyed
her with a wariness she appreciated—one should always be wary of near strangers.

One girl wore glittery pink fairy wings over a solid
pink outfit, with some dark purple stain on the collar.

The older of the two wore a fussy-looking dress and pink sparkly cowboy boots that could be of no actual ranch use.

"Summer is dress-yourself season," Cade offered, nudging the older girl through the door. "It cuts down on some of the arguments during the school year about fairy wings."

He picked up the fairy-winged child and carried her inside.

There was something mesmerizing about a big cowboy carrying a little girl dressed like a fairy. Enough of *something* it took JJ a few moments to realize she was standing there with the door open, flies and bees buzzing in, while she stared at a big muscled arm hefting the weight of a small sparkly girl.

JJ blinked and shook her head. She didn't have a clue what was wrong with her—and she had no desire to find out.

"Well, I guess there's no dress code down at the farm."

Cade smiled that crooked smile. "Lord knows you never had one. You used to wear your grandpa's old stained T-shirts, if I recall."

"That was only because I ripped all my good shirts, and he wasn't needing them anymore." She only had fuzzy memories of her grandfather before he'd died when she was a little girl. They were fond fuzzy memories, but nothing more than that. She had always liked wearing his shirts, though.

Cade placed a large, scarred hand at the crown of his daughter's flyaway blond hair. "Hopefully you can show these girls as much fun as we had when we were this age." He lowered the younger girl to her feet, though she clearly didn't want to be put down.

Cade looked from the girls, standing hip to hip, still not saying a word, to her. "Are you sure you can handle this?"

JJ smiled reassuringly before she glanced at the girls, who were staring wide-eyed at her. Unease swept through her, but it would be silly to be intimidated by two children.

"Sure I can. Grandma left me a whole book of instructions, games to play, what kind of food the girls like. She was well prepared, and therefore, so am I."

"We sure miss her around here."

"Yeah, well." JJ had never known what to do with missing. Add sympathy on top of it, and she was pretty keen to get Cade going. "You probably have work to do. I wouldn't want to keep you."

"Right. I appreciate it, JJ. You doing this for me is a real lifesaver." He pulled a small card out of his pocket. "I'm sure June left you this information, but just in case, this has my cell, the ranch number and anyone else you could get a hold of if you need me. Just call through these numbers until you find me—you know, if something goes wrong."

It was the first sign of uncertainty she'd seen in him. He was trying to hide it, she could tell, as he handed her the card casually. The way he slowly let out his breath told her he wasn't as okay with this whole thing as he was pretending.

"It'll be fine," she said as brightly as she could manage, though bright had never been in her wheelhouse. "Your girls are in good hands."

"Of course they are." He smiled, but it didn't reach his eyes. "But you'll call if you need anything?"

"Absolutely," she replied, pushing away the thought she should reach out and give his arm a reassuring squeeze. How weird would *that* be?

Cade tipped his hat. He opened the door, then gave his girls a stern look. "You be good for Ms. JJ now. Got it?"

The girls silently nodded in unison.

"Call. Really. If you need…anything. I'll be back to take them for lunch."

Then he was gone, leaving his two children with her. JJ was trying to figure out how that had happened when the youngest, Lora, looked up at her with tears in her eyes, mouth trembling.

"I miss Grandma June," she wailed.

JJ didn't wail, but inwardly she added an item to her list.

Figure out what to do about little girl tears.

CHAPTER TWO

CADE DIDN'T CONSIDER himself an overprotective father. When a man had two little girls, and only brothers to help with the raising of said girls, there was only so much worry a man could bear.

So he was desperately trying to let go of his nerves over letting JJ watch Ellie and Lora. June would have never suggested such a thing if she hadn't thought JJ could handle it.

And Cade *knew* JJ. Maybe not as well these days, but June cared too much about his girls to entrust them with someone who wasn't capable.

Had cared. It was still just…sad. June had been like a surrogate grandmother to him, and in some ways a mother, considering his had died when he'd been eight. He remembered bits and pieces of a small woman with a gentle way, despite six thundering boys. June, though, had been a part of his life for these almost thirty years.

He tried to give his girls all the gentleness he could find, but there was only so much to be had at the Mathewson Ranch.

JJ Frost. Not exactly his idea of *gentle*. She'd been one of the boys in those youthful summers. With a tenacity to prove herself just as good as anyone around her.

He supposed his girls could use that, too, if there was no feminine gentleness to be gleaned from JJ. Maybe he'd secretly wondered why Grandma June hadn't tasked Lila, or even Keira, with the responsibility, but it didn't matter now.

The small note Grandma June's lawyer had brought to his door, while the girls had been miserable with chicken pox and he had been miserable with single parenthood, had made it impossible to refuse her:

Dearest Cade,

Sad to leave you in the lurch this summer, but you know I always have a plan. The girlies need stability. I'm sorry I won't be able to be around to give it to them. JJ will be in the house this summer, and I've asked her to take on my role. She can step into my shoes easily enough. Let those darlings have the house again this summer. It'll be good for all of you.
Looking out for you always,

Love,
Grandma June

Grandma June had always looked out for him, and he couldn't ignore that she was doing so even after she'd left this earth.

He doubted JJ was feeling the same at the moment. So he picked up the grocery bag full of the sandwiches he'd made for the girls and himself. He'd take them somewhere on the property for a quick picnic. It might lift Ellie's grumpy spirits. She always loved a picnic.

Which wouldn't assuage his guilt that he wasn't doing enough for his girls, but it'd at least give JJ a break and maybe a chance for her to tell him she couldn't hack this.

Which would make his life exponentially harder. Something he was intimately acquainted with. He wouldn't even know what to do with easy.

A good night's sleep, a quiet morning and the persistent worry knot in his gut gone?

A pipe dream.

He dreamed about all three as he drove out to the country highway and over rolling hills until he reached Grandma June's gravel drive.

As the house came into view, he wondered if JJ would let him do a few repairs June had always told him not to bother with. Somehow, he doubted it. JJ and June had a lot in common when it came to stubbornness.

He parked next to JJ's truck. Lora came running out of the house, a big grin on her face. Her fairy wings, more than a little crooked, flapped in the wind she made as she ran toward his truck.

He got out and opened the gate of the picket fence that surrounded the house. He scooped up Lora into his arms when she launched herself at him. He knew from experience with Ellie that she'd be out of this phase of loving on him soon enough, so he soaked it up while he could.

"How's it going, princess?"

"Ms. JJ gave me candy when I cried."

"Did she, now?" he returned, trying for stern even though it amused him that JJ would immediately resort to bribing. "Why were you crying?"

She laid her head on his shoulder and sighed. "I miss Grandma June."

"I know, baby—me, too."

JJ stepped onto the porch with Ellie, who had her

arms folded across her chest and a disapproving look on her face.

"How goes it?"

"Good. Everything is…good." JJ didn't look frazzled exactly. Cade wondered if she was a woman who ever looked *frazzled*—but she didn't look so perfectly in place as she had when she'd opened the door this morning. Some of her straight, dark hair had fallen out of its band, and she had a smudge of chocolate on the hem of her shorts.

She also had very nice legs. Which he probably shouldn't be noticing while holding his daughter.

He put down Lora and gave Ellie a questioning look.

"It was fine," she muttered with a jerk of her shoulders.

"We'll get out of your hair for about an hour, then. Got big plans for your lunch break? A nap? Maybe sixty minutes in a silent-proof chamber?"

She didn't laugh at his joke, just answered him seriously. "The garden needs work."

"Ellie always helps with the garden," Lora said, earning a sneering look from her older sister.

"Oh," JJ replied, blinking. "Well. Grandma June didn't mention that, but—"

"I don't want to help with the stupid garden," Ellie said petulantly.

A petulance Cade thought they'd moved past. "Since when?" he asked, trying to sound cheerful instead of worried.

"Since *now*."

"Then I'll stay and help," Lora said resolutely, moving over to JJ and sliding her hand into JJ's. Stubborn little chin lifted. "I'll eat lunch with Ms. JJ so she doesn't have to be alone."

Sometimes Cade worried about Lora following Ellie around blindly, doing whatever her older sister said, but once in a while she put her foot down and reminded Cade people weren't quite so simple.

"Well, you don't have to..." JJ trailed off as Lora looked up at her with what Cade called Lora's sad puppy-dog look. JJ moved her gaze to him, a desperate plea for help in her expression, but he shrugged—he enjoyed Lora using that look on someone besides him.

"We could make an afternoon project out of it, I suppose. I'll redo my list and—"

"Why don't we all go eat out on the back porch? Then Ms. JJ can work in the garden and whoever wants to help out can. And no one eats alone."

Lora cheered. JJ stared at him openmouthed, as if he'd suggested they all go skinny-dipping.

"Or not?" he added when JJ did nothing but stare.

She looked down at Lora's pout, then back at him. "No. No. It's fine. Good idea. Really. Yes. I just have to rearrange my... It's fine." JJ plastered a completely fake smile on her face.

Ignoring her clear discomfort, and Ellie's daggers, Cade smiled. He wanted to get to the bottom of Ellie's sullenness, and it'd be easier to do with them all together. "I'll grab the lunches then."

Lora let out a whoop and then began hopping around the house, making her fairy wings bounce as she headed for the back porch. Ellie marched behind her as if facing a firing squad.

"I'll just make myself a sandwich," JJ said faintly.

"No need. Long as you like PB-and-J, I've got plenty."

"Oh...kay."

She stood on the porch looking lost, and Cade nodded toward the truck.

"Sorry to spring that on you, but Lora is hard to say no to," he offered as she followed him.

"That she is."

"Besides, Ellie's in a mood, and I'd like to get to the bottom of it. That requires some finesse and some company most of the time. Plus, it gives me a few minutes with them out of earshot to ask how it *really* went." He grabbed the bag out of the truck and then they walked slowly toward the back, where the girls were.

JJ touched the leaves of the dogwood tree in the front yard as they passed, her eyebrows drawing together. "Well, it's a first day. First days aren't perfect."

She didn't seem too happy with that truth.

"Grandma June really stepped in after Melissa left," Cade offered. He didn't mind JJ showing a little discomfort—he knew from those first months or maybe years of parenthood that overconfidence caused the most problems. But she seemed more...sad now. "Don't take Ellie's attitude personally. She just misses June."

"Oh, I don't mind Ellie's attitude at all. It's Lora."

Cade stopped in his tracks. No one in her entire six years of life had ever had problems with his sweet, darling baby.

"She's so...emotional," JJ said, an indictment.

"She's six."

"Oh, I'm not complaining, Cade." Like this morning, JJ made the slightest move as if she was going to touch him, then stopped herself. "Your girls are both well-mannered and follow all the rules. I'm just not... I'm not cut out for tears and..."

"Feelings?" he supplied, trying to work through how JJ had an issue with *Lora*.

JJ frowned, but she didn't argue with him. "I'm a practical sort."

"So was Grandma June."

"I'm no Grandma June."

Which, for someone who was the *practical sort* was an awfully emotional admission.

"No one expects you to be," Cade said gently, because living up to Grandma June was a lot of pressure to put on oneself.

JJ shook her head as they rounded the house, the back porch coming into view. She stopped, and Cade took in the overgrowth—the lawn that needed mowing, the garden that was spilling over its fence and the big trees that offered some shade.

"I don't know why Grandma picked me," JJ whispered, as if it was the gravest admission she'd ever made.

"Me, neither." When her head whipped up, expression offended and maybe a little hurt, he smiled kindly. "But she did. So we'll both make the best of it."

He reached out to pat her shoulder—a perfectly friendly gesture—but his hand lingered there. His pinky finger and ring finger brushed the bare skin at the cuff of her sleeve and something sparked to life in that touch of ragged skin to soft.

It might have been interesting, something to explore, but she quickly jerked her shoulder away and walked toward the girls.

And he was a man left with a bag full of peanut-butter-and-jelly sandwiches—crusts cut off—with no earthly clue what to do about *attraction*.

CHAPTER THREE

~~Weed~~ *Show the girls how to weed*

JJ DID NOT ADD "figure out what that shoulder pat was" to her list, because she didn't want to know why she'd felt…jittery all of a sudden. Or like she wanted to stay precisely there, in the midday heat, with Cade's hand on her shoulder.

Very *big* hand.

She marched toward the girls, a smile plastered on her face. Wondering what on earth had compelled her to say she didn't know why Grandma had picked her. There was just something about being the constant caregiver for two children for those endless morning hours that made things want to pour out of her mouth.

I don't know how to do this.

I want to cry when other people cry, and I'd rather run in the opposite direction than deal.

I really like the way Cade smiles.

And fills out his jeans.

She sucked in a breath and blew it out. Okay, so he was good-looking. When had that ever mattered? Hot guys looked at her about the same as any not-hot guys, which was not at all. She was Cade's *babysitter*.

She had three months to heed her late grandmother's

wishes, and she was determined to do it. Even if it made her nauseous.

JJ approached the duo as Lora was desperately trying to get Ellie to participate in some game about flowers and fairies, but Ellie had her arms crossed and her chin in the air.

"I don't want to play your dumb baby games," Ellie said snottily.

It was like watching herself and Lila in those painful months Mom and Dad had spent deciding what to do about *them*. Lila had surrounded herself with the happy and the fanciful, and JJ had wondered how Lila could ignore all that *pain* in the air.

JJ had probably said that exact same sentence to her: *I don't want to play your dumb baby games*. Not when she'd known everything was changing, and not for the better.

Let yourself feel. Those three words from Grandma's letter haunted her, because she was so afraid if she started…she'd never be able to stop.

"Come on, kiddos. Time to eat," Cade said, and JJ didn't know if he was ignoring the tension between sisters or didn't see it.

He plopped the bag of sandwiches onto the table in the middle of the screened-in back porch. The girls greedily grabbed sandwiches and unpacked them from baggies with clear practice. This was something they did a lot. With Grandma June.

JJ pulled out her phone to avoid the lump in her throat.

Give the back porch a good scrubbing
Figure out the mowing situation
Stop looking at Cade's arms

With those additions to her list, she gingerly slid into the seat between Ellie and Cade and took a sandwich—no crusts.

Cade handed her a juice box with a wry twist of his lips. "I was all out of fruit punch, so you'll have to settle for grape."

He made her want to smile, and JJ wondered why she felt like she shouldn't. Her father never would have gently poked fun at the lunch he'd brought her.

"Daddy makes the best sandwiches because—" Lora licked a chunk of jelly that had fallen through the side of the sandwich and plopped onto her palm "—he uses extra, *extra* jelly."

Cade leaned close to JJ. "I had to secretly switch to sugar-free before she rotted her teeth out," he whispered companionably.

"I guess I should tell you that I let her have a few pieces of candy earlier."

He didn't get irritated or lecture her like she might have expected. He grinned. "I suppose it's only fair if you three have your secrets. Lord knows June did with them."

JJ frowned. Her father had impressed upon her that she should *never* keep secrets. Even with Grandma June. He was her father, and he had to know everything going on with her life.

As she'd gotten older she'd come to realize he was most worried about her having any contact with her mother, and Grandma June facilitating it. Even now he sometimes seemed worried she'd suddenly want a relationship with the woman who'd had no qualms about disappearing from her life.

Did Lila feel that way about Dad? She'd been even

younger when Mom and Dad had divorced, so at six she'd gone to live with Mom and had next to no contact with Dad. Did she wonder what was wrong with her that Dad hadn't wanted to have a relationship with his own daughter?

"Rowdy!" Lora screeched, almost upending her chair with how quickly she jumped out of it. She ran off the porch, Ellie at her heels.

"Who's Rowdy?" JJ asked, glad for the distraction from her depressing thoughts as the girls scrambled through the overgrowth in the back corner of the yard.

"Stray cat. Grandma June or the girls feed him whenever he comes around. He'll let them love him, then break their hearts and disappear for weeks at a time."

"Then why do you let them feed him?"

"*I* didn't let anyone do anything. Grandma June did what she did." He nodded toward the girls as he polished off his second sandwich. "Besides, we live on a ranch. Animals come and go. And sadly, those girls already know people do, too."

"They shouldn't know that yet," JJ murmured, watching them enthusiastically pet the gray cat that appeared through the weeds. She hadn't thought about Cade hearing it, even less him responding.

"We both did. My mom died when I was in between Lora's and Ellie's ages. Your parents divorced when you were what? Ten?"

"Eight," she replied.

"Grandma June always made it sound like you don't have much to do with your mom."

"No, I don't."

"Then maybe that's why she picked you."

JJ blinked, coming back into herself—a herself

that was horrified they were having this conversation. "Huh?"

"Your mom walked out on you. Their mom walked out on them. Maybe she thought you'd understand."

"It's… It was different."

"I'm sure it was. That doesn't mean you don't understand."

JJ didn't know what to do with *that*. It made sense, and yet… She didn't want to understand her own pain, let alone anyone else's.

"Sorry. You didn't sign up for us hijacking your lunch, and you certainly didn't volunteer for conversations. I'm just used to making it." He pulled the straw off a juice box. It should look ridiculous, this man eating crustless PB-and-Js and drinking out of a juice box.

The corded muscles of his forearms didn't seem ridiculous. At *all*.

JJ turned her attention back to his words. "You used to eat lunches with Grandma June," she said carefully. No doubt Grandma June made Cade and the girls sandwiches herself, offered Cade a listening ear, sage advice, and he left feeling better. He probably loved summers because of Grandma June, just like she always had.

"Sure. That doesn't mean—"

"We should talk, then," JJ decided. "I'm stepping into her role for the summer. Whatever she did, I'll do." She was a doer. She helped people, and maybe that usually meant work at the greenhouse, and now it would mean…people things, but she could do it. Grandma had entrusted her with this task. She *had* to do it.

"So we're…friends?" he asked, not so much as if he didn't believe it, but with a certain amount of cautiousness that made her double down.

"Of course we're friends." She didn't have all that many, but she could be Cade's friend for the summer. Just like all those old summers. With less tree climbing.

"I bet I could beat you in a footrace now."

Her mouth twitched. The problem was she'd always liked Cade. He had an easiness about him, and that hadn't changed with his circumstances. He never made her feel awkward or out of place.

He was hot now, though, and that was awkward in and of itself.

"You know, I have a list of things I've been dying to fix around here," Cade said, eyeing the house behind them.

It's got nothing on my list, buddy.

"Maybe you'd let me come out in the evenings and fix up some things. After the girls are in bed, my brothers can sit at the house. I'm usually up for a while yet anyway. Might as well be doing something worthwhile."

"Well, yeah, I guess that's…" Cade here by himself. Fixing things. She honestly didn't know how to respond to that.

He shrugged. "Up to you."

She was used to doing things on her own, and for everyone around her, for that matter. But the farm had always been her respite from that. Instead of JJ taking care of Dad, Grandma June had taken care of her.

So maybe she'd let Cade take care of a few things here. What could be the harm? "I guess if it wouldn't be too much trouble."

"None at all."

"Okay, then."

He finished off the juice box and called the girls back over. They grudgingly finished their lunches while chatting excitedly about Rowdy. Cade left again, making sure to say goodbye to both girls and reminding them to be good.

When he left, JJ didn't let herself feel out of sorts. She jumped right into the parts of her list she could do with the girls.

They walked through the overgrown garden together and while JJ instructed Lora on the difference between weeds and the vegetable plants Keira must have planted during her spring, Ellie moved through the opposite side of the garden adeptly pulling weeds without JJ's instruction.

Lora faded quickly, long before JJ and Ellie were done with the garden. She started to whine about the dirt, the heat, the bugs and how much she hated *every* vegetable growing.

JJ stood from where she'd been instructing Ellie on how much water to give each plant, though Grandma had clearly taught Ellie plenty.

"I'm hot," Lora whined for the millionth time.

"I can fix that," Ellie said cheerfully, turning the hose on her sister. Since JJ wasn't standing too far away, the frigid blast of water sprayed against Lora and splattered onto JJ, as well.

Lora let out a primal scream and ran for her sister. Ellie was smart enough to run out of the fenced-in garden, still holding the hose and occasionally pointing it back at Lora.

Once the shock had passed, JJ scrambled after them. Lora was alternately yelling at Ellie to stop, and letting out little sobs of frustration, while Ellie laughed like a maniac.

JJ didn't know *what* to do, except catch up with Ellie

and take back the hose. Of course, by the time she got the hose in her possession they were all soaked.

Both girls, bedraggled and sopping wet, stared at her with big blue eyes—just like their dad's, except instead of Cade's usual humor, she saw solemn worry as they watched her.

JJ didn't feel *here* exactly. She felt like she'd fallen back in time, to summers under the hose. Grandma would set up a sprinkler or a plastic pool, and her, Keira, Lila and Bella would splash around. When Keira had gotten too mature and elegant for such things, JJ had once taken the hose to her.

A chase much like the one she'd just witnessed had ensued. Except Keira had wrestled the hose away from JJ and laughed as she'd gotten JJ back. Then Lila had run into the fray, and Bella.

JJ wanted to forget those happier days, the way childhood memories cut with a pain that was matched only by the warmth of joy that seemed to echo across the time between then and now and shimmer in the late-afternoon sun.

"Are you mad, Ms. JJ?" Lora was brave enough to ask.

"No," she retorted without even thinking it through. How could she be mad at two little girls having fun? *Here*, of all places. She did almost say something about their dad being upset, but then she remembered what Cade had said about secrets. She knelt into the now squelchy grass so she could be eye to eye with them. "In fact, it'll be our secret. How does that sound?"

Lora grinned, and Ellie didn't scowl, so JJ decided then and there that her first day of babysitting was a success.

So she turned the hose on both of them to their screeching delight.

CHAPTER FOUR

WHEN CADE PICKED up the girls that night, he was surprised to find them smiling. Ellie even gave JJ a quick hug before she hopped off the porch. Both girls bounded to the truck, heads bent together whispering.

All without arguing.

"What happened after I left?" Cade asked, feeling shell-shocked by this new development.

"Garden kindred spirits," JJ replied with a smile that hinted at secrets.

Yeah, June knew what she was doing—even if none of the rest of them did.

"Do you know anything about porch maintenance?" JJ asked, toeing one of the weak boards beneath her feet. "It'd be nice to get the porch swing back up, but I'd want the foundation to be strong enough to hold little feet jumping on and off."

Cade studied the porch. "Maybe. I'd have to see what's underneath. I can come by later tonight, scope it out, then figure out what we can do. If that works?"

"Okay."

Not an enthusiastic *okay*, but *she'd* brought it up. "Honestly, it's amazing how quickly the house has taken a turn. You'd think Keira didn't spend the spring here with all the issues that still need tending."

JJ frowned at that, but then shrugged. "I suppose

she was busy with the cattle more than keeping an old house up and running."

"Well, I'll be back. A little after eight, okay?"

She hesitated, but then she nodded. Cade couldn't say he understood the hesitation, but if he agreed to fix the porch, at least it gave him something to do.

Something that didn't involve his disapproving older brother or the encroaching loneliness once the girls were asleep.

"See you in a bit," he said, tipping his hat and walking back to the truck and the girls. They were already in their booster seats, buckled and conspiring.

"Just how much candy did Ms. JJ give you?"

Lora giggled. "We made cookies after…" He watched in the rearview mirror as she and Ellie exchanged a look and then burst out laughing.

He shook his head. He'd learned many years ago that sometimes it was best not to know what they were up to.

Besides, Lora almost always spilled the beans if he didn't press.

He drove them home, enjoying the rare but always reassuring bout of friendliness between his girls.

Once home he made dinner—enough for an army, because inevitably his brothers would trickle through his cabin, grabbing this or that. When Mac came in, Cade decided that of all his brothers, he'd ask the fewest questions.

"Can you stick around after bedtime?"

"Sure," Mac returned, filling his plate with the last of the mac and cheese and most of the chicken nuggets.

Cade frowned since he still hadn't had a chance to get a bite—but what else was new?

"Can you pick up some paper towels for the main

house? I swear to God I'm going to punch Hudson if he doesn't stop using three sheets when one would do."

"I'm not going into town."

"Where are you going?" Mac asked around a mouthful of nugget.

Cade busied himself with scraping a few noodle remnants from the pot and shoveling them into his mouth. "Just up to Grandma June's. Some repairs to help out with."

Mac nodded, then settled himself on the couch and flipped on the TV. As Cade predicted, he didn't ask any questions.

Thank God.

Cade managed to snag a few chicken nuggets before Tate waltzed through and cleaned him out. Cade went through the bedtime routine with the girls. There was one minor meltdown over the pink bubblegum toothpaste running out and having to use the *gross* adult stuff, but other than that the girls crawled into bed, listened to a story and smiled at him when he kissed them good-night.

He closed the door, listened to their quiet whispers they thought he didn't hear, then headed back to the living room.

Mac was dozing to a baseball game, and he'd likely fall asleep, but he'd also wake up at the slightest movement from the girls' room. His brothers might irritate him, but Cade could count on them.

"Gonna head out. Text if I need to be back."

Mac grunted in response while Cade got together his wallet and keys.

"Condoms at the main house."

Cade stopped midstride. "Condoms? Jesus," Cade hissed, leaning closer to his brother so they could keep this conversation at a reasonable level. He whispered, "I don't need condoms."

"Better be safe about it, bro."

"I didn't mean… I'm not going to…" He trailed off, almost certain his daughters would hear him utter the three-letter word he wanted them to never, ever know. "I'm just fixing some stuff. Nothing else."

Mac shrugged. "You say so."

"I do," Cade said resolutely.

He went to his truck, grumbling about Mac's utter insanity. He drove, resolutely trying not to think about sex.

But Mac had brought it up and now the idea was just *stuck* there.

Cade hadn't been with anyone since Melissa. He'd been busy, and it was a small town. He knew everyone, and everyone knew his sad sap story. It was complicated, and he hadn't even had time to consider how complicated, or what he was missing, because he was always busy.

Now it was lodged there. *Sex.*

He was thirty years old and hadn't had sex in years. *Years.*

He stopped in front of Grandma June's house. He might have felt bad about thinking about sex with her granddaughter in her front yard, but JJ was already outside, bent over some plants in front of the porch.

He was *human.* Sex in his brain, pretty woman in front of him—it was only natural to think about putting the two together.

Natural thought process didn't mean he'd *do* anything about it.

The day's sun had already faded as the world edged toward the beginnings of dusk. JJ finished up whatever she'd been working on in the dirt, brushed off her hands, then shaded her eyes against the fading sun to greet him.

The low sunlight made her shimmer gold. His gut clenched with a surprising amount of intensity.

He *was* attracted to her. No doubt there. He didn't really know her all *that* well, but it felt as though he did thanks to June. She'd made his daughters smile, and whisper to each other over bedtime instead of the usual arguments.

And she was here for a *summer*. Which was not conducive to trying to start anything up. If he had the time or wherewithal for some temporary fling, it wouldn't be with June Gable's granddaughter.

Which meant he should stop being the creeper sitting in his truck staring at her. He cut the engine and hopped out, trying to find casual friendliness somewhere in the midst of his brain being an idiot.

"Hey," he offered, opening the gate and closing it behind him.

She smiled. It looked forced at best. "So the Mathewson boys babysit? They don't seem the type."

"They're not. They are the do-what's-needing-done type. They're also the biggest pushovers when it comes to those girls, so the babysitting has to be limited."

"That must be nice."

"I guess. It's also loud, frustrating and more often than not a giant pain in my ass."

Her mouth curved a little more naturally, but then her gaze moved to the dogwood tree behind him and everything about her seemed…sad. Which wasn't the first time he'd seen that emotion wash over her. He could make an easy parallel between talking about his brothers helping out, and what he knew about her relationship with her sister, thanks to June.

As a man who spent a lot of time trying to cheer up sad women, even if they were the under-ten set, he couldn't help but ask her about it.

"You and Lila don't talk?"

She blinked. Then turned toward the porch. "So some of the porch boards are rotting, but I looked through Grandma's files and she'd had the house inspected for termites before…"

She couldn't seem to avoid all the uncomfortable topics she wanted to, and Cade felt sorry enough for her to jump in and focus on the not-hard stuff. He knelt at one of the boards she pointed to and pushed on it.

"Looks like we just need to replace a few boards," he said. "I can do that. We'll take up the boards tonight, make sure there's no structural problem underneath, then I'll take some measurements. Should be able to get that done before we lose the light. Let me grab my tools."

"Oh, I have a toolbox right here." She pointed to a rusty contraption that might have been around since the house had been built.

Cade smiled. "I'll get tools from this century if you don't mind."

She rolled her eyes and gestured him toward his truck. He retrieved the tools, then went through the work of pulling up the floorboards that gave. A few had even splintered, but the joists looked good.

"Do you want me to get you some lemonade or something?"

"Sure," he replied, though the heat of the day was cooling off pleasantly. JJ disappeared as he pulled off the last weak board. He discarded it with the others, then, satisfied with what he found in the opening, took a seat on the stair.

The sunset was a quiet one. With no clouds in the sky, it merely faded from brilliant blue to a peachy rose.

He heard the screen door squeak open and slam. "I've got brownies, too," JJ announced.

He looked over his shoulder at her and grinned. "My hero."

She eased onto the stair next to him, handing a glass of lemonade to him. "You called me that when I punched your brother in the nose that one summer."

Cade laughed. "Oh, right. Grant pushed you into the creek, and you did not take it lightly."

JJ handed over a brownie and kept one for herself as her nose wrinkled. "He deserved it."

"You're damn right he did. Sometimes I fantasize about that when he's really pissing me off."

"Didn't he tell everyone it was Everett McCall who hit him?"

"Couldn't stand the fact a girl had bloodied his nose."

"You made me an award. Painted 'world's best right jab' on a very nice rock."

This time he flat-out laughed. "Oh, right. I hope you kept it."

"It might be stuffed in a closet somewhere," she said with a ghost of a smile. She nibbled her brownie thoughtfully, squinting out into the sunset. He should have done that, too. Instead he watched her against his better judgment.

"What are you going to do after all this?" he asked.

Her eyebrows drew together. "After summer, you mean? Well, I'll go home, of course. Dad's pretty worried he won't be able to run the greenhouse without me. I think it's the first time…"

He let the silence settle for a few seconds while she took a big bite of brownie to have to keep from finishing the sentence. He had a feeling finishing the sentence was exactly what she needed.

"First time what?"

She swallowed the bite, frowning out at the darkening mountain horizon. "The first time I went against what he wanted. He never particularly *liked* my visits with Grandma June, and sometimes something at work would crop up and I'd have to cancel. This time, I couldn't give in. I couldn't even give him a good reason. I had to come. She…"

"She asked you to."

JJ nodded, letting out a shaky sigh. "Exactly."

"That's reason enough, JJ."

She shook her head. "It wasn't for him." She squeezed her eyes shut. "Why on *earth* are we talking about this?"

"Why not? We're friends, right?"

"That doesn't mean you sit around discussing your… issues."

"Sure it does."

She laughed, though there wasn't much joy to the sound. She turned her gaze to him, eyes widening when she realized he'd been staring at her the whole time. She swallowed, cheeks turning an interesting shade of the faintest pink. "Well. Anyway. Thanks for your help."

"Here's your hat, what's your hurry," he murmured as she quickly got to her feet.

"Huh?"

He forced a cheerful smile. "Nothing. I'll work on ordering the lumber to fix up those gaps soon as I can. Might be a few weeks, but not too long. Just keep the girls off that side of the porch."

"Great. I can pay you back however you'd like."

"Oh, don't worry about—"

"Grandma left money for the house. It should go to the house."

Cade wanted to argue, but she seemed a little fragile, so he only nodded.

"Thanks for your help."

"Anytime." He stood and handed the empty glass back to her. It felt like an odd way to leave things. Unsettled. Wrong to walk away while she stood in the shadow of this old, lonely house.

He stopped halfway through the yard and turned. She was still standing on the porch, a shadow in the quickly falling evening. He knew she wasn't watching him, and there was some weird part of him that wanted her to be.

That was stupid. As stupid as the thought that June would be disappointed in him for leaving her here all alone—when that was clearly what JJ wanted.

He couldn't shake the feeling there was more to say, though. Another hand to reach out.

"I spend my days working with my brothers who communicate in grunts and lectures. I spend my nights with the two most important people in my life, but sometimes a man does not want to referee yet another fight about My Little Pony. If you ever get a little lonely, I'm only a ways away."

Something struck him as starkly *painful* about her expression then, but she only nodded and offered another thanks before heading for the front door.

He had been firmly and utterly dismissed.

Regardless, that look on her face haunted him all night.

CHAPTER FIVE

JJ HAD NEVER felt alone in Grandma's house because the house had always been home. The place she went to feel whole and at peace.

She wished Grandma was here just about every second of every day, but the feeling dogging her lately was edgier and antsier. It wasn't *sad.* It was the feeling of missing something. A heavy isolation that had wrapped itself around her ever since Cade had driven away. Out of nowhere the house felt cold and empty, despite the stubborn summer heat that clung to the air.

Why did he have to go say things like *a little lonely*? She wasn't lonely. Couldn't possibly be, because she was used to being alone.

She had Keira, but no matter that they'd once whispered secrets to each other late at night in this very house, JJ had never been the type to call someone and unload her feelings. They texted, they kept each other up-to-date, but they didn't have heart-to-hearts anymore.

Just the thought of one made JJ cringe. Even when Keira had called to tell JJ about getting back together with Remy, JJ hadn't been able to offer much in response. She was so happy for Keira, but she didn't know how to get past the discomfort of *showing* that.

Because being alone was her best default. So there

was no *loneliness* when loneliness implied missing something.

She curled up in the twin bed she'd always slept in at Grandma's, perfectly content. She had some tea that was supposed to help her sleep and one of the romance novels off Grandma's shelf.

Lonely? No. This was *great*. A vacation of sorts. She *would* enjoy herself.

But when Cade showed up with the girls the next morning, that heaviness she hadn't been able to escape, even in sleep, eased. She settled into Ellie's and Lora's chatter, even if it was about unicorns, of all fanciful things. They ate lunch the same way they had the day before, though she and the girls had cleaned off the porch that morning *and* made a few more things besides PB-and-J.

Cade left them with another tip of the hat that made something in JJ's stomach flip. Then it was her and the girls again. They didn't have a water fight this afternoon: instead, they worked on the garden. JJ discovered if she let Lora play in the dirt with her toy ponies, she didn't care how long Ellie and JJ weeded.

When Cade picked up the girls that night they were bickering over the most inane detail of some television show they both loved, and JJ was sure she was glad to see the back of them.

The heavy loneliness returned as darkness settled. That yearning for something she couldn't name. Whether she cleaned or cooked or worked on replacing the window screens, what she really wanted to do was curl up in a ball and *cry*.

Which was wholly unacceptable.

Even her list brought her no comfort. She was half

tempted for the first time in her life to delete it completely.

After two *weeks* of this unnatural phenomenon, she sat on the front porch—alone—wondering what the hell Cade had done to her. Clearly it was *his* fault.

She'd never, ever felt lonely before and then he'd put that word out in the ether. Eaten lunch with her every day. Made her laugh. Trusted her with his children.

When Cade's truck appeared on the horizon, her heart twisted with irritation and something far lighter. A kind of hopeful relief.

She clung to the irritation.

He parked and waved her over to the truck. She got off the stair, reminding herself that her irritation was her own problem, not his.

"Lumber's all cut to the measurements, so we shouldn't have any problems," he explained, walking to the bed of the truck. "If we have any problems, I can adjust whatever doesn't work and come back another night."

The fact that she wanted something not to work out so he would come back was absolutely unacceptable. "I could probably do it myself," she offered, too sharply to sound like a friendly offer.

He stood to his full height, which made her feel smaller somehow. Not just in size but in…everything.

"Did you *want* to do it yourself?"

It was such a reasonable question, she didn't know what to say. She wasn't used to being…overdramatic. Which was the feeling clawing at her chest.

Let yourself feel.

Why? So everyone around her could know what a mess she was on the inside?

"I don't want you to feel put out," she said, trying for casual instead of as sharp and brittle as she felt.

"Here's a tip, JJ. If someone is happily helping you out, acting like you might be putting them out is annoying as hell."

She frowned as he hauled the lumber to the porch. Cade wasn't usually short with her, but that had been testy. Even if she probably deserved it.

"How were the girls tonight?" she asked, trailing behind him. He'd seemed fine when he picked them up. Now he was… Well, she wasn't sure. Tense.

He dropped the lumber in front of the porch, rolled his shoulders and then marched back to the truck. "Fine," he grumbled.

"I find that hard to believe."

"Suit yourself," he replied, hefting the toolbox out of the bed of the truck before returning to the porch.

She couldn't figure out why she kept following him around, why she felt compelled to poke at whatever was bothering him. He didn't want to share. She should be thrilled.

But Ellie *had* been quiet today, and even Lora had been subdued. JJ had figured they'd just had a busy Fourth of July—Cade had invited her to a party at his ranch. JJ had politely declined, but she'd assumed the kids were wiped from that.

Cade took one of the boards up to the first spot that needed repairing with none of his usual cheerfulness or *ease*. Inwardly, every instinct she'd ever honed told her to be quiet. To let him work in silence. But words she could control anywhere and everywhere else seemed to bubble out of her *here*.

"The girls weren't themselves today. If there's something I can help with, I want to."

He shook his head, putting some glue underneath the board. "Ellie's birthday is August 21," he said, his voice a shade rougher than usual. "She wants a sleepover, and I wanted to get it all planned in advance because of vacations and stuff, but her best friend's mother isn't *comfortable* with her daughter spending the night on a ranch full of men. And, oh, she'd love to have Ellie over, but her husband works nights and she has a baby and so on and so forth."

"Ellie's upset?"

"She's detached, which is worse. Looking at pictures of Melissa, which is even *worse* worse. Why am I telling you this? Ignore me." He picked up the board and began fitting it into the hole, looking serious and…angry.

Cade angry was all wrong. "I care about them, too, you know," she said before she thought that sentence through. Before she admitted how true it was. How quickly and easily they'd woven their loud, pink ways into her heart.

In some ways it was because it was like watching her and Lila with the distance of adulthood. In some ways it was because Grandma had loved them, so how could she not? And in some ways it was just *them*. Boisterous Lora with her bouts of affection or honesty that JJ never knew what to do with, but made her feel warm and important somehow. Serious, quiet Ellie, whom JJ identified with so completely.

They made her heart hurt, reminded her of her happy summers here and poked at her insecurities over her relationship—or lack of one—with her sister. Yet the girls were lodged in her heart so deep already the thought of the summer being over…scared her.

JJ didn't want to leave Grandma June or those girls, and that was what September would bring.

"I could…do whatever for the party."

He stopped fitting the board into the hole and looked up at her in complete confusion. "Huh?"

"If this mom wants a female chaperone or whatever. I might not know the mom, but if she knew my grandma it might put her at ease."

"You want to chaperone a sleepover with ten-year-old girls?"

"Well, *want* isn't the word I'd choose, but if it's a solution to a problem, then I'd volunteer."

"Because you like to solve problems?" he asked carefully.

She wished she could say *yes, that is the reason.* But he was looking at her like he understood all too well, and she had the insane thought if she lied he'd be disappointed.

She shouldn't care if he was.

"Because I care about Ellie, and she should have a nice birthday party. I *was* at her baby shower. It's not like she's a complete and utter stranger to me."

Cade rocked onto his heels and tipped back his hat to stare at her, a stark pain moving across his expression. He didn't seem embarrassed by it, even though it made JJ want to fidget. How could you just *let* someone see the pain inside of you like that?

"I didn't realize you'd met Melissa," he said, turning his attention back to the work.

Good one, JJ. How many times had she accidentally brought up Mom in that first year after the divorce and then had to sit through one of Dad's tirades that ended in weeping before she'd learned to think through everything before she said it?

She really didn't want to see Cade weep, and she really wanted to stop making mistakes she'd learned to eradicate at the age of ten. "Just the once."

Cade didn't rage or cry—he went back to work. "So, you probably saw it coming, too."

"Saw what coming?"

"Her leaving. Everyone loves to tell me they knew it would never work. Apparently Grant thinks that's supposed to be some great comfort when the girls are sad about their deadbeat mom. So, go ahead. Tell me."

"No, I never thought that. She seemed…happy."

He let out a harsh breath that might have been a laugh if it wasn't so filled with disgust. "Didn't she just?"

There was a bitterness she hadn't suspected. Because he always acted so…amiable. She wouldn't have thought Cade had an edge to him, but here it was.

This was the kind of thing she'd spent a lot of time learning to avoid. Dad's sore spots. Her own, so as not to upset the balance.

Cade upset and bitter wasn't balance at all.

"So you didn't have problems?"

He made the nonlaugh sound again. "We did, but *I* thought it was the kind you worked through. I certainly didn't think they were the kind you abandoned your kids to go 'find yourself' for." He pounded a nail into the board.

"Sometimes people can't see beyond themselves, I guess." Because that was the only reason someone could leave sweethearts like Ellie and Lora. JJ's mom had been disappointed in her, hadn't been able to love her past all her unfeminine flaws. So that was on her. No one could think Melissa had left because of Ellie or Lora, or even Cade. Who would leave Cade?

Her stomach hurt and her chest burned and too many feelings fought in between the two. A hard weight of discomfort and competing thoughts.

Maybe a mother abandoning her children never had anything to do with the children. Maybe it had everything to do with not being able to see beyond themselves.

Mom kept Lila.

"Honestly, I think I'm over it," Cade said, putting down the hammer. "It's been *years* and you learn to accept things—it isn't all that different than a death. But it's birthdays and holidays. They should have their mother, because she's out there. I couldn't have mine. She died. Then I get mad again, because it's the one thing they need that I can't give them."

It cracked her heart in two.

"I just have to remind myself that someday they're going to grow up and understand they have so many people who love them." He forced a smile that didn't reach his eyes, and the words were…wrong.

"They'll always know their mother didn't." Which she hadn't meant to say out loud. Not about those girls. Not to *him*.

He looked up at her with all that *hurt* in his gaze that he wasn't afraid of like she was. "Well, stab me in the heart, JJ."

It was horrible knowing she'd said something to hurt him. That she hadn't thought through her words like she *always* did, but had been wrapped up in her own stuff instead. "I'm sorry. I shouldn't have said that. I just…"

"It's true. It's true for you, so it'll be true for them."
He swore and scraped his fingers through his hair.

"You know, this is why I don't talk to people," she
said, hating the rust in her voice. "This is why *lonely*
is just fine, because at least you're not making things
worse for people." She was absolutely horrified that
tears were filling her vision. She practically lunged for
the door, ready to barricade herself away from all the
emotion in the air, but Cade's hand curled around her
arm before she could get the door open.

Gently, he pulled her back until she was forced to
look up at him.

He looked…sympathetic. Which was awful.

"You didn't make anything worse for me, JJ," he
said with a gentle calm. It was sad, and it was hurt, but
it wasn't… She didn't have the vocabulary for all this
emotion. For the way Cade seemed able to deal with it,
to take it and accept and not rage or run.

All she'd ever known was the rage and the run.

"Life sucks sometimes, you know? My parents were
good people and loving parents, but they're gone. Before
they even met my kids. Because life isn't fair. I wish I
could make it fair for my girls, but it's not. We've all
got our hurts that don't heal."

"That's a bleak thought."

"Only if you think hurt is the worst thing you could
possibly be. If I go back and erase all the ways Melissa
hurt me, I don't have Ellie or Lora. So hurt isn't the
worst thing I could be."

She lost her fight with tears and wished the ground
would swallow her whole. Instead, strong arms wrapped
around her and held her gently. A hug. A comforting hug.

No one hugged her except Grandma June, and now

Cade. It wasn't even awkward or uncomfortable. It was nice to relax into him. He was sturdy and perfectly calm.

"Shh, sweetheart. I didn't come over here to make you cry," he murmured, rubbing her back.

Which made her want to sob into his shoulder all the more. "I shouldn't have…" She couldn't even get out a good response. "I'm such an idiot."

"Come on, now. You can't think I'd be felled by a few tears? I have two girls. I practically drown in them on a daily basis. Tears are normal."

Not for me.

She had to get ahold of herself if she was *ever* going to face him again. She blinked hard, trying to get out all the tears. She attempted to extricate herself from him, but he held her by the shoulders, keeping her from moving away completely. He watched her, a crease appearing in his forehead as if he was thinking very deeply.

He was probably wondering why he'd gotten himself into this mess. Why Grandma June had trusted a woman with so little control over herself with his beautiful, wonderful girls. He'd said he wanted to be her friend, and now he was regretting it.

Luckily she knew what to do about people regretting their connection to her. Cut them off and out. Make it clear you understand, so they don't feel compelled to tell you.

"I don't think you picked a very good friend to have, Cade."

He used the backs of his fingers to wipe her wet cheek. "I think Grandma June knew what she was doing giving us each other for the summer."

There was such a genuine *kindness* in the dark blue

of his eyes, and he still had one hand on her arm and his fingers on her cheek.

She swallowed. He had that *thing* about him that made her chest flutter, and her stomach get too tight. Even with puffy eyes and a sniffly nose, she felt that jolt.

She knew what it was, but she was afraid to call it what it was. Then his gaze dropped to her mouth and her whole stomach flipped. He couldn't actually...

She'd just cried all over him. She was delusional to even think attraction could be mutual. She tried to pull away, needing distance and... God, any sort of control of the situation.

He held firm.

"Now, you've got two choices. I go back to fixing the porch, and you get some lemonade—or hell, something stronger if you've got it. Maybe round up a few of those brownies. I finish up. We have a snack and talk about Ellie's birthday. Or I can go home, finish this up another day and we can pretend this whole conversation never happened. Before you decide, I want you to know I'd prefer to do the first."

He was insane. Who wanted to hang around and act like this whole fiasco was just normal?

Cade Mathewson apparently.

It must be catching, because he made it seem less like a nightmare scenario and more like the only option.

"I'm out of brownies, but I could probably scrounge up some cookies."

He grinned and released her. "That'll do."

CHAPTER SIX

THE COOKIES DIDN'T DISAPPOINT, and there was an intense satisfaction in actually accomplishing something. The porch wasn't exactly good as new, but it was safer than it had been.

So often in ranching—and parenting—nothing ever got fully *accomplished*. It was constant work and a constant up-and-down cycle of never knowing quite where you stood.

Tonight Cade sat on a porch he'd helped fix with a glass of lemonade and a handful of chocolate chip cookies—with Grandma June's special orange peel touch.

The stars had come out to play, a twinkling blanket above. The air had cooled, but JJ was sitting next to him on the step and it was warm here in their little pocket of space.

"We'll have to rehang the swing tomorrow."

"I bet the girls would like that," she said. Her voice still had a tightness to it, but she hadn't told him to leave and he'd given her the opportunity.

"They'll love it. Now, are you sure you want to volunteer for Ellie's party? I don't know if the mom will agree, but if you're good with it, I'll see what she thinks."

"I've been the girl with the single dad. There was

always…weird stuff. When you're too young to understand the world isn't about *you*, it can hurt your feelings."

It was a careful way of putting it. JJ was always so *careful* about feelings.

He didn't understand embarrassment or fear over honest ones—and not just because of being a dad, but because the Mathewsons had always had *big* emotions. Maybe it was losing Mom so early, or losing Dad so suddenly, but he'd never been afraid to express an emotion to his brothers.

He should be heading home, not thinking about feelings—certainly not the oddly warm and *strong* ones worming around his heart when it came to JJ. But the night was all star shine and crickets chirping, and the woman next to him was…something.

"Since I cried all over you like a sap, can I ask you something really personal?"

"Crying doesn't make you a sap, JJ. But sure."

"You said Melissa seemed happy, so why—why did she leave?"

Cade shifted. He didn't like to talk about Melissa. In some ways he'd gotten over the end of his marriage. What choice was there? But no one liked to trot out their failures in front of someone else.

Of course, JJ considered crying in front of him a great failure, so maybe this was tit for tat.

"She never wanted to stay here. We weren't planning to. Then Dad died and I couldn't…leave. Then she got pregnant with Ellie and it was supposed to be fine. I built the cabin away from the main house. We'd fight now and again about moving away, but mostly Ellie came and she was perfect and parenthood was hard and… I don't know. Then we had Lora. It was hard, balancing the ranch and family, but I never got the sense *we* weren't what she wanted."

"So she just woke up one day and left?"

"It felt that way to me. We weren't even fighting. Distant, maybe, but not fighting. I come home and she's packing her bags. She says she'd been unhappy for years, thought Lora would fix it, but the kids just made it worse. She didn't know what she wanted or who she wanted to be, and we were in the way. She needed a life without responsibility to figure it all out."

JJ was quiet. Her gaze was on the stars, and much like two weeks ago, he watched her instead. She had her hair pulled back, leaving the sweep of her jaw visible. Her chin was a tad too pointy, and her eyes were too big, really, to be considered *beautiful*.

She was *compelling*, and even in the midst of talking about his ex-wife of all things, he wanted what he hadn't wanted in a long time.

And couldn't want. Not from her. Not in a temporary summer.

Remember that, dumb ass.

"So you just let her go?"

"You can't fight people who want to leave, JJ. They have to do the leaving. For a while, I thought she'd come back. When the divorce papers showed up, I had to accept what she needed was somewhere we weren't. Doesn't mean I'm not bitter or don't think she should have made better choices, but I can't… I can't control her. I can only deal with what's here."

"And if she'd wanted to take the girls?"

He didn't have to be a mind reader to know she didn't mean *the* girls, she meant *one* girl. "I would have told her to go to hell." Not a very fair truth when JJ was asking for herself. "I can't judge your parents. I don't know why they made the choices they did, but you're an adult now. You can ask. Or you can accept that the choices they made didn't have anything to do with you—even if you were the one who had to deal with the consequences."

"I thought…" She cleared her throat, and she gazed hard at her hands clasped together in her lap. "You know, I never talked about this with anyone. Even Grandma. I mean, partially because I think she might have been able to read my mind and knew it all already, but partly because I thought if I didn't try to figure it out, it would just go away."

"So what changed your mind?"

"I look at your girls and I see me and Lila. It hurts, but not the way it used to. I don't know how to explain the change. I just know… I couldn't do what my parents did—not even to those kids who aren't my own. So if I couldn't, maybe it didn't have anything to do with me."

"I imagine Grandma June tried to tell you that a time or two."

JJ laughed softly. "In more ways than one. There's something about someone you love telling you something you want to hear and actually seeing yourself in someone you…" She trailed off, shifting next to him on the stair.

"It's okay to say you love my kids. They're pretty lovable."

She huffed out a breath. "They're yours."

"They're anybody's who loves them. They're my brothers', June's, each other's. Yours."

She nodded, and he thought maybe this was the first

time she didn't try to wipe that pained expression away, or hide it from him by attempting to run into the house.

So he slid his arm around her shoulders and gave them a squeeze. She sat straight for a while, but she didn't pull away or get up. In fact, after a few minutes she relaxed, even leaned against him.

He didn't know how long they sat there, and he didn't particularly care. It was nice. It was good.

Eventually responsibility called. "I should head back."

"Yeah."

She stood, his arm falling off her shoulders with the movement. So he stood, too.

"Well, thank you for the porch. I appreciate it."

"And the shoulder to cry on, right?"

She wrinkled her nose and he had to laugh. And resist the urge to touch her hair. Hell. He could close the distance in less than a second. Follow that yearning spark he'd forgotten could exist between a man and a woman. The thought was so tempting, so *new*, he couldn't help but lean in, closer and closer.

He heard her intake of breath mixed with the raucous buzz of crickets. He could smell the hint of her vanilla shampoo over the sunbaked grass scent that surrounded them. And he could imagine, all too easily, discovering what it would feel like to kiss JJ Frost after all these years.

The years were what stopped him, because wasn't he well acquainted with what people who didn't plan on staying did to a person's heart? He cleared his throat and stepped back. "You know, that's probably a bad idea."

She blinked at him, like she was coming out of a

trance, then practically fell over trying to back away from him.

Not quite the reaction he knew what to do with. In the end, maybe he should take that as a sign. Don't *do* anything. "Night, JJ."

She didn't respond, and he left trying to pretend the whole *moment* hadn't happened.

CHAPTER SEVEN

JJ SAT AT the kitchen table and stared at her list. She hadn't added anything to it in weeks. She hadn't deleted anything off it, either. In fact, even with the plans for Ellie's party in full swing, her list had been as far from her mind as anything outside of Jasper Creek.

The summer was flying by. There were days with the girls, lunches with them and Cade and some evenings of Cade coming out to work on something around the house. It felt so real, so full. Vibrant and *happy*.

She didn't want the lists and the boredom. She wanted...life.

It had been weeks since Cade had almost kissed her. If that was what he'd been about to do. She honestly wasn't sure, and his behavior ever since just had to mean...

She'd been crazy. Because he hadn't tried anything, or looked at her in that special way, and he certainly didn't keep his distance, like he was afraid he couldn't keep his hands off her.

But then *what* had been a bad idea?

She allowed herself a groan before turning away from the list she didn't want to deal with. Ellie's friend had been given permission to spend the night with Ellie at the farmhouse, with JJ chaperoning. Ellie had said she wanted to sleep out on the back porch so it felt like they were camping, which meant JJ needed to round up some extra blankets for cushioning.

She'd searched through the attic for the old sleeping bags, but came up empty. Maybe Keira had an idea. She'd been here in the cooler months and might have moved things.

JJ hadn't reached out to her cousin much since she'd come to Jasper Creek. She felt strange about interrupting Keira's new life with Remy. On occasion, Keira had texted, or extended a dinner invite, and JJ always found an excuse to say no. Keira, and probably Remy, too, would want to talk about Grandma. Or ask how things were going at the house. JJ didn't want to expose herself that way. Even with Keira.

Keira. Who'd started a new life here. What would starting a new life feel like? JJ couldn't imagine, wasn't sure she wanted to, and yet the thought of going back to the greenhouse and Dad... She couldn't imagine it the way she should be able to.

She shook that thought away, because of course she was going home. Like those childhood summers, this was a special time away from the real world—to do what Grandma asked. Maybe come to terms with Grandma being gone.

Practicality would always beckon. In this case, JJ needed blankets. She dialed Keira's number and half hoped Keira wouldn't answer.

"Hey, JJ. What's up?"

"Hi. I'm not bothering you, am I?"

There was a pause. "Is that why you've been scarce? You're afraid you're going to bother me?"

"I... I've been busy."

"I can't imagine. The babysitting is going well, then?"

"It's… Yes." Better than she could have imagined, which made her stomach clench for some reason. "Um, listen. Do you know where those sleeping bags Grandma always had us use are stored? I checked the attic."

"I could have sworn they were there. What do you need them for? I might have something here you can borrow."

"Ellie's having a sleepover here next week. Her friend's mom wasn't comfortable with her daughter sleeping over at Cade's what with him and all his brothers being the only adults, so I offered to chaperone."

"Wow. You're really getting into this."

"They're—they're really good kids. So it's easy." *Easy* was not the right word. It was the opposite of *easy.* All the ways Ellie and Lora reminded her of her and Lila. All the ways they stirred the deepest feelings she wanted to run away from and simply couldn't because she wanted to sink into them more.

She was *different* because of the girls. And Cade.

Or was it simply being away from home, being sad over Grandma and reliving those long-ago summers? Maybe it had nothing to do with the people at all. She'd go home and go back to being the same old JJ.

She didn't want to be the old her anymore, though. She wanted this new thing to be permanent. Things hurt more, but she was happier, too.

Let yourself feel.

"Did Grandma's letter to you… Did it give you advice?"

JJ could practically hear Keira's smile over the phone. "Of course it did."

"Did you take it? Did you feel like staying here…
changed you?"

"I don't know if it was a change, or some kind of
awakening, but yeah. I didn't at first, then eventually
I had to admit Grandma was right. That changed me,
I guess. Plus, having Remy back… I know you won't
believe me, but I think Grandma knew we all needed
a season there. Not to say goodbye so much as to find
what we lost."

Keira said it so unequivocally. Like it *should* cause
change—or awakening, as she'd put it. It wasn't about
goodbyes or even Grandma, but something Grandma
knew they needed. That they'd lost something.

Let my spirit guide you in all that you do.

"Everything okay, JJ?"

"Yeah, I just… How did you…" It would be so trans-
parent to ask Keira about Remy, and Keira wouldn't hesitate to call JJ on it. But JJ needed someone to talk to.

When she never needed anyone to talk to. If you kept
everything to yourself, you didn't get hurt.

Wasn't she just always low-level hurting, though?
She'd never realized that, not fully. Not until Cade and
the girls had come into her life. That peaceful feeling
she'd always found with Grandma wasn't just a break
from having to do everything for Dad.

It was that she was surrounded by love and care here.

"Come on, JJ. Spit it out."

"Cade…" Normal women knew how to talk about
men and kissing and *feelings*, but that was so not JJ.

"Ah, Cade," Keira said with all the knowing of a *normal* woman. "Well, I couldn't keep all the Mathewsons
straight if I tried, but they are nice to look at. I assume
you like looking."

"Keira. I…" Was it so awful to admit that *yes*, she liked looking? Keira knew a lot of JJ's embarrassing stories. What was one more to add to the list? "Yes and…" She blew out a breath. "He almost kissed me, I think."

"If you *think*, he didn't do anything, JJ."

"No. I'm not explaining it right." She had to get all the words out and then maybe hang up and run away from everyone and everything. "I thought he was *going* to, then he said it would be a bad idea and walked away and hasn't done or said anything since. So I don't know why I brought it up. Because clearly—"

"*Clearly*, you want to kiss him."

JJ nearly dropped the phone. It felt like such an *accusation*. She wanted to deny it, but the words wouldn't come out of her mouth.

"You still…haven't had a relationship exactly, right?" Keira asked very carefully.

JJ made a face. "Right. Anyway, I better find these sleeping bags."

"J—"

"I have a lot to do and this is a silly topic. Who cares? It was, like, weeks ago and nothing has happened and it's dumb. I have to go." Far away from this clutching in her chest and the awful cramp in her stomach that was embarrassment and, worst of all, *fear*.

"Okay," Keira said, sounding sad. "One little tiny piece of advice, since Grandma isn't here to knock some sense into you. You're never going to have what you want if you don't go after it. Playing it safe only keeps you safe."

"I guess it's a good thing I like being safe," JJ returned, feeling even more accused and called out. "I have to go."

"Think about coming over for dinner sometime."

She wanted to refuse or hedge, but she wasn't a child. She just had to get away from this conversation. "Yeah. Definitely. Bye."

All she needed was sleeping bags, not…advice. Or anything. So she marched herself over to the one place she hadn't looked.

Grandma's room.

JJ hadn't stepped foot in this room in the weeks she'd been here, but it was time. She had to find those sleeping bags.

So she opened the door. It squeaked, and even that sound was a memory. That squeak would echo through the hallway and JJ would know Grandma was up and about.

Not anymore.

JJ almost closed the door, retraced her steps and gave the *hell* up. But she tripped, somehow, and the door pulled her forward as she stumbled into Grandma's room.

It smelled like her. That uniquely Grandma June scent of something floral and comforting—a slap in the face now.

Grandma's bed was exactly as she'd likely left it— neatly made with a faded quilt she'd created with her grandmother when she'd been engaged to Grandpa and impatiently waiting for their Christmas wedding.

The windows that bracketed the bed were somehow perfectly clean, the glowing pink sky clear as day through the sparkling glass. Grandma always liked to watch the sunrise here, and the sunset on the porch.

Sunrise had been Grandma June's alone time. Sunset had been their time together.

The lump in JJ's throat was huge and it fizzled painfully as she tried to swallow past it. She turned blindly away from the windows and the bed, the floorboards protesting underneath her.

Against the wall was Grandma's bureau, mismatched picture frames angled across it. JJ wondered how it still looked polished and perfect, as if Grandma June had dusted just this morning.

There was the picture of Grandma's parents, then Grandma's daughters. JJ stared at her own mother's face. Becky looked like Grandma, though more delicate. She was smiling and JJ couldn't say she remembered her mother ever doing much of that.

Do you *do much of that?*

She had lately. This summer was hardly her real life, though. She looked at the picture of her, Lila, Keira and Bella from their last summer together. All standing on the back fence with their arms hooked around the top rung. Even Bella was smiling.

She'd thought of those summers as a fantasy, or a dream. They weren't real because she'd been happy. Because she'd been cared for and loved and surrounded by family who were also friends. That couldn't be *real*.

Maybe she'd had it all backward. Or it was all real. Every second of her life, a choice she made. An experience she reached for or shied away from. She could spend her life being safe and trying to avoid hurt, but… Did she want to live for eighty-some years like that?

It was a confronting thought, so she moved her gaze to the next picture. Grandma and Grandpa on their wedding day. In contrast to the frowning pictures of Grandma's parents, the picture of June and Fred featured big smiles and palpable love.

Grandpa Fred. She had fuzzy memories of a gentle man who'd always smelled like cigars. More, she remembered Grandma talking to him…long after he'd actually been gone.

JJ had thought it was odd, but also that Grandma must not have felt sad. Not the way JJ had after Mom and Lila had left.

Now, JJ understood. Grandma *had* been sad, but she'd also still felt him there. So she'd talked to him like he was there, because it had made her feel like he was.

Something shifted in JJ's chest, and that lump in her throat expanded and dissolved. She sank onto the edge of Grandma's bed, the urge to find her here so overwhelming, and so scary, that she could hardly do anything.

Until the cracked, ragged word escaped her mouth. "Grandma." God, this was stupid. No one was here. She didn't believe in ghosts or spirits. The words spilled out anyway. "I miss you. And I don't know what to do."

There were no answers.

And yet, something inside her that had been knotted tight eased. Because maybe there weren't ghosts, but there was all that Grandma June had been.

JJ didn't need her here to know what she'd say. It was what she'd always said to JJ, and what JJ had always had such a hard time believing.

You deserve to be happy in your own way. Not the way anyone else wants you to be.

Once she'd gotten past the fear that if she was too emotional or needy, Dad might abandon her, she'd believed that life would reward her for taking care of her father. For staying, the way Mom and Lila hadn't.

Belatedly she realized she'd stopped believing that somewhere along the way. She'd become completely self-sufficient, like he'd always told her to be. She could run the greenhouse with him or without him. Nothing had changed. She'd kept putting Dad and Frost Greenhouse first.

Because it was habit. Because it was easy. It didn't require her to take risks or make mistakes. This summer, she'd put a part of herself first. It was the happiest she could remember being since that last summer with everyone here.

She stared at the picture of two happy people in love, of her own summer happiness reflected back at her in the other picture, and her mother captured as just a person, not the missing part of JJ's life she'd built her self worth around…and she wondered.

What would change if she did what Keira said and went *after it*? Happiness and experiences and something beyond the safety of never trying for more when it came to people.

"Don't be stupid, JJ," she muttered aloud, then shrieked when the door slammed shut. Even though it wasn't unheard of for a breeze to sweep through the windows and open or close an unlatched door, the unexpected burst of sound had scared the crap out of her.

Some picture frames fell over, so that only the picture of her and the cousins was up. Staring back at her. Happiness.

Just do it. Just ask. Why not?

She could think of a million reasons why not, but

she stood from the bed and righted the frames that had fallen over as she pulled her cell out of her pocket.

She dialed Cade's number, and that certainty started to fade, but she looked at the pictures when Cade answered. She gathered her courage from Grandma's eyes, and herself as a kid. Smiling.

All she had to do was ask. That was it. Hadn't she survived worse rejection? Didn't she know that she had a perfectly comfortable life waiting for her no matter what happened with this thing she couldn't seem to stop wanting?

"Hey, JJ." Cade's voice was cheerful, maybe even happy to hear from her. Because he liked her well enough. They were *friends*.

"Hi, Cade. Um." Oh, *God*, what the hell was she doing? And why did her voice sound so high-pitched? "Do you...think you could come over?"

"I think so," Cade replied, as if it was a normal request. "Gotta round someone up to stay with the girls. What's up?"

"Oh." She couldn't tell him over the phone. No. "I just need some...help with something," she said, wincing at how horrible the lie sounded.

"Okay. Give me a few, yeah?"

"Yeah. I'll...be here."

They said their goodbyes and for a while JJ simply stood staring at pictures from a past that was gone. No matter what she did or didn't do, losing Grandma was always going to be a part of her life. No matter what happened next, Mom had already hurt her. Dad had taken her for granted. She didn't even speak to Lila because there was no common ground there.

Especially not now that Grandma was gone.

All of these things existed regardless of her wanting them or not.

She was so *afraid*. Of letting anyone in—of letting them see the things she felt or the fears she had. As if there was some magic recipe for taking care of everything and keeping to herself that would give her some kind of reward.

She was creeping up on thirty, and the only rewards in her entire life were Grandma and this place—and neither had ever felt like a *reward*. Not even a cosmic payment. Grandma and this house were the heart of JJ's life.

With Grandma gone, maybe it was time for JJ to become the heart of her own life.

She moved to the door, and it opened on its own. She really needed to make sure that was just the breeze outside and not a draft from somewhere.

She didn't move to put it on her list. She walked through the house and down the stairs. She walked out onto the porch, which had held up quite nicely after Cade's patching-up job.

Then she sat on the porch swing until Cade's truck came into view. He parked and waved as he got out, then walked through the gate and headed for the porch.

JJ stood, heart hammering in her chest. She wanted to take it all back, but Cade approached, the sun glinting his hair gold, and he had that easy, handsome crooked smile on his face.

She liked him. More than she liked just about anybody. He made her chest hurt and made her nerves hum—but in a nice way, which was certainly not a nervousness she'd ever known.

"So what needs fixing?" he asked. He didn't climb the stairs. He stayed at the bottom of them. There'd been a distance he'd put between them since that moment—right here, weeks ago.

It was only a physical distance—not a personal one. So that had to mean... It had to mean he was aware of it. He *had* been going to kiss her, but for some reason, he thought it was a bad idea.

She had to know why, and if she knew why... Well, anything was possible.

"Actually, I have a question."

His smile dimmed a little as his eyebrows drew together in confusion, but nothing ever fazed Cade for long. "Okay. Shoot."

"Why would kissing me be a bad idea?"

He blinked, and in that horrible moment when Cade rocked back on his heels, looking anywhere but at her, JJ knew Keira had been all wrong. Asking for something she wanted was the absolute worst, stupidest thing she could have ever done.

She whirled away from him. "Okay, yeah, never mind." She lurched for the door.

"Hold on."

"No, it was a dumb question. Stupid... Stupid and you weren't and—" She grasped the door, pulled desperately at the knob, but it stuck.

"Whoa, whoa, whoa. Hey, no. You're reading me all wrong."

"Well, of course I am!" she shouted, hating the anger in her voice, and the way she was blushing and shaking and... Damn it, why wouldn't this stupid door open? She pulled with all her might.

He took her arm, but she shook off his grasp. "It was dumb. You weren't going to. So if you would just leave." Why did people ever want to deal with feelings *ever*?

"Would you stop?" he said, a surprising note of sharp command in his voice. Enough of a surprise that she did stop yanking at the door.

When he took her arm this time, she was too over-whelmed with stupidity to do anything but let him pry her hand off the knob and turn her to face him.

Her instinct was to look down at her feet, but she was embarrassed enough. She would not *cower.* Maybe her face was red as a balloon, and maybe she wanted to disintegrate and blow away on the nonexistent wind. She would at least look him in the eye and *pretend* like she felt nothing.

It was her great superpower after all.

His eyes were an intense shade of blue, glowing somehow in the midst of dusk, and the air was hot and still around them. She couldn't pretend not to feel when it was swallowing her whole.

"I never should have said anything." God, she would beg if this would *stop.* "Please, can we just forget—"

Then Cade's mouth was on hers and she *couldn't* talk or think. There was only…feeling. Not the kind that made her wonder why people would put themselves through it, but the kind that made her wonder why on earth she'd been avoiding *this.*

His mouth was soft, but the kiss wasn't. He held her too tight, and the short whiskers of his jaw rubbed against her skin. Then there was his body, which sud-denly seemed entirely forged out of steel. Against hers. Hot, hard.

She could hardly take all that in when his tongue traced her mouth, and despite the fact no one had even come close to kissing her or touching her like this, she knew she wanted more than lips.

She opened for him, and was met with the taste of
Cade. She couldn't have described it with a normally
functioning brain, let alone *now*. She could taste him,
and he sampled her. Everything seemed to make perfect, blinding sense as long as they were kissing.

The noise she made in the back of her throat was as
foreign to her as this sensation of being perfectly and
utterly melted, then devoured.

His grip on her loosened, the kiss ebbing until Cade
pulled his mouth from hers—though only by an inch
or two.

He eased her back, and his hands came to her arms
again, holding her steady. She wasn't planning on going
anywhere. Not when she knew what was possible if you
asked a man the right question.

The right man, the right question.

"Are you ready to listen now?" he asked, his voice a
rough whisper against the muted evening around them.

"No," she whispered back, and this time lifted to her
toes and fitted her mouth to his.

CHAPTER EIGHT

CADE WAS HALF convinced he was having a very vivid dream. It wouldn't be the first time since JJ had appeared in June that he'd end up waking to thoughts of JJ's mouth on his.

But she was too warm, and he could smell the flowers she tended and the grass he'd helped mow the other day. He could hear crickets and frogs, and she smelled like an old house. He held on to her and she was *real*.

It wasn't a dream. Thank God for that, but it was hardly...simple. Especially when her hands slid up his chest and across his shoulders—as if she was testing the breadth of them, and the muscle underneath.

It would take absolutely nothing at all to let this moment spin out. All those *bad-idea* reasons were a lot harder to access when he was drowning in her.

"We need to talk about this," he said against her mouth, incapable of making any effort to pull away.

"Why?" she asked, her fingers running through his hair, her mouth not quite leaving his.

"I don't...know." Not with her touching him. Not when he finally knew what she tasted like, and the fact that their bodies matched up like someone had designed them to come together just like this.

What was there to talk about when there was so much to explore? The way rigid, contained JJ softened in his arms, opened herself up and poured into him and through him like a revelation. The way finally—*finally* that armor she held around herself seemed to not just unlock, but fall off.

Completely, in this moment, and all he wanted was to be part of it. Part of her.

The feeling was too big, too all-encompassing, and he knew the kind of disastrous roads that led to. He had to believe if he was a man with less responsibility this would be easily handled, but he wasn't just *him*. "We have to think." If he could just stop touching her.

"Do we?" she asked, her voice dreamy in a way he'd never heard it before. "I think I'd prefer not to."

He laughed, had to, though it was a mix of actual humor and some kind of cosmic—and physical—pain. He nudged her away, then back, then took a good three steps away, so as to put distance between them.

Her hair was messed up from his fingers, her cheeks flushed from *him*. She was... Too much.

"*I* have to think," he said, more to himself than her, as he ran his fingers through his hair and tried to *focus*. Because he had responsibilities and he'd made a promise to himself when he'd finally realized Melissa was never coming back that it was a responsibility he'd always take seriously. "I have two little girls at home who... I have to think, JJ. Of them. You're leaving. That is why this was a bad idea all those weeks ago, and more now. The summer is more than half over. It's bad enough the girls will miss you like crazy, they don't need..." *Me to do it along with them.*

He was starting to wonder if he wouldn't anyway. No matter what or how. Two months wasn't a very long time, but she felt like an integral part of his life. Dropping off the girls, lunches here. How *lonely* life would go back to being when she left.

But she *was* leaving. He wouldn't fool himself this time. He knew too much. He didn't want anyone staying against their will. That only bred more problems—the kind he'd had enough of.

"They won't miss me because I'll visit," she said, hands fisted on her hips. "And call. Email. I won't abandon them." Anger flashed in her eyes, and determination. "How could I do that?"

Their own mother did. Why should I trust you not to?

He knew too much about JJ to say that to her, even though he wasn't sure he had any trust left in him. He believed she loved those girls, but he also believed that love faded. She wanted to keep in touch or whatever she told herself, but it didn't mean she would. Not forever.

Her expression changed, something like hurt chased across it, as if she could read his thoughts just from the way he was looking at her. For a second he thought she was going to do what she always did—wrap herself in armor, turn off the emotions and retreat back into that protective shell.

She shook her head and stepped forward instead. She took his hands in hers and turned them over, as if studying his palms would hold some answer.

"I love those girls," she said carefully, frowning down at his hands in hers.

"I know you do."

"I would never do anything to purposefully hurt them, but I guess I'm beginning to realize we often hurt people without meaning to. Especially if we're mired in our own hurt." She looked up from his hands, though she kept her grip firm on them. "I know your life is about Ellie and Lora, but this moment isn't."

"J—"

"So I'm going to tell you something kind of embarrassing."

"Okay."

"I don't have any experience with this."

"Okay." He stared at her as he was starting to get a clearer picture of what all this was. "What exactly do you mean by *any?*"

"I mean *any.*" She cleared her throat. Her cheeks were pink, he would have said with embarrassment, but her gaze was frank. "It's not for any philosophical reason. It's because I've always kept people at a distance. I don't exactly put off a kiss-me vibe."

"JJ—"

"Let me finish. I've never been all that compelled to try to have any kind of physical thing with a guy. It's not like anyone's offered to climb all those walls I put up. I like you, Cade. And I really liked kissing you. The walls aren't as high where you're concerned, for whatever reason. Yes, I'm leaving come September, but we're friends. I don't know why we couldn't be…friends with benefits, regardless of how long I'm going to be in Jasper Creek. People do that…don't they?"

People. He was sure *people* did that. He'd just never had much of a middle ground between *try to get into a girl's pants* back in high school and then marriage not that far removed from high school.

But sure, people did that kind of thing, and he was people, wasn't he? "I suppose they do."

"So we could. It wouldn't be about anyone but us. For as long as… Well, my point is…" She dropped his hands, a pained expression moving across her face before some of that armor clicked on. "I guess I don't know what my point is and—"

"I know. I know what your point is." He stepped forward and kissed her again, like he had when she'd been babbling about this being stupid. Hell, he wasn't so sure it wasn't irrevocably stupid, but he was sure it would be worth it.

JJ had never done this, and maybe it was wrong, but *he* wanted be the one to give it to her. He wanted to be someone she remembered, even if she ended up fading away, like people usually did.

That was potent enough to risk all the stupid. That and the promise of this being something about just him and just her. Even if he wasn't sure he'd ever be a *just him* again.

"Well, we should go inside," she said, her eyes half-closed, her mouth a whisper from his.

"Hold on. I—I have to get something out of my truck."

"You know the thing I needed help with was fake, right? You don't need your tools."

"Condoms, JJ," he replied, unable to help the grin that spread across his face as he backed away from her. "I'm going to get condoms."

"Oh. Okay. I'll...be inside."

He nodded and strode for his truck. Feeling like half a fool and half the luckiest damn guy in the world, he grabbed a condom from the box Mac had jokingly thrown in his truck when he'd come over to watch the girls.

Cade shoved it in his pocket, but stopped halfway through the yard on his return.

He looked at the house, which seemed to glow there in the near-gone light. Maybe he should feel bad that he was about to take advantage of Grandma June's granddaughter in Grandma June's house, but it looked welcoming.

He had the funniest feeling that if this was frowned upon, there'd be some sign from that house, from the *air*. But the door was open for him, and JJ was waiting for him, and he knew without a shadow of a doubt that whatever ways this messed him up, it'd be worth it.

CHAPTER NINE

JJ STOOD IN the middle of the living room having no earthly clue what to do with herself. The courage to kiss him was one thing, even the courage to suggest they have a friends-with-benefits sort of arrangement.

But waiting for him to get condoms.

Condoms.

She blew out a shaky breath, reminding herself she wanted this. She wanted him. If sex was anything like a kiss with Cade... She might die, and it might be worth it.

If it wasn't? If it was weird and awkward and terrible, well, she'd know. It'd make the time left a little weird, but wasn't it better than *not* knowing?

Cade walked in the door—which she'd thought she'd closed, but was wide-open as he stepped over the threshold. It was dark outside now, and she'd only turned on the lamp in the living room. It gave a weak light that made him looked shadowed and dangerous, if she hadn't known it was Cade.

Cade, who was tall and broad, who had an easy smile and blue eyes that would make her think of summer no matter the season. He was sweet to his girls and good to her, and he kissed her with very little of the sweet or good.

A few weeks of awkwardness was worth the gamble.

Slowly, he closed the door behind him. Hadn't she closed that door? She tried to remember herself *not* closing it, but Cade was walking toward her. Did doors matter?

She'd been brave enough to start this, but her thoughts scattered under the potent heat of his steady gaze.

"Did you want something to…drink? Or…eat? Or…?"

"Nope," he replied, striding right for her, apparently completely unfazed by the squeak in her voice. "You'll do." His mouth was on hers again, and there was a desperate *need* inside of her that he brought out. Not just by being him, but because he seemed to feel it, too.

His arms slid around her, so she returned the favor, linking hers around his neck. It was amazing that it only took Cade's mouth touching hers to release all those things she kept held inside so tight. A tightness she hadn't even realized existed until he loosened it.

It wasn't just attraction or even that she liked him—it was that she trusted him. With who she was, with this. It had been a very long time since she'd trusted anyone, aside from Grandma. She hadn't even *meant* to. It had sneaked up on her and now it just was, whether she was particularly comfortable with the idea or not.

Something she'd have to mull over later when Cade's hands weren't sliding over her *butt*. Which might have caused her to laugh with awkward nerves, except the move was so possessive, the threat of laughter died on a shiver of excitement.

He lifted her off her feet with an ease that brought back the laugh, though with none of the nerves. It simply felt good to laugh against his mouth as he started walking, as if he could carry her.

"I really like your smile, JJ."

She didn't know what to do with the ache in her chest, or the way that simple statement made her want to cry. She was looking down at him for once, because he was holding her up. The only words she had were the truth. "I don't know what to say to compliments."

"Usually a thank-you will suffice. Upstairs?"

"You can't carry me—"

"Upstairs," he said with a firm nod, as if she hadn't said anything at all.

She renewed her grip around his neck as he took to the stairs. Like he was just *used* to this kind of thing.

"I wrestle cattle, and sometimes my hardheaded brothers. I can carry you up a flight of stairs, JJ," he said as if reading her thoughts.

"But you don't *need* to." Though it made her understand the word *swoon* for the first time in her life.

"No, I don't need to."

"So why would you?"

"It's called romance, I think." He grinned at her as he crested the stairs.

"I'm not sure romance is something I want." She was already taking a space shuttle outside of her comfort zone. Romance seemed like an added intimacy she wasn't sure she'd be able to bear.

"Well, don't you worry, I don't have a whole heck of a lot to give. What I've got, I will. This one?"

She nodded as he inclined his head toward her bedroom door—it was the only one open in the hallway, which was weird. She didn't have time to think about that as he strode inside, *still* carrying her.

"You make your bed," he said, an odd note to his voice.

"Of course I make my bed," she replied, trying to wriggle out of his grasp, but he only held her more firmly to him.

He laid her on the bed, as if she weighed nothing, and whatever she'd been about to say was lost. Then he stood there looking down at her with such intensity she wanted to squirm.

"You're sure?" he said, as if the making of her bed proved to him she didn't know what she was doing.

Which was enough for her to double down on the sure. "I'm a twenty-six-year-old virgin, Cade. Not stupid. Just slow and a hater of mankind." She rolled her eyes, trying to sound far more flippant than she felt. "Get over it."

"I'll be your first."

"Yes." It didn't *have* to be weighty, but it felt that way. More so when he smiled down at her. "Why are you grinning?"

"I don't mind giving you something to remember me by."

She liked the idea a little too much. That she'd always have a piece of him. Not just fuzzy memories of a happy summer, but an actual specific *first* from him.

He lowered himself over her, and it was all so… much. The breadth of him, the heat, the fact he wanted her in some way. His warmth and the intense intimacy of someone else's body being on *top* of hers.

It wouldn't matter what it felt like—just *him* would always make this special and amazing.

Somehow she had to let him know that, to make him understand it wouldn't matter. "I know first times aren't necessarily good. I won't hold it against you."

He choked out a laugh and rested his forehead against hers. "It'll be good."

"You don't know that," she returned. It wasn't like she had any practice to know *how*. He couldn't just *say* things that weren't true or proven fact.

He grinned down at her, pressing a kiss to her mouth before leaning back. "Sure I do."

"Cade."

He ignored her admonition and moved onto his knees, pulling her into a sitting position. He lifted the hem of her shirt and tugged upward until it got through to her sluggish brain to lift her arms so he could pull the T-shirt off her.

He cupped her face and held her there, his eyes darker blue here in the low light of her room. She could still see the outline of stubble around his mouth—just like she could still feel the scrape of it from those kisses downstairs.

Then his hands—rough from ranch work, but gentle in every other way—slid down her cheeks and moved featherlight over her neck. Her heart was beating so hard she was certain it was shaking her body in time with each beat.

He molded his hands over her shoulders, taking the bra straps with him as he moved his hands down her arms. He didn't kiss her again. Instead, he watched the journey of his hands as more and more skin was exposed.

He nudged her onto her back again, hands trailing down her body as she moved. Then his fingers were on the button of her jeans. Nerves threatened, but there was something about the way he held himself—tense and ready—that, along with all these sensations, made her too curious to worry.

No lists. No what-ifs. Just a pulsing need that expanded from the deepest part of her, out to the tips of her fingers.

Cade slid her jeans off her legs, taking the underwear with them. She wanted to cover herself up, but that would be cowardly and the antithesis of the point of what they were doing. Sex was nakedness. She was here, which meant she was brave enough to be *here*.

He lay next to her. "Aren't you a picture," he breathed.

She wanted to shake her head, because how could she possibly be anything worth a look? But he kept staring at her, like he wanted to. Like to him she was pretty as a picture. She didn't know how to accept it was true. "Cade...don't..."

"Don't what?" he asked, tracing a line from her shoulder, the side of her breast, her waist, to her hip and leg. All the way to the ankle and back up again.

She was afraid he'd stop if she didn't tell him the truth, so it fell out like a toad's plopping jump in the grass. "I don't think I'm very pretty."

His gaze whipped to hers, though his touch remained lazy and gentle. "Well, I do," he said firmly, as if there wasn't a doubt. "Why don't you let me tell you?"

"No, you don't have to—"

He shushed her. *Shushed* her. She might have found some outrage, but he got off the bed and undid the button of his jeans. "I remember when you opened that door the first day I dropped off the girls, and it struck me speechless for a second."

She wanted to shake her head, but he was slowly taking off his pants, revealing long, powerful legs.

"Then there's your eyes. Always so serious, so *intent*." He held her gaze as he knelt back on the bed. "Filing things away and I know you'll remember them all, or at least write them all out on a list, and I don't know why I think that's sexy, but I sure as hell do."

"You should take off your shirt, too," she said, too interested in what he revealed to be embarrassed that her voice shook.

He grinned, reached back and lifted his shirt off him in the way men seemed to do that was so fascinating. He was just that. All hard angles and delicious ridges. She could trace the outline of the days he spent out in the sun on his skin—so when he got back on the bed, that was what she did.

"Sometimes all I want to do is lean in and..." He didn't say it, demonstrated instead, pressing his open mouth to the curve of her shoulder. "You've been driving me crazy for weeks."

"Oh" was all she could manage.

"I suppose I could tell you all the things I've imagined, but I've always been better with my hands than any flowery words. So let's try this." He cupped her neck and pulled her into a kiss.

It was fierce with teeth, and so potent she didn't even tense when his fingers explored her, touched her, drove her to a peak she hadn't known could exist, so sharply, so exquisitely. It rolled through her, and that should be it.

But she wanted more. She rolled onto her side, pressing her mouth to his, indulging in another heated kiss that made his grip on her tighter. She slid her hands over his body, just as he had hers, outlining his muscles and spanning the entire shape of him with her fingers.

Up to this point she'd been thinking about her—
the way he made *her* feel, whether he thought *she* was
pretty, what this meant to *her*.

It dawned on her he was having his own thoughts
and feelings. She could feel the way his heart beat hard,
hear the sounds of pleasure he made. *He* would get
something out of this, too, and she wanted to be active
in giving it to him.

When she worked up the courage to tug away his
boxers, she forced herself to look him in the eye. To
close her hand over him while she watched the reac-
tions chase over his face. Then she stroked.

His head fell back, a groan escaping his mouth. He
was hot and hard, and the sound he made when she
touched him made her pulse jump. He wanted *her*, just
as much as she wanted him. For the first time in her
life, she didn't feel like she was on uneven footing with
someone else. They were equals—power to power.

*You really want to find out all the things you'll have
to leave behind?*

She pushed away that depressing thought, that *better-
safe-than-sorry* thought. Maybe she'd be hurt. Maybe
she'd be sorry.

But she'd always have Cade in this moment. She
wanted him to have that, too—a memory of her, something that would make him smile. So she touched him,
learned him. When she was sure and ready, she slid her
hands back up his body, then cupped his face as he had
hers. "I want…" Her throat was closing up, some mix
of nerves and overwhelming emotion, but she swallowed. "I want *you.*"

His gaze held hers, and though not one tensed muscle

on his face moved, his eyes seemed alive with passion and need. Still, he held himself so still, so…controlled.

She wanted to break it. For whatever reason, she *needed* to break all the ways he was holding himself back *for* her.

"Get the condom, Cade."

He didn't break, but he moved away, pulling the packet out of his discarded jeans. He rolled on the condom, the whole process fascinating, and JJ was so flushed with pleasure it didn't even occur to her to be embarrassed.

When he settled himself between her legs, his blue eyes held hers. She didn't want to meet that frank, searching gaze, but she couldn't seem to look away.

"I promised it would be good," he said, his voice gentle, but there was a scrape to it, as if he was holding himself back. "Trust me."

She hadn't trusted anyone. Not like this. But she did trust him—both in control and out of it. So she nodded.

He slowly moved inside of her. All her breath got caught up in her lungs, because it was too much. The moment, the physical feeling of him inside of her—too much pressure in her chest and where he entered her.

She wanted to cry, and she wanted to grab onto him. Hold on to him. Squeeze her eyes tight and let him take care of all this building inside of her.

"Breathe, J. Just breathe."

So she did, and all that *pressure* eased some. He kissed her cheek, her temple. He touched her, gentle caresses meant to soothe.

It didn't matter that there was a part of her that wanted to wriggle away from that pressure, it was Cade.

She wanted this with him no matter what it felt like be-cause…because it was him.

He thought she was pretty, and he'd wanted to kiss her long before he'd done it. He had a good heart and an easy way, and what was a little discomfort?

She'd always have the memory of him filling her for the first time.

If she breathed, if she touched him like he was touch-ing her…

She dragged her fingers down his back, steadied by the strength there. The pressure eased more as he moved, as she breathed. The scrape of his rough cheek against hers, the mix of sweet and erotic things he whis-pered to her, until she forgot all about that pressure.

"Cade." Something bigger and brighter was building inside of her. The discomfort was gone and there was only his body and hers—joined and pressed together, moving together toward that elusive end.

There was a break, and then pulsing pleasure. She shuddered, and he did, too. Wrapped together. Her and Cade. Like it was just where she was meant to be.

After a few minutes of even breathing and something close to pure bliss, he rolled off her. She was ready to mourn the loss, but he wrapped her up against him. Like the night on the porch, where he'd put his arm around her and she'd leaned into it. It felt like that elu-sive belonging she seemed to only find here at Grandma June's.

She would feel this way with Cade no matter where they were, and that was new and overwhelming—more so than the rest of it.

Cade was her first. She'd had *sex*. She turned her

head, all but touching her nose to Cade's. He had his arms wrapped around her, and their faces were so close.

It was too hot for all of this, the air heavy and sticky in midsummer, and she didn't care one bit.

"You know what's one thing I always wondered?" he said, pressing a kiss to the corner of her mouth, one of his hands tangling itself in her hair.

"What?" she murmured, happily buzzed on *everything*.

"What does JJ stand for?"

She winced, some of that sweet warmth evaporating into a chill—despite the fact nothing in this house was remotely cool. "Nothing," she answered automatically, rolling onto her back again, away from his face and gentle kisses.

His grip didn't loosen, and he moved to his side so his face loomed over hers. "Liar," he murmured, pressing his mouth to that spot on her shoulder that *almost* distracted her enough to tell him. But no. She didn't want…that weight here. Ever.

He didn't press the subject. Instead, he sighed. "I have to go."

She'd known that all along, so that it caused a jolt of pain was beyond stupid. "Of course."

"I want to make it clear, I don't *want* to go. I *have* to go." He dropped a kiss on her mouth before rolling off the bed.

"I know. I…appreciate that. It'll never hurt my feelings that you put them first." She understood too much what it was like to be put second, or last, by the people who were supposed to take care of you.

She sat up, pulling the sheet with her. Cade got dressed and she watched, marveling at the fact he had just been *inside* her. He was so beautiful, and he'd made *her* feel beautiful somehow. Desired.

Dressed, he turned back and bent down to kiss her. She lifted her mouth to his, but he paused. His expression went grave for a moment. "We'll have to be careful around the girls. I wouldn't want them getting their hopes up that there might be…"

Her brain shied away from finishing that sentence for him—from wanting things she'd never be able to have. She nodded, maybe a little too vigorously so he wouldn't find the words. "Yeah. Definitely."

"Free tomorrow?"

He wanted to come back. She'd hold on to that. "I think I could clear my schedule."

Finally, he dropped his mouth to hers. Just a peck, but then it lingered, heated, ignited. Until she was pulling him back down on the bed, and he was going willingly.

"What's another hour?" he murmured against her mouth, already pulling off his shirt. She laughed with him as he wound himself around her and they lost themselves in each other all over again.

CHAPTER TEN

IT WAS SOMETHING of a revelation there were so many different kinds of sex, and more of an amazement that JJ got to experience them all over the next few evenings. Soft and sweet. Desperate and a little rough. A million other things in between.

She sighed happily the Saturday morning of Ellie's party. This—*this* was what content was. Except for that little reminder in the back of her head, always, that time was running out.

Today was no time to think of that. She was going to help Ellie celebrate her birthday, and that was the most important thing.

JJ spent most of the day getting things ready. She hummed to herself as she hung the streamers and decorations Ellie had picked out—all pink and unicorns. JJ had even braved the overheated attic to find some of Grandma June's birthday boxes.

Ellie might not like the aesthetic, but JJ hoped she'd appreciate the gesture. Grandma had always made a big deal about JJ's summer birthday, and JJ had always dreaded it. Her birthday signaled the end of most summers. In a few days Dad would come pick her up.

Mostly he forgot she ever had a birthday.

So Grandma always gave her a big celebration with whichever cousins were still about.

For the first time in her life, in a very real way, JJ could put herself in her grandmother's shoes. She wanted this party to remind Ellie that it didn't matter what she *didn't* have, she had lots of people who loved her.

Grandma had never let JJ forget it. JJ couldn't look like Grandma, or sound like Grandma, or even decorate a cake like Grandma, but she could give someone what Grandma had always given her.

She took the box of Grandma's birthday decorations into the living room and began to put them up just as Grandma always had. The tattered Happy Birthday sign hung over the couch. The sparkly, rainbow-tinsel rope across the mantel over the fireplace, with two of the big paperweights from Grandma's collection anchoring either side.

Keira must have dusted right before she'd left. JJ certainly hadn't taken on the chore. Still, the mantel was clean as a whistle—all of Grandma's paperweights looked as sparkling as they ever did. Even the silver frames looked freshly polished.

JJ smiled over the photographs. All four of Grandma's granddaughters in separate frames at different points in time. Lila, a young, smiling woman making cookies in Grandma's kitchen, Keira's college graduation looking so adult and proud. Bella was still a little thing in her picture, since her mother had cut off almost all ties with Grandma long ago. Grandma hadn't let that stop her from trying to keep Bella in their lives.

In JJ's picture she was thirteen and had a giant clutch of summer wildflowers in her hands. She was grinning in a way she didn't think she was in any of the pictures her father had of her.

She'd once asked Grandma why she kept the young picture of her when surely she had more recent ones, and Grandma told her she couldn't bring herself to. JJ finally understood. In how many pictures did she look *that* happy?

June's daughters had done quite the number on their children, but June had given them a place to survive those wounds.

Then, she'd given them each a season. Keira had certainly found something in hers. More than just Remy— an awakening, as she'd called it.

JJ hadn't ever meant to let herself feel as Grandma had instructed in her letter, but it had happened anyway. She had been changed already by the quiet moments of grief, by those sweet girls. By Cade.

Her phone rang, jolting her out of thoughts of Cade. It was the man himself and JJ felt more than stupid that her face got a little hot when she answered.

"Hi," she greeted.

"Hey, listen. Beth canceled. Stomach bug or something."

"Oh, no."

"Can't say as I buy it since her mom was all cagey about rescheduling. Ellie's crying in her room. Lora's trying to cheer her up, which is only causing Ellie to yell and Lora to cry and—"

"Bring her over anyway," JJ said, unable to stand that thread of hurt and failure in his voice, as if it was his fault Ellie had a crap friend, or her friend had a crap mom.

"J—"

"I know it's not the same, but I've already decorated and I bought a cake. I'll make a big deal over her, just like Grandma June would do. It won't be the same, but it'll feel special."

He was quiet in response, so she pressed on.

"She'll have her sleepover. A night where she's the star of the show. Let me try, Cade. I have it ready anyway."

She heard his intake of breath, and then all that *failure* in his voice again. "All right. We'll be over in a bit."

"I'll be ready."

She ended the phone call, worrying over Cade feeling overly responsible for Ellie's disappointment. She fretted over Ellie's disappointment and what she could do to soothe it.

She wanted to wrap them both up in her arms and... and... She didn't have a clue. She just wanted to fix it all for them, but she couldn't.

Yeah, she was getting more glimpses into what Grandma June must have felt as a grandmother.

When she heard a truck puttering up the drive, she hurried to the front door. Cade got out of the truck first. Unlike their weekday morning routine, where the girls raced out of the truck, eager to see her, both Ellie and Lora had to be lifted out of their seats and plopped onto the ground.

Cade carried a little pink backpack and a cupcake pillow. Lora kicked rocks on the way to the porch, a scowl on her face. Ellie kept her gaze on the ground.

JJ's heart twisted at the clear *dejection* hanging over all three of them. She smiled brightly as they approached.

"Well, hello, birthday girl."

"It isn't even really her birthday yet," Lora muttered irritably.

Ellie stuck her tongue out at Lora, who made a screech of outrage, so Cade stepped between them.

"Here's her things." He looked down at the two angry girls. "You sure you want to take this on?"

"Of course I do. Come on, Ellie. I have lots of fun planned." JJ held out her hand, but Ellie didn't take it. She downright trudged up the stairs as if she was pulling herself through mud.

"Call if you need anything." Cade smiled, but it was a defeated thing.

JJ wanted to kiss him, or even give him a reassuring hug. It got harder and harder to fight those impulses in front of the girls when she knew it was something he'd accept behind closed doors. With Lora and Ellie watching, she could only reach out and give his arm a little squeeze—a silent *don't worry*.

JJ gestured Ellie inside, and the girl trudged forward as if she was walking to the guillotine. Lora complained bitterly as Cade nudged her back to the truck, and as much as it twisted JJ's heart to be leaving one of the girls out, the one thing she'd always had too much of was exactly what Ellie was missing.

JJ had always been alone when she was with her dad. In some ways there had been a comfort in that, but what would it have been like to have someone to share that attention with?

Ellie, on the other hand, had nothing but split attention. A little one-on-one time would do both girls some good. Lora would have Cade—who she'd probably never truly had all to herself. And Ellie got her.

JJ stepped inside behind Ellie. Ellie's solemn, red-rimmed eyes took in the scene. Streamers and balloons that Ellie herself had picked out in the hallway and dining room. The decorations from Grandma's box in the living room.

"Those were Grandma June's. She used to—"

"I know," Ellie said curtly. "She told us."

"Right. I made your favorites that you requested," JJ offered with all the cheer she could muster, moving forward to the kitchen.

"It won't be like Grandma June's."

JJ let out a pained breath, stopping halfway to the kitchen. "No. It won't," she agreed, because nothing she could do would live up to Grandma June. Or the hopes of a sleepover with a friend.

Why had she thought she could handle this? Cade would be better at knowing what to do for his hurting daughter. "I bought you a present!" she blurted, grasping for every last potential straw.

That lifted Ellie's gaze. "You did?"

"Two, actually. One is something I got you because I thought you'd like it, and one is something I had when I was your age. You sit down on the couch and I'll get them."

JJ gathered up the two gifts and hurried back to the living room. Ellie was sitting dutifully on the couch, frowning at the Happy Birthday sign on the wall.

Just keep pushing forward. JJ arranged the gifts on the coffee table in front of the couch. "Here we go."

Ellie leaned a little forward with *some* interest. "I can open them right now? I don't have to wait for dinner or anything?"

"This is our party and you're the star. We can do whatever you want."

Ellie let out a sigh and flopped back on the couch. "What does it matter?"

"It's your birthday. That matters."

"Not to anybody else. Not to my friends or my mom."

JJ opened her mouth to point out Cade was planning to take her to her favorite restaurant the evening of her actual birthday, and she'd likely be showered with gifts from her uncles and her sister on top of what Cade would do.

But JJ knew from experience having people tell you what you had and how lucky you were didn't get rid of the emptiness that took hold when the people you wanted to love you didn't.

So she went for a different tactic. One she never would have taken two months ago. *Let yourself feel.* She never had for herself, but it seemed for other people she could. "You know, my mom left me, too."

Ellie's head whipped up, but the surprise in her expression faded to a cynicism too sharp for her age. "You mean she died."

"No. My parents decided they couldn't be married anymore. My mom took my little sister, but she didn't want me. So my dad took me. I pretty much didn't see my mom anymore." They hadn't even spoken at Grandma's funeral because Dad had stuck close since he'd never cared for the "old ladies" of Jasper Creek. Mom had kept a wide berth.

"She took your little sister?" Ellie whispered.

"Yeah, can you imagine that? If it was just you and your dad. And you never saw much of Lora."

Ellie shook her head. "It might be nice sometimes," she said, but her voice was squeaky and not at all sure.

"I think you'd miss her. Just like you miss your mom. But you know what you and your sister taught me this summer?"

Ellie looked up, her big blue eyes, just like Cade's, wide and waiting.

Tears threatened, but JJ wanted to be strong and matter-of-fact for Ellie. So she understood. So she believed. "I used to think it had to be my fault that my mom left me with my dad. I know you know what that feels like."

Ellie ducked her head, but JJ didn't have to see the pain on her face to know it was there. "But I know you. I've taken care of you. Nothing you are or could do would drive anyone away, so it has to be something wrong with them. My mom. Your mom. It's them. Not us."

Ellie poked at a spot on the couch, kicking one of her legs. "Grandma June left."

"Yeah." JJ's voice broke, and all she could do was move to sit beside Ellie on the couch. She didn't reach out to touch, for fear she'd break, but she sat right next to Ellie and tried to find the right words. "She died. And that's life. She would have stayed if she could. Which is why sometimes I feel her here."

"Like a ghost?"

"No. I don't believe in ghosts. I think… She left us this house, and each other." JJ looked down at Ellie, understanding in a way she hadn't fully grasped until this moment that Grandma had known. Known that this little girl needed this conversation…and that JJ did, too. "She asked me to watch after you and Lora. She gave us each other, because she knew we'd be friends."

"You're going to leave at the end of the summer." Ellie looked up at her imploringly. "Why do you have to go?"

JJ could clearly hear Cade's voice say *stab me in*

the heart. "My life is in another town. It doesn't mean I won't visit. Write and call. Maybe I can come back next summer and watch you again."

"Maybe," Ellie echoed, clearly disbelieving.

"I know you don't believe me, and you don't have any reason to. I'm going to prove it to you—just like Grandma June did. You'll always be able to count on me, Ellie."

"I have Daddy."

"You have the best daddy. And a really sweet little sister, even if she irritates you. You've got all those uncles who help your daddy take care of you. That doesn't mean you can't have me, too." She was going to have to say it. Lay it all out there because Ellie needed it, and maybe just like all the other things, JJ needed it, too. "I know I'm not your mom, but I love you."

Ellie stared at her solemnly, then slowly...slowly leaned against JJ's side. She didn't tense or push her away when JJ gingerly wrapped her arms around Ellie.

"I love you, too," Ellie whispered. "But you're going to leave."

"When I was your age I used to spend summers right here, but I went to school where I live with my dad. I would miss Grandma June so much, but she always sent me letters and called me. So I promise you, Ellie. I *promise* you. I might not always be here, but I will always be right here." She placed her hand on Ellie's chest. Even if it was cheesy, it was what Grandma June had given JJ growing up, and it had made all the difference.

"Can I open my presents now?" Ellie asked, her voice muffled against JJ's side.

"I say we do presents, then cake, then games, then more cake."

Ellie giggled. "I don't have to eat dinner?"

"As long as you can keep it a secret that all we ate is cake," JJ said solemnly.

So they snuggled on the couch and Ellie opened her presents—a sparkly pink doll complete with unicorn sidekick, then the old copy of *Little Women* that had been JJ's favorite whenever she'd visited Grandma.

JJ knew Ellie wasn't as excited about that one, but maybe someday she'd appreciate it.

They ate their cake, played princess games and watched a princess movie. They even slept outside on the porch together after counting stars and making wishes.

Through the whole thing, JJ held it together, because she had to. Because Ellie needed it.

For the first time she truly understood that at the end of this summer, even when she went back home to Frost Greenhouse, everything would be changed—because she was changed. There was no going back now.

There was only going forward.

CHAPTER ELEVEN

CADE TRIED TO wait for JJ's call that Ellie was ready to be picked up, but lazy Sunday mornings weren't his thing on a good day. Add Lora's inability to entertain herself, he was on considerable edge.

"Daaaaaaaaddddyyyyyy," Lora whined, with an impressive high-pitched note that made him want to cut off his own ears.

"All right. Fine. You win." Not that he needed all that much imploring. Not having both girls unsettled him. Even trusting JJ completely...

It wasn't right. He was the dad. He was the one who was supposed to make things *better*. Not some woman. Even if she was connected to Grandma June. Even if Cade had slept with her.

Over and over again, for weeks on end. Getting deeper into something he was struggling to define. Struggling to keep his head above water when all these feelings swamped him.

Lora already had her sandals on and was pawing at the door. Cade grabbed his hat off the hook and settled it on his head. He looked down at his youngest daughter and tried to work out what this squeezing, panicked feeling clawing at him was.

Especially when it had been nice to spend some one-on-one time with Lora. He so often looked at his kids as a set, but they were individuals. Girls who needed individual attention. He'd even considered asking JJ to watch Lora when he took Ellie out on her actual birthday so they could have the same type of evening.

Something in him told him to ask one of his brothers instead. Stop insinuating JJ into so much of their lives. She wasn't permanent. He was setting up the girls for hurt.

What about yourself?

"Let's go-o-o-o," Lora whined.

"Yup." He walked outside with her and helped her into her booster seat in the back of the truck, though she could buckle herself now. Both girls were getting older at such a rapid rate. What would he do when they were teenagers and needed a woman to talk to?

Ellie and Lora needed someone besides him, much as it pained him to admit it to himself. JJ had promised to always be there for the girls, but that didn't mean she would be. And she wouldn't be *here*.

She wouldn't be yours.

He shook his head. Lack of sleep was making his brain think stupid thoughts.

He pulled up to June's house. JJ and Ellie were already on the porch, swinging on the porch swing.

His heart clutched painfully at the picture. Perfect. And fleeting. Just like June's last years with them. Nothing lasted. Why was he letting them build this up only to lose it? Not much longer and he'd believe— No, not him. The *girls* would believe this was real life.

Ellie was smiling as he and Lora approached—a marked change from when he'd dropped her off. JJ was smiling, too, though there was something worrying around the edges.

Ellie immediately produced a doll and began bragging to Lora about the grown-up book JJ had given her.

JJ handed Cade Ellie's backpack and pillow. "We had a great time." She looked down at Ellie, and he could *see* the love she had for those girls as she looked at them. "Thanks for spending the night with me, El."

Ellie smiled brightly. "Thank you for my party and my presents." Then, without even one piece of encouragement, she stepped forward and gave JJ a hug.

JJ whispered something in her ear and Ellie laughed. She pranced back to Lora, waving the doll in the air to gloat some more.

"Thanks again, JJ. I appreciate it."

She studied him, and if he fooled himself into thinking anything like *love* was in her gaze, it was just leftovers from Ellie. It wasn't for *him*.

"Anytime." She clasped her hands in front of her, and she watched him with too-perceptive eyes, so he turned away and walked to his truck, the girls following in his wake. He dropped Ellie's backpack in the passenger seat, but he didn't open the back door for the girls.

"Can you two play out in the yard for a second? I have to tell JJ something."

They nodded, and Ellie immediately gave Lora a hard push and screamed, "You're it." Which was met with a screech of Lora's own, complaints about that not being fair and the immediate pounding of little feet on the ground as she began to run after Ellie's retreating form.

Cade strode back to the house. He just had to…say something. Thank her but tell her no more of this. It was going to crush him. The *girls*. It was going to crush the girls.

They had to go back to the original arrangement. Just babysitting. Not friends with benefits. Not a woman who swept in and took care of *his* girls like they were her own.

She wasn't June. She didn't have the right.

He gave a perfunctory knock and then pushed open the door. He immediately jumped forward into the living room because JJ was sitting on the couch *crying*. Not just crying, but downright sobbing into her hands.

Everything else was forgotten. "Christ. What is it?"

She jumped a foot, but settled when he sat next to her on the couch. "You scared the crap out of me," she said, sniffling and wiping at her face.

"What's wrong?"

"Nothing. No, really," she insisted when he opened his mouth to argue. "I... I had to hold it all in when she was here and then—"

"Hold all *what* in?"

"Really, Cade. It's nothing to worry about." She sucked in a ragged breath, then rested her head on his shoulder. Like it belonged there.

He closed his eyes, swallowing the groan of pain. He wished he could rip his stupid heart right out of his chest and throw it away. Apparently it couldn't learn its lesson, because this...

He wanted this. Not for a summer.

Abruptly, far too abruptly, he pulled away and got to his feet. "JJ." He had to find the words to fix this mire of crap he'd plopped himself and the girls into. The girls most of all.

"You want to know what happened with Ellie. I know." She smiled reassuringly at him. "It's just so weird. I don't cry in front of people. I didn't even like to cry in front of Grandma, and now here I am crying in front of you for the second time and it doesn't feel wrong."

Her eyes were still wet, but she looked at him with such certainty, as if she had it all figured out. He wished like hell he did.

"We talked about mothers," JJ said. "It was good, though. I promise." She stood and crossed to him, reaching forward and placing her hands on his chest. The warmth of her palms was a soothing balm to everything that churned inside of him. "Good for her to realize she's not the only one in the world who had a mother walk out on them."

Yes, no doubt it was. No doubt Ellie and Lora needed someone exactly like JJ in their lives. No, not someone like. JJ. Just JJ. June had known. She'd put this together.

Had she any idea of how much harder it would make *his* life?

"You don't have to blame yourself for that," JJ said softly.

"I don't blame myself," he replied stiffly, feeling too...seen.

She cocked her head, studying him. "Maybe not all the time, but sometimes you do. I've blamed myself for a thing or two that wasn't my fault. I know what it looks like. What it feels like."

"The girls are waiting." *The girls are waiting and I am somehow in love with you, so if you could just stab me in the heart, that'd be great.*

Her eyebrows drew together, as if she was realizing he was being jumpy.

"Are you coming back tonight?" she asked carefully. He shouldn't. He should end this right now. He couldn't be in *love* with her, and more sex was definitely not the way to nip that horrible thing welling inside of him in the bud.

She looked up at him hopefully and he had no refusal in him. "Yeah."

Her mouth curved. "Good."

"Good. I have to…go." He moved for the door, but no matter what was going on with *him*, JJ had given Ellie something last night. "Thank you for being what she needed."

"You don't have to thank me for that."

"Yes, I do." Then he broke his own personal rule, giving her a brief kiss even with the girls running around outside. He stared down at her knowing he felt too much, and regardless of what he wanted to see reflected in her eyes…it wasn't there. Or whatever *was* there wasn't big enough to leave her life over.

Because Jasper Creek was his life and her vacation. His girls were his *responsibility*, and her occasional enjoyment. Nothing worked the way it should—the way it would need to.

"Bye, JJ."

"I'll see you later."

He tipped his hat and left. He gathered up the girls, though they whined and asked to stay with JJ or ask JJ over to their house, and Cade refused them at every turn—probably too curtly to be fair.

It was time to start easing away. To start protecting…his *girls*.

Because this was about them. Not his own heart.

CHAPTER TWELVE

THERE WAS SOMETHING up with Cade, that much JJ knew. The five days since he'd picked Ellie up from their sleepover, he'd been…so serious. He still dropped off the girls with a smile, but he hadn't eaten lunch with them. He came by every night, aside from the night he'd taken Ellie out for her birthday and JJ and Lora had entertained each other with a dinner party of their own.

Whenever Cade or the girls were *here* there'd be hours of time the heavy band of worry would disappear. Then he'd leave, as if the weight of the world was on his shoulders.

Everything between them seemed so fragile—adding any weight scared her. She hadn't even told him tomorrow was *her* birthday.

Worse still, the clock was ticking down. She needed to start thinking about going home. About packing her things and hiding the key under the mat so that Lila could take her place here. Maybe do more to pack Grandma's things than she had.

She stood in the middle of Grandma's room overwhelmed with all different kinds of sadness. Grief over Grandma. Dread over leaving. *She* might have changed, but the world around her hadn't. Her job was with Dad at Frost Greenhouse. Her home was a little apartment above the bakery in Plainview.

That wasn't home.

Home.

Why couldn't this be…her real home? Where the people she loved—and who loved her back—were. Maybe Dad loved her, but not the way she needed him to.

She blinked at the familiar quilt on Grandma's bed, the lacy curtains fluttering in the almost-cool late-summer breeze. Outside, the world was dark and crickets chirped their incessant song.

What if this person she'd changed into needed a new life?

The idea shivered through her like fear. It shook her and part of her wanted to run away. To go back to Dad's house and Frost Greenhouse, where she knew exactly what was expected of her.

What kind of job could she have *here*? What…what would a life of her own design look like?

She heard the distant sound of a truck's engine outside.

Thank God. She left Grandma's room exactly as it was. Everything remained exactly as it had been when Grandma had left this earth.

JJ didn't know how she'd ever be able to face packing up Grandma's things. It was as scary and challenging as the idea of changing her life.

So she hurried to the door and opened it to Cade's grim face. What had made sweet, cheerful Cade so *grim*?

She smiled at him, hoping to see some flash of the man she'd… It hit her then, in a way she hadn't allowed it to yet—this overwhelming pressure in her chest that swelled into hope every time she saw him, the need to reach out to him, give him pieces of herself she'd never wanted to give anyone before.

That was love. She was in love with him.

"Hey," he offered.

"Hi." *You love him.* She wanted to laugh, but she knew that would not make sense in the moment. She wasn't sure anything made sense in the moment...standing in the entryway of Grandma June's house, head over heels in love with Cade Mathewson.

"Are you going to let me in?" he asked, and there was *almost* that hint of humor she so loved about him. *Love.*

"Cade..." She wanted to tell him, but she remembered that fragility even as she stepped aside and let him enter.

He was the strongest, best man she knew, and for some reason the past few days made her think he was made of spun sugar and he'd float away at the wrong move.

His phone ringing interrupted the tense, awkward silence. Cade frowned and answered, frowning deeper based on whatever the person on the other end was saying. "I'll be right home."

JJ practically leaped forward to grab onto him. "Is everything okay?"

"Lora had a bad dream. She told Mac she wants me. I better head back."

"Of course. Poor thing."

Cade picked up his hat and settled it on his head. He looked lonely, she decided. Too solitary. He needed help. Not just a babysitter, but a partner. Someone to shoulder some of the responsibility—not separately, but together.

He wouldn't *ask* for that. Not after what had happened with Melissa. So she had to offer it. She had to offer herself in some way. It still scared her, even knowing she loved him. But she'd learn how to deal with the fear—and put herself out there anyway.

"I could go with," she offered, even with nerves multiplying in her throat. "I've never seen your place."

The change in his expression was like watching everything she'd built shatter. Just as fragile as she'd thought. His gaze shuttered, blanked, and it was almost as if he physically withdrew into himself.

She would know what that looked like—she'd built her life on that move.

"You leave in two weeks, JJ."

"Yes." She held her breath. Would he ask her to stay? She couldn't…but she wanted to. Wanted to figure out a way. Surely there might be *some* way. If he asked she could battle all that fear and try. She could try for him.

Can't you try for yourself?

"We can't do this anymore," he said roughly, everything about him tense and scraped raw.

It took a few moments—as if he'd spoken in a foreign language she knew the basics of and slowly, oh so slowly, came to understand what he meant.

This was what had been coming. The inevitable end. She'd just been stupid enough to think it didn't have to be inevitable.

She'd been fantasizing about change and love and new beginnings. When she was still JJ Frost. And nothing ever *really* changed.

Least of all her.

CADE HAD NEVER been the one to break off something. He'd always been the one left, so this was new.

Horrible.

"It'll be easier that way."

"Easier," she echoed. She was gripping the table like it was holding her up and she looked…blindsided.

Of course she was blindsided. He'd handled it like crap. "I'm sorry."

She shook her head, lifting her chin, and tears glittered in her eyes, but they didn't fall. "Don't be sorry. *I'm* not sorry. We had our… Now it's over. Because it'll be easier." There was a note of derision in her voice, but her expression remained blank, if a little fierce.

"I should go. Lora can't go back to sleep until I—"

"Of course. I'll see you Monday morning."

"Yeah. Right. Monday."

She stood there, chin in the air, eyes a little cool, but she didn't rage or say anything mean. She didn't cry or demand answers. She didn't say she was changing her whole life for him. Or that she wanted to stay.

She just dismissed him.

Had he been hoping for something else? He shook his head and turned back to the door. Of course he hadn't. This was the decision he'd made, and it was the right one—regardless of what her reaction was.

But he couldn't stop thinking about the way she'd folded it all in, iced him out. The whole drive home he replayed the few words she'd said to him. As if she wasn't hurt at all. Maybe a little miffed. Not…the devastation he felt swallowing him whole.

So he'd made the right choice.

He parked his truck and went inside his cabin—his real life with his two girls and no women. He got Lora settled back into bed. Kissed both his girls good-night again and determined everything was fine.

He was surprised to find Mac still sitting on the couch when he slipped out of the girls' room.

"You can head back if you want," Mac offered, eyes on the TV.

"No," Cade said, surprised to find his voice rusty. "I probably won't need you in the nights much anymore."

"She dropped the ax, huh?"

"No," Cade returned. "I did."

Mac sat up straighter on the couch, looped his arm around the back of it and stared at Cade. "I'm sorry. You were getting sex every night and *you* dropped the ax?"

"She's leaving," Cade replied. Because that was the bottom line.

"Did it occur to you to ask her to, you know, not?"

"She has a life somewhere else." Cade opened the fridge with a jerk, swore when there wasn't a beer in it. He didn't keep any hard stuff at the cabin, and he couldn't get drunk anyway, because two little girls were sleeping down the hall.

He slammed the fridge shut. Ask her to stay. It sounded so simple when Mac said it. But it wasn't.

Besides, she'd stay if she wanted to. She would have made that decision on her own. So she didn't want to stay. End of story.

"It was just a fling-type thing," Cade insisted, not that Mac had argued with him. But he needed to expel all the reasons he had inside of him, because JJ had dismissed him.

She hadn't needed reasons.

Well, he damn well had them. "I was overdue for one of those," he said to Mac's inscrutable expression. "And it ran its course. So now it's over."

"So why are you so pissed?"

"I'm not pissed."

"That dish towel you're strangling says otherwise."

Cade looked down at the towel he was indeed squeezing within an inch of its life, then tossed it into the sink. "You can go, Mac."

Mac unfolded himself from the couch. "Listen, baby brother." At Cade's warning growl, Mac only smiled. He walked to the door casually, and even the way he spoke was casual, but that was Mac's greatest strength. He was always so *casual*, you never knew when he was going to knock you out.

"When a cow kicks you in the head you don't just get to avoid cows for the rest of your life."

"You're right. You get brain damage."

"Just consider for a second that the pain of one thing doesn't mean you avoid the thing for the rest of your life. Life's going to kick you around, no matter what you avoid."

"Gee, you should sell these pep talks. Wisdom from Mac Mathewson. Until everyone's so depressed by your advice, they jump off a mountain."

Mac merely shrugged and slipped through the door, closing it behind him. Cade glared at the door.

He agreed with Mac—hurt was a part of life. That was fine for him, but he would not inflict it upon his children when the big bad world out there would do it plenty—and in some ways already had.

It was the right thing, regardless of kicks to the head.

Life would go back the way it had been before this summer.

Cade collapsed onto the couch, cradling his head in his hands.

Before this summer. When he'd been lonely, working too hard and trying even harder to give something to his girls he'd never actually be able to give them— something to make up for the fact Melissa had left.

Then June had given them JJ, and now everything was a mess.

But he hadn't been lonely.

CHAPTER THIRTEEN

JJ WASN'T SURE how long she stood gripping the table. Night crept in and still she stood there, inexplicably holding the tears at bay. She was alone and could certainly let them fall.

There was no point in crying, of course. There was no point in *feeling*.

Grandma's advice sucked.

It was the first thing that jerked JJ out of the trance she'd been in. JJ could almost feel the rap on the back of her head over such blasphemy as thinking Grandma's advice sucked.

She let go of the table, surprised to find a vicious ache in her hand. Surprised to find hours had passed since Cade had walked out of the house.

Out of your life.

He'd said it would be easier. What would ever be easy about not having him? Hadn't she been considering changing her entire life for *him*?

He didn't want that. Just *we can't do this anymore.*

She trudged up the stairs, but instead of turning into her room—and the bed she'd been spending hours in with Cade—she turned to Grandma's room.

She stared at the darkness, then did something she hadn't considered doing this entire summer.

She crawled into Grandma's bed. JJ spread her body

out, trying to take up as much of the bed as possible for some reason she couldn't put into words.

She needed to feel like Grandma was here. Like there was someone here who cared about *her* at least as much as they cared about themselves.

The breeze drifted through the window, cool enough to feel like Grandma's roughened palm sliding over her forehead. JJ closed her eyes and let that silly fantasy lull her into sleep.

She awoke to the sun shining on her face. There was a strange noise outside. An engine, puttering.

She bolted into a sitting position. Oh, Cade was back. He was *back*. She darted into the bathroom to look at her reflection. Puffy and blotchy, so she quickly splashed cold water over her face. It might not fix everything, but it could hide a few things hopefully.

He was back and he'd changed his mind. Her heart danced with anticipation, and her chest swelled with hope as she moved down the stairs to the front door.

When she opened it, it wasn't Cade climbing the stairs of the porch.

"Dad." Her heart sank, but if she was waiting for signs from the universe, wasn't this it? Her father, the man she looked so much like, was actually visiting her on her birthday.

Time to go back to your old life, JJ. Your real life.

"You haven't honestly been *living* here, JJ. My God. It looks like a serial killer's house."

She ignored the harsh words because he'd remembered her birthday. Hope and love twisted knots in her stomach that she thought she'd untied long ago.

She'd finally done it right so *someone* cared. "Dad, you're here."

"I knew I couldn't convince you over the phone."

He still hadn't said *happy birthday*. He wasn't even pretending to be happy to see her. He was annoyed.

Didn't she know better than to get walloped, let alone twice in one twenty-four-hour period? "Convince me?" she echoed flatly.

"To come home early. We're barely scraping by without you. You've only got a few weeks left of this nonsense. Come home. You did your duty to June. You can leave a little early."

There it was. The hard crash when he inevitably wasn't capable of giving her what she hoped for. "What day is it, Dad?" she asked, exhausted beyond measure.

"Huh?"

"What is today?"

"How am I supposed to know? You're my calendar, JJ. You take care of everything and we are lost without you. I muddled through for months, but you've had your time. Come home now. So things can go back to normal."

Normal *sucked*. She thought Cade's rejection meant she could go back to her old life. That she had to.

She couldn't. The changes she'd made this summer made going back impossible. "I don't want to take care of everything anymore. Not like this."

"I knew this summer, this awful house was a mistake," Dad muttered as he spun away and kicked at the porch's front post.

"It's not awful." It was her heart, this house. When she thought of home, she thought of this porch, and Grandma's kitchen. *And Cade's girls, and him fixing the porch, and love.*

"Look at it," Dad returned, whirling around and

flinging his arms toward the house. "It's falling down around your ears. This is just another one of June's schemes."

Dad had always called the ways Grandma had made her feel loved *schemes*. Twenty-six years she'd tried to be good enough, useful enough for him to notice, but he was incapable. He couldn't—or wouldn't—change, not while she kept running his life for him.

She was glad he'd come and reminded her. Reminded her that she'd changed, and she couldn't go back. No matter *what* had happened with Cade. This wasn't about Cade. It was about her.

"I quit," she said, maybe too loudly in the quiet morning.

"Well, I'd quit this house, too."

"No, Dad. I quit my job. I quit Frost Greenhouse. All of it. I'm not coming back to Plainview. I'm staying here."

"You can't quit. You can't stay *here*." The horror in his tone might have swayed her, but she saw too clearly that horror was born of never, ever trying to understand *her*. Only ever seeing her how he wanted to see her— as a helper, as the scheduler and organizer of his life.

"I *have* to quit. I can't be your calendar or your cleanup crew anymore. I have to be something for me."

"Frost is yours, too."

"I don't want it." It was a shock how true that was. "I never really did."

"News to me."

"Me, too. I put all that work into it because you wanted me to, and I wanted you to notice me. Not because I cared. Not because it mattered to *me*, but because it mattered to you." *And you'll pretend you just*

*love your job, not that you've been trying to ensure
your father's love and pride since you were a little girl.*

Grandma had known, of course. She'd seen it, and
tried to show JJ all the other options she had, but JJ had
refused to listen.

Until this summer.

"It's my birthday, Dad. My birthday."

Dad grinned. "Well, of course it is, princess! Why
do you think I'm here? To bring you home on your
birthday."

I am home. "Don't lie to me like that. Not now."

"If it slipped my mind today is your birthday, it's
only because you weren't home to remind me. I'll take
you home and I'll take you out to dinner. Chinese food.
Your favorite."

"That's not my favorite, Dad."

He looked so puzzled by that, she couldn't even muster anger. He couldn't look outside of himself. And that
was his cross to bear, not hers.

Not. Hers.

She walked back inside and grabbed the keys and
purse hung on the hook by the door. Then she marched
past him and toward her truck.

"Where are you going?" he demanded.

"I don't know. But not with you. Go home, Dad.
Find someone to replace me. I've made up my mind."

"No, you haven't."

She wanted to laugh, but she swallowed it down.
"Yes, I have."

"You'll change your mind. You will. I will be gracious enough to take you back. I can't hold that job forever, JJ. You remember that. A week, tops, and then I
expect you back."

No. She wouldn't be back. Couldn't go back. So she got in her truck and drove away.

She drove into Jasper Creek and parked at the edge of town. It was her birthday. She wanted cake. She'd buy a book for herself at the pretty new bookstore. She'd treat herself to…something.

Maybe she was alone, but she was home.

She got out of the truck, the heat of day already making the air sticky. She was still in the clothes she'd worn yesterday and probably looked like some lost hiker stumbling out of the woods.

She didn't care. She walked up the sidewalk, taking in the pretty shops and restaurants that brought in tourists despite the isolated location.

She'd walked these sidewalks with her cousins and her sister, buying treats from the little general store with the change Grandma had given them. Poking through the junk at the old antiques store until the surly old man who used to run it had told them to buy something or get out.

This was the landscape of her childhood, and she had given it up trying to be something she was never comfortable being. She'd lost so much time, but she was still young enough to fix that. To *change*.

She was twenty-seven as of today and she'd finally found home. She barely noticed stopping in the middle of the sidewalk, tears tracking down her cheeks. It was both joy at a new beginning and pain at Grandma not being here to see it.

"Are you all right, dear?"

JJ looked down at the small woman who took her in with great concern.

"You're one of June's, aren't you?" the older woman asked.

One of June's. Always. "Yes, Mrs. Kim. I'm JJ."

"Of course you are. You're crying, dear," Mrs. Kim said, delivering that news on a whisper.

"I know. It's okay. I just miss her, is all."

"Of course you do." Mrs. Kim bustled her off the sidewalk and nudged her onto a bench. She then dug in her purse and pulled out a crumpled tissue. "Clean yourself up."

JJ did as she was told.

"I don't suppose this has to do with that Mathewson boy. Word is he's been spending a lot of time at June's."

JJ managed to smile at Mrs. Kim even though tears still fell. "No, it doesn't." It had to do with *her*. She would cry over Cade, no doubt, but in this moment she needed to let go of a future she'd been dead set on, even though she hadn't really wanted it.

"JJ? Are you... Oh, my God, what's *happened*?"

JJ looked up at Keira rushing over and managed a smile. "Nothing."

Keira squeezed onto the bench next to her. "You're crying. In *public*." She glanced at Mrs. Kim, who nodded firmly, as if all was taken care of, before she walked away. No doubt to spread the word JJ had been crying about Cade.

"Apparently that's not the end of the world," JJ offered to Keira.

Keira slid her arm around her, squeezing tight. "Amazing, isn't it? What changes in that house?"

JJ nodded. "I'm not going back to Plainview. I don't know what I'm going to do, but I'm staying. This is home." Keira had stayed. Maybe it wasn't Grandma's plan for all of them, but maybe it *was*.

"Does this have to do with Cade?"

JJ shook her head. "No. It doesn't. It has to do with me." No matter what happened in the future with Cade, this decision was hers and hers alone.

"Okay. I wasn't going to press because I thought you'd have... Well, come over tonight. I'll bake you a birthday cake."

"Can you two come over to the farmhouse instead? I want my birthday there." She wanted to celebrate this new year with Grandma and the house that had built her.

"That's perfect. And don't do a thing. I'm bringing dinner and cake and everything." Keira squeezed.

JJ nodded. "Thank you. It'll be fun."

"Yes. I can kick Remy to the curb for the night, have it be a girls-only party."

"No. Not tonight. Remy's part of your life, and that makes him part of mine." She looked into Keira's dark eyes, and even though she'd kept in the best touch with Keira, it hadn't been good enough. "We're family. We should all start acting like it."

Keira grinned. "I have the strangest feeling that's what Grandma had in mind."

CHAPTER FOURTEEN

BY DINNERTIME THE day after, Cade was about ready to lock both girls in their room and blare something depressing and painful to drown out the bickering and cartoons.

Instead, he opened the door to their room to get them to wash up for dinner. Lora made an odd noise and quickly shoved something under the messy covers of her bed.

Cade frowned at her. "What did you just hide from me?"

"Nothing," Lora said, sitting straight up on her bed, hands shoved under her butt, blue eyes wide.

"Lora May. What are you hiding from me?"

"Nothing!"

"She stole something from Grandma June's house," Ellie blurted.

Cade could only stare, dumbfounded, at his angelic, good-hearted youngest. "You *stole*?"

"Yesterday. She took one of Grandma June's paperweights from JJ's room," Ellie continued. She didn't even sound like she was smug over getting Lora in trouble. She seemed troubled.

"I wasn't stealing!" Lora shouted as she glared at Ellie.

"Taking something from someone without them

knowing it *is* stealing, Lora May Mathewson. I'm so disappointed in you."

Lora's face crumpled and she immediately burst into sobs. "It's pretty and… I just wanted to have it."

He wanted to bundle her up and tell her it was fine, but of course it wasn't. She'd stolen something. His baby, who *was* old enough to know better.

"Get it. Then get your shoes on. We're going to JJ, and you're going to tell her what you did."

Cade didn't wait for the wailing and begging. He marched into the living room, trying to keep some semblance of calm.

He'd never had any real problems with the girls. Sure, tantrums and talking back. But they were angels at school, and only tried his patience at home.

Lora had *stolen*. Something from JJ, the number one woman he didn't want to see right now.

He couldn't be a coward if he didn't want his daughter to be one, though. He gathered his wallet, keys and hat, then put on his shoes while Ellie gently pulled Lora to the door.

At least *that* he could be proud of. When push came to shove, the girls loved each other and helped each other out.

Lora sniffled and begged all through getting her shoes on and marching out to the truck. Cade didn't know how many times he almost caved, but it only took a look at the little paperweight clutched in Lora's hand to remind him this was necessary.

Lora had taken something of June's. It wasn't just a dollar, or some random toy. It was a prized possession of June's—irreplaceable to those June had left behind.

Cade drove to June's in relative silence, only punctuated by Lora's occasional sniffles and Ellie's sad sighs.

As Cade pulled up the drive, he frowned at the fact there was a truck in the drive. A strange twist of jealousy and longing, completely out of place, washed through him.

"Daddy. Can't *you* tell JJ?" Lora implored from the back.

Broken from his reverie, Cade shook his head. "No. We're all going up there and you're going to tell JJ what you did."

Lora sniffled, and Cade had no doubt she was crying again. No matter how it broke his heart, he would not let his daughter ever think taking just because she wanted was acceptable.

He pulled her out of her booster seat and set her down even when she held on to him.

"You'll walk, young lady. You'll walk up there and explain what you did and give it back."

Lora stalled and dragged her feet and took approximately a million years to make it up to the front door, but Cade refused to snap or give in. He held Ellie's hand behind Lora's interminable progress, and didn't go up the stairs until she did.

When she looked back at him with tears in her eyes, he only nodded toward the door. With a trembling mouth, she turned back and knocked so lightly on the door Cade doubted a mouse would have heard it.

Then Ellie about broke his heart and stepped forward and knocked for Lora.

JJ opened the door with a bright smile on her face, but it died when she saw him. Which broke the rest of his heart. Then she looked down at the girls and immediately dropped to a crouch. "What's wrong?" she asked, resting her hands on Lora's shoulders.

Lora held out the paperweight. JJ took it with a confused frown. "How did you get this?"

"I... I'm sorry, but I put it in my pocket and took it home."

JJ cocked her head, studying Lora and then the paperweight in her hand. "You meant to take it home with you?" she asked gravely.

Lora nodded, hanging her head, and making little crying noises again. JJ took a deep breath, but if she was angry she didn't show it.

"Taking it without asking me was wrong," JJ said quietly. "I know you know that."

Lora launched herself at JJ, nearly knocking her over. "Please don't hate me," she sobbed.

"No. I don't. I could never hate you." JJ held her tight, giving Cade a brief pained look before returning her gaze to Lora. "I'm sad that you took something from me, but I'm proud of you for apologizing and admitting you did something wrong. People make mistakes, sweetheart—it's fixing them that matters."

"Daddy made me," she whispered dejectedly.

"But you did it."

"I'm sorry, JJ."

"I know you are." She gave Lora a squeeze, then gently set her back on her feet. "Thank you for coming to tell me the truth. Apology accepted."

Lora sniffled and stepped back toward him.

"Well, I wanted her to give it back and apologize," Cade said, sounding stiff and ridiculous to his own ears.

Because he wanted this—her. A partnership. Someone to help him with this incessantly hard parenting thing. He wanted her in his house and them in town together as a family. But he'd eased away instead.

Because you had to. Because her life isn't here. It wouldn't be fair to ask her to take all this on, and even if she wanted to *now*, he knew how quickly that could all change. Better safe than sorry. For his girls. "So we'll be going now."

JJ frowned at him as she stood back up. She didn't say anything, so he took the girls by the hands and led them back to the truck.

"Can't we stay, Daddy? It looked like JJ was having a party," Lora whispered.

"Not tonight, sweetheart." Or any night. She would still be in their lives what little she decided to be, but he couldn't…do it with them.

Then what does that make you?

He picked Lora up, plopped her into her seat and, unable to hold on to his anger with her, gave her a kiss on the forehead.

"Buckle up, girls," he murmured, closing the back door.

"Cade?"

Cade looked back at the house, lit up in the dark. The days were starting to get shorter, inch by inch. Fall would be here before he knew it—back to school and then winter and Christmas, and this house would not be part of any of those things anymore.

It was the *house* he was worried about losing, not the determined woman walking toward him.

He swallowed, wishing he could run away. Wasn't that what he'd always done? Used Ellie and Lora as shields against the hurt in his life?

JJ stopped on her side of the gate. "I wanted to let

you know I'm staying," JJ said, her voice firm and sure. Her words...nonsensical.

"Staying where?"

She frowned. "Here. In Jasper Creek. I quit my job, and I'm staying. You know, beyond summer. Forever."

"Here." It echoed around the hot summer night and still it didn't make sense. Staying. Here. Forever.

"That's what I said."

"Oh." He didn't have anything better to say because he didn't...believe her. Yes, that was that panic clawing at his chest again. Not fear. Not hope. Disbelief. "Okay."

"Okay? That's all you're going to say? Okay?"

"I..."

"Forget it," she muttered, whirling around and stomping back in the house filled with *other* people, apparently.

Which was fine, because they should all forget it. All of them.

He got in his truck and shoved the key into the ignition, ready to drive away from June Gable's house, and granddaughter, *forever*. Because running was what he did, damn it.

But when he turned the key, the truck didn't make any sound at all.

CHAPTER FIFTEEN

WHEN JJ REOPENED the door, she could only stare at the sheepish man in front of her and try not to punch him in the nose as she had his brother all those years ago.

He cleared his throat, both girls on either side of him reminding her to keep her fists to herself.

"My truck won't start."

Of course not. This was a good reminder of what staying meant, though. She'd have to see him and want to punch him in the face regularly.

"I forgot my cell at home. So I thought maybe I could use your phone. To call one of my brothers. To pick us up."

JJ couldn't find her voice. Because what she wanted to do was yell at him and tell him he sucked, but the girls were staring at her, then Cade, like they could sense the tension.

JJ's stomach sank. Even if she wasn't their mother, she knew what it was like to sense that tension and have it sit inside of you like a black weight of fear. She looked at the paperweight gripped tightly in her hand.

"Maybe the girls would like some birthday cake while we wait?" Keira asked.

JJ watched with a mix of amusement and pain as the girls' heads whipped toward their father, all imploring hope.

"Uh, sure."

"Follow us, girls. Don't worry about a thing, JJ. I'll handle it," Keira said, her and Remy bustling the girls into the kitchen, Remy's dog trailing behind them and sniffing the girls with interest.

"I make the *best* birthday cake," Keira stage-whispered conspiratorially to the girls.

Leaving JJ in the foyer alone with Cade. Not by accident, JJ was sure.

"It's your birthday," he said, sounding a bit like he'd actually been punched in the gut, not just in her imagination.

She folded her arms across her chest. "Yes, it is."

"You never mentioned..."

She wanted to feel indignant, but she felt chastened. She hadn't told him. She hadn't told him a lot of things.

Just like she hadn't told Dad that she liked cultivating far more than running the greenhouse. That running his life hadn't felt useful—it had made her feel trapped. Love had trapped her.

It suddenly dawned on her, as Lora and Ellie quietly chattered with Keira and Remy in the kitchen, that Grandma had told her to let herself feel—but what she'd really meant was to let it out.

JJ had talked to Cade about some things in her past. But when it came to how she felt about him? How he made her feel or what she wanted out of life? Just a few minutes ago she'd told him she was staying.

She hadn't told him why.

Or that she loved him.

Or that she wanted more from him than this summer. She'd wanted Cade to do it first, to smooth the way for her—not consciously, but that was what she'd been waiting for. Someone to make it *easy*.

JJ had always *felt* without any help from Grandma, but she'd had to learn to lock it down in that house of tense silences and angry, bitter fights.

She wasn't in that house anymore. She was in Grandma's. To let herself feel meant letting Cade know. Regardless of if it was easy, or if he reciprocated. It meant making the first move sometimes.

Because she didn't need him to prove himself. She only needed him to love her back.

He hadn't moved for the phone, and they stood there in darkened silence. In that darkness, she recognized something beyond her own feelings—much like the first time they'd been together.

It wasn't just *her* that was scared—it was him, too.

His first wife had *left* him and his girls. A nice smile and an easy way with people didn't eradicate fear. He had every reason in the world to be afraid to trust, to make the first move.

If she loved him—and she did—she couldn't wait for him to be the one who stepped over the fear. She had to let her fear go—not just for herself but for the people she loved.

"Jessamyn Joy," she said into the weighted silence.

"What?" he replied, eyebrows drawing together.

"Jessamyn Joy. My name, what JJ stands for. Joy was Grandma's suggestion. I used to ask my parents to call me that, but Mom insisted on calling me Jessamyn—never Jess or Sam, no matter how much I begged. Dad insisted on calling me JJ. They each used the name they liked, as though it was some battle they had to win."

"JJ."

"I used to think love was overrated, because all they ever did was try to use my name and Lila's feelings like pawns in some scorecard of who loved who more. They could never give if they weren't getting back, and you can't have a relationship—any real relationship—like that. You have to be willing to give sometimes, without the scales being equal. You have to be willing to get sometimes without making sure you give the exact number back. Grandma June never made me feel like I *owed* her. She only made me feel loved."

He stood there, still as a statue. Scared. He had to be *scared*. He'd trusted her with his daughters—with their care and a birthday and a million other things. He'd made love to her time and time again, and he wasn't the kind of man to make a lie out of that.

He was scared, like she'd always been. But Grandma had given her the example of how to be brave—how to love fiercely and no matter what.

"I used to believe it was better to be safe than sorry. Being safe never really gave me anything." She stepped forward and placed her hand on his heart, her own thundering. "So I'm done being safe. I love you, Cade."

He didn't move, as if the words *I love you* were a curse. Then he swallowed.

"I love you, too, JJ." She practically leaped into his arms, but his next words stopped her in her tracks, undercutting that momentary burst of hope.

"I wish it was that easy."

He said it so sadly, with such finality. Like because it wasn't easy, it wasn't possible.

She knew that feeling *so* well, but didn't that mean she knew how to fight against it? "When I was growing up, I was deathly afraid of hoping for anything good happening. Lila was so *optimistic* and happy while our world was crashing down around us and I decided then and there it was much better to think the worst was going to happen."

"It's not that I—"

"No, let me finish," she said softly, still holding her palm against his heart. "I know what it's like to plan a life around the worst that could happen, about what you *might* lose, without ever realizing it."

"It's not just me."

"Yes, it is." When he opened his mouth to argue, she shook her head. "I've already told you, and I think you believed me. I love your girls. My relationship with them isn't based on my relationship with you. You could tell me to go to hell, and I'd still show up the next day to throw them a birthday party or talk to them about crappy moms. That's separate from this. Me staying is, too. I made my decision to stay thinking we were over. Maybe I don't have the details worked out yet, which is a new one for me, but I have family here. Family who'll help. So I'm staying no matter what. I made that decision knowing it would hurt like hell to see you around town knowing you didn't love me, but I was going to do it anyway. Because this is home. This is the life I want. And I'm lucky it's possible, so I'm going to grab it with both hands. Regardless of you."

"I don't know what you're trying to do," he said as if she was trying to tear him apart.

"I'm trying to tell you what I should have told you when I realized it. I love you. I wanted you to say it first, to prove something, but that's silly—and it's more like what my parents had than what I want."

"What you want?"

"Yes. I want a life in Jasper Creek. I want to start the flower business Dad always said was putting too many of my eggs in one basket. I want to love you, Cade. And your girls. Forever. I probably will, whether you do anything about it or not."

He stared at her a bit like she was speaking a foreign language, but underneath her palm his heart beat, steady and sure.

"You can't want…"

"I want you. I want a *life* with you and the girls. Jasper Creek is my home, and something about this house is my heart, but you guys? You're my family."

His jaw tightened, everything in him going rigid again. But she understood him, didn't she? She had to be brave enough to reach into that pain and hurt, and be the shoulder he needed. Like he'd always been for her.

"I know you're scared," she said, her throat tightening because the thought of him scared or hurting made her sad.

He nodded. "Yeah, I… I'm afraid. For me. I've gotten so used to being afraid for them, I convince myself I always am, but it isn't true. Not with you. With you I'm afraid for me. Because I lose everything."

"What? Like you're cursed?"

"No… I don't know."

"Sometimes, it's better to have tried and be a little sorry about how things went than to stay there in the safe place where nothing changes. You're the one who told me that hurt isn't the worst thing that could happen. You got the most beautiful things out of some of the hurt in your life. Well, I want some beautiful things with you and them, even if it hurts."

"JJ." He sucked in a breath. "We have a garden,"

he said, his voice rusty, the statement coming out a bit like a question.

"Huh?"

He cleared his throat, and this time his voice sounded more sure, and *this* time his hand came up to cover hers over his heart. "On the ranch. Mom always grew flowers, and when she died Grant kept tending them. I don't know that he's any good at it, but year after year, there they are. Mom's flowers."

"Are you offering me…flowers?" she asked tentatively, not at all sure where he was going when she'd only meant to show him her heart, her plans.

"No. Well, sort of, I guess. I'm offering you… I love you. I thought it would be easier to end things, before everyone got in too deep. Because it was starting to feel real. Like you were my partner. A mom to the girls, and a…" He looked down at their hands. "I told myself I bailed because you were leaving."

"Well, I'm staying. Problem solved. And apparently you're offering me a garden."

"I'm offering you… I'm… You didn't even get mad that Lora took that paperweight."

"I did the same thing when I was a year older than her."

"You did?"

"I did. Only I never told Grandma. I never apologized. I took it home with me thinking she'd never notice. Then she wrote me one of her letters, and in it she mentioned how sad she was she'd lost it. I felt guilty for a month before I got to come back, but I…put it back. I never told her. She knew, of course, but I never admitted it. I was too afraid. I don't even know why. She loved me no matter what."

"I guess sometimes, when we blame ourselves for things going wrong, we're afraid the people who love us might find out and realize what a mistake they made."

It put it into words so perfectly, and she thought back to when she'd told him he blamed himself for Melissa leaving. He'd denied it, but sometimes deep down the feelings you had didn't match with the rational thoughts in your head.

"You'd never be a mistake to me, Cade."

He took in a ragged breath. "Okay."

"Okay?"

"I'm scared to my toes and back, but I love you. I want a life with you. I probably would have figured that out in a week or two and come begged you to take me back, truth be told. So thank God for broken-down trucks, and a beautiful, brave woman…named Jessamyn Joy."

"I swear to God, I will bloody your nose like I did Grant's if you ever, ever call me that again," she said, though a tear trickled down her cheek.

He laughed and pulled her tight to him. "God, JJ. I do love you." He kissed her temple, her cheek, then her mouth. "I've been miserable," he murmured against it.

"Good," she replied, wrapping her arms around his neck. "I hope you learned your lesson."

"I'm sure I've got a few more to learn, but…we love each other, and our girls. I figure we'll work it out."

Our girls. That got a few more tears out of her, but then his mouth was on hers and that was all that mattered. Cade loved her, and no matter what fears they both had, they'd learn to face them together. A family.

"Daddy?" Ellie's voice said, tremulously, like she

was seeing Santa Claus in the flesh and wasn't sure what to do about it.

"They're *kissing*," Lora screeched, rushing into the room with a grin on her face.

"I think that's our cue to leave," Keira said. JJ made a move to protest, but Keira shook her head and opened the front door. "Soak it in, J. Happy birthday." Then she and Remy and the dog were gone and she had one very handsome cowboy staring at her, and two very curious little girls looking up hopefully at her.

"Are you and Daddy going to get married and have babies?" Lora asked.

"You can't ask them that," Ellie hissed.

"I want a baby sister."

Cade turned an admirable shade of red. "Let's hold off on the baby-sibling wishes for a bit there. But, uh, JJ does have some good news."

JJ knelt down so she could be eye-to-eye with both of them. "I'm staying in Jasper Creek."

"For how long?" Ellie asked suspiciously.

"For good. I'm going to work here, and live here and…" She glanced up at Cade. "Love you all right here in Jasper Creek. I suppose I'll have to figure out a place to live here first. My sister is moving into Grandma June's house soon. You guys don't know anywhere I could live, do you?" she asked, trying to maintain a serious expression.

"I think I know of a bed you might be able to crash on," Cade offered.

"Oh, mine!" Lora shouted.

"No. *Mine* is bigger," Ellie argued.

"*I* have princess sheets."

The girls bickered, and Cade drew JJ up to her feet. "You sure you want to take all this on, all so quickly?"

"Yeah." It didn't feel quick. It felt like she'd been waiting for this for far too long. Just like Grandma had said. *I have the upmost confidence you'll find that thing you've been searching for that you never admit to yourself you're searching for.* Here it was. Finally. "I'm sure."

A breeze fluttered through the open windows, bringing with it a familiar floral scent that reminded JJ far too much of Grandma's perfume, though of course it couldn't be it. Unless maybe Keira had sprayed some.

It seemed to wrap around the four of them, and even the girls quieted, until the scent and breeze died away.

Lora grinned at everybody. "See, even Grandma June is happy."

JJ blinked at the tears, and Cade wiped them away. Because he always would. And she'd shoulder his burdens, and he'd shoulder hers.

So with Grandma June's blessing, JJ knew everything wouldn't always be perfect, but they would always have love.

CHAPTER SIXTEEN

JJ WATCHED CADE cart the last bag of her stuff out of Grandma's house and to the truck—the truck that had magically started later that night two weeks ago. Cade was convinced it was Grandma June magic.

JJ scoffed every time he said it. But deep down, she wondered.

The girls were picking clover out of the lawn and trying to braid it into crowns. JJ hoped they could spend summer days out here next year.

Because next year she'd be watching them, living with them, loving them. She glanced at Cade, who was watching her carefully.

He knew this was hard for her. Like saying goodbye to Grandma all over again. At least, that was what JJ thought she'd been going to feel. This was different.

She looked at the house. "Lila's next."

"That makes you sad?"

"I don't know. I want to fix things with her, or build new things. I think she needs her autumn first, though. I know I needed my summer." She leaned against Cade, because he always knew when to lend a shoulder.

He gave her shoulders a squeeze. "Leave her a note. I hear those are quite popular."

It wasn't a bad idea. So while Cade put the rest of her things in the truck, she penned a note to her sister.

She set it in the middle of the table, then grabbed the paperweight she'd stolen all those summers ago, just as Lora had this summer.

Smiling to herself, JJ slipped it into her pocket. She went over to Grandma's collection and picked one that reminded JJ of Lila—instead of one purple flower in the middle of it like hers, it was a riot of colored flowers multiplying under the glass.

She set it on top of the letter.

She took a deep breath and looked around. It was sad to leave, and yet she had such a life to look forward to.

So she walked out to it, not noticing that the closing of the door jiggled the paperweight, and the note slipped out on a summer breeze and floated across the room and onto the floor.

JJ stepped onto the porch to find Lora swinging on the swing with Ellie, whispering and giggling while Cade crossed the yard from the now-packed truck.

"When are you going to get married?" Lora asked, as if quizzing them what was for lunch.

Ellie gave an exasperated big-sister sigh, but she looked at Cade with the same imploring expression as Lora.

"Shh. We have to convince her first," Cade said in a stage whisper. "You have to be on your best behavior. You better run away now before you scare her off."

Giggling, the girls darted off the porch and ran around the dogwood tree whose leaves would turn red soon enough.

"How long are you going to use that?" JJ asked.

"Long as I possibly can," he returned with a grin. "You ready?"

"One more second."

As if understanding, Cade nodded and started chasing the girls to their delight.

JJ looked back at the house. She hadn't done much cosmetically, but it looked less ramshackle than it had when she'd first arrived. The sun was shining so it must have made the paint look a little whiter, the shutters a little straighter.

"Thank you, Grandma." She still didn't believe in ghosts, per se, but she believed Grandma heard that.

"Good luck, Lila," she added for good measure, because no doubt her sister's life was about to change.

JJ just hoped she got to be a part of it.

* * * * *

Fall

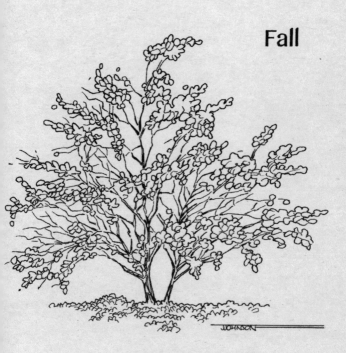

Maisey Yates

To my amazing friends and authors, Caitlin, Nicole and Jackie. This project was a joy because I got to work on it with you. I'm thankful not only for your talent, but your friendship. Without you, who would I send raccoon GIFs to? You are all truly the best.

FALL

Dearest Lila,

It's a very strange thing to get old, to know that eventually the world will go on without you. To see clearly your successes, and your mistakes, and still not know what you could have done about either.

You, my head-in-the-clouds girl. How I've missed your imagination and your spirit brightening my summer days. I know this autumn will be hard on that soft heart of yours, but the simple truth of life is that one can never wish away all the bad or hard. Sometimes, a girl has to roll up her sleeves, make an apron for a chicken tea party and find her spot in the real world.

I have many things to ask of you this autumn. You'll hate most of them, and they'll test all of those skills you doubt yourself on. But you'll always know, if you can organize the Red Sled Holiday Bazaar, you can survive anything.

Let my spirit guide you in all that you do, let this house take care of you as it has always cared for me, and I have the utmost confidence you'll find that anchor you've been searching for.

Love always,
Grandma June

CHAPTER ONE

LILA FROST STOOD in the center of her grandmother's driveway. Her feet were firmly planted in the gravel, her eyes fixed on the white, weathered farmhouse. On the dogwood tree in the front, with its red leaves burning bright, standing in evidence of the fall season.

She had never seen the dogwood tree in fall.

She had only ever come to see Grandma June in the summer. When everything was bright and green, the rolling hills stretching back to the mountains and touching a bright, faded denim sky.

The sky was still clear, but the blue was different. An intense jewel color that seemed to ignite the tree, making it look like a burning bush in the middle of the desert. Alight, but not consumed.

It was different. And Lila didn't like it. Not at all.

It was different because the tree wasn't as it should be. Because the house looked weathered and worn.

Grandma June was gone.

Life was different, and it would never be the same again.

She swallowed hard, squeezing her eyes shut for a moment before taking a deep breath and walking up the two front steps to the porch. She knelt down and lifted the mat, where she found the key.

She held it in her hand, flat. It was a skeleton key with a compass on the top.

She could hear Grandma June saying *North, south, east, west, and at the end of the key is home.*

Jasper Creek had not been home for a very long time.

It had never been her home for real. But it had been her home away from home for many summers when she had been a child. After she'd grown up, she'd still visited as often as possible in the summer. But jobs and life had gotten in the way. Her work at a florist's in Portland was demanding in the summer, all of the June and destination weddings taking up her time.

But she was home now.

Only the thing that made it home—the person that made it home—wasn't here. And she never would be again.

She stepped forward, inserting the key in the lock and turning it. The door gave easily, and she stepped inside.

The house felt empty. Cold.

She knew that her sister had only left a week or so ago. And that JJ was now living with a single father just a few doors down on his ranch.

Lila would have never suspected that JJ would do something quite so spontaneous or…domestic. She had certainly never figured her sister for the type to fall for a single dad. Much less a cowboy. Not because JJ didn't like the outdoors—she did—it was just that that type of man seemed to get JJ's hackles up more than anything else.

Lila wished that cowboys weren't her own personal weakness. But sadly, they were.

Or, rather, one in particular. Who she was not thinking about. Not now. Not in her first moments in the farmhouse since her grandmother had died.

That would be incredibly inappropriate.

Sadly, Jasper Creek was inevitably bound up in thoughts of Everett McCall. Always had been, and... well, she hoped after this, no longer would be.

She didn't have time to think about Everett—and wouldn't the whole time she was here, since the task that her grandmother had given her to complete was organizing the Red Sled Holiday Bazaar, which June had spearheaded every year for the past thirty years.

There would be a whole committee of women for Lila to organize. And she... Well, the very idea made her want to lie down and wrap herself in a soft blanket and never, ever emerge.

Lila was not a take-charge person. Lila did not like confrontation.

Lila did not like lists, she did not like making decisions and she did not like raffia scarecrows.

All of which the Red Sled would require an abundance of.

But it was up to Lila not to let it down, and that was a whole lot of pressure on someone who had barely ever planned out a birthday party successfully without getting distracted.

But she could do it. She could. If her grandmother needed her, she would be here. Maybe she hadn't been here the way that she could have for the last few years. It was difficult. With her mother sinking deeper into her bitterness and needing Lila to make sure that she left her house, that she bought groceries and that she ate.

Especially since just mentioning June often upset her. Lila's mom had always felt that her own mother had disapproved of her greatly. Especially after her divorce from Lila's father.

Lila knew that her mom's relationship to Grandma June had fractured long before Lila was even born, but for as long as Lila had known her grandmother, she'd been trying to fill the cracks. Whatever had happened back then, she'd always been good to Lila, and she'd always tried to reach out to Lila's mom.

But that hadn't been enough for her. She'd been hypersensitive to Lila's relationship with Grandma June and any mention of the farmhouse, or of June, created drama that Lila didn't like being in the middle of.

She had no time for drama, not now. Not drama from her mama, and not drama in the form of Everett McCall. Not that he cared about her at all. Or ever even thought of her.

But for her, thoughts of him would always be tied to Jasper Creek.

The last time she had seen him she had made a ridiculous fool of herself. She had been seventeen to his twenty-seven. And had tearfully confessed her undying love to him at a potluck one hot summer afternoon.

Okay. Not just a *generic potluck*.

The potluck that had been thrown down at the river to celebrate his engagement.

His engagement to a woman who was very much not her.

It was the one time she'd broken her rule about confrontations.

Thankfully, he had not returned the sentiment, and if he had, she would have lost respect for him forever, really. The kind of man who would run off with a teenager at his own engagement party was not the kind of man that you would want returning your declarations of undying love.

A thing that she knew now at the ripe old age of twenty-four.

It hadn't felt like a good thing at the time.

The pain and humiliation had faded, but when she came to stay with her grandmother, she avoided town and town get-togethers. She helped with chores in the yard, clipped flowers from the garden and enjoyed freshly made strawberry lemonade with berries from the patch out back.

She stayed for a week, and then she left. And managed to avoid the cowboy that had ground her heart to pieces beneath his boots.

And she would be avoiding Everett McCall until she left here at the end of November, if she had anything to say about it.

It should be easy enough. The man was the definition of a *dude*.

He was certainly not going to get anywhere near the Red Sled. And maybe Tonya, his wife, would. But seeing Tonya wasn't going to hurt her. It wasn't like she was still in love with him or anything like that.

Maybe, just maybe, he was still the one and only thing that stoked the fires of her passion. And maybe that was the reason that she hadn't quite been able to...

Maybe it was the reason her dating life was a little bit of a nonstarter.

He probably had a beer gut by now. He had probably gone bald. Yes. Men like him had a very short shelf life. Hard bodies did not stay hard forever.

That was just a fact.

And now, she was done thinking about Everett.

She took a breath and turned around in the entryway of the house, the wood planks creaking underneath her feet. It felt damp inside. And old. The paint was peeling, not just from the outside of the house, but inside, as well.

Had it always been this derelict, and it hadn't felt that way because of June's spirit?

She could see it.

Her grandmother had been so warm and sensible. A wealth of wisdom that Lila herself didn't seem to have inherited it all. Lila was a dreamer, a constant disappointment to her mother, who was decidedly grounded on earth, and bitter about most things, particularly since her divorce from Lila's father.

Although, Lila had always felt that she had much more call to be bitter about it than her mother did.

The breakup between the two of them had been so acrimonious that they had basically pulled a *Parent Trap* on herself and JJ. Separating the two of them.

Of course, they had known about each other, which was a little bit better than the movie. Though, neither of them had meddling nannies or butlers to help them bridge the gap, either.

Still, for all that they knew about each other, they were not close—something that wounded Lila and seemed to be somewhat neutral to JJ. But they had grown up in different states. They had different lives.

And while they had come together here at the farmhouse as girls every summer, even then it had been difficult for the two of them to connect. JJ had run around with the boys and Lila...

Had typically sat under trees trying to make chickens engage in tea parties.

For the record, it was very difficult to get a chicken enthused about a tea party.

Of course, your sister is a stone's throw away. You could go to her. Right now. You don't have to stand in this drafty house by yourself.

Lila did not care for her own internal musings. JJ might not want to see her. She had responsibilities and things now.

Lila sighed and tapped her feet on the floor.

This was home for the foreseeable future. Her boss at the florist's in Portland had allowed her an extended leave. Gretchen had seen this as a trip to Lila's own true self and had given her blessing for Lila to go. She had more than one artist who worked on arrangements, and since Lila's current obligations were filled, she'd been fine with giving her space, and also had made it clear she was welcome to come back after the three months were up.

She was happy with where she was, but it wasn't her dream. Some time away from it…well, it would only be a good thing.

And she had a holiday bazaar to plan. So she had better get settled in and get to work.

Starting, she decided, with her grandmother's garden. There hadn't been a frost yet in Jasper Creek. She had checked before she had come. And that meant that there was a possibility for early-fall tomatoes, and most definitely the possibility that there would be zucchini. A horde of it. And that meant Lila could bake zucchini bread as a peace offering for the old crones—the distinguished ladies of Jasper Creek—who would likely take a dim view of Lila spearheading this year's event.

Grandma June understood, though, that Lila could

do this. Yes, Lila could be scattered. And, yes, sometimes Lila left important paperwork in a kitchen cupboard. Or the fridge. But she was also a dreamer. And she already had big plans for the decor of the Red Sled.

She went into the kitchen and opened up one of the distressed wooden cupboards, the green paint beginning to wear thin.

She fished around inside until she found a bowl, one large enough to take on the tomatoes. Then she grabbed a basket from a hook just above the sink. She stacked the bowl inside the wicker basket and made her way out the front door, down the steps and around to the back of the house.

The garden was surrounded by a very, very high fence designed to keep the mule deer out, although, occasionally a very ambitious one found its way inside, and then often found itself being chased back out by Grandma June and her broom.

Lila snuggled into her knitted sweater and pushed the gate open, smiling as she looked down at the rows of vegetables. There were even pumpkins, transitioning from green to orange, knobby and hideous, as a good heritage-garden pumpkin was wont to be.

She bent down, her copper hair falling into her face as she began to pull zucchini off the vine and put them into the basket. She wrinkled her nose when she encountered a cluster of aphids, wiping her hands desperately on her jeans, but continuing to work.

A flash of movement caught her eye, and she saw a little gray cat picking through the dry weeds on the other side of the fence.

"Kitty," she said. "Kitty, kitty…"

"There you are," a familiar and booming voice said from behind her.

The cat bounded off. And Lila froze.

Just the sound of the voice sent shivers all the way down her spine and caused something warm and not entirely unpleasant to pull in her stomach.

Everett.

She recognized that voice seven years later. Without even a visual. How annoying.

Grandma June had been close to the McCall family, and Lila had grown up with a starry-eyed crush on the much older Everett. But she had been a fool then. And the sad thing was, she was a little bit of a fool now.

You're not foolish. You're optimistic. It's not like being a pessimist makes anything better.

No, that was true. But then, pessimists probably didn't confess their undying love to remote and unreachable men in public spaces. And she had most definitely done that.

"Yes," she said, picking up her zucchini-laden basket and clutching it with both hands. She steeled herself, taking a breath before turning around.

He will be ugly, she said to herself. *Maybe he has a wart on his nose. Maybe he has a peg leg.*

She turned. And her stomach crashed down into her boots.

Oh, there had been no way to prepare herself for this. Even with the wicker basket held tightly in her hands like a lifeline, she felt like she might become unmoored from the earth and float away into the clear fall sky.

Everett McCall had somehow taken his good looks and multiplied them at least tenfold in the past seven years.

Granted, Lila herself was much better-looking than she had been when she was seventeen. Her face no longer round with youthful puppy fat. But still, her improvements were nothing compared to his.

He seemed taller, which she knew wasn't true, because he had been twenty-seven the last time she'd seen him. But he was definitely, and most assuredly, broader.

He was wearing a black cowboy hat, pulled low over his eyes, but she knew exactly what color they were. A blue not unlike the sky she had just been pondering falling into, and she had to wonder if that was a coincidence, or if it was, in fact, related to Everett McCall's eyes.

In addition to the cowboy hat, he had on a snug black shirt with three buttons at the neck and long sleeves. And though his arms were covered up, she could tell that years of manual labor had only served to increase his physical strength.

His jaw was squarer, the whiskers on his chin darker. His hands were larger, she was sure of it.

Neither leg was pegged.

Drat.

"Of course I'm here," she said. "My grandmother asked me to be. I would do anything that she wanted."

"Except come back to visit more often," Everett said, leaning against the open gate, his arms crossed over his broad chest.

That galled her. "I came to visit quite often, actually, Everett," she said. "It's just that I didn't look you up when I came."

"You hadn't been for more than two years. Don't think June didn't tell me. Every time she came by with a jar of preserves or some zucchini bread." He looked meaningfully at the basket in her hand.

"It just so happens," Lila said, "that I am going to make some. But it's not for you." His wife could make him some. That was not Lila's job. "It's for the ladies who help run the Red Sled Holiday Bazaar. If you don't know, I am planning it this year. My grandmother left me the responsibility." She flashed him a grin.

And take that. She was not young, impetuous, irresponsible Lila Pauline Frost anymore. No, she was dedicated, responsible, creative and cheerful Lila Pauline Frost, and Everett and his mysteriously compelling disapproval were not going to change that.

"I do know," he said, his tone going very grave. "The Red Sled is being held at my ranch this year. And June didn't just ask you to plan it. She asked me to help."

CHAPTER TWO

THERE WEREN'T VERY many people on God's green earth that Everett McCall would consider taking on babysitting duties for. And actually, the person he would do it for was no longer on God's green earth.

June Gable had been a guiding light in his life, and even though she was gone now, he would not want to disappoint her.

The letter that he had gotten the night after her funeral had caused an uncharacteristic shift of emotion inside of him.

The delicate script, written out in June's unsteady hand, had been simple, direct and to the point.

Lila is coming. She's going to need your help.

Then, there were dry, detailed instructions on what June expected from the Red Sled Holiday Bazaar, and Lila's involvement in it.

And frankly, he could think of nothing less suited to Lila Frost than the planning of anything.

Except maybe a birthday party for a hedgehog.

That had been about Lila's speed, at least as he remembered her.

But then, he also remembered her with a tangle of gingery hair, sunburned cheeks and freckles across her nose.

And the Lila that stood in front of him now was…
Different.

Different in a way that itched like the kind of ancient wool sweater his mother had always forced him to wear when the colder months rolled around.

The kind he did not wear now that he had full control of his life and the means to buy clothing that hadn't been stored in mothballs for half a century.

Yeah, looking at her itched like that. Under his skin.

She had been at the funeral, he knew that. But he had never interacted with her. And in fact, he hadn't been certain which person in attendance was her.

He could see why now.

Gone was the wild ginger hair—now it was tamed into something a bit sleeker, darker. More of an auburn.

Her cheeks were no longer sunburned. Though he supposed that stood to reason, given that it was fall.

And she probably also doesn't go out running in the sun anymore.

For some reason, that thought made him feel unaccountably wistful.

Lila Frost would always be bubbly vim and vigor and hot summer days to him. Part of those wild months they'd spent running all over June's property when they'd been kids.

He hadn't been around for much of her childhood, given that he was ten years her senior and he had essentially been grown before she was knee-high to a grasshopper.

But he'd taken work on June's ranch until he bought his own place, and he'd always taken time to visit with Lila, who had been a strange and fascinating creature to him. Eternally smiling and brimming with the kind of effervescence that he should have found annoying, but didn't.

Her cheeks turned slightly pink when she looked at him, and somehow that made her look more familiar.

"Everett," she said.

"Been a while," he said.

"Yes," she said. "It has. Did you go to the funeral?"

"I did," he responded. "But I didn't recognize you." She tilted her head to the side, and he couldn't read her expression. "Your hair is different."

"Than it was seven years ago? I hope so."

"Mine isn't."

The corners of her mouth pulled back slightly. "Uh, no. Well, I dye mine. So there you go."

Well, that hardly seemed fair. How was he supposed to recognize her if she changed her hair?

"I never saw you," she said. "At the funeral."

"I stood in the back. Made kind of a quiet exit. I'm not family, so I didn't want to…"

"I feel like everyone in Jasper Creek was June's family, don't you?"

"I don't know. I mean, the whole town certainly turned out for it."

"They did," Lila said. She blew out a hard breath. "Of course, my cousin Bella didn't even come, and she was *actual* family. No one can get ahold of her…" She trailed off. "We got letters."

"Me, too," he said, putting his hand against the breast pocket of his waxed canvas jacket.

"Right. Well, I guess…hence your presence."

She just stood there, looking at him with those luminous eyes, like she always had, and that looked familiar enough. And made him a little uncomfortable.

That itch again.

He cleared his throat.

"Bella…" He tried to think back, to the troupe of girls that had descended on June's every summer when they were kids. "I'm not sure I remember Bella."

"Oh. She and her mother quit coming around when she was a teenager."

He had the vague memory of a small, sullen girl with wide blue eyes. "I might remember Bella," he said. "But I'm not here for Bella. I was sent here to talk to you."

"You were sent?"

"I was. June let me know that she wanted you to be involved in planning the holiday bazaar. I've been hosting it the past few years."

"You don't…seem like the type. To enjoy a holiday bazaar, I mean. Felted animals and spiced cider seem a bit fanciful." Then she bit her lip and looked away. He couldn't read that expression.

"I don't know that I'm the type to enjoy a holiday bazaar, but I am the type to accept space rent for the use of my barn."

"All right, fair enough," she muttered.

"Why are you muttering?" he asked.

"I just… I don't see why Grandma June would have put the two of us working together."

He frowned. "Why not?"

She blinked, clutching her basket, which was filled to the brim with all kinds of vegetables he'd rather not eat in this lifetime, and gave him an owlish stare. "Because of our history," she said.

He arched a brow. "Our what?"

"I… The last time we talked to each other was at your engagement party."

He cast his mind back. He didn't let himself think about that warm summer night seven years ago all that often. It had been the beginning of a long and painful train wreck. Where everything he'd spent his life fighting to become had suddenly been seen as wrong by the woman he'd married.

And he'd bent and twisted his whole life.

To find a way out. To find a way to better.

And she'd wanted him to leave it all behind. To be more fun. More flexible. To consider moving away from Jasper Creek, if it made him so *unhappy.*

Unhappy. Like happiness had much to do with life and getting through it.

"So the last time you saw me was at my engagement party and…?"

"And I humiliated myself by confessing my love for you," she said, utterly deadpan. "I am traumatized by it."

"You… You did? *You did,*" he said.

He *could* remember that, now that she mentioned it. But only a little bit. She had pulled him aside and had quite earnestly said that she loved him.

He'd felt… Well, he thought it had been sweet, actually, and he didn't think much was sweet. But Lila had been a sweet presence at June's every summer, and as Everett had gotten older he'd had a hard time letting go and enjoying playing with the other kids.

He'd been focused on the future. On figuring out what he was going to do to find a life with more stability than his parents had.

But when June's farmhouse had been full, with her granddaughters, with the Mathewson boys, sometimes the laughter had been bright enough he'd been able to join in for a while.

So, yeah, Lila saying she loved him had seemed sweet. Like a good omen, really, because if Lila could find some affection for a guy like him, then maybe he was more than just a boring, steady rock.

But she had been a *kid*. He sure as hell hadn't thought she'd loved him in the way he'd loved his fiancée.

Lila had always been...*fanciful*. The word she'd just used for the holiday bazaar fit her to a T. It had been cute when she was little, slightly annoying when she was a teenager, but nothing he had given that much thought to overall.

"Do you...*not remember*?" The words were a half-whispered squeak.

"It was my engagement party, Lila. So I was mostly focused on that."

Her hands dropped to her sides, the vegetables in the basket bouncing slightly. She looked... Well, she looked enraged. He didn't have the best track record with women, but this was the angriest he'd ever made a woman in such a short span of time.

"You don't *remember*."

"Now that you mention it, I do. But I haven't... thought of it, no."

"That was..." She put her hand to her chest and looked past him, and he had the feeling she wasn't standing in this space and time at all. "That was the most devastated I have ever been in my life."

He went out of his way to avoid this stuff. He'd married young to avoid it. And here he was being accused of hurting her when he hadn't done a damn thing. "I'm sorry."

He didn't mean it.

"My heart was *broken*."

"You still seem to be standing," he pointed out.

Her face contorted, and he knew then that he had spoken with that kind of unfailing practicality that his ex-wife had despaired over.

Unfailing practicality that wasn't sensitive, or romantic, or any of the things that his ex had wished he would magically transform into after they'd married.

Everett was a man who had grown up on a farm. There wasn't much space for frilly sentiment in the life they'd had.

If the crops froze, then there was no money. And if there was no money, there was no food. Handouts—from the church pantry or from the government—were beneath the McCall family, and they were not something his mother or father would accept.

Better to go to bed with a growling stomach than wounded pride.

Everett's father had been a farmer. One of the last holdouts on a family farm without "fancy machinery" and fields rented out by "fat cats in monkey suits."

He had been a man who had worked the land that they had owned for generations, the way his father and grandfather had done. No innovation. No invention.

Everett had wanted more than that. Because while his father had fancied himself the soul of practicality, Everett had found the kind of sentiment that found the man clinging to a land that was becoming increasingly less profitable the antithesis of *real* practicality.

His father was *sentimental*.

Everett had gotten into horses. His old man had rolled his eyes at that, but Everett had known that there was up-and-coming money in certain breeds, and he'd found a way to get in on the ground floor by buying into Irish Cobs before the value on them skyrocketed. And now, he was one of the premier breeders in the United States. That equaled money. But he never put all his eggs in one basket.

Which was why he also had eggs. And beef. And why he rented out his barns to events like the Red Sled Holiday Bazaar.

He was also financially secure. So his ex-wife could dog on his practicality all she wanted. Could talk about happiness and fulfilling dreams and whatever else she'd been convinced was missing from their lives. But he didn't go to bed hungry. Not anymore. A man could love the land and still go to bed full—Everett believed that. And he lived it out. For all his sins.

And it appeared that he was sinning greatly now, at least in the eyes of Lila Frost.

"I can't believe you don't remember it." She still wasn't looking at him and he had to wonder if she was yelling at the him from seven years ago. "I have literally been avoiding you for the past seven years because of it. I come back to town and scamper between stores with my head held low because I'm afraid that I'm going to run into you."

"Well, you didn't have to do that," he said.

"Apparently," she snapped, drawing her basket in front of her and tramping back toward the farmhouse.

He followed along behind Lila, up to the front porch, and the board gave way beneath his foot. He frowned. "For all that Cade Mathewson was over here with your sister, I would have thought that he would have fixed the front porch."

Lila whipped around. "Cade Mathewson. That's who she's with?"

"Did you not know the details?"

She stiffened. "I don't know much of anything about JJ."

"I see."

It appeared that he wasn't the only person that Lila avoided.

"Yeah. Me, too," she said, sounding weary. "I'm going inside and I'm making zucchini bread."

"We need to discuss the Red Sled," he said. "June left me a list."

"Lists," Lila said, the word dripping with disdain. "I *hate* lists. And I don't like you very much right now."

"Join the club. I'm sure there are T-shirts."

She paused, narrowing her eyes. "Who else is in that club?"

"Well, you. Though I hate to break it to you, but Tonya is probably the founding member."

"Your *wife*?"

He chuckled. "When you go into avoidance mode, you really avoid. I've been divorced for two years. Didn't June tell you?"

Her lips twitched. "Funnily," Lila said, "your name didn't come up often. Or ever."

"Oh, did it not? Sad for me."

"So sad," Lila said. "I'm sorry. About your divorce."

"Yeah, me, too. She's not."

"I don't really know what to make of that. Any of this. I've been avoiding you for years because of my embarrassment. And also felt partly uncomfortable about it because I knew that you were happily married. Except...you aren't."

"No, I'm not."

"Maybe I'll make you some zucchini bread, then," she said, sounding terribly long-suffering.

"Well, in that case, maybe I'll fix the board here on the front porch."

"I guess you can," she said. "If only because I'm certainly not going to fix it, and…maybe Bella is coming after me."

"You aren't sure, though."

"I told you I'm not. Nobody's really sure about her."

"So do *none* of you speak?" He shook his head. "I have a hard time imagining that. You all seemed close enough back then."

"Well, that was before that last summer. When Bella left. And JJ became impossible to talk to. Keira was lost in all of her drama with Remy…"

"But Keira and Remy are engaged now," he said.

"Yes," Lila said. "I am invited to the wedding, so I guess there's that."

"Did you have a falling-out with Keira, too?"

"No. I think Keira had a falling-out with Jasper Creek. Well, with Remy. And as a result, the town."

"June said you still came to visit."

"Of course I did. I was avoiding *you*. Not her."

"I honestly didn't realize you were avoiding me. And I didn't interpret what you'd said to me to be a confession of…romantic feelings. I was engaged."

"There's nothing wrong with making sure people know your feelings," she said stubbornly.

He disagreed. There were a lot of things wrong with making sure people knew your feelings. There was no point, first of all. People were going to do what they were going to do, no matter what your feelings were.

An old stubborn man was going to allow disease to eat away at his body rather than go to a doctor, leaving his wife saddled with a ranch she couldn't afford, and a kid she didn't have the energy for. Stubbornness—stiff-necked idiocy—masquerading as practicality.

Emotions over reality.

"I'll never know," he said, "why people rage against reality."

"Because often reality is terrible. And hope is much brighter."

"And causes you to go into hiding for the last seven years."

"Fix my porch, Everett," she said. "I'll pay you in bread. And then you don't have to put up with me and my hope any more than is strictly necessary."

"Sounds good to me," he said. "Now, where can I find a hammer?"

CHAPTER THREE

By the time the zucchini bread was out of the oven and on the cooling rack, Everett seemed to have finished with the boards on the porch.

The temperature outside had cooled, but sadly for Lila, her face had not.

She didn't know who she was angrier at.

Everett or herself.

Him, *obviously*. Clearly, what had been a defining moment in her life had not been…even a blip on the radar to him. And at herself, because she could never just…keep it in.

It was her fundamental problem in life.

She was too much. And she didn't know how to be anything less.

When silence was the better part of valor, she could usually be counted on to blurt. And when she was in an emotionally thorny situation, she usually ran straight for the brambles and got herself tangled up.

Her mother was a runner.

She had run from her father, and from every subsequent relationship thereafter. She had given up hope before hope should've been lost, in so many situations. More than Lila could even count.

She had often felt obligated to be the unfailing optimist to her mother's pessimism.

Because what else was there to do?

Her mother had often said that a good attitude wouldn't change the outcome of something, and she was right. But a bad attitude didn't change it, either, and it certainly didn't blunt the pain of the disappointment when you didn't get what you had hoped for. It just made you miserable all through the waiting.

Lila didn't see the point in it. She'd made choices about how to navigate the world, choices that had been a necessity growing up in her house, because if she hadn't made cheer, no one else would have. She could have grown up in somber darkness that never had a break in the clouds. She hadn't been interested in that.

But then there were times like this. When she couldn't control it. When she just led with all that bright, burning emotion inside of her chest, and even while she was doing it, she knew it was a bad idea.

And yet.

And *yet*.

If her sister could've seen that…

Practical, list-making JJ would have been horrified. JJ certainly would never make an idiot out of herself for a man.

Lila had. More than once.

In fact, her last date had been a complete and utter disaster of her making a fool of herself.

It had been her fourth date with that particular man, and he had clearly imagined that it was time for them to take their relationship to the bedroom.

But Lila hadn't felt ready.

The problem was, she had felt more for Everett McCall at seventeen than she had for any man thereafter.

If they couldn't top that feeling, she didn't see the point of taking her clothes off.

She didn't necessarily need the first guy to be *the one*, but she did need him to be important. Significant. He would have to create a sea change inside of her in order to be allowed into her body.

She knew who she was. And she knew what she wanted.

Of course, she had also known who she was and what she wanted when she was seventeen and professing her love to Everett at his engagement party. And she had known who she was back in the garden a little while ago.

Just because she knew who she was didn't mean who she was wasn't occasionally *annoying*. Even to herself.

She made an exasperated sound and whacked at the zucchini bread with a knife.

"What did that bread ever do to you?"

She turned around and saw Everett standing in the open doorway, looking at the kitchen.

"Was that a joke?"

He lifted a shoulder. "Probably not. It's well-documented that I don't have a sense of humor."

She would never have said that. Not about the man she'd known all those years ago.

Yes, he was the kind of man you had to work to get a smile out of, but she had always enjoyed that. From the time she was a kid, she had counted herself lucky if she could tug a smile out of Everett McCall.

His smiles had become dear to her, things she counted and collected. Until she had to stop. Because of her own stupidity.

She was glad that he was here, actually. If she could

set aside all humiliation, all the ridiculousness that she had built up inside of herself for the last seven years, she liked Everett. She always had.

He was a part of her childhood, and while so many pieces of it had fractured and splintered, he was here. And so was this house. The same as it ever was.

Maybe she could never be close to Keira again. She was thrilled her cousin had invited her to the wedding—and really, she wouldn't have expected different. With the three of them, it wasn't as if anyone had taken a pair of scissors and cut their connections.

It was more like the years had stretched them. Made them thin. Made it hard for Lila to imagine how they might find a way to connect with each other. Really connect.

She was younger than Keira and JJ, and they were the two who'd always been closest. And sometimes she'd resented Keira for her effortless closeness to Lila's own sister. She also felt a little resentful that Keira had managed to snare her crush, Remy West, who was also older than her. While Lila could not get Everett's attention at all.

But now Lila was just happy Keira and Remy had come together. Of course, it was also what had kept her from seeking Keira out since she'd come to the farmhouse. She didn't want to intrude. But that might also be an excuse.

Maybe she could never be close to JJ. And maybe they would never even *see* Bella, ever again.

But this house was here. And June had brought her here to stay in it for a reason. And maybe she could look at the inclusion of Everett as a gift.

She eyed the zucchini bread. There was an awful lot of it. "Does Noah Faraday still live next door?"

He'd been Bella's stepbrother for all of a year before she and her mother had left Jasper Creek forever. But Noah had stayed, and had stayed close to Grandma June, even though she wasn't his grandma by blood.

"He sure does."

"Maybe I'll give some of this to him." She looked back at Everett. "Do *you* want some bread?"

"Sure," he said. "If you can promise you didn't poison it."

"That isn't my style," she said, smiling sweetly as she lopped off the end of the loaf. "I would never stoop to subterfuge. There is no performance in that." She shoved a piece at him.

"Well, that I believe."

She wasn't even wounded that he thought that. It was true. Lila didn't do things by halves, and she didn't do them quietly.

So she had been told often by her exasperated father, before he'd left and taken the child who caused him no fuss with him.

"Now, about the Red Sled—" Everett began.

"There's a binder," Lila said. "Grandma June mentioned that in her addendum to my letter."

"Well, that's good. We should start making lists of what we need—"

"I won't need to make a list," Lila said. She bustled around the small, cozy kitchen and wiped things that were already clean. "There's already a binder. I won't have to do any of that. The organization has been done for me, thank God."

Lila was many things, but organized was not one of them.

At the florist's she worked for, she had no administrative duties. Her job was to arrange the flowers. To be creative, and to create works of art, which she was very good at. When it came down to the artistic part of this entire event, she was very confident.

Grandma June had seen to the organization. At least, Lila assumed so.

"Okay," he said slowly. "Let's see that binder."

"It's somewhere," Lila said. "I think in the hall closet."

She tramped out to the entryway and regarded the closet across from the base of the stairs. That had been where June had kept the games when they were children, and perhaps she kept other things in there, too.

She opened the door and said a small prayer that she wouldn't come up with a handful of spiders when she went digging around.

The small, enclosed space was cold, and she shivered slightly as she stood up on her tiptoes and began hunting around. She pushed aside one of the board games they'd often played as kids.

Game nights were just one of the many gifts Grandma June had given them.

Summers spent outside, without TV. Without their creature comforts. Nothing but board games, stacks of books and afternoons spent down by the creek.

She suddenly had a flash to an evening they'd spent in the house. It had been a summer rainstorm, the air heavy with the scent of rain, water on stone and the swollen river.

It had been back when Bella had still been around,

and they'd all been cooped up and restless. So they'd spent the time playing sardines, a game of hide-and-seek that saw everyone eventually joined together with the hider. She could remember well all of them being cramped up inside this closet, their mouths covered by their hands as they tried not to giggle.

If she closed her eyes, she could almost put herself right back there.

Her fingers brushed up against something that was not a board game and she brought it down.

It was a binder with a red-checked cover and felt letters stuck to the front.

Red Sled Holiday Bazaar.

"Aha!" She made a grand show of exiting the closet and shutting the door. "I found it."

"Great," Everett said, his voice filtering in from the kitchen.

"Ever organized was Grandma June," Lila said, setting the binder on the table before going and procuring herself a piece of bread and sitting down.

She opened the binder and immediately, her eyes glazed over. The first page was a layout of booths. Numbered. Along with a time frame for when booth rental began.

"Yeah, that's going to be contentious," Everett said, looking at the page.

"It will not," she said.

"Yes," he responded. "It will be. There are preferred locations, booths that the women fight over every year."

"It will be first come, first serve," Lila said resolutely. "I'm not having any squabbling over booth placement. That's easy enough."

"Sure," he said.

"First come, first serve," Lila said. She turned the page. There was information about which businesses had donated food in the past, and the balance of items that was ideal. And for something that involved crafting, it was all a bit too close to math for Lila's comfort.

"Okay, there's a lot of information in there. But it seems like the first thing will be to handle the booth rental on the date. Is everyone aware of the date?"

"Well," Everett said, "they will be when you make and distribute flyers."

"It doesn't say anything about making and distributing flyers in here."

"Well, how do you think the word is going to get out, Lila?"

Lila scowled. "Fine. I will make sure that there are flyers to disseminate. I can make flyers."

She was a decent artist, whether by hand or on the computer, so flinging together a flyer wasn't going to be difficult.

"I suspect that Grandma June doesn't have a printer of her own?"

"You might just want to take them down to the print shop," he said.

"How many will I even need?" She looked at him. "Do *you* have a printer?"

"There's a print shop," he said, as if that was all the answer she could possibly need.

"Well," she said, "fear not. I will put together a flyer with all the relevant information. Including when people can call about booth rental."

"They're going to start bugging you before then," he said.

That calm certainty of his was only annoying.

"How many years has the Red Sled been at your barn?"

"Three," he said. "Believe me, I've witnessed some cutthroat behavior to get prime booth space."

Prime. Booth. Space.

She couldn't fathom what that would even mean.

"I'm just going to keep things the same way that Grandma June did. The last thing I want to do is get into fights with women who want things done the same way they've always been done."

"The only person who wants things done the same way they've always been done is Mrs. Kim. And that's because she has the best booth every year."

"It's going to be fine," she said. There was no point catastrophizing anything. Things would turn out one way or another, and it didn't matter if she let herself get all knotted up about it.

"Well, I best be getting on home," he said.

"Yeah," she said. "I hope you have some free time tomorrow, because I need someone to help me find the print shop. And figure out where I need to hang these flyers."

Everett looked at her for a long moment, and her heart jumped.

No. Oh, no. She had made an idiot out of herself with this man too many times already. And she was not going to do it again.

Then Everett stood up, unfolding his long, rangy body from the table, stretching, the material of his shirt going tight across his broad chest. And somehow, her eyes were drawn right *there*.

To the front of his jeans.

To the bulge there that seem significant to her,

though what would she know, considering she was nothing more than a virgin who had no visual or hands-on experience with what was behind that compelling denim.

Well. It was one thing to get her heart to settle down, and apparently quite another to get her body to take the memo.

"Great," she said, smiling broadly. "I'll see you tomorrow then."

He nodded slowly, tipping his hat. "See you tomorrow."

And then Everett left, leaving Lila to wonder how she had managed to bake bread, humiliate herself and finagle a way to make sure she and Everett spent the day together tomorrow, all in the space of just a couple of hours.

CHAPTER FOUR

EVERETT WASN'T ENTIRELY sure why he found himself idling in his truck outside the farmhouse's front door that next morning.

June.

That was what he told himself. It was what June wanted him to do. And he wasn't about to argue with what June wanted.

It had nothing—so he told himself—to do with the current occupant of the farmhouse.

When she burst out of the house, hair curling and flying wildly behind her, her body draped in a ridiculous mixture of scarves, fringed boots, a long, flowing sweater, woolen leggings and a short dress, she reminded him much more of that girl he'd known.

But she wasn't a girl, and he couldn't ignore that.

"I emailed my files to the shop," she said as soon as she got in the car.

"Okay," he said.

"They said they would get them printed right away since it's such a small order."

"Okay," he said again.

He wasn't sure why Lila thought he needed to know about the minutiae of the entire thing. He certainly felt he didn't.

And yet, Lila continued to talk about every minor

detail during their ten-minute drive down a winding two-lane road that led into the redbrick-lined main street of Jasper Creek.

The little print shop at the end of the main drag also served as a post office, a place where the townsfolk could accomplish any number of small office-related tasks. In a town like Jasper Creek, where many of the residents were aging, and most didn't own their own computer, the place did pretty good business.

Everett parked his truck and Lila bounced out before he could go and open her door for her. Then she was into the shop ahead of him in a flurry of movement as she gave her name and all the details of her order, and was handed a small stack of paper a moment later.

She paid, and Everett barely had time to tip his hat to Tim, the owner of the place, before they were back on the street.

"We should walk," she said. "And that way we can canvass the whole town."

"I thought you brought me with you to help limit the canvassing."

"Well, I suppose so. But I haven't been down into town in…ages. When I come visit Grandma June, I…" She trailed off. "I'm going to miss her. I already do."

"June was one of a kind," Everett said.

He wasn't very good at comforting people, particularly women, but he would miss June, too, and he knew well enough that sometimes the only way to help people with grief was to let them know you shared in it.

"I don't know that she was an optimist," Lila said, musing. "But she was determined, and in the end, that's almost the same thing. She never gave up. Not on anything or anyone. And I've always admired that in her."

"Are you an optimist?"

"Yes," Lila said cheerfully. "I'm an optimist, because pessimism does not produce a different result, just a different attitude on the journey." She looked up at him. "What are you?"

"A realist."

She barked out a laugh. "Right. So you're a pessimist, then."

"No."

She stopped, standing in front of a little corkboard that was hanging on the side of one of the little cafés. "In my experience, pessimists tend to think that they're more realistic, when in reality the odds that things turning out badly aren't actually any better than all the things turning out well."

"Absolutely untrue," he said. "In many cases, it's pretty apparent how things are actually going to turn out."

"Right. Doom and gloom?"

"Not at all. But look, avoiding things doesn't change the outcome. Wishing for better doesn't change the outcome. The only thing that changes the way things work is action. There are things you can do, and things you can't do. I guess pessimists focus on all the bad things you can't change, and to my mind, optimists often engage in blind hope without doing much. A realist does what needs to be done."

"Okay. So you are a practical soul," she said dryly, moving on down the street, her heel catching on one of the cracks in the weathered sidewalk. She made an exasperated sound but traipsed on.

"Why are you an optimist?"

"Why not?" she asked.

"It seems to me that then you're always blindsided by bad things."

"I'm never blindsided by bad things. What will be, will be."

"You're a fatalist," he said.

"Maybe," she said. "But a cheerful one."

"I don't believe in fate, either. If you work hard, and you work smart, you can make things better for yourself. If you go to a doctor when you have symptoms of a disease, you might be able to have that disease be cured. Sitting around, hoping it's nothing bad, isn't going to help you. Sitting around knowing it's bad and doing nothing won't help you, either." He shrugged. "If you die because you didn't go to a doctor, that's not fate."

"I suppose not."

All of it skated a little bit too close to his actual life, and he didn't need to be talking about his dad.

"Well, it's not like I do nothing," she said. "I do. I just don't see the point of doing it with a bad attitude."

"Are you little Lila Frost?"

Both he and Lila turned and saw a small older woman standing there, her hands clasped in front of her, the smile on her face broad. Everett knew that it was Linda Anderson, but he didn't know if Lila did.

"Yes," Lila said, returning the smile with equal breadth. "I am."

"So you're June's granddaughter. The one that she put in charge of the Red Sled this year."

"I am."

"We were all so sorry to lose your grandmother, dear. She was truly one of a kind."

"Yes," Lila said, her smile turning wistful. "She was."

"But I'm sure that you'll do a wonderful job running

the bazaar. I sell handmade jewelry," she said. "Very popular. Last year alone I earned a thousand dollars with my booth for the local school. I would really love to have booth number seven."

"Oh… Well, the booth reservations actually open up in two weeks' time. All the information is on the flyer."

"Never mind that," Mrs. Anderson said. "I just thought that I would make it clear how important my contribution to the Red Sled is. And how much I would like booth number seven."

Lila's smile stayed firmly fixed. "Well. Two weeks. The information is on the flyer."

Mrs. Anderson reached up, took the flyer that Lila had just freshly tacked onto the board and removed it. She folded it up and put it in her handbag. "Thank you, dear. I will keep that date in mind."

The older woman crossed the street, leaving Lila standing there staring after her. "What just happened?"

"I believe they call that being railroaded."

"She took my flyer."

"She probably wants to make sure that she's the only one who knows when the booth registration opens up."

"You weren't kidding," she said.

"Do I look like someone that kids?"

She turned to face him. "I guess not."

"I don't. For the record."

"No. Kidding doesn't fall into the realist code." She took another flyer off the stack and pinned it back to the bulletin board.

"That's just a taste of what's to come," he commented.

"Well," she said. "Just *well*."

"Still think you're not going to make a list?"

Her expression turned fearsome. "I will not make a list."

"She's just the beginning."

After that, Lila became extremely cagey about the hanging up of the flyers. By the time they reached the coffeehouse at the far end of the main street, she was hunching over her task. He might have left if he hadn't known that all of this was serious small-town psychological warfare. And Lila was not local enough to deal with it. Oh, sure, she might have spent scattered summers in Jasper Creek, but it wasn't the same as being local.

Before they left the coffee shop, she got herself some insanely oversweetened concoction that she called a breve, which she explained to him was made with half-and-half instead of milk. He stuck with tried-and-true black coffee.

As they walked back to his truck, Lila in all her excess and he in his jeans and long-sleeve black shirt, he felt like their personalities might have been written across them for all the world to see. She with her bright hair, trailing yards of fabric and excessive beverage. He with his...

Well, nothing other than what was strictly necessary.

"I'll drop you back by the house," he said when they got back to the truck. "But I have to go be about my business."

They got into the truck together, and suddenly he became aware of how cramped a truck cab was. "What is your business?"

"Irish Cob horses," he said.

"What does that...mean? You...train them, eat them, teach them to dance wearing toe shoes?"

"No."

"Then explain to me what you do."

They began to drive back toward the farmhouse, and he found himself counting the seconds until he had deposited this chatterbox off where she belonged.

"I breed them. They're very versatile horses. Good for showing, good for cart pulling. Just in general and all-around great temperament. They've become an incredibly sought-after breed."

"That's interesting," she said. "Your father owned a farm, didn't he?"

"Yep. And he died poor."

It was clear to him that Lila had no idea what to say to that.

"I didn't intend on dying with an empty stomach," he said.

"Right. So...not a passion project for you."

He shrugged. "As much of one as any. This is where I'm from. I love the land. I love the community, the people in it. I imagine that I would raise a family here."

"Right."

"I didn't want to go off and be a banker or a doctor. School was beyond us financially, anyway, and it's not like I got good enough grades to justify anyone giving me a scholarship. So I figured I had to find something that I could do that connected to this place. The land."

She paused for a beat. "And you don't think you're going to raise a family here anymore?"

"I don't think I'm going to raise a family anymore."

"Why?"

He shot her a glare.

"Just because you got divorced once?" she pressed.

"How many times does a man need to get divorced to find out that marriage doesn't suit him?"

"Did marriage not suit you, or did *she* not suit you?"

"Optimist," he said. "Realist."

"Pessimist," she insisted.

"I don't bend," he said. "I don't know how to. Marriage, in my experience, requires a bit of bending. I couldn't do it. She left."

"That sounds like an incredibly abbreviated version of whatever actually happened."

His expression shifted to something sort of resigned. Lila recognized that look. People often got it when she was tenaciously digging for something, as if they knew they'd been beaten. She didn't feel guilty.

"She thought that working the land made me miserable. She thought living here made me miserable. That I worked too hard, didn't have enough fun. She thought that I was consumed with getting the place off the ground and being successful. She wasn't wrong. She thought we could pull up stakes and go somewhere new. She didn't want my kind of life, and in the end, I didn't want her kind, either."

"Well, you'd think that's the kind of stuff you talk about before you got married."

"Tonya was local as they come. I didn't have any damn clue she might want to live somewhere else. And she didn't know that a life on a ranch would make her miserable. The fact is, Lila, we thought we knew what each other wanted. We were as ready as any two people could be for marriage. Still didn't work."

"Well, then, she wasn't *the one*," Lila said resolutely.

"Don't believe in *the one*," he said.

"How can you not believe in *the one*?"

"Because that's magical thinking. It's not reality. Two people get married, and they can either bend enough ways without breaking that they can pretzel into some kind of life together, or they can't. Tonya and I couldn't. It made me ask a lot of questions about whether or not I actually ever wanted to."

Lila frowned, and right then, they pulled up to the farmhouse. "I don't think that's true," she said softly.

"What? My experience of marriage?"

"Oh, I'm sure your experience of marriage was the experience it was. I'm just not sure your conclusions are correct."

"Have you ever been married, Lila?"

She shook her head. "No. Because I haven't found him yet."

"How do you know he exists?"

"He has to. Everyone has a—a glass slipper. Or... The person that can change them from a frog into a prince."

"Life is not a fairy tale," he said.

"Not if you don't want to be," she said. "I think you have to at least believe in magic a little bit to have some in your own life."

"I don't believe in magic," he said. "I believe in hard work. That's it."

He stopped the truck, and Lila sat for a moment before getting out. But he didn't feel relieved. Not like he thought he should. No, instead it felt like she had taken some of the air right out of the cab of his truck with her, making it difficult for him to breathe around what she had left behind.

And as he watched her walk into the house, trailing scarves and sweaters in her wake, he wondered if Lila Frost was a little bit magic herself. At the very least she was the only person he'd ever met who made a case for it.

CHAPTER FIVE

THE DOORBELL RANG, and Lila jumped. She squeezed her eyes shut and counted to ten before getting out of her chair, where she was staring at a binder, resolutely *not* making a list, and walked cautiously to the door. She quickly looked out the lace curtains to the side and saw a small woman with graying black hair standing there holding a plate of some kind of baked good.

Another bribe.

They been stacking up for days. Food, doilies, tea towels. It never seemed to end. She had been hoping to… Well, she had been hoping to lie around, read, plan the Red Sled Holiday Bazaar and mostly enjoy a little bit of the vacation away from her job, but no. She had spent the past days entertaining all of June's old friends.

She hadn't seen Everett since that day in town when they hung up flyers, and she had the feeling that he was avoiding her. It was too bad she couldn't avoid her current visitor. She jerked the door open, a determined smile on her face, and she looked down at the tiny woman standing there.

"I brought cookies," she said.

"Hi," Lila said.

"I'm Mrs. Kim," she said.

"It's very nice to meet you, Mrs. Kim."

"I just wanted to bring these cookies by," she said, "and remind you that—"

"You always have booth number seven," Lila finished. "The most coveted booth in the entire space. Positioned handily just next to the kettle corn and the spiced cider, and directly across from the entry."

She had questioned what prime booth space was. She had since been educated.

Thoroughly.

"Yes," she said. "How did you know?"

"This is not the first sales pitch I've had. And I'll tell you what I told everyone else. You may officially reserve the booth October 5. The first phone call gets the booth. But I will take your cookies. And it was very nice to see you again."

Lila took the plate and Mrs. Kim gave her a scowl, turning and walking down the front steps, just as a faded old Volvo pulled up the drive.

Lila blinked in total disbelief. The lady that got out of that car was even smaller and more shrunken than the one that had come before. As if they were little pushy matryoshka dolls. One tiny cute one appeared, then a tinier cuter one.

This lady did not have a plate. She had a little woolen bag that was clearly stuffed full.

It was not—she didn't think—Lila's imagination that Mrs. Kim shot her new visitor a death glare from her car as she pulled away.

"Hello," she said, smiling widely, patting her salt-and-pepper hair, dark eyes glowing. "I'm Ms. Jones."

"Hi, Ms. Jones," Lila said from her position in the doorway.

"I just wanted to bring you by some of the items that

I sell in my booth." And from her bag she produced two of the smallest, cutest felted mice that Lila had ever seen.

"Oh," she said.

She itched to take the mice. She didn't know what she would do with small felted mice. All she knew was that she wanted them.

"I just wanted to make sure that you knew also," she said, "that I have my heart set on booth number seven. It's just—"

"The best booth," Lila finished.

"Yes, dear," she said.

Lila was suddenly sorely tempted to offer the booth in exchange for all of the felted creatures. No one would ever know. *Someone* had to have booth seven. Why couldn't it be Ms. Jones?

No. Everyone expected her to do things like bend rules. Bend rules and be disorganized and give in to bribes that involved small animals. But she wasn't going to.

She was going to do this *right*.

Grandma June believed in her. She wasn't sure anyone else ever had.

"That is very kind of you," she said. "But booth rental does not open until October 5 and I cannot guarantee anyone a particular booth. You just have to be the first to call on that date."

"Why is that, dear?" the other woman asked, her tone as sweet as her brown-sugar skin.

"Because *Grandma June said so*. And if that's how she wants it run, then that's how I'm going to run it."

The older woman snapped her fingers. "Darn. I was hoping you might be a softer touch than June was."

"I'm not," she said, privately thinking she absolutely was.

"You can expect a call from me very early."

"I welcome it," she said. The older woman turned to go. "I don't get the mice?"

"I didn't get the booth," the woman said, putting the creatures back in her bag and striding down the porch steps.

Lila could only stand there and stare, shocked. She had no idea the women of Jasper Creek were so cut-throat.

She was ruminating about that when there was yet another knock on the door. She threw her hands up over her head in a silent entreaty to the sky to deliver her from the hell of *booth number seven*.

"What would they do if I changed booth number seven to booth number...? Booth number *twelve*. What if I just moved them? And then, they didn't even know where they were going to end up, they just ended up where I put them."

She jerked the door open and was completely surprised to see not a tiny old woman, but a very large cowboy.

She did her best to calm the sudden uptick in her heartbeat. "Are you here about booth number seven?"

"I am not," he said.

She growled and stepped to the side, allowing him entry.

"I take it you had visitors." His gaze was behind her, on the side table full of goodies.

"I did. And I want you to know, I nearly sold my scruples for a couple of felted mice."

He stared at her blankly. He was handsome even when blank. "I don't understand any of the words in that sentence, and I'm not asking you to help me."

She growled and stamped into the kitchen.

"I had some questions for you."

"You know," she said, "there is a thing called a phone, and it means that you don't have to suddenly materialize in the middle of someone's house every time you have to tell them something."

"I don't have your number."

"June's landline?"

"Well, she used to yell at me. Tell me I lived not fifty paces down the way, and there was no reason for me to startle her to death with a telephone call when I could easily pay her a visit in person."

"Different times," Lila said. "I would prefer someone send me a text so that I don't even have to be startled by the sound of their voice."

"See," he said, "this is the kind of thing I don't get. People think I'm antiquated, but they can't even have a conversation anymore."

"Do you consider yourself a sparkling conversationalist, Everett McCall?"

"Hell, no. But I sure as hell know how to speak with someone face-to-face."

"A realist without a smartphone," she said in fake lament.

"I never said I didn't have a smartphone."

"Do you?"

"Yes. It's a practical way to keep tabs on potential buyers for my horses. And to update listings and the like."

"Right. The practical soul of reason. How quickly I forget. Would you like cookies? I am drowning in them."

"Yes," he said. "As a matter of fact I would love some cookies."

"Now, why are you here?" she asked, traipsing over to the side table and picking up a plate.

"I have some questions for you about vendors. I'm going to need to figure out exactly what I have to provide. Sometimes there's a requirement for power supplies and the like. If Ace Thompson is coming over with beer from Copper Ridge, then I'm going to need to help with that setup, because it gets pretty complicated."

"Beer?" She affected mock shock. "What kind of wholesome family fun is this?"

"The redneck kind," he said.

"Well, I'm not sure. I know that I talked to… I did write it down." Frustration bubbled up inside of her. She wanted to do this on her terms. Grandma June had asked her to do it, and she knew she could. She hated that she was forgetting now. It was Everett's fault, anyway. Standing there being distracting.

"You have a list?"

"I don't need a list," she insisted.

"I think you need a list."

"I don't want to need a list," she said. She huffed into the kitchen and went back to the binder. "I have some notes. That's not the same."

"Why, exactly, don't you want a list?"

"Because I'm not JJ," she said. She was overreacting, and she knew it, but she wasn't sure how to stop it. "I'm not organized, practical JJ. And that's why my father took her instead of me. Because I am a disaster. An explosive, messy disaster, and I have been since I was a little girl. I had the temerity to cry when I fell and scraped my knee. My room was always a mess. I left stuffed animals and dolls everywhere. And I never cleaned up after my tea parties."

Her issues felt so perilously close to the surface here. In this farmhouse, doing this task that was frankly so far out of her comfort zone it made her want to run back to the safety of Portland and Burnside Blooms, where she was never asked to be anything but creative and where she didn't have to try to stretch herself.

Didn't have to try to be something or someone she knew she could never measure up to.

A person her father might want.

"I knew you when you were a kid," he said, his voice even. "You were not like that."

"I was. But it's fine. I don't care. I'm me. I can't do anything about it. I am who I am. And I'm sorry if everyone seems to think that I should be something else. Except Grandma June."

"Is that what you think?"

"Grandma June is the only one who believed I could do this. No one else would have ever assigned this to me. They would have thought that I would mess it up. But I'm not going to. I'm going to do it my way. I'm going to do it with my whole chicken-tea-party-giving self. Grandma June knew me. And she loved me. My dad didn't want me. I drive my mom insane. I'm still not sure how she lost the draw to get JJ. I bet you they fought over her. If they'd been thinking, they would have traded weeks off with JJ and shunted me off somewhere else altogether."

Everett didn't say anything, and now that her temper was cooling slightly, Lila felt silly.

"I kind of proved my own point," she said.

"You know, there's a lot of ground between being asked to change and keeping a list to make your own life easier."

"Is there?"

"Yeah. I would say there's all the ground in the world between those two things," he said.

"Says the man who already told me his marriage fell apart because he didn't want to change."

He regarded her for a moment, his eyes stormy. "So you're telling me that nothing in your life has been made harder because you refuse to do something an easier way out of sheer stubbornness?"

"I'm an idealist," she said. "Another *ist* for you, to go with your grand self-claims."

"You're really going to stand there and lecture me," he said. "You. The girl—yes, *girl*—who confessed her love for a man at his engagement party."

Something inside of Lila snapped. "Well, I was right. Wasn't I? I mean, let's face it, Everett, you certainly shouldn't have married Tonya."

"Couldn't have married *you*, either," he said. "Given that it would've been against a few different laws. And I'm into *women*."

"Well, you still made a marriage mistake, didn't you? You were wrong. Maybe that was it. Maybe I was your sign, and you were supposed to listen to it."

"Or maybe you were just some silly little girl, and I took what you said as the word of a silly little girl."

She walked forward and slapped her hand against the center of his chest. Damn. That was a lot more rock-solid than she had expected. "Well, I'm not a little girl," she said. "In case it had escaped your notice, I'm a woman now. And my observation is still that you're a stiff-necked stubborn asshole who has no right to stand around and judge what I do or don't do given the state of your own existence."

Suddenly, she found herself trapped against that rock-hard chest, his arm wrapped around her. And she didn't know what was happening. Her heart was thundering hard, the pulse between her legs pounding heavily. He was angry at her, and she should probably shout about him manhandling her, all things considered. Except…it didn't feel scary. It didn't feel like manhandling.

It didn't even feel anything like dangerous.

It felt like something else altogether, and she wasn't sure she had a word for it.

Except…

The heat in her belly felt familiar. When she was young, it had bloomed in her chest, like a bright white hope that seemed to guide her to Everett, whatever the situation.

It had burned the hottest in her chest at his engagement party, when she had been so desperate to stop him from making a terrible mistake.

She had never known such an injustice.

That Everett McCall hadn't even been able to wait *one more year* for her to be a grown-up so that they could have a chance. Just a chance.

That was all she had wanted. But she had always been racing against some kind of clock, given that he was a decade her senior. And, of course… Of course, some woman had fallen in love with him. Lila had fallen in love with him when she'd been a girl, but the least that Everett could have done, the very damn least, was wait until she could compete on a level playing field.

Just one more year. Just until she was eighteen.

And then she could have kissed him.

But now, that feeling was situated lower. Her belly, and blooming outward, blooming down.

You could kiss him now.

Angry, grumpy Everett McCall, who had now been married and divorced and had given up on love, with her still a blushing virgin.

But maybe that was it.

He wasn't *the one*. He couldn't be.

If he was *the one*, they wouldn't want to kill each other on sight after all this time. If he was *the one*, it would feel sweet and airy and glorious, and not like this dark, gnawing desire that nearly hurt.

But he was…a *something*.

She didn't need to be with only one man, but she needed it to be significant.

And for her, Everett McCall was significant in every way.

Somehow, as she rose up on her toes just then, she felt like she was tipping forward. Off the edge of something. And when her lips met his, it was like an explosion.

CHAPTER SIX

LILA WAS ROCKED. This was the kind of kiss that unleashed a storm of devastation inside her.

It felt big enough that it should have created an explosion. But no. Green cupboard doors didn't burst open, the china didn't rattle. All of it was still, while her insides were anything but.

He was motionless. A rock.

Which was, in many ways, what Everett had become in her life.

This immovable rock, a thing she could not excise from her soul no matter how hard she tried.

So maybe she would do it this way.

Mouth-to-mouth.

But then suddenly, he took part in the kiss, and once he began to move, there was no room left for thought.

It was Everett. His lips, his big, calloused hands cupping her face, his tongue sliding against hers so that she was ready to strip off her clothes right then. No first, second, third or fourth date required.

Because she had loved this man for longer than she could count, and okay, maybe she could admit now that there was no way she actually *loved* him, considering she didn't know him. Considering she hadn't seen him at all in the last seven years, and she had assumed that he had been married to someone else.

But she felt *something*.

Something deep. Something raw. Something real. Something she couldn't fight and didn't really want to.

His hands were large and warm, and his thumbs skimmed over her cheeks, making her shake. Making her shudder. She had put her hand on his chest—the barrier that his shirt created between her fingertips and his muscles a barrier she intended to demolish. And now. She pushed her hand beneath his shirt, and suddenly, Everett drew back.

"*Not* a good idea," he said, his voice rough.

"So what?"

"What?"

"Since when does sex have to be a good idea?"

He huffed a laugh that sounded more like pain than humor. "It's a pretty long bridge between a kiss and sex, Lila."

"Not the way we were doing it. That's a short bridge. And I'm really okay with crossing it."

"No," he said firmly.

"Why not?"

She watched his face, and with some grim satisfaction realized the man could not come up with one good reason.

"Because June asked me to help you," he said. "And you're going to leave."

"Yes to both," Lila said. "So that sounds fairly perfect to me. You can help me plan the Red Sled. And you can help me keep warm at night."

As a general rule, she knew what she wanted, and wasn't shy about getting it. Or not getting it, as the case may be. And as strange as it sounded, she felt like turning down any number of men over the past few years had made this feel perfectly reasonable, and perfectly easy.

She'd always been confident that when the time was right, she'd know. And it was time.

"I…"

"You don't have a reason," she said. "Not a single reason. Unless you're not attracted to me."

Then she sucked in a breath and did possibly the boldest thing she'd ever done. She placed her hand directly over that bulge that she had looked at earlier.

And, with great satisfaction, she found him hard.

"I think you do want me," she said.

"Lila," he said, his voice rough. "I haven't had sex in two years."

Lila stepped backward, stunned. "You haven't… In two years? Not since your divorce."

"No," he said.

"Why not?"

"With who? Half the women in this town used to be friends of my ex-wife, and the ones that weren't hated her, and I don't exactly want to be the spite sex that somebody has to get back at a girl that they fought with in high school."

"I didn't think men cared about things like that."

"Well, I do."

"That doesn't seem much like a realist. I would think that realism demands that you acknowledge that having an orgasm—with an interested party—is much more fun than not having one." She was running her mouth now about things she didn't fully comprehend, but she was hoping that leading with enough bravado would cover up that she was talking out of her ass. In her experience, it usually did.

She continued. "I *would think* that one would acknowledge that realistically, your pride will not keep you warm at night, but a naked woman will."

"Oh, but experience says that inviting a woman into your bed for the wrong damn reasons doesn't end well."

"There's no wrong reason between us."

"You're way too young for me," he said. "I have known you since you were a child."

A very nice try. She had to admire him for the attempt.

"And here I am," she said, "not a child. Must be confronting."

"You're going to stand here and beg for me, then?"

She knew he'd said that to make her feel shame. But it had come out sounding much more like a dare, like an invitation to something sinfully wicked, than it had a deterrent.

And so she leaned in again, keeping one hand on the front of his jeans, rubbing him through the fabric. Lifting her other hand and tracing his cheekbone with the tip of her finger. "Please?"

And that was when she found herself being consumed again. And if there was any more discussing to be done, it had turned nonverbal. Because their mouths were occupied, and his hands were on her body, and she wanted nothing more than to keep on like this. Rushed heat and liquid desire, a heavy, aching pulse between her thighs, and a tingling in her breasts.

As long as things kept on like this, there would be no room for virginal nerves. And she found herself being swept up, caught up, whisked up the stairs.

"My room is the one at the end of the hall," she said.

And he carried her right down that hallway and pushed the door open.

Her bed was as she'd left it, frilly and made up like a

picture-perfect fantasy room. An oasis, as it had always been, from the drama of her real life in her apartment with her mother in Portland.

She had dreamed of Everett McCall late at night in this room. Imagining—when she was a girl—that someday she might marry him, her in a frilly dress and him in a tux, and her with no knowledge of what passed between men and women between the sheets.

Then later, as a teenager, when she had thought of kissing him with all the passion inside of her, with only a bit of hazy knowledge about why men's bodies were so mysterious and wonderful and different.

And it seemed fitting now, that this would be here, and it would be him.

Suddenly, that it was autumn seemed fitting, as well.

It was such an achingly transient season. The leaves changing from all that summertime glory to fiery red, before fading to brown and passing away.

You couldn't stop time. Couldn't stop seasons. Couldn't stop the people in your life from losing all their color, fading away and drifting off in the wind.

But she could seize what they had now.

Her own personal moment of brilliant, bright red glory, here in the arms of Everett McCall.

She pushed her hands beneath his shirt, stripping it up over his head, hungrily testing his muscles with her palms, his skin hot and glorious beneath her hands. How she wanted him. How she needed him.

Needed this.

The satisfaction of all that she had ever been.

And if she could go back in time and tell that seventeen-year-old girl who had been crushed by the marriage of this man to another woman, she would love to tell her...

You're going to get naked with him someday.

And that nearly made her laugh, because seventeen-year-old her would have been much more concerned with whether or not she might marry him, than whether or not she got to see him naked.

That was the difference seven years made. She didn't need him to be her perfect white knight or any of that. But she did quite want to see him naked. Twenty-four-year-old Lila had a slightly different fairy tale in mind, and if something was going to fit perfectly…it didn't need to be a glass slipper.

It just needed to be his body.

She drew back and turned the bedside light on. Old-fashioned and made to look like an oil lamp.

She sat back and appraised him, waiting for him to remove the rest of his clothes. His shoulders were broad, and so was his chest, covered with just the right amount of hair. Her palms itched to touch him there. To take in that contrast. That roughness. That broad chest tapered down to a lean waste, a washboard stomach that she thought one could indeed have scrubbed some clothes on.

"Is this a show for you?" he asked.

"Yes," she said.

Not just because it was going to be the first time she had ever seen a naked man in the flesh, but because of who the naked man was. Something hot lit his dark gaze, and it made her feel a bit breathless. A bit in over her head. But his hands went to the belt buckle on his jeans, and he undid it slowly, then the button, and then the zipper.

He shrugged his jeans and underwear down quickly. Easily. Of course, he had no nerves to speak of. But then, why would he?

She, on the other hand, was trembling now. Because he was...

He was so very much.

And she had no experience.

She felt very suddenly like a very small kitten that had claimed it was a lion, pitted up against an actual predator.

But then he closed the distance between them, joined her on the bed and gathered her up against his naked body, kissing her until she was dizzy. And her clothes seemed to disappear like magic, and his hands were magic, and his hot body up against hers was magic.

For a man who didn't believe in it, he sure created a whole storm of it.

His hands between her thighs created sparks that shimmered over her skin, and when he secured protection and positioned his whole body there, she shuddered.

His dark eyes bored into hers, and she trembled. This was the thing she had held herself back from all this time, because she had known that for her it would be impossibly intimate. And she had this one moment to turn back, she knew she could.

Somehow, she just knew that if she told Everett now that she was afraid, that she couldn't do it, he would get dressed and walk out without argument. But she wanted him as much as she feared this, and she knew, beyond a shadow of a doubt, that if it wasn't him now, it would be no one ever.

So she grabbed hold of those broad shoulders and whispered in his ear. "Please."

And he didn't have to be asked twice.

He was inside of her in one hard stroke, the pain of it taking her breath away. And she could do nothing but scrunch her face against his shoulder, a sob wrenching her throat.

He froze, and the storm in his eyes wasn't a gentle one. She watched as indecisiveness contorted his handsome features, and then a grim kind of acceptance firmed his mouth into a line, and he withdrew slightly, then thrust forward.

And with each stroke he replaced the pain with a fraction more pleasure, until she couldn't remember her name.

But she remembered his.

Everett McCall.

The man that she had loved since before she knew what it meant.

Since before she had known it meant *this*.

Skin and bodies and hands and hearts. Sweat and tears, and very likely blood.

She squeezed her eyes shut as release broke over her, as the warmth, that bright brilliant light that she had carried inside of herself for all this time, bled through every part of her. It wasn't just her chest, it wasn't just between her legs.

It was everywhere, and it was everything. So all-consuming that she thought it might destroy her.

But in the end, he froze above her and came apart, the masculine sound torn from his lips so perfectly devastating that she could do nothing but revel in the intensity of it, because it matched her own. But afterward… When their breathing had slowed, and their heart rates had returned to normal, he looked at her.

And she felt again like a girl of seventeen who had demanded the impossible. But this time she had gotten it.

And the man was no less angry with her.

CHAPTER SEVEN

EVERETT COULDN'T BREATHE. Not around the tangle of emotion in his chest, and not through the burning in his lungs.

This had been...

It had been indulgent, and it had been as impractical as it got.

And she had been a virgin.

And, God help him, if June knew what he'd done to her granddaughter in this frilly floral bed...

"You don't think you might have wanted to tell me that you were a virgin, Lila?"

"I wasn't a virgin," Lila said, glistening eyes round in the lamplight.

"You were very clearly a virgin."

There was no mistaking that. The way she had tensed up, cried out in pain. How tight she'd been. He wasn't a man who'd had a whole array of experiences, but he knew enough to recognize *that.*

"Have a lot of experience with virgins?"

"No," he said. "But I hurt you. It's not supposed to hurt."

"I'm sorry," she said finally. "It didn't seem relevant. They say that for some women it doesn't hurt, so I thought maybe it wouldn't hurt me. Apparently, I was wrong."

"Are you okay?"

"Yes. Of the two of us, you are the only one surprised by my virginity. I have been very aware of it for the last twenty-four years. Well, no, that's a lie. I've probably only been aware of it since I was about fifteen. But you get the point."

"Why?" he asked. "Why me?"

The anger drained out of him. He was just awed. She had chosen him. It all bled away, that anger. And he wished that he could hold on to it. Grasp it and keep it up against him, because it would protect him.

"It was you because it had to be," she said. "Don't you… Isn't there any unfinished business in your life?"

He thought back. And no. All the business in his life had been firmly finished. His father was dead, and there was no yelling at him. His mother was taken care of. His ex-wife was very much his ex-wife and he had said everything to her that needed to be said, and she to him. And then some.

"No."

"How? How are there not…? Things that you want to… Everett, you're the reason that I'm a virgin."

He froze. The words replayed themselves over and over in his mind. And for some reason, he could think of only one response. "Actually, I think I'm the reason you're not one," he said.

"Okay," she said, forcing a small laugh. "Fair play. But I mean…you were my unfinished business. My… white whale."

He closed his eyes, and his lips twitched. And he didn't know why in the hell he wanted to make a joke now, because he never made jokes. "Are you saying that I'm your Moby—"

"It's too easy," she shouted, sitting up and flinging her hands wide. "I can't even respect that."

"You were the one that said it."

"I was being sincere."

"And I was being funny. First time for everything."

"I'm *always* sincere," she said. "It's one of my greatest flaws."

"While it's not a flaw to say what you mean and feel real things." He thought about his own life, practical and pieced together in perfect ways. His marriage had been messy, and he had resented that, because there was no way to rationalize what was going on between himself and Tonya. If he made her happy he had to disassemble the life that he'd created, and it was the most important thing to him. He couldn't think of another way to take care of her, and she had only been cavalier about it because she didn't know what it was to be left uncared for.

He would never have married if he couldn't take care of his wife's physical needs. Shelter, medical care, food. He would never bring children to the world if he couldn't do it, and the only reason Tonya thought that was something he could stand to care less about was because she didn't know what it was like to exist without those things.

His mother had been strong. A farmer's wife had to be. She'd carried the weight of his father's burdens, and her worries for her son, for herself, on her slender shoulders.

She'd done it all without complaint.

She'd kept the unspoken parts of the vows that were made between a woman like her—dutiful, faithful, traditional—with a man like Everett's father, stubborn, determined, tough.

She'd made dinner with what food there was, every night. There might not always be breakfast beyond coffee, or much lunch to speak of, but his mother could stretch ingredients like no one else. And she'd never said a damn thing about it.

Not when the money was gone. Not when the house was cold because the electricity had been turned off, or they just couldn't afford to heat it.

She'd cared for them both when they were sick, while never taking time off for her own illnesses.

He was convinced that his mother had died of exhaustion, at the end of it all. She'd gone only three years after Everett's father.

He'd sworn to himself he'd never put that burden on a wife.

"It hurts, though," she said. "To be such a big...ball of feeling."

"It can hurt to be a brick wall, too," he said, and he didn't know why, or where it came from. But she was naked, and so was he, and his guard felt a little lower than it ever was.

Anyway, she was Lila Frost, and she was soft and as pretty as ever, and in no way scary.

Except as he let his gaze drift over her soft, pale shoulders, he felt a little bit afraid. Damned if he knew why.

"Well, I'm here," she said. "I can stand beating my head against a brick wall, for a while."

When she reached out and brushed her fingertips against his chest, he realized how lonely he'd been. How long he'd gone without being touched. And how much he missed it. Not just sex, but being around another person.

Practicality didn't seem to always make a space for that. He put his hand over hers. "For a while," he repeated.

"I need an ally, anyway. All these women are going to henpeck me to death when I don't give all of them booth number seven. I could always call them all booth number seven…"

"Yeah, you would just be setting yourself up for a good old-fashioned brawl."

"Definitely don't want any part of that."

"They're all harmless," he said. "Somebody's going to be disappointed. There's no avoiding that. Everybody can't have what they want."

Lila looked incredibly thoughtful. "I guess not. That's…depressing."

"They're just craft booths," he said.

"No," she said. "I mean, yes, I guess. But it's more than that. It's… I guess I can't just smile a lot and make sure that everyone is happy, when they're not going to be happy. Because they want different things. Or they all want the same thing, and there's only one of it. I'm probably going to have to give in and make some lists," she said.

"What made you change your mind on that?"

"Would you believe that the sex was a transformative experience?"

He thought about it. "I'd love to say yes, but no."

She laughed. "I just… Actually, it was kind of this. Us. I can't stay the same forever. And I think I keep trying to. I keep doing everything I can not to disrupt the balance of my life and not to change too much. I kept thinking that happy made it okay. I'm optimistic, and I'm cheerful, and I get my work done. So…I've been functional. And I've never had to confront any of the things that I've failed at in the past. My relationship with my father, my relationship with JJ. Organizing anything. Having an intimate relationship with another person," she said, looking at him meaningfully. "But I think this has clarified some things for me.

"Change isn't always bad," he said. "Change isn't always good, either. Usually, it's kind of a mixed bag."

"Yeah."

He shifted. "I thought that getting married would solidify some things for me. It was part of that practical life that I had laid out for myself. That was the one thing about my parents, Lila. What they had together was real. I figured that if I set up a life that didn't have the burdens of poverty, that my marriage could only be stronger. It wasn't something I was ready for. Wasn't something I was even particularly suited to. I've learned that I'm better alone."

"You didn't love her enough," Lila said softly.

The soft words were like a bullet, cutting straight through to his heart.

"What?"

"She didn't love you enough, either. If she had, she would have stayed. I think about that a lot. Because the way my parents did it… That straight fifty-fifty split, to me that is a lot about the way they saw their marriage in general. I've always thought you had to be willing to give all of yourself, to let go of everything. And the person who loves you would never ask you to do that. But you've gotta go all in, one hundred percent. You can't give fifty percent. That's the kind of thing that leads to you being able to easily take your half right back. Divide your assets, divide your kids."

"Maybe you're right. But I could never give all that to someone else. I didn't have any control growing up. Everything was the way my dad said it had to be. He worked that land like a man possessed, and that didn't make it give us anything that we could hold on to. It was useless. Worthless. Failed us more often than it yielded anything valuable. My mother supported that dream with all of herself. She went hungry, and as a consequence, so did I. I couldn't do that to any woman in my life. To any children I might have. My father never knew what a support system he had in her. He used her until she was broken and I know he didn't mean to do that, but she stood by him and never complained and... I never wanted to build a life like that. One where I took and another person gave and I never even knew it was happening."

"I guess it's complicated," Lila said, sounding sad. "I always want to think that I can figure all this out. But I'm going to find some magic amulet, or something someday, and it will help it all click."

"You really do spend a bit too much time on fairy tales."

"Maybe that's part of the problem. But fairy tales are simple. They punish the bad and reward the good, even when it all seems impossible. People with pure hearts and optimistic minds win in the end."

"Yeah, sadly not any life I recognize works that way."

She looked at him for a long moment, and he could feel a gulf expand between them, in spite of the fact that they were both still naked. "I think it probably is for the best if this just happens once."

He didn't know exactly what had caused that reversal, and he couldn't figure out whether he was relieved or disappointed to hear it.

"Reason being?" he asked, because she was one to fling pushy questions around whenever she felt like it, and he didn't see why he couldn't do the same.

"I think I learned what I needed to."

He didn't like the idea of this being a lesson for her.

"I didn't learn anything."

"Well, maybe I'm not a lesson for you. Maybe I'm just…another experience."

"You have to make everything mean something, Lila?"

"I try. Because otherwise, my father didn't want me, and my mother is too distracted to care about anything but herself. The one person who really loved me is gone, and all I have left is her house. What happened between us years ago was just me being overdramatic and hurting myself. I'd like to think it's all connected. All threads that go together to make the tapestry of a person's life. Intentional and beautiful when you stand far away from it, even if you can't see it up close."

"I think that's optimistic, honey," he said.

"Well, I'm still an optimist. Even if I acknowledge the need to make some lists."

"All right," he said. "I better get dressed and head out."

Once was for the best. He couldn't give her anything. She was the kind of woman who needed promises made to her.

Because if everything she told him about her life was true, then the poor girl needed someone to care. And he just wasn't the right guy.

Lila said nothing. Instead, she tucked herself into bed and watched as he dressed.

"You still going to help me," she said. "Right?"

"Yeah," he said. "June asked me to."

Lila nodded. "Right. Of course."

"I'm not going to let you down, Lila. My word is my word. I don't break it."

Except marriage vows, he supposed. It wasn't death that had broken him and Tonya apart, just his own hard-headedness, and while he didn't regret the end of that marriage, the reality of that—a broken promise that size—seemed to linger between them and call him a liar.

"I believe you," she said.

Everett finished dressing, and the last thing he did was put on his hat. As ridiculous as it seemed, it also felt like the right thing to do to tip it once before walking out of her bedroom.

"See you soon," he said.

"Yeah," Lila said. "See you soon."

CHAPTER EIGHT

LILA HAD SLEPT terribly every night for the past two weeks. Her body was restless, and her heart was sore. As was her hand, since she had been making lists constantly, trying to keep track of everything, and in general be responsible with everything that Grandma June had entrusted to her.

Grandma June hadn't asked her to change, but Grandma June certainly needed her to try her hardest.

Though, none of that was why she hadn't been sleeping well.

The *why* was the same big, dumb cowboy that had been keeping her up for years now.

But she had slept with him.

Well, not *slept* with.

She'd *had sex* with him. And then told him they shouldn't have sex again.

She felt utterly betrayed by herself, and while she knew why she had done it, she was still mad.

The way that he talked about marriage, the way that he talked about love… It wasn't what she believed in. And it wasn't what she was going to end up wanting if the two of them kept on…

She could accept that she had never known him well enough to love him in the past, but the fact of the matter was, she was also a very short distance away from being pushed right into love with Everett now.

And while she was an optimist, she wasn't quite optimistic enough to hope against the words that came out of a man's mouth.

At least she tried to believe that.

There was always that little voice inside of her that said *What if?*

But what if you gave it a try? But what if he could change? What if Dad invites you to spend Christmas there one year? What if, magically, JJ will understand you? And you'll magically be able to understand her... and what if clouds really were cotton candy?

Always.

So it had seemed smart to keep herself away.

Which had resulted in sleeplessness, and now, her sleep was being interrupted by the ringing phone.

And it was still dark outside.

Lila scrambled downstairs and picked up the phone. "Hello?"

"Am I the first?" Lila recognize the thin, elderly voice on the other end of the phone, but she couldn't quite place which of her many visitors it was.

She looked at the clock on the wall and saw that it was 4:30 in the morning.

"I—"

"It's booth day. And I want booth seven."

Technically, it *was* booth day. And this woman was the first to call.

"Yes," Lila said, a bit dizzy. "It is indeed booth day."

"Put number seven down for Ms. Jones."

"You've got it," Lila said.

"Andrea Kim is going to be enraged," she said glee-fully. "Thanks, dear."

And then she hung up the phone.

The only thing that made Lila cheerful later that day, given all of her sleep fog, was the felted mice that she found on her doorstep later, a clear gift from the victor, and one that secretly pleased Lila.

After that, her day was filled with an unpleasant se-ries of phone calls and the tricky situation of assigning booths and answering questions about the particulars of what would be next to each one, and how it should all be spaced.

The two weeks that followed weren't much better, and still, she didn't see Everett.

Her own choice, but she didn't like it all the same.

She tried to focus on planning the event—exactly as Grandma June had done, because she was determined to live up to her high standards.

She'd checked in with Gretchen a couple of times at Burnside Blooms and had been told all was running well. It surprised her how much she didn't miss it.

She had pleasant feelings about the shop, about her rotating coworkers, but it felt like a phase of life she was moving away from, and she wasn't sure what that meant exactly. Only that it…felt like another time and place, and not a home she needed to get back to.

She missed her work, the creative side of it, but plan-ning the Red Sled filled some of that.

Mostly, she was obsessing about Everett, and she hated herself for being such a cliché.

And then one evening, late, the phone rang.

"Hello," a masculine voice came down the line.

"Hi," she said, her heart leaping into her throat. "I

didn't think that you…" She cleared her throat. "What I meant to say was I didn't think you used this line, when you could just as easily make a call to the house."

"Well, I figured I'd give it a try. I was wondering if you wanted to come over tomorrow. We're going to have to start assembly in the barn. And I might need your help."

"You don't need my help," she said.

"I don't have all your charts and lists. I most definitely do need your help."

And if the next morning, when she got ready with all of her charts and graphs and lists, she spent a little bit of extra time fussing with her hair and putting on a bit of makeup, that was just totally normal for working in a barn and doing menial tasks, and had nothing to do with the idea of seeing Everett again for the first time since they'd slept together.

She had never been out to his place, but the instructions he'd given her were easy enough to follow. He really was close to Grandma June's, although fifty paces was quite the exaggeration.

The wide, wrought-iron gate opened with the push of a button. The paved drive led to an expansive house and an even more beautiful equestrian facility that was incredible.

Everett wasn't just successful. He was…rich.

Out in the pastures were some of the most beautiful horses she had ever seen. Tawny gold with shimmering manes and tails—absolutely incredible animals.

For one moment as she sat there clutching the steering wheel in her little Camry, she imagined a life there. With horses, and a beautiful farm and a man whose big hands felt like magic on her skin…

No. She wasn't going there. Once. That was it. Everett didn't want more than sex, and she'd accepted it.

So there.

She knew it.

And maybe if she *knew* it, she would start to *believe* it.

At least, more than she did.

Maybe she could finally stamp out that little bright light inside of her. That was the point of sleeping with him, wasn't it?

Liar. You wanted to sleep with him because you want him. And deep down you always think things are going to turn out.

She gritted her teeth and got out of her car.

"You don't know me," she muttered to herself.

She stopped at the barn, where there was already a light on, and she assumed Everett would be there working already.

She was right.

There he was, halfway up the ladder, a bundle of wood in his hand.

"What's that?" she asked, walking into the gorgeous, gleaming barn made of high-gloss wood that seemed to glow with a honeyed warmth all around her.

"Pieces of the booths," he said, opting to jump down the last three rungs instead of continuing to climb.

And her eyes fixating on the way his muscles in his arms flexed, how thick and fit his thighs were. And, well, his butt. Because his butt was amazing.

"Everett," she began, "this place is amazing. I can't believe that you… You made all this for yourself."

"Well, the contractor did most of this for me," he said, his tone dry.

"You know what I mean," she said. "I remember how hard you worked for Grandma June. I admired that so much. It's funny what sticks with you. I was never going to be college-bound like Keira. I didn't like school enough, plus I wasn't good enough at it to get scholarships like she did. JJ did all this hard physical work. She's fearless. I was better at sitting and doodling, dreaming. But I watched you—I watched you step away from your family work, pour your effort into Grandma June's ranch. It was your own path. I started believing I just had to find my path. Like you did."

His expression was unreadable. "And did you?"

"I do floral arrangements. Bouquets, whole wedding shows."

"Are you going to do anything for this?"

"It wasn't included in the regular list of things. I hadn't considered it."

"I heard that JJ has quite the flower garden going up at the Mathewson place now," Everett said.

She ignored the hurt that lodged in her chest when she thought of her sister.

JJ was growing flowers. That they were so different, but were connected by that love of nature and things that grew. It made her wonder why she couldn't bring herself to try and bridge the hurt that seemed to grow wider between them by the year.

It wasn't even because of a fight. There was no spoken anger at all.

When their parents had split, at first it had been a wonderful thing to see her sister at Grandma June's.

But as the years passed, JJ seemed to dig into her toughness, to an attitude that if she just put her head down she could move any mountain.

Lila had… She had felt so many things, and she had begun to annoy her sister, she knew it.

JJ and Keira seemed to have a lot more to say to each other in general.

And wide-eyed Bella seemed overwhelmed by Lila more than anything.

Then Bella had left and never come back.

Keira had fallen in love with Remy West and had been consumed with him in her pursuit of a better future, and later in her heartbreak. She and JJ were just still there, and with none of the chaos, none of the noise, and no one else around them to be a buffer, it had become clear that the two of them didn't have much to say to each other.

It was always on the tip of Lila's tongue to ask, though.

How things were with their dad. Their dad, who clearly loved JJ, and didn't love her. Her dad, who didn't even speak to her at the funeral.

God forbid he look her in the eye then, when he'd been breathing the same air as his ex-wife.

The ex-wife he hadn't been able to be in the same room with, he had claimed years ago. Which was why they'd split the family. Split the sisters. Treated them like a set of salt and pepper shakers. One to one house, one to another. Easy as that.

She wondered if it would ever quit hurting.

And if JJ hurt the way she did.

Always on the tip of her tongue to ask if she wanted to come see Mom, because JJ would probably be a steadying influence on her, and that was something that Lila could never be.

Lila had chosen to try to be a sunbeam in a dark space, and she had learned that sometimes the darkness could just swallow the light whole. No matter how hard you tried to shine.

She knew JJ didn't understand that. She tried to be an optimist because everything around her was so grim. JJ just found her annoying.

"Think about doing the flowers. And in the meantime," he said, taking the pile of lumber over to the corner, "you can help by crawling up there and ferreting out the scarecrows."

Lila grimaced. "That sounds like nothing I want to do."

"You don't like scarecrows?"

Creepy vacant faces. "I admit I'm not overly fond of them, no."

"Are you a bird, Lila?" he asked.

He might be teasing her and that made her stomach feel strange. She resented him for that.

She frowned at him. "No. I'm not a bird."

"Are you sure?" he asked. "It's typically birds that have an aversion to scarecrows."

She tossed her hair back behind her shoulder and did her best to look regal. "I have more of a rodent energy."

He stared at her, his face totally flat. "That's the most ridiculous thing I've ever heard."

"It's true," she countered. "Vibrant, cheerful, easily spooked."

"You are *not* easily spooked."

"I am," she said, keeping her expression serious.

He moved in her direction, his eyes blazing with heat, and she froze, all the air drawing itself out of her body. He stopped when he was less than a foot from her, and she could feel the heat radiating off his body. Could feel it echoing inside of her in a scorching wave.

She wanted him.

She didn't want to stand here having an inane conversation with him about flowers or her energy. She wanted to tear his shirt off of his body and get a good look at those muscles again. Feel his heat and hardness on top of her, surging inside of her.

The idea made her ache between her thighs. Made her clench her teeth.

"See," he said. "You're steady as a rock, girl."

"I'm not afraid of *you*, Everett McCall," she said. "I'm afraid of *scarecrows*."

And you. Down to my soul. But more myself than you, and the things I could let myself feel.

But she didn't say it. A rare win for her self-control.

She went up to the ladder and regarded it before starting her ascent. "It better hold me," she shouted down.

"It just held me," he said, as if that put paid to her ridiculous fear.

"Yes, but you're not taking into account the weight of my emotional issues," she called back.

She had meant it as a joke, but in light of her recent ruminations, it didn't feel all that funny. She did occasionally feel swollen with her emotional issues.

Like now.

"Again," he said. "It just held me."

Now she really did want to jump down off the ladder, and she wanted to ask him about all of those emotional issues. Wanted to pull her own out and compare and have him…

Understand her.

She wanted someone to understand her. And who better than this man? This man who had seen her naked and touched her body. Been inside of her.

"Get a grip, Lila," she muttered as she reached the top of the ladder and catapulted herself over the top and into the loft, landing inelegantly on her knees. It was tall enough for her to stand up there, but she imagined that Everett would have to bend slightly.

"Okay," she shouted. "What am I looking for?"

There was a stack of lumber that she assumed was the disassembled booths, and beyond them, in the corners, which were lower, there were other things.

"Are there mice up here?"

"You have a rodent energy," he called up. "Commune with them."

"I do not want to commune with *actual* rodents. I only like rodents that are ceramic, felt or knit."

"I imagine there's a full spectrum of mice up there."

She huffed and crept toward a covered pile of something in the back. She breathed an intense sigh of relief when she removed the cover and found no creepy crawlies of any kind, but did find a stack of large raffia scarecrows.

"These are huge," she said.

"They go out front."

"They're not that scary," she said, looking down at their smiling faces.

"June made them," he said.

Lila stared at them and blinked. Okay, maybe she was never going to be a huge fan of scarecrows, but knowing that Grandma June had made them made her pause for a moment, letting her fingertips drift over the material.

She had always known that Grandma June liked to make things. Pies, blankets, quilts. Seeing this kind of handiwork made her feel connected to her. The way that the garden did. The way that the house did.

Grandma June was part of her. More than her own mother ever would be.

She felt angry sometimes, at the way her mother had lived her life. The way that she had cut everyone out of it because of her failed marriage. As if that one heartbreak had destroyed her on such a deep level she had refused to allow anyone to matter to her ever again.

Her father was the same.

But Lila's mother had Grandma June, and Grandma June would have been there for her, Lila knew it.

She was there for you. That's what matters.

"You okay?" Everett's voice came from much closer this time, and she hadn't realized he had come up behind her.

"I'm fine," she said. "It's just… It's been months now, but sometimes that she's gone takes my breath away. I know that we were at the funeral, I know that we said our goodbyes. But it doesn't feel like it."

He reached over and put his hand over hers. It was big and warm, calloused and reassuring in ways that she didn't want to ponder too deeply. She looked at his hand, and then up at his face. And she just…didn't feel alone.

Even dealing with the realization, harsh and stark, that Grandma June was gone, she felt warmth. Deep in her heart. Comfort.

A sense that she was there, in her heart at least, if not beside her, where she could see her.

"Thank you," she said, pulling her hand out from beneath his, because taking that kind of comfort from Everett was only dangerous.

"I loved her, too," he said. "She believed in me, like

you said she believed in you. It's amazing what belief from one person can do for you. Just the one."

Lila nodded. "It's true. And I think I got my creativity from her. I think if my mother had just learned to knit or something, she might have gotten over some of her bitterness."

"You think that knitting cures bitterness?" His tone was incredulous.

"I think learning to create changes something in your soul," she said. "No matter what it is. When you can bring beauty into the world, it forces you to appreciate what's beautiful in the world. When I was little, Grandma June taught me to knit, and I learned something from that. That if I could add a little something to this planet, even if it wasn't strictly useful, I at least felt like I was more than just…me. I can leave little things I've made wherever I go, and that makes me feel connected. To the world." She moved her fingertips over the scarecrow. "And now to Grandma June."

"Working the land is what makes me feel connected to it," he said. He moved away from her, going over to the wood that was stacked up against the wall and grabbing another bundle. "You can't stay disconnected when the dirt has some of your blood in it."

"I don't imagine so."

"It's the one thing that makes me understand my old man," he said. "The connection to the land. I can almost sympathize with him. For the way that he clung to it until it killed him."

He said that as firmly and practically as he did everything else. Something about that, those words of grief so flatly and simply spoken, made them even more painful.

She could tell it wasn't something he'd talked about

before, somehow. And the honor of being the one he did talk to made her glow inside, even as she hurt for him.

"Did it?" she asked, her chest hollowing out with a pang of horror. "Did it kill him?"

"Cancer killed him. But it didn't have to. If he'd been able to take care of anything other than that piece of ground that he poured his whole life into, he might have gone to the doctor and spared himself. He ignored it until *treatable* became *a death sentence*. But you know, it was the land in the end. Because he could never have done anything that might jeopardize that land. He had sacrificed our happiness. Our health, our safety, for that land. And so, nothing could ever come before it. Sometimes I wonder if I'm not that different."

"Why? Just because this is important to you? It isn't the same. It's been productive, and it's been profitable."

"And it was more important than my marriage."

"Are you…?" It hurt Lila to even say it. And it shouldn't hurt. "Are you still in love with her?"

It did need to be asked. Because, after all, Everett hadn't been with a woman other than her in the last two years, and he could give any reason he wanted, but she had to wonder if it actually had to do with feelings for his ex.

He shook his head. "Not at all. But you know that stubbornness is in my blood. That feeling that giving up is its own kind of sin."

"So is holding on when you're meant to let go. You can see that. And what happened with your dad. With his farm."

"I suppose that's true enough," he said.

They didn't talk more after that. He gathered the wood and went back down the ladder, and she took hold of the scarecrows, making her way down after him. The scarecrows were slightly flat from being stored for a year, but since they'd been under a tarp, and Everett's barn was clean and well-maintained, they were not really the worse for wear.

As scarecrows went.

There were other small pieces of decor in the loft, and while Everett set about assembling booths, Lila brought all of those down. Then they got out her seating chart and began to figure out where everything was supposed to be arranged.

Each booth had about six pieces involved in assembly, and Everett was quick. And watching him swing a hammer was…

Well, it was way too interesting. It shouldn't be. She should know better. And she didn't seem to.

Woe is her.

The way his muscles moved, the flex in his forearms, the strength in those broad shoulders…

"Are you going to keep on staring a hole through my back?"

She scrunched her face. "I'm not staring at *you*. I'm admiring the *scárecrows*."

"Well," he said, letting it go as he took a step back, "there it is. The infamous booth seven."

Lila could not see a difference between this booth and any of the other booths.

"It's just…where it goes?" It was at the center of the back of the barn, so she imagined when you walked in it was one of the first things you saw.

"Yes, prized for its visibility, proximity to refreshments and where it lands on the shopping route. Because people don't want to buy too early into their walk-through, but if you're at the end it might be too late."

"Very clever," Lila said. "Well, these little guys are going to be here this year." She stuck her hand into her bag and retrieved the mice, setting them on the booth.

"You had mice in your bag the whole time," he said, looking slightly stunned.

She blinked. "They were a gift."

"Were they a bribe?"

She affected an expression of mock outrage. "I'll have you know, I did not take them as a bribe, and Ms. Jones happened to call the earliest, and she gave them to me as a thank-you."

"Seem suspicious. I think you might be tainted."

"I'm *not* tainted," Lila said, sniffing. "I am the soul of integrity."

She smiled and looked up at him. And there was something about the way their eyes held in that moment of shared humor, the way that the conversation had flowed along and built to this, and now seemed to wrap itself around them.

From mice to grief and back again.

The inane and the essential. And now…a sense of companionable friendship and…well, desire.

Because she knew exactly what those hands of Everett McCall's could do. And she wished very much that they would do it again. Everything was still for a moment, a perfect beat where everything was swollen with possibility, but nothing had happened.

And then she took a breath, and it tore the air, and Everett closed the distance between them, and in that split second before their lips touched, Lila already knew that she was lost.

CHAPTER NINE

SHE'D SAID THIS wouldn't happen again, and he had taken her at her word. Hell, he needed to. The last thing that he wanted to do was spend even one night pining over Lila Frost.

He had woken up hard and aching more times than he could count over the past month, and he had gritted his teeth through it every time. Hadn't allowed himself to find pleasure at his own hand, because it was a damn travesty that this woman—who had once been a girl he'd known—had begun to obsess him in a way that he couldn't really afford.

But she was here. And she had kissed him. And maybe, just maybe, another taste would be okay. Maybe this was actually what they needed. What they both needed.

Just a little. Just for now.

His body was all in. For a man who prized control it was a strange experience. He wasn't sure he could stop now if he wanted to. She had done something to him.

Reached inside of him and rearranged things that had been carefully placed over the course of his life.

And he didn't understand how she had the power to do that.

But it didn't matter. Not now. Because her lips were soft, and so was the rest of her body. Because she fit perfectly in his arms, and she melted into him like she wanted to stay forever, and it was what he wanted, too.

But forever was hell. Forever was being tethered to land that couldn't give you a damn thing. A commitment to misery and, even worse, to death.

Forever could never be.

Because eventually they would just end up holding each other back. And that wasn't feeling sorry for himself, it was just the damn truth.

And if they didn't hold you back, then you held them back.

He had lived it. The way that farm had been an albatross around his father's neck, and the way it had dragged them all down right along with it. The way that that kind of deep sentimentality could ruin a person.

And not just one person—everyone who touched him.

That, at least, Everett had got right.

It had been the better thing, the more practical thing, to let go of a relationship that didn't work. That didn't fit with the life he had chosen.

Whatever he wanted to do, he would do it. But he would never, ever bring somebody else down with him if he was going to make a mistake.

Not anyone. Certainly not Lila.

Forever. Not for them. Not for *him*.

But for now…

She moaned softly against his mouth, and his arousal pushed him right over the edge.

He didn't do this. Ever. He didn't do impassioned encounters…anywhere. He hadn't been a hookup guy before he'd been married, and he hadn't pursued any since.

Everything he'd done, he'd done with measured control, and in the end, that was why his failed marriage offended him so much. Not because he had loved Tonya so passionately. But because he had chosen that relationship so carefully.

This was something else entirely. Kissing Lila was like that glimpse of sun breaking through the autumn leaves. Bright. Vibrant. Igniting everything it touched with a golden glow that shimmered all around him.

The closest thing to magic that he had ever witnessed, and the kind of deep, hard-to-define beauty that a man like him would usually say was frivolous. The kind of thing a truly practical soul didn't need on this side of eternity.

But just now he wanted to bathe in it. Submerge himself completely. A baptism in gold, red and fire that was Lila Frost, who was anything but her name. She was warm and sweet and inviting a rest for his soul.

A soul he hadn't realized was weary until she had touched him.

As a man full of practicality, a man who valued the things that he could touch, the things that he could see, he would have said that sex served a physical need. Like eating or drinking. But this was reaching somewhere it never had before. And she was reaching parts of him that he had long denied. He moved his hands down, cupping her denim-clad ass, then gripped her thighs and lifted her so that her legs were wrapped around his waist and he could carry her over to the nearest surface.

Booth number seven.

He set her down on top of it and stripped her top up over her head.

She had made him give her a strip show during their first time together, and now she owed him.

He stripped her bra off, revealing pale skin, round, lush breasts and rosy nipples that made his mouth water.

Then he moved down to the button on her jeans, undoing it, taking the zipper right along, too. He worked the jeans down her hips, grabbing the waistband of her panties along with them, and cast them onto the floor.

Her cheeks went fiery, a blush that spread down her neck.

"What?" he asked. "Are you embarrassed?"

"A bit," she said, locking her knees together primly.

He chuckled and spread them apart, stepping between them and consuming her mouth. By the time he was through tasting her, she was panting again. He put his hand between her thighs and stroked her, finding that however embarrassed she was, she was also ready for him. As into this as he was.

"Still embarrassed?" he murmured against her mouth.

"No," she panted.

He stroked her deep, until she went rigid and let out a harsh gasp, climaxing hard around his fingers.

She tore at his shirt, stripped it up over his head, taking his hat along with it. They both went down to the floor, and he unbuckled his jeans, freeing himself as he reached into his back pocket to take hold of his wallet and hunt for protection.

"Do you just carry that with you?" she asked.

"No." And then he laughed. "It was…just in case. Just for us. I suppose it was the first truly optimistic thing I've ever done."

"Apparently," she said, taking the packet from his hand, "it was realism."

She tore the package open and protected them both with shaking hands. His breath hissed through his teeth as that delicate hand took hold of him and squeezed gently.

He pressed himself to the entrance of her body and flexed his hips forward, entering her slowly, achingly so. What he wanted to do was take her hard and fast and obliterate all the strange, aching sensations that had spread from his chest down to his bones. But he tortured himself.

And he took it slow.

Let himself feel.

It was more than just pleasure, more than just the building climax that he thought might break him apart. It was something else. Something that surged through him like an electrical shock, made his teeth hurt. Made his chest hurt. It was something he didn't have a name for. And it didn't fit anywhere into the plan that he'd made for his life, or into one of the acknowledged practical needs that he possessed.

Because it wasn't something that he could easily define, wasn't something he could hold in his hands.

Wasn't something he could see with his own eyes.

It simply was.

Stretching from the top of his head, through his fingertips, and down to his toes. As inevitable and undeniable as the seasons changing.

Which didn't feel right or fair, because how could something he couldn't grasp with all his senses possibly be this real?

But it was.

And it consumed him.

Then, he was just lost. In the bone-deep pleasure of being inside of her, in the rhythm of claiming her.

Each and every thrust, each and every gasp of pleasure on her lips.

She grabbed hold of his shoulders, fingernails digging into his skin, and she cried out her pleasure in his ear. And then, he let go. Let himself fall over the edge into nothing.

Into everything.

They clung to each other, and she kissed the edge of his mouth. "Okay. Maybe just the twice."

"Hell, no," he said, gathering her up and setting her down on her feet in front of him. "Until the season ends. But as long as you're here. You're mine."

He didn't know what possessed him to say those things, because a practical man certainly wouldn't have ever uttered those words.

Nothing wrong with it. It's concrete. And what's concrete is real.

True enough.

Yes, that was real. But he could have her until she left. That they could be together without that unraveling, that degradation of what had once been good.

"Okay," she said. "Twist my arm."

She looked up at him with those luminous eyes, and he traced a line along her jaw. "You're beautiful, Lila."

"Thank you," she said.

And he realized that she accepted that praise with the kind of ease that a lot of women didn't. But then… why would Lila ever doubt her beauty? She had always been pretty, and the fact was, waiting to be with a man had very much been her choice.

Lila had plenty of insecurities, but her beauty wasn't one of them.

So he looked around the barn, and then he looked

back at Lila, and he pressed his forehead against hers. "You've done a good job on this. And June must've known that you were the right one to do it."

Her eyes went bright then, a sheen of moisture clouding them. "Thank you," she said, this time more softly.

"You should do flowers," he said. "If you have time. As great as the scarecrows are, and as much as keeping the tradition alive matters, she gave *you* this job. So don't be afraid to be you."

Much like being the one he confided in, this…being someone he believed in, felt like glowing, too.

She wanted to do this, to find a way to make it hers. But she'd been afraid. Like it might not be right or good enough. Not what she'd been left behind in the binder.

She gave you the job. Do it your way.

"Okay," she said, her voice scratchy. "I guess I better talk to JJ."

And when she moved away from him and began to collect her clothes, he felt like a piece of him had gone with her.

And he had no idea what in hell to make of that.

CHAPTER TEN

LILA WAS IMPETUOUS, and she was headstrong, and she often led with her mouth. As a result, she often found herself in situations she hadn't meant to get herself into.

But never had any of those situations landed her in a temporary affair with a smoking-hot cowboy. And they had also never landed her on the front doorstep of her sister's new house.

The sister that she had been avoiding since she'd come back to town.

Because there were just so many things that she always wanted to say to JJ, and they stuck in her throat, and stuck in her brain, and stuck in her heart, and made her feel like a mess. But here she was. Hoping to get flowers, which, as the Frost sisters went, were something of an olive branch.

She knocked and held her breath and waited.

She heard the clamor of feet, squealing and excited voices, before the door opened.

She looked down and saw two little blonde pixie-like girls, whispering and laughing as though they shared secrets. And somehow, Lila was thrown right back to when she and JJ had been little.

To when they had huddled together like that, conspiring. To simpler times when their lives, and themselves, hadn't been divided down the middle.

"Hi," she said.

"Hi," the tallest one said.

"I'm Lila. I'm—I'm JJ's sister. I'm here to see her. Is she here?"

"JJ!" The littlest one ran off, her bare feet slapping the hardwood.

The oldest one regarded her with an intense amount of seriousness. "I'm Ellie," she said.

"Very nice to meet you," Lila said, matching her seriousness.

"You're JJ's sister that's staying in Grandma June's house now."

"I am," Lila said.

Her face looked mutinous. "But you haven't come to see JJ."

Lila felt thoroughly chastised by this very small person, and she wasn't sure that she liked it at all.

"You must be… Cade's daughters," she said.

"And JJ's," Ellie said, sticking her chin out, defiant.

Lila's heart crumpled. JJ had slotted into this family, clicked into place, been the missing piece that they needed.

The whole family.

Lila would never find that.

Lila would never find that because…

Well, she was brewing powerful feelings for a man who wanted nothing like it, and she just wouldn't ever…

"Lila?"

She looked up and saw JJ standing there, so very firmly her, with her brown hair tied back in a low ponytail, her simple, serviceable outfit something that could easily be called plain, but that gave her that kind of effortless, tomboyish beauty that made it look like she hadn't even tried.

Possibly because she hadn't. Lila knew that.

JJ had a spark about her, a kind of bewitching charisma that she didn't think her sister had any idea she possessed. It was in her fierceness. That layer of toughness that she wore like armor.

It was still there, but there was something softer there now, too, and it made her that much more compelling.

"I wasn't expecting you."

"I know," Lila said. "I—I figured I would ambush you. So that you wouldn't find an excuse to be busy."

"What makes you say that?"

"Well, we haven't seen each other. I mean, I haven't come here. But you... You haven't come to see me, either."

"I know," JJ said, keeping her voice measured. "But... I had the opportunity to be in the house when you weren't here. And I think... I think Grandma June has a lesson for all of us. And I don't think it would do you any favors if I jumped in the middle of it. I am, however, happy enough to have you jump into my life. But I didn't feel it was my place to intrude on you. Not right now."

That made Lila's eyes feel scratchy. And it created a whole buildup of words she didn't know how to untangle. It was disconcerting, for a woman who was used to having to hold words back, to find herself speechless. Which seemed to be what often happened with her sister.

But she thought of Grandma June's letter. And of her time with Everett. And all those affirming words he'd said to her yesterday in the barn, when they'd still been close together, skin to skin, and everything in her had still burned as if he was still inside of her.

"I—I guess... Yes. That's true. She sent us four different letters. And she didn't have us going to the house all together. There must be a reason for that."

"I didn't stay away to hurt you," JJ said.

It only hit Lila then that part of her was hurt and felt like while JJ might not have done it on purpose, she might not have thought of her at all and might have hurt her accidentally.

"I know," she said.

"This is the house. And those are the girls. Lora and Ellie."

They waved. They had that look about them, particularly the younger, of bedraggled fairies. And the idea of JJ parenting such soft, feminine things seemed...

Well, perfect.

If Grandma June had intended to change JJ, to provide some missing piece for her, then she'd certainly done it.

More than.

Because she had *love*.

She had Cade. Lila ignored the burning in her chest that might have easily been labeled as jealousy.

"I don't want to take up a lot of your time," she said. "I mean, I want to catch up. I do."

JJ quirked a smile at her that seemed to say, *do you?*

Lila ignored it.

"I—I wanted to know if I could buy some flowers from you," she asked.

"Flowers?"

"Everett mentioned it. Everett McCall." She tried to suppress the blush she could feel mounting in her face. "He's working on organizing the Red Sled Holiday Bazaar with me."

JJ nodded. "I took over the garden here on the property. All the seasonal flowers are blooming right now."

"I want them. All of them. I want to arrange them for the bazaar. Put them up all over the place." She hesitated. "If you're here, you left Dad's business, then."

JJ's smile turned rueful. "Uh. Yes."

"And…are you going to do it here as a business?"

"It's all I know. So I was mostly planning on continuing with it, yes."

"Well, I'd love to advertise for you. And then people will know that they can get their flowers from you. And that you'll do their landscape."

"That's nice of you." It was such a cautious thing to say. Too cautious for two sisters, but Lila didn't know how to shift it. How to fix it.

"Well, it'll be good. Because I know how to arrange them, and you're good at growing them… And it'll be…a fantastic way to showcase them."

"Let me take you out to the garden."

It was a truck ride away to the fenced-in flower garden on the property. The Mathewson Ranch was a huge spread, which stood to reason. It was worked by Cade and his five brothers, and she could easily see how a place like this, with so many wild acres, needed all hands on deck.

The garden area seemed manicured when compared to the rest of the wild around them. The sharp green mountains blanketed with pine, the uneven fields with green grass and intermittent patches of weeds with spiky purple flowers.

In the garden, white gladioli with deep purple centers, begonias in sherbet hues and cheerful yellow aconite were planted in regimented rows behind a deer-proof fence. It spoke so very much of her sister. Wild by nature but tamed into something deeply practical by necessity.

"These are beautiful," Lila said.

"They'll be perfect for the holiday bazaar," JJ said.

"They will."

And, as always, there were about a thousand more words that she wanted to say. Something that she wanted to fix.

But she couldn't figure it out.

She couldn't find the way.

"I'll take them all."

JJ grinned. "Okay."

"For money, obviously. I have cash for the event."

"I wasn't going to give them to you for free, don't worry."

Lila laughed. "I wouldn't expect you to."

"Hey, did you—did you find anything on the table when you got to Grandma June's?"

Lila blinked. "I... No."

"Oh. Okay."

"Why? Did you leave me something?"

"It's not important."

But Lila sensed that it was. She just wasn't sure if she could, or should, push her sister for more info.

They worked in companionable silence, and even though Lila wished that she could make it more, it felt good to work with her sister. She was glad that even if she and JJ couldn't find a way to blend their lives, they could blend their talents this way.

At least, she tried to be happy about that.

But when she drove away from her sister's house, she just felt a bit achy and raw.

And she couldn't for the life of her figure out why sometimes it was so difficult for two people who wanted to find a way to close a rift to be able to find the materials to bridge that gap.

But she didn't have answers.

No answers, but a car full of flowers.

And tonight, she was going to spend the night at Everett's.

So there was that.

CHAPTER ELEVEN

IT HAD BEEN years since Everett McCall had woken up with a woman tangled around him in bed. But here he was, wrapped up in Lila Frost, whose soft, naked body was a hell of a lot more effective at waking him up than his early-morning chores ever could be.

It was late. The sunlight was already beginning to turn the sky around them gray, and that he was still in bed when pale light was beginning to signal dawn spoke more volumes about how significant and strange the morning was than anything else ever could have.

Everett McCall was up before the sun. Always. Nothing was more important than this ranch, and even with employees helping to manage the spread, he considered it a necessity he be out there working, too.

But the sky kept getting lighter, and he kept lying there.

He only stirred when delicate fingertips began to trace shapes over his abs.

"Good morning." Her voice was sleepy and somehow that was incredibly erotic.

"Good morning."

"I've never woken up with anyone before," she said, burrowing more tightly against him. "This is weird."

"Well," he said, "that is quite the greeting."

"Seriously, though," she sighed. "This place is amazing. And your bed is amazing. It's been wonderful to stay in the farmhouse and have all those memories, but I could ignore a lumpy mattress a lot better when I was fourteen than I can now."

"Was that mattress lumpy?" he asked, feeling strangely buoyant and cheerful. He almost didn't recognize himself. "I didn't notice."

"Well, I didn't notice that night. But I've noticed it every night since. When I struggled to sleep. Without you."

Those words hit him funny. He didn't want Lila struggling to sleep just because he wasn't there.

In another month or so, he wouldn't be there. And she wouldn't be here.

That shouldn't make a strange arrow of pain lance through his chest. But it did.

"Well, in a bed that size you wouldn't have slept better with me in it," he said, deciding to sidestep with something light, which he typically didn't do, but he always wanted to with her.

He didn't want to give out heavy, practical answers that might dim the smile from her face, and he couldn't remember when in hell he last cared about something like that.

"But it's very, very hard to sleep," she said, scrabbling over his body and flinging her thigh over his waist, sitting on him, looking down at him.

And wasn't that a picture.

Lila Frost naked with that fiery, autumn hair all around her shoulders and her eyes gleaming bright.

The way she was sitting brought her hair and arms down to obscure her breasts, and that tempting triangle between her thighs. And there was something even more luxurious about her when she was being a tease.

"It's really hard to sleep when you want a man to touch you, and he's not there to do it."

"Yeah, it's hard to sleep when you want a woman the same way." He reached up and curled his fingers around the back of her neck, drawing her down and kissing her hungrily.

He did not have time to indulge in this with her. He needed to get out and get to work. But she was here, and she was naked, and he was desperate.

He had intended to make it quick, but with Lila it could never be quick.

He had gotten lost in her. Her colors and textures and flavors. And by the time he was exhausted and ready to fall asleep again, the sun was well and truly in the sky.

Lila extricated herself from his hold and walked into the bathroom. He kept watch the whole way, entranced by her curves. While he was propped up, he reached over to the nightstand and grabbed his phone.

He had eight missed calls.

"Shit," he muttered, getting out of bed and checking his voice mail.

It was from his foreman, Richard.

One of the horses had foundered and was down in the field.

The vet was there.

They couldn't get her to stand up.

He bit off a curse and dressed quickly.

"What's going on?"

"I wasn't there when I should have been, and there's an emergency. I have to go."

"Can I go with you?" Lila sprang into action. "What's happening?"

"One of my horses is sick."

"I want to go with you."

"Dammit, Lila," he said, complicated emotion rising up inside of him and building behind his teeth. He clenched his jaw, clenched his fist, and tried to breathe through it. "I was here, and I should have been out there. I have responsibilities, and sex with you isn't one of them. I let myself get distracted, and I can't do it again." He shook his head. "You should just go home."

She looked wounded, drawing back into herself, covering her breasts with her arms, as if that would shield her. As if it would mean he hadn't seen her naked.

But he had.

And he had let it distract him.

He had let it take his focus away from this thing that was the most important.

But none of his justifications felt right. He just felt angry, and he couldn't place why that was exactly. So he kept his excuses right there, because they gave him something to hold on to.

And he was a man who needed something to hold on to.

"I'll see you later."

"Okay," she said, her voice small. "Everett, call me and let me know how the horse is."

He couldn't stay mad, not really. She actually cared. That wasn't something he could fault her for.

"I will."

But then he walked out the door and left her standing there, pushing his guilt off to the side.

He had responsibilities.

And Lila Frost wasn't one of them.

CHAPTER TWELVE

LILA WORKED ON flower arrangements until her fingers were raw.

She had knotted and twisted and cut ribbon and fussed with various shapes until her knuckles ached. Until she had split the skin on a couple of them.

Until she was covered with unpleasant green fuzz from foam blocks that she had stuck some of the blooms in. She tried to do it until her eyes hurt, until they were gritty from staring at the flowers. Instead of gritty over a lack of sleep from last night, and a whole lot of crying later in the morning.

It was silly. He was upset, and he had to handle things the way that he wanted to. And, really, there was no point involving her in his life.

It was one thing to have her working on the Red Sled Holiday Bazaar, which was temporary. Like what they had between them. It all worked and it all fit.

But he wouldn't want her on hand to deal with a sick horse.

That was part of his real life. She got that. She wasn't going to be immature about it. Or… Lila about it.

She wasn't going to run back to his house and yell at him for hurting her feelings or stamp her feet and try to make him see her point of view.

She was going to focus on this.

The flowers were beautiful, so there was that. And she had cleared out the entire fridge so that there was a place to keep them cold.

But now she was in the sitting room, at loose ends, with throbbing hands and a wounded heart. If Grandma June had been here she would have told her. Oh, not everything. Not the part about sleeping with him. The thought horrified her.

"You wouldn't approve," Lila said, not sure why she felt compelled to speak directly to her grandmother.

She hadn't, not since arriving in the house.

The house had felt different when she had arrived, and she attributed that to the lack of Grandma June. Feeling that lack, it didn't seem like there was any point or purpose in addressing her. But now... Well, she didn't have anyone else to talk to.

"You wouldn't approve of me giving my virginity to that man in the bed upstairs. I know you were old-fashioned like that. You would have told me you were practical." She smiled, a small, wistful smile.

What happens when your book runs out of battery, Lila?

I charge it.

Call me old-fashioned, but a book that needs to plug in doesn't seem practical to me.

"Everett always tells me how practical he is, too. But I know that I'm not supposed to get involved with him and still... Everything about him breaks my heart. I don't know what I'm supposed to do about it. I don't know how I'm supposed to stop myself from having feelings."

I'm heartbroken. I'll never be able to show my face in town again.

Lila Pauline, no one else saw you talking to him. No one else knows.

I know! But I know! And I feel like I might die. What if I did the wrong thing? I mean, he rejected me. But I couldn't let him marry someone else without telling him.

You could have. But that's not the choice you made. Maybe you did make the wrong choice, honey, but that's not a bad thing. It's how you learn.

I've learned that I'm destined to be alone!

"You told me to be okay with doubting myself. Back then and in your letter. And... I think you're the only person who ever knew how much I do. Everyone thinks the way that I move through life, like a bull in a china shop, means that I'm confident...but I question everything. And I just...try to use my smile as a Band-Aid. But he won't let me. He wouldn't let me be there for him today, and I don't know what to do."

You're going to have to do things you don't like. You can't wish all the bad or hard away.

She wanted to, though. *Dammit*, she wanted to.

"What am I supposed to do? Just...feel *bad*?"

She didn't want to do that, either.

She got up and wrapped her arms around her midsection. Suddenly chilled. It felt like there was a window open somewhere. She followed the draft into the kitchen and saw that the curtains over the sink were wafting in the late-evening breeze.

She frowned and walked over to the window, leaning over the sink and closing it resolutely, the wind fighting back and giving a final great gust as she shut it firmly. That last gasp of outdoor air kicked up some papers in the kitchen, sending her seating map and vendor list swirling to the floor.

Lila made an exasperated sound and ducked down to the scarred floor. Then she saw a small, folded piece of paper lying there near the edge of the wall, and she paused. That hadn't been in her pile.

She crawled forward and unfolded it, her heart slamming into her breastbone when she saw her name written across the top.

Lila,

In some ways I'm sorry my summer has ended, but I'm happy for your fall to begin. Grandma June knew what she was doing when she asked us to stay here. Keira and Remy found each other again. I found Cade. And Lora and Ellie.

I found some healing.

I've been hurting for a long time over the way Mom left me. Seeing my hurt reflected in those two little girls gave me a lot to think about. It gave me some peace.

Whatever happened between Mom and Dad, it wasn't our fault. And I'm tired of letting their choices come between us.

When Grandma June's letter makes sense to you, come and see me.

Love,
JJ

Lila's heart felt cracked and sore. She moved her fingers over her sister's resolute penmanship and fought back tears. No wonder JJ had seemed expectant when she'd gone to see her about the flowers. She'd left a letter.

But Lila hadn't found it until just now.

It's wasn't our fault.

I'm tired of letting their choices come between us.

She did feel that. She'd held on to it. An unfair resentment for her own sister because she'd imagined their father loved her best. But JJ hadn't felt any better about their mom taking Lila. And all that resentment was unearned. Directed at a sister who would have been there for her if Lila hadn't let their parents' games make her bitter.

She'd been so convinced of her own optimism and cheer. Of her brightness. And she'd missed the glaring darkness down inside of herself. How had she missed it?

Because you didn't want to see it. You wanted to blame other people.

The revelation made her face hot, made her ears pulse. It was her fault, too. It always had been.

There was a knock on the door.

Her head popped up, and she looked around. But if she was waiting for an answer from Grandma June, it wasn't going to come. So she stood, and she made her way to the door. She knew it was Everett before she opened it.

"Is everything okay?" she asked.

She wasn't going to waste her time being angry at him. It all kind of evaporated, anyway.

They were both carrying the weight of their emotional issues, after all.

Her own heart was exceptionally heavy. Her own shortsightedness, her own selfishness when it came to JJ, had nearly taken her breath away.

But Everett was here.

And suddenly her whole chest was a mix of good and bad, and she had no idea what to do with that.

"She's all right," he said. He came in, and she couldn't help but notice how haggard his expression looked.

He pushed past her and into the farmhouse, and she watched as a sense of relief seemed to roll over him.

She touched her hand to the wood panel on the wall, and said thank you, even though it was a little bit silly.

"Everett—"

"I don't want to talk," he said.

And he pulled her up against his body, wrapping his arm around her waist and claiming her mouth and a kiss.

It was hard and dark and desperate. It was full of a dark intensity that rolled over them both like a wave. And she didn't know if there was enough sunlight in the world to light it up. Didn't know if she could.

But he needed her.

And somehow, in that moment, she thought that maybe Grandma June had known that this would be one of the things she'd find difficult.

She had been thinking of Everett and her relationship with him in terms of what he could do for her. The ways in which he could help her put to rest her long-held feelings for him, the way that he could help her move on and be a normal woman, rather than a twenty-four-year-old virgin who couldn't seem to get an old crush out of her head.

But this wasn't about her. Or an old crush.

It was about whatever had grown between them over the past weeks. It was about what Everett needed.

Whatever it was that had caused him to choose a

ranch over a marriage. Whatever it was that had created a man so stalwart and rock-hard that he had married a woman he didn't particularly love, just to create the picture that he was after.

A man who'd lost his father, and whose mother hadn't been far behind. A man who had created an empire from the ground up and had no one in his life to share it with.

She wondered about *him*.

Not just that surface fantasy that she had built up with him when they were young. That man who had been tall and strong and compelling as he'd worked on her grandmother's ranch. He was still all those things. But he was broken, too, and she could see that now clearly. No amount of optimism would put the pieces of him back together.

So he just needed her to be there. Needed her to hold him, to kiss him. To be his.

His.

That word bloomed in her heart like a flower. One that she couldn't arrange or rearrange. One that grew wild. Wrapped itself around her like a beautiful, bright vine.

The idea of that. The security and belonging…

It made her heart lift, made her chest feel like it couldn't contain the emotion that was expanding inside of it.

She could hardly believe that this was the sort of magic that Grandma June wanted her to get from the farmhouse. But it was the magic she'd gotten. Everett. His hands, his mouth, his body.

Everett.

The reality and not the fantasy. Everything.

Everything.

That word beat in her heart like a drum as he stripped her clothes off right there in the prim sitting room, and she felt the need to yelp in protest.

Because Grandma June's refined sitting room was hardly the place for down-and-dirty sex.

But as he brought her down over him on the floral couch, where she had sat and had any number of conversations with her family members, it didn't feel so wrong.

It felt like freedom.

Like opening up places inside of herself that she had ignored for so long. Like finding a fullness in herself. Bringing together all these pieces of what and who she was. She had tried to be happy. A ray of sunshine to all.

Because she had thought it might help make up for the rest of her. The messy parts, her dreamer soul that seemed to get her into trouble from time to time.

The impractical part of her that wanted to give chickens tea parties and stymied her father so that he didn't actually want to spend any time with her.

So she had taken one part of herself—just one—and honed it until it was a sharp blade cutting through the resistance of others. Because she had thought it might be the best thing. That she could offer optimism when other people could only see the dark side. That she could bear the emotional burdens of others because her own always seemed so light. And that she never gave any of her own back.

But there was something about this. This thing with him that reached all the way down deep inside of her and opened up those dark and messy spaces, that made her feel like she didn't have to try to be anything.

Didn't have to be so resolute in being the one who saw the bright side for everyone else.

Why should she? Why couldn't she be sad? Why couldn't she be overwhelmed?

Why couldn't she *be*?

In Everett's arms, she felt like maybe she could.

She pushed his shirt up and off his body, dragged her hands down his muscular chest and stomach, undid the belt buckle on his jeans and freed him, stroking him before he arched up and pulled his wallet out of his pocket, producing a condom.

When he slid inside of her, she felt whole. Felt like all that intensity and darkness inside of him was coursing through her, and she welcomed it.

It was freedom. To feel everything. Even the dark, hard, intense things.

And when her orgasm broke over her, it was something deeper and more intense than she'd ever experienced before.

She stayed on the couch like that, straddling his lap, her forehead resting against his as their breath mingled.

And it was like something in her chest broke open. Like there had been a web of dividers and compartments holding different feelings at bay, and suddenly they were all gone, and she was flooded with everything.

She shivered and shook, her eyes filling with tears, sliding down her face freely. And she couldn't even be embarrassed.

She looked up at Everett, into those stormy blue eyes, and she knew.

This was love.

And it hadn't been love until she had been willing to take on the pain with the pleasure.

It hadn't been love until everything in her had opened up.

Love wasn't just rainbows and fairy-tale endings. Love was acceptance. Love was patient. Love gave. And love shouldered the burden of the other person.

Love wasn't fifty-fifty.

Love was everything. In her mind that had always meant a haze of happiness, but that wasn't it. Not when it came to her family, and not when it came to Everett.

Love wasn't an optimist or a pessimist. It wasn't a realist. Love didn't sit back and receive. Love was action.

Love bore burdens. Love hoped.

And most of all, love *believed*.

Through the hard things, through the dark moments.

Love pushed through when things got tough. And it was only that love—love that was a poet *and* a warrior—that did all those things.

That could conquer anything.

Rifts created in childhood that had widened over time. Scars cut in deep by distant fathers and mothers who didn't care.

That was the love that endured. *That* was the love that never failed.

It was rolling through her now in waves—not gentle waves, not waves that moved over her gently, but waves that left her feeling storm-tossed, battered against the rocks. And she realized then that for all her debate with Everett, she had been wrong about the function of optimism. That was just about the way you saw what life gave you.

What she needed to worry more about was what she gave back to life.

And so, not knowing at all what she believed might happen, not knowing at all if what she was doing would turn out okay, she looked up and met Everett's eyes directly.

"I love you," she said. "I love you, Everett McCall. And just so we're clear, I mean like a woman loves a man. Because I've said this to you twice now, and the first time you didn't seem to understand. So now I need you to. I love you."

CHAPTER THIRTEEN

THIS HAD BEEN a mistake. And Everett had known it. From the moment that he had come to find Lila, he had known that it was a mistake.

Things had fractured this morning, and he should have gone ahead and made a break.

But he hadn't been strong enough.

For all his talk of realism, what had he gone and done? He'd let himself get involved with Lila to an extent that he was no longer thinking clearly. To an extent that he was no longer doing what needed to be done.

He'd let himself begin to believe she might not be wrong about magic. About fairy tales.

And he knew better than that.

He *knew* it.

Lila didn't love him. Not really.

Lila had been a virgin. Lila had a big, soft heart, and he had taken advantage of that.

He had been selfish, and he had only looked after what he had wanted, and he had told himself a whole bunch of lies to get there. And it hit him then that he was no different than his father.

What had his father told himself all those years?

That he was practical. That he was a realist. And that firm belief in himself had set it up so that he never questioned what he did.

And damned if Everett wasn't the same.

Everett had used the trappings of his financial success to convince himself that he wasn't like his old man at all. Hell, he wouldn't work the land if the land didn't give anything back.

But they were the same. Different excuses, same outcome. Money was just a big glittery shield that let him pretend he wasn't like him.

It sneaked up on him.

But there it was. In the way that he bent this woman around his life to suit him.

And she would just… She would just end up getting hurt.

Is that really what you're afraid of?

He wasn't afraid of a damn thing, but he could recognize well enough when he was being a prick.

He moved Lila away from him, trying to keep his movements gentle.

"Lila," he said. "This is just really good sex."

"Don't say that to me," Lila said, scrambling to her feet, naked as the day she was born.

"I can't have a conversation like this," he said, indicating his current state.

He went into the bathroom and handled the practicalities, gripping the edge of the sink and looking at himself full in the face. Here in Grandma June's house… She'd been the woman who had taught him that he could work hard for what he had, that he could step away from his father and the family land and make something of himself, make something of his own. And he was hurting her granddaughter.

Right in this farmhouse that should have been sacred in some ways, hallowed ground for the way that it had taught him what kind of man he wanted to be, and he was…

A long way off from that.

He turned to walk out of the bathroom, and he tripped on that loose floorboard and cursed Cade Mathewson yet again for the lack of care he'd given the place when he was here messing with JJ.

And then he asked himself how he was any better.

Cade Mathewson had proposed, and Everett wasn't prepared to do anything like that at all. He returned to the sitting area and found Lila still naked, perched on the edge of the couch like a small, angry queen daring him to comment on her lack of dress.

He didn't understand this woman. Didn't understand how she opened herself up like this, how she conducted herself with such fearlessness and defiance.

"I still love you," she said. "Just in case you were wondering, I changed my mind in the last two minutes or so."

"Lila, I appreciate it—"

"Don't you dare," she said, standing. And she stamped her foot. "Don't you dare patronize me. I don't want you to appreciate my love. I want you to accept it. Everett, I have loved you forever. And I believe in fate, just a little bit. I think that it brought me here this autumn and threw me together with you. Fate. Grandma June. I believe in it. I believe in her, and I believe in us. In this. And I just think that some things in life we can't see or touch, we can only feel them."

"I just don't believe that," he said, his voice hoarse.

"Well, you're not going to like the rest of my revelation," she said. "I also believe that we can have all this magic, but if we don't put the work in behind it, then it doesn't matter. We have to show up. And we have to give. But if we do that, we can make it. And, Everett, I know you're a man that makes miracles. If you weren't, you wouldn't have the ranch that you have. I'll bring the magic, but let's both bring the work. I can understand that you need to be up at four thirty in the morning for work. I can do better at supporting you. I can be whatever it is you need me to be."

Everything in him rejected what she had to say. Because he couldn't believe it. No one had ever given a damn what he needed, and he didn't know why in hell they should start now.

Most of all, it seemed to him like this offer required him to need her back.

And the very idea filled him with dread.

He couldn't quite capture that dread, couldn't define it, couldn't explain it, and he didn't really want to.

"No," he said. "I don't want to have a fight with you, Lila, and I don't want you to humiliate yourself."

"Shut up," Lila said, moving toward him like a fiery ball of rage and indignation and beauty. "I want everything. And I always have. From you. I'm so tired... Why should I always take half, Everett? Why? Half of my parents. My sister. Why? *Why is that my life?* Is there something fundamentally wrong with me?"

"There is nothing the hell the matter with you, Lila. There something wrong with me. Stop loving people who are broken and see how far you get."

He couldn't even figure out where those words had come from. But the moment he'd said that, he'd known it was true.

He was the one with the problem. It wasn't her, it was him.

His own father had loved the barren, useless piece of land more than he had loved him.

There was a flaw in him, and it was nothing that he could ever overcome.

His wife had married him, thinking that she could change him. And when it turned out that he was exactly who he had shown he was, she had wanted out.

And he hadn't wanted to change.

"We're all broken people," she said. "If we can't love each other in spite of the brokenness, the world would be a sad, dark place."

"It is a sad, dark place, Lila. At least to me. Find a guy like you," Everett said. "Find a guy who sees the bright side of everything. Find a guy who's your age. Who isn't married to a ranch already. Who isn't... Who isn't so damned walled-off that he can't figure out how to feel anything."

"You feel things," she said, her voice small. "I know you do. You were torn up about your horse this morning..."

"It's a responsibility," he said. "If you can't take care of horses, you shouldn't have them. It's my job to take care of them. I slacked. I got distracted... And, honest to God, Lila, if it weren't for that, I might let you go ahead and love me and live with me. Except it wouldn't last. It wouldn't last—you would get tired of it and you would want to leave, and I wouldn't be able to blame you. So just go now. Finish out your time here. But it's not going to be with me."

"You're a coward," she said. "And you need to stop acting like a wounded child."

"I *was* a wounded child."

"So was I. But I grew up, and I want... I want healing. A wounded child just turns into a wounded man, a wounded woman, unless we heal our own selves."

She looked down, twisting her hands together. "My sister wrote to me about healing, about how she found hers. We have to take control of it. Of this life, of what we've been given. That's what Grandma June did, leaving us this place. I know that her daughters broke her heart. Over and over again, but she's trying to fix it. With us. She's giving us something. Something to work with. But we have to be willing to take it. My mother had all this, but she kept waiting for life to fix itself. But we can't do that. We have to make our own magic, Everett."

"There's no magic."

"Well, then, that's it," she said, shrinking back, all small and sad. "There won't be any if you won't let us make it. I believe in happy endings, but I believe you have to work damned hard for them. And if you don't want to work—"

"All I do is work," he said. "That's the problem."

"No, the problem is that you're afraid. You haven't seen enough good to believe in it. I would believe in it enough for the both of us."

"That's your optimism," he said.

He dressed the rest of the way and gritted his teeth against the pain as he turned away from her. And he walked out the front door, and it seemed to slam itself behind him.

Like the farmhouse was giving him a shove right on out.

"Don't be like that," he growled. "You taught me about hard work. And now I'm doing it. It's why I have a home. It's why I have a life. It's why I'm not starving.

It's why I can go to the doctor when I need to. So don't get mad at me now."

But he was just yelling at a slammed door. And for a man who had claimed superior practicality, he had to admit that it was a little bit ridiculous.

And as he walked out to his truck, the night felt oppressively black, and not even his headlights on the two-lane highway could do anything to make that feeling go away. And he pulled into his ranch, through the giant wrought-iron gates and up to the massive house.

And for the first time in his adult life, he wondered why the hell it mattered.

Right now, he just didn't know.

CHAPTER FOURTEEN

LILA WAS FEELING completely deflated, and she had the Red Sled Holiday Bazaar to get through the following day. But all she could seem to do was drag herself around the house, feeling nothing at all like herself. And nothing like there was hope on the other side of *anything*.

Maybe that was her lesson. Her real lesson.

But sometimes things didn't work out the way you wanted. Sometimes, there was no amount of optimism that could fix the situation. Sometimes, everything just kind of sucked.

Lila wasn't sure she particularly liked the conclusion, but she didn't know what other one she was supposed to draw.

Somehow, she was going to have to get through a bazaar at Everett's place. And she didn't think she could ever handle seeing him again.

It was going to crack her open, utterly and completely.

"Was this your plan?" she asked the empty farmhouse. "To let me get my heart broken, to teach me the lesson that sometimes it'll never be put back together? Because as lessons go, I kind of hate it."

But there was no forthcoming answer, and Lila wasn't sure why she had expected one at all. Her sis-

ter texted her, which was an unexpected surprise. Lila
wanted to talk to her sister. She really did. She wanted
to tell her about the letter and everything else, but not
today.

How is everything going?

Lila couldn't even muster up an emoji.

Okay.

She went about the rest of the day completing her
checklists and doing last-minute confirmations with
vendors. And was completely surprised when there was
a knock on the door.

She was even more surprised when she opened the
door to find JJ and Keira standing there.

Keira and JJ. Together.

She hadn't seen Keira since the funeral, and she suddenly felt silly over that. Guilty. She'd had her excuses
about why she hadn't reached out, how she didn't want
to bother her and Remy, but it had never been about that.

It had been about her own heart. Her own hurt. Her
own anger.

"What are you doing here?"

"You said you were doing okay. There was no ex-
clamation point or anything. There was no smiley face.
There wasn't an emoji of a small mammal. That means
you're seriously depressed," JJ said.

Keira nodded. "We came to see what was wrong."

"Who said anything was wrong?" Lila asked. "You
know, *okay* can just mean *okay*."

"Not when *you* say it," Keira said.

Funny how her cousin could be so insightful, no matter how little they spoke anymore. She looked at Keira and JJ now. They were women, different than when they'd been girls. Keira looked every inch the elegant cowgirl, her blond hair tamed into a braid, and a denim jacket over a fitted white top. JJ was ever herself. Simply and serviceably dressed. Except her sweater seemed to have llamas knitted into it.

"Are you wearing llamas?" Lila asked.

"The girls chose it for me," JJ said, frowning.

Another reminder of how things were just a bit different now. In strange ways and wonderful ways.

"I'm just busy. I'm putting together flower arrangements and everything for the Red Sled Holiday Bazaar," Lila said.

"And?" JJ prompted.

"And *nothing*," Lila said, turning away from the door and stomping into the house.

"You seem edgy," JJ said. "Which is weird. Because you are many things. But edgy isn't one of them."

"I found your letter." Lila looked down. "Just now. Last night. And I was going to text you, but some things happened and I… I'm sorry. I don't know how to talk to you. You're so practical, and I'm not. I'm just… I'm a pest to everyone, and I know it."

"You're not a pest," JJ said. "And I admit that your cheerful demeanor horrified me a little bit when we were younger. As did your insistence on embarrassing yourself sometimes with your…open declarations of feelings. But that's my stuff. It's not yours. You don't have to take that on board."

"Yeah, my sister finds me horrifying. I don't have to take that on board."

"Well, you find me *mean*. And you find me not very fun. So I have to deal with that."

"Maybe we're just too different."

But the lovely words from the letter stood between them now. Not their differences. And Lila, even in her diminished state, felt hope.

"Who said that different was bad?" JJ asked. "It's not like I think you're wrong to look at life the way that you do. In fact, I'm a little bit jealous. I always had to be the practical one, and I always had to keep things together. And you just…didn't."

"I was always jealous of you," Lila said. "People could depend on you. And they didn't think they could depend on me." She blinked. "Because Dad loves you best."

"Well, Mom took you," JJ said. "Our mother let our father just *have* me. How do you think that made me feel?"

"Both of your parents suck," Keira said. "And I say that as someone whose parents also suck. But they didn't have another kid to play me off of. So they could only screw me up between the two of them. But for the record, neither of you are bad people. Your mother and father are, though. And all the stuff between the two of you comes back to them."

"I…" Lila looked at Keira, and her heart twisted. "I know," she said. "I mean, I think I really do. But I just…"

You're going to have to do some difficult things. Things you won't like.

She found herself crying again. Which she hated more than anything. Grandma June had been right, and it hadn't even been about Everett. It hadn't even been about the Red Sled Holiday Bazaar.

"I'm sorry," Lila said. "I'm sorry that I spent so long pretending I didn't have any bad feelings that might have made it impossible for you to get to know me. I just couldn't… I thought that if I started crying, that I would never stop. I thought that if I was practical, I would have to acknowledge that we might never have a relationship again. That Mom and Dad were never going to reconcile. That Dad might never actually want me.

"That the man I loved might never actually love me back. And so I didn't want to be like that. I didn't want to be anything but resolutely positive, and that made it so no one could really get close to me. It made it so I couldn't even be close to myself. Because I just shoved aside everything hard and I couldn't even figure out what I wanted anymore." She closed her eyes. "I know now. I want a relationship with you, JJ. I want one with you, Keira. I don't want to be alone anymore. I don't want to be resentful. Hiding it all behind blaming you."

"I don't want that anymore, either," JJ said. "We're never going to be the same. But I think the problem was thinking we might have to be."

"I would rather be more like you right now. Everything worked out with you and Cade. Everett…"

"I *knew* you still had a crush on him," Keira said.

"It is not a crush, Keira," Lila said, her immediate reaction to be overly sincere. "I am *devastated*."

And it was so comically similar to the epic performance she'd wailed all through her grandmother's farmhouse seven years ago that it was almost funny.

Except for the broken heart.

"Sorry," Keira said, suppressing a smile. "I mean, really. But what happened?"

"He said that he doesn't want me to love him."

"Did he say he didn't love you?" Keira asked.

Lila frowned. "Well, no. But he said that we couldn't be together. He thinks we're too different." She made a broad gesture. "Because he's very practical. And I'm very not."

"Is that what he said?"

"I don't know. I think he's afraid. And he's been hurt. But so have I."

"I know you've been hurt," JJ said. "But one of the things I've always admired about you, Lila, is that no matter what, you've always felt like you deserved to be loved. You might have been angry about it, but along with that cheerful optimism was a lot of stubbornness that I think other people missed. You have a stubbornness about you, and a strong sense of who you are. You were angry at Dad because... Well, you thought you deserved his love, didn't you?"

"Yes," Lila said slowly.

"And you told Everett that you loved him when you were seventeen because you thought you deserved for him to love you back?" JJ pressed.

"I guess I did," Lila said, her tone grouchy.

"And you told him that you loved him this week because you thought you deserved for him to love you back still."

"Yes," Lila said. "I guess that's true. But I—"

"A lot of times when you've been hurt like we all have...you don't believe that. I know it's something that I struggled with. Maybe he doesn't believe that he deserves it."

"I…"

She thought about Everett. About everything he told her about his father. A man who had clung to the land even while his wife and son suffered. A man who had sacrificed his own health, let himself die of a treatable disease rather than going and getting it checked.

Leaving his wife and child alone with that same albatross. And she wondered how in the world he would feel like he deserved anything.

Then there was his ex-wife. His ex-wife had never truly loved him. She loved the idea of him. And maybe, just maybe…

It wasn't that he didn't love her, it was that he didn't believe that she loved him. Because he couldn't believe that anyone loved him.

"Well, he didn't say any of that to me," Lila said. "And I'm tired of… I'm tired of humiliating myself." His words echoed inside of her. "I can't hope forever that things will turn out. I can't believe for everyone."

And suddenly, she found JJ's arms around her, followed by Keira's. "You don't have to," JJ said.

Keira kissed the top of her head. "We believe in you."

Lila blinked. "Grandma June said that I was going to have to do some things here that I wouldn't like. I thought she just meant being organized. I thought she meant making lists. I think she meant that I had to understand some things about the world. That sometimes not everything is going to turn out. But also that it doesn't mean it's a waste."

She swallowed hard. "I want everything to connect up, and I want it all to mean something. And a huge part of my heart wants to believe in destiny and fate. In *the one*. But no matter what happens with Everett, I have learned things here. And I'm here with you. With both of you. Maybe it's okay that not everything can be fixed and perfect."

Keira frowned. "I've always liked that you thought it could be," she said. "I don't know what it says for the rest of us if you can't believe in the best outcome, Lila."

"Well, sometimes you're not going to get the best outcome," she said. "Sometimes you're just going to get your heart stomped on. But then your sister and your cousin show up and hug you. And you're all together in your grandmother's farmhouse. So maybe that has to be enough."

The three of them looked around the room. "We're missing Grandma June," Keira said. "And Bella."

"I know," Lila said. "But maybe that's just going to be the way it is, too. Grandma June is gone. Bella is who knows where. Maybe we can never have everything wrapped up in a neat little bow in life. Maybe I want too much."

"I've always loved your dreams," Keira said.

"You can have a tea party for chickens, Keira," Lila said. "But it does not mean the chickens will *like* the tea party. Or something like that."

"I like to think they did," JJ said. "It's just that they couldn't pick up the teacups."

Lila laughed at the absurdity of it. At the fact her sister was engaging in the absurdity at all, because it was deeply un-JJ of her.

"Thank you," she said. "I don't really want to include the chickens, but maybe we can all have some tea."

"I would like that," Keira said.

"Me, too," JJ responded.

"And if you need anything else for the Red Sled Bazaar... You know, we can come and help you."

"That would be good," Lila said. "Yes. I would really appreciate it if you could be there. Everett might be there. I might do something we all regret."

"Like?" JJ asked.

"Like beating him to death with one of Grandma June's raffia scarecrows."

"I'd help," JJ said cheerfully.

"Well, if nothing else, I appreciate the support."

They all set about to making tea, getting out the floral teacups that Lila had always used with the chickens.

And for some reason, without talking about it, they got out five cups, and set two extras in the empty spaces at the table.

Grandma June.

Bella.

Even in her diminished state, those cups felt a little bit like hope.

Enduring, believing, love.

And no matter what, she wasn't ready to give up on all that entirely.

JJ and Keira were here.

There was no way to feel utterly hopeless.

CHAPTER FIFTEEN

EVERETT WENT OUT the next morning and rode his horse around the perimeter of the property, taking in everything that he owned.

Everything that was his.

But whatever he expected, whatever he was waiting for, didn't seem to be there.

It hit him then, like a revelation dropped out of the sky. He was waiting for the same thing that perhaps his father had been waiting for.

For the land to love him back.

Because the land was less of a risk than a person.

And Everett had tricked himself into thinking that perhaps his land did love him back. And so he didn't need anything else.

His land gave back to him. It sustained him.

But sitting out here now, on the back of his horse, surveying everything that he had decided made him a man worthy of calling himself one, he knew that it was hollow.

Money wasn't love.

And dirt was just dirt.

It was fear that made a man pour everything into that dirt rather than into the flesh and blood around him that cared.

He saw his father for what he was clearly for the first

time. Not a realist and not a fool. But a man who was deeply afraid of what he didn't understand, of what he couldn't have dominion over.

Who held himself at a distance from his wife and child, and gave to his farmland, because in the end, that was easier. And he thought of his father, and he thought of Grandma June.

His father had died and gone back into that dirt. That dirt that had been the ultimate love of his life.

And that felt like *it*. It felt like he was gone.

But then there was Grandma June, who had loved people, whose love had filled up that farmhouse, her love for those who came into it far greater than the structure itself.

And it felt like she remained.

Woven into the fabric of who he was.

Her love felt soaked into every board of that house, her caring stitched into the quilts there.

It was love that made places like that matter. Love that gave things meaning.

And love that gave a man a real purpose.

Lila was right. He was a coward. Because on some level he had always imagined he might not be worthy of love. He'd never intended to give his whole heart to anyone for fear he wouldn't get it back.

Lila loved, anyway.

Fearless, strong Lila.

He'd thought of her as silly before. An overly enthusiastic, frothy kind of girl. But he could see now. The bravery in everything she did. In everything she was.

In her resolute hold on the hope that made this life worth living. In her willingness to love a man like him and to hold fast to that love even in the face of rejection.

Again.

What had he ever done to earn the love of a woman like that?

He didn't think he *had* earned it.

Maybe it was magic, and that settled uncomfortably over his skin, made everything hiss and crackle beneath.

He didn't want to believe in something he couldn't hold on to.

But right now he needed to. Needed to believe in the fantastical and the wondrous and the invisible.

Lila.

Like a golden thread that held together all those other pieces in his life, without which it would all fall apart.

He loved her.

He loved her no matter how terrifying that was, no matter how little he understood it.

She had put herself out there for him, not once, but twice.

And he owed her nothing less.

He was going to give Lila Frost the declaration that she deserved.

CHAPTER SIXTEEN

EVERYTHING ABOUT THE Red Sled Holiday Bazaar had come together better than Lila could have ever imagined.

She had to credit Keira and JJ for their help. They had doubled the flowers that she had created, and now, bright brilliant blooms were everywhere, linked by garlands done up in fall colors, tied with spectacular burlap ribbon.

There was apple cider, apple bobbing and apple cake. There was pumpkin-spice coffee and pumpkin-spice beer, and pumpkin-spice bread that Lila had been told was superb.

Kiera had a cart set up, and was making coffee as fast as she could, handing it out in cheerful blue cups that said *June's* on the side.

The felted animals were selling at a good clip from booth seven, and all of the ladies with their crafts seemed to have forgotten about the rivalry to get that booth, as they were all being particularly successful.

Indeed, the bazaar had drawn a near record crowd this year.

Tourists driving in from Copper Ridge, Jacksonville and Gold Valley. A great many people had made the trek down from the Portland metro area, too.

There was a band playing country music outside the barn, and a dance floor, with heaters set up around it so that people could have a good time without freezing to death.

It was a great and grand kickoff of the holiday season. With decor fit for Halloween, Thanksgiving and going all the way to Hanukkah and Christmas. For Lila, though, the success was somewhat muted.

Here she was in Everett's barn, holding a piece of apple cake in her hand that she couldn't bring herself to take a bite of, staring at booth number seven, not because the felted animals were cute, but because she and Everett had made love on that booth.

She had sanitized it. Because she was thoughtful that way.

But that didn't erase the memories.

Someone looped an arm around her shoulders and gave her a light squeeze. She looked to the left, at JJ, who stood a good four inches taller than she did.

"You okay?"

"I will be."

She looked around and saw Lora and Ellie running around the barn, Cade keeping watch over them like a paranoid hawk.

Lila reached into her purse and pulled out the two felted mice that Ms. Jones had gifted to her.

"Here," Lila said, handing them to JJ.

"What are these?" JJ asked, looking askance at her. "I don't want your rodents."

"They're for Lora and Ellie. They should have them."

"Thank you," JJ said, clearly still in deep unwant of them, but obviously willing to have them for the girls' sake.

"Tell them they're from Aunt Lila. And that…I want to see them more. I think… I think I want to move here.

I've been thinking, JJ. I know that none of this went exactly the way I wanted it to. But…this did," she said, gesturing around the barn. "The arrangements, your flowers. I think we could really have something. I don't want to go back to the florist's in Portland and work for someone else. I want to build something with you. I want to be…here. Where the best part of our childhood was. And I want to be near you and Keira. Because you're my family. The only real family that I have. And…whatever happens with Everett, that's not going to change."

JJ pulled her in and gave her a hug. "I want that, too," she said. "Really. Everything down to the flower shop. As long as you deal with the people."

"I'm happy to deal with the people."

"Good. Because I'm not. I'd rather dig in the dirt."

"That's fine with me. I mean, that's what makes us a good team. That we're different."

JJ grinned. "Yeah. I guess that is what makes us a good team."

Then she took the mice over to Lora and Ellie, who squealed, and Lila had a feeling that JJ and Cade were going to end up buying quite a few more from Ms. Jones before the day was up.

It took Lila a moment to realize that the music had stopped. Suddenly all she could hear was the sound of voices rising up over the crowd. "Excuse me for a moment."

That was when she heard Everett.

She blinked, beating a hasty retreat out of the barn, and to the stage area.

"Hi, Lila," Everett said.

He was standing on a stage. And she could think of

nothing that Everett McCall would like less than to be standing on a stage.

"What are you doing?" she hissed.

"I have a little bit of public humiliation to engage in. Though, whether or not it ends up humiliation might be up to you."

A whole crowd had gathered now, people filtering out from the barn to come out and watch what was about to happen.

"Lila Frost," Everett said. "You have told me that you loved me in good faith more than once now. And I was too much of a fool to recognize that it was the thing I needed most. I see that now. I hope it isn't too late. I love you, Lila. I want to marry you. I want to have babies with you. All those things I said I didn't want, I want them, because it would be with you."

A ripple went through the crowd, and Lila was part of that ripple. Because she couldn't believe it. She knew that most people in town wouldn't believe that staid, steady Everett McCall was confessing his love to *airy fairy* Lila Frost.

Frankly, neither could Lila.

"This can't be real," she said.

"It is," he said, still speaking into the microphone. "It is, and I'm going to stand up here and keep on telling you that I love you until you give me an answer. Until I embarrass us both, which really wasn't the idea, because I'm trying to even the playing field."

"I love you," she shouted. "I love you, even though you were a little bit of a… Well, you were a jerk." She would've said a stronger word, but there were children present.

"Will you marry me?" he asked.

"Yes!"

She scampered up to the stage, flung her arms around his neck, kissing him, hard.

He dropped the microphone. "You were right," he murmured. "I was scared. But my love for you is bigger than fear. And it's what I want. More than my ranch or my horses. More than what I considered to be success. I'm not a success if I don't have you, Lila Frost. And that's the God's honest truth."

"I love you," she said, kissing him again.

And she looked around, and saw everyone watching them, the whole town witnessing her triumph. And right there in the front were Keira and JJ. And, somehow, she felt like Grandma June was probably watching, too.

She had always believed. In her heart she'd believed that she could be loved. That the world was beautiful, even though it was hard sometimes. That if you just hoped, and kept on hoping, your day would come.

It was even better, though. She'd learned over these past weeks. It was more than hope, more than optimism. If you were willing to take a chance, if you were willing to change, if you could reach down deep and find a way to heal some of your own hurts, you could free yourself up to hold a lot more love.

"I guess sometimes you have to do things you don't like to have the one thing that you need," he said.

"I guess so."

"And you know what…? You were the one, after all."

She'd been right all along. Her heart that was too big, too loving, too soft, hadn't been any of those things, after all. It had been true, and it had been for him.

And it had been just right all along.

"And so were you."

CHAPTER SEVENTEEN

LILA AND EVERETT stayed in the house for the rest of the fall. It was inconvenient for him to move back and forth between his ranch and the farmhouse, given the early mornings that he had to put in, but it was worth it to him.

And Lila felt like she had to finish out her season.

It was wonderful to be able to finish it up with him.

Two things happened before she left the farmhouse.

The first was that she took hold of one of the little floral teacups that she'd once used for chicken tea parties, and that she'd used again to bond with her cousin and sister, and wrapped it in fine paper, so that it could come with her to her new house. Her new life.

So that she never forgot who she was.

That girl with the tea parties, and the fanciful imagination.

The one who had always believed in love, and rightly so.

The second thing that happened was that Keira called her, breathless.

"Grandma June's lawyer said they finally found an address for Bella. She's coming."

After she got off the phone with Keira, she put her hand on the door frame. "Something tells me that Bella is going to need one of your miracles," she whispered. "It would sure be nice if you could give her one."

She made sure to leave the house warm, a fire running in the woodstove. Something bright and welcoming for the cousin none of them had seen for so long.

But when she left, and closed the door behind her, a breeze kicked up.

And unbeknownst to Lila, the fire went dark.

On she and Everett went, to their own house, where they created enough heat between them to warm the impending winter.

And all the winters thereafter.

* * * * *

Winter

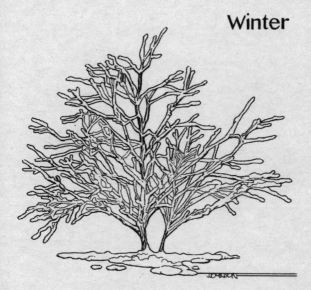

Jackie Ashenden

This is dedicated to the wonderful ladies
of Voltron (let's do this again some time)
and to all the words that got cut from this novella.
Gone, but not forgotten.
You shall live on eternally on my hard drive.

WINTER

Dearest Bella,

It's a very strange thing to get old, to know that eventually the world will go on without you. To see clearly your successes, and your mistakes, and still not know what you could have done about either.

Oh, my serious girl. How I've ached for you these past few years. But a grandmother can only do so much, and a person has to be willing. You know that even better than I. I've missed that quick wit of yours (minus the swearing, young lady) and that quiet way you have of always knowing just what someone needs.

Except yourself.

I have many things to ask of you this winter. To make sure the old house is ready for sale, if that's what you, Keira, Lila and JJ decide. But what you'll have to do (and fight tooth and nail against—never let it be said I don't know you) is ask for help. Over and over again. Until you realize help doesn't make you weak. Opening yourself up for a partnership will be as sweet as those summers we all remember so fondly.

Let my spirit guide you in all that you do, and

I have the utmost confidence you'll find that hand to hold, like you used to hold mine when you didn't think anyone was paying attention.

Love always,
Grandma June

CHAPTER ONE

THE TREE IN Grandma June's front yard was dead.

Bella Jacobson stared at its blackened branches as the snow soaked through the canvas of her worn sneakers, not sure why it being dead should be so surprising when it was winter and every other tree surrounding the old white farmhouse was also dead.

She wasn't sure what sort of tree it was, she just remembered it in summer, when its gnarled branches and trunk were softened by green leaves and sunlight.

Now it was black and twisted and...dead.

Like your heart.

The thought made her laugh hollowly in the privacy of her own head. It was something her mother might say, except Bella didn't want to think about her mother right now. Though that was hard, considering she'd just arrived back in Jasper Creek, the tiny town she and her mother had left over ten years ago and hadn't been back to since.

No, these days Bella called Seattle home.

Not so much anymore.

She hauled the one bag she'd brought with her higher on her shoulder. No point thinking about the mess she'd left behind in Seattle, either. Better to concentrate on what was happening now and the reason she was here— to spend winter in her grandmother's old farmhouse.

Evening was coming on, the wind cutting through her jeans and clawing under the worn leather of her jacket. Her blue beanie seemed little protection from the elements right now.

Hunching her shoulders as snow swirled down from the gray sky, Bella glanced at the farmhouse itself, sitting in a dainty square of white, the pale pickets of the fence surrounding it almost lost in the snow.

It was a lovely old place and always had been, with dormer windows and a wide, deep porch around the outside. In summer, ivy climbed around the porch supports and along the awning above it. But there wasn't any ivy now. The house looked cold, the windows dark. Deserted.

Bella shivered. She had that lonely feeling sitting inside her again, that one that had always been there, that didn't ever go away.

But with the ease of long practice, she forced it down, pushed open the white gate and walked up the snow-covered path. Dwelling on it didn't help and it was a stupid feeling, anyway.

She *liked* being alone.

Going up the wooden stairs that led to the porch, she grimaced as the steps creaked.

Presumably fixing those steps was one of the numerous tasks she had to do while she was here for the winter, all detailed in the letter from Grandma June that had finally found its way to her, months after it had been sent judging from the postmark.

Apparently her other three cousins had also gotten letters. Bella didn't know what her cousins had had to do, but she had to fix the house up for its eventual sale. Though fixing up old houses wasn't in her wheelhouse, the chance of a place to stay for the winter hadn't been something she could pass up. Not when she'd lost her room in the apartment she'd shared with a couple of others only the day before.

It was either doing what her grandmother asked or finding accommodation at one of the homeless shelters in Seattle.

She couldn't bear the thought of a shelter. Her pride wouldn't allow it.

The situation made her angry. But she'd had no choice. Coming back to Jasper Creek was her only option. Plus there was the added bonus of the chance of money from the eventual sale of the old farmhouse. Once she'd fixed it up, of course.

The thought of selling her grandmother's house made her feel bad, but she needed the cash if she wanted to get her plan of getting a café up and running, especially now all her savings had gone. She'd been on the point of finally having enough, after years of scrimping and saving, to buy out a little café business just down the street from the apartment she'd had to give up. The elderly owner had wanted to sell and move somewhere warmer, like Florida, and he'd wanted to sell to her.

But then she'd had her wallet stolen and even though she'd canceled her debit cards as soon as she'd found out, it hadn't been soon enough; they'd cleared out her account completely. The bank had been awful to deal with, refusing to refund the money, insisting she'd been negligent in not safeguarding her cards properly. It had been a terrible blow and one that she was still recovering from.

Grandma June wouldn't mind. And hey, if she *really* hadn't wanted Bella to sell the house, she wouldn't have mentioned it in the letter.

She stopped on the porch in front of the old front door, bending to grab the key from where Grandma June had said it would be, under the mat. Her hands were freezing and she fumbled the key, her fingers numb.

It was *really* time to get inside before the temperature dropped and get some kind of fire going, though she had no idea how to light one.

The idea made her feel even tireder, but she ignored it, her breath puffing out in white clouds in front of her face as she pushed the antique-looking key in the lock and turned it.

But there was no well-oiled click, the door opening in welcome.

The key stuck instead.

Bella cursed, turning it harder. But it wouldn't budge.

She tried to turn it back and pull the key out, but that didn't work, either. The key remained stuck in the lock.

Frustrated, she fiddled around, pulling at it, but apparently nothing was going to get it out.

Great. What did she do now?

The cold was biting deeper, but unless she smashed a window, that door looked like it was going to stay closed.

Bella gritted her teeth.

Her grandmother had left her the number of the owner of the ranch next door to call in case of emergencies, but calling that number was the last thing on earth Bella wanted to do.

Because that would mean having to ask her exstepbrother, Noah Faraday, for help. And she'd rather die than do that.

Unfortunately, if you don't get inside, that could become an option.

She turned and scowled at the snowy yard.

Asking for help made her feel like her mother, who couldn't do anything for herself, at least not if she had a man around to do it for her, and calling Noah in particular made her uncomfortable.

Nothing at all to do with how she'd once had a giant crush on him.

But that had been years ago, when she'd been thirteen and he'd been her nineteen-year-old stepbrother. Tall, dark and wickedly gorgeous. Brooding and protective…at least of his father. Not so much of her.

He'd never liked her and that had hurt—at least until her mother had divorced his father a year or so after marrying him, and moved to Seattle, taking Bella away.

He probably wouldn't even remember her.

Damn. She was going to have to call him. It was either that or smash one of the windows, which would just give her something else that she didn't know how to fix.

"Okay," she muttered. "You can do this. It's only a problem with the door. And it's just stupid Noah."

"Who are you calling stupid?" a deep, gritty male voice said from behind her.

Bella went still, shock freezing her in place.

A footstep resounded on the wooden planks beneath her feet.

"Lila mentioned you might come back," Noah Faraday said. "But I didn't believe it until now."

Bella whirled around and sure enough, down one end of the porch was a tall male figure.

And somehow she couldn't move as he came closer,

the last rays of the setting sun chasing the shadows from his face.

Her heart contracted, a wave of familiar longing washing over her.

She remembered that face, with its high forehead and blade of a nose, slightly crooked from when he'd broken it playing football. The strong jaw that had been once been clean-shaven, but was now shaded with black stubble. The full curve of his lower lip that had once fascinated her...

Except this face wasn't that of a nineteen-year-old anymore. This face was very much that of a man— older, harder, more defined, more masculine.

He lifted a hand and pushed the brim of his cowboy hat up, and a pair of familiar dark eyes looked into hers.

Those eyes were the same. Dark as black coffee and just as fathomless.

In addition to the cowboy hat, he wore a pair of worn jeans sitting low on his lean hips, boots and a dark green coat that highlighted the width of his powerful shoulders.

An unidentifiable electricity whispered over her skin. *Noah*...

"Wh-what are you doing here?" she stuttered like a fool.

"What do you think?" He gave her a long look, encompassing her soaked sneakers, damp leather jacket and the shiver she couldn't quite hide. "I'm here to make sure you don't freeze to death getting into Grandma June's house."

IT HAD TAKEN Noah Faraday a minute to recognize the petite woman standing on Grandma June's porch.

Lila had told him the day before that she thought Bella would be taking up winter residence in the farmhouse, but she hadn't been certain, so could he please keep an eye out for her? And if she did turn up, could he make sure that she was okay?

Noah had been leery of that. He hadn't wanted to concern himself with Avery Jacobson's daughter, not that he remembered much about Bella other than she'd been a quiet little thing who barely said boo to a goose.

He remembered her mother, though, and how she'd used his father for a place to stay, divorcing him as soon as she'd gotten a better offer from some rich city guy up in Seattle.

It had taken Hank a long time to get over that, and since Noah had been the one who'd had to pick up the pieces, it had taken Noah even longer.

If he ever had.

He wasn't a man to hold grudges, but he held one against Avery. Because he was damn sure she was the one who'd made his father turn back to the drink that had killed him not long after she'd left.

It wasn't Bella's fault, but she was a reminder of the past, and he didn't need reminders.

Still, he wasn't a man to leave a woman without help if she needed it and he was certain a city girl like Bella would need help.

Whose damn fool idea was it to wear sneakers and a leather jacket in the snow?

"I'm not going to freeze to death." Bella lifted her chin, her slightly husky voice edged.

She didn't look how he remembered, but then his memories of her weren't exactly vivid. She'd been small and her hair was still black as the night sky and as straight as the road that ran along the front of his property. She'd had bangs back then, dark blue eyes peering out from underneath them, and though the bangs were gone, those blue eyes were still looking out from beneath the beanie she wore.

But they weren't as shy or fearful as they had been. They were as guarded and wary as a kicked dog's.

"Sure looks like you might," he said slowly. "You need to get inside and get warm."

The wary expression didn't lift from her delicate, pale face.

Grown up pretty, hadn't she?

"I would if the stupid key hadn't stuck in the lock." She lifted her shoulder, as if it didn't matter. "I was going to call you, so that was good timing. If you could give me a hand with the key and the door, that would be great."

Her tone was polite, but he got the feeling that she definitely didn't want him to be there.

Interesting.

"The door, huh?" He glanced at it. "Can't get the key out?"

"No. I tried, but the damn thing is stuck."

Giving her another assessing glance, he shrugged out of his jacket and came over to where she stood, draping it around her shoulders. It was warm and she looked like she could do with it.

Then he turned and, ignoring the frigid bite of the wind through his black thermal, went to the door and fiddled with the key.

It took a bit of strength, but he managed to turn it and get it unlocked—clearly the mechanism needed some oil or maybe even replacing—except then the door jammed as he tried to pull it open. Looked like the hinges needed attention, too.

Pulling hard, he finally got the door open with a screech.

"Thank God," Bella said with feeling, sidling around him as she stepped into the hallway.

It was dark inside and only a fraction warmer than outside.

Bella fumbled around for the light switch, but since he knew the place, he reached for the switch himself and turned it on.

She turned around, scowling as light flooded through the hallway. Then the scowl vanished, replaced by a very forced smile. "Thanks for the door. And it was, uh, good to see you again." Her smile became fixed. "But I'm okay now."

She definitely didn't want him around. Fine. If she didn't want help, he wasn't going to insist.

Looking ridiculously small and vulnerable wrapped up in his coat, her eyes were dark, her hair tumbling over her shoulders in an inky waterfall.

Something odd shifted in his chest. Something he didn't much care for.

"You know how to light a fire?" he asked, because he needed to make sure. "Get the heating working?"

"Hey, I'm not a kid anymore." She'd already begun to unwind herself from his coat. "I'm okay to do all of that."

"I never said you were a kid."

"I know, but just in case you did." She held out his coat, that smile still fixed to her face. "Thanks, Noah. It's been great and, honestly, I do appreciate your help. But it's all good now."

Unease sat inside him.

The old central heating needed the woodstove to get it working and getting that lit required a certain knack. A knack he bet this little city girl didn't have. Which meant she was in for a cold night.

"I can stay if you like," he offered, not taking the coat. "Help you get things sorted out heating-wise."

"Nope." Her smile became less and less natural. "Like I said, I'm good. I'll let you know if I need anything."

He got the sense that "when hell freezes over" was implied.

Well, if she wanted to be stubborn, he wasn't going to force her. Besides, she was inside now. There were blankets upstairs if she got too cold; she wouldn't freeze like she would have out on the porch.

"Suit yourself." He took his coat from her, shrugging it back on, not missing how her gaze followed his movements.

Interesting. What was all that about?

The faint fresh and flowery scent clung to his coat and something inside him tightened in response.

Her eyes were very wide and for a second a deep blue spark leaped in the depths.

Then she blushed. "Good night, Noah," she said quickly.

And a moment later, he was standing on the porch in the cold, the front door slamming shut in his face.

CHAPTER TWO

BELLA PRESSED HER fingers to the front door and waited, barely breathing, listening to the sound of Noah's footsteps on the porch outside.

Was he going away? Please, let him be going away.

Sure enough, the footsteps receded, but it wasn't until they'd finally faded that she let out the breath she'd been holding.

"Idiot," she muttered. "Idiot, idiot, idiot."

Her heart thumped from the shock of seeing him and she still felt the heavy weight of his coat around her shoulders, warm from his body and smelling of wood smoke and cedar, a masculine scent that had made her mouth go dry.

Still felt the pull, the longing that she'd thought was a product of her overactive teenage hormones, that she'd felt whenever he was around. Whenever his dark eyes had met hers.

She'd always wished he'd smile at her, but he never had.

He hadn't now. In fact, the only reason he was here at all was because Lila had asked him to come check on her.

Did you want him to be here for you?

Bella snorted and pushed herself away from the door.

She didn't need anyone. She never had. And now he was gone, she never had to think of him again.

Bella turned, taking a look around the narrow hallway.

She only had vague memories of this house, but she remembered it feeling a lot more welcoming than it did now. Though that might have been to do with her grandmother.

A funny pain lodged in her chest at the thought of Grandma June. She hadn't had a lot to do with her grandmother, but the few memories she did have were of a gnarled but warm hand enveloping her smaller one and a pair of kindly blue eyes. And a smile that made her feel like she was standing in a beam of sunlight.

Bella couldn't say she missed her grandmother, not when she'd never really had her, but the thought that Grandma June was gone made her eyes prickle. Her mother hadn't cried when she'd told Bella the news and made certain Bella knew that she wasn't going back for the funeral. So Bella hadn't gone to the funeral, either, though why she couldn't exactly say.

She'd told herself it was for solidarity with her mother—Avery had never gotten on with Grandma June—but she was afraid it was more because she didn't want to step back into the past here.

Jasper Creek hadn't been a place of happy memories.

Coming cautiously into the kitchen, Bella fumbled again for the light switch and found it this time. The darkness fled, revealing a worn and old-fashioned kitchen, with green painted cupboards both above and below the counter, and an ancient woodstove up against one wall. A large window with a sink beneath it looked out over the front yard. With night descending hard, the glass was a big square of black, making everything feel depressing and cold.

Not what she remembered of this particular room. Her memories of the farmhouse might be vague, but the kitchen had always been special, with an atmosphere of warmth and togetherness. Her grandma standing at the stove cooking, talking or humming, delicious scents filling the room.

Food, good company and that nurturing atmosphere had always made Bella happy. Made her feel connected to people even when she wasn't. It was what had made her decide on her dream of opening her own café, because even though she couldn't cook, she loved the thought of providing people with a place like Grandma June's kitchen.

A place for lonely people to reconnect.

Right now, though, Grandma June's kitchen looked like a place where teenagers in horror movies were murdered by serial killers.

She grimaced and moved over to the scrubbed wooden table in the middle of the room. After putting her bag down on one of the chairs, she went to investigate the woodstove.

It was full of dead ash, and though Bella didn't know much about lighting fires, she did know that a fireplace had to be cleaned first before a fire could be lit in it.

She spotted a metal shovel and brush hanging from a nail jammed into the wall. Grabbing both implements, Bella knelt and tried sweeping the ashes into the metal shovel. She felt clumsy, her fingers numb and her hands awkward. The ash drifted in the air, some of it going on the floor and sprinkling down the front of her jacket, getting on her damp jeans.

She ignored it, sweeping until she had a shovel full of ash and a cleanish-looking stove. Not knowing where to put the ash, she settled for leaving the shovel by the stove; getting the fire lit was more important than cleaning up.

Finding some kindling and twigs in a basket nearby, Bella dusted off her hands then stuffed both kindling and twigs into the bottom of the stove in a heap. She rose to her feet again and looked around for something to light it with.

No handy box of matches leaped out at her.

Her breath puffed in front of her face as she began pulling out drawers, cursing her own idiocy for not thinking to get a box of matches or a lighter.

You didn't even stop to get food.

Bella slammed a drawer back in. Yeah, she really *was* an idiot.

Eventually, in a drawer in the hutch dresser that stood opposite the woodstove, she found a matchbox. It didn't have very many matches left, but it was better than nothing.

Crouching down in front of the stove, she lit match after match, only to have each fledgling fire splutter and die.

Frustration curled in her chest.

Why couldn't she get it to light?

Give up for the night. Go upstairs and go to bed.

No. Hell, no. If she couldn't even light a fire, she might as well give up and go back to Seattle right now. She was *not* going to let this get the better of her. She'd left home at sixteen, when her mother had told her it was time to leave, and she'd found herself a job and a place to live, so surely she could handle lighting one small fire.

Resolutely, she rearranged the pile of kindling and reached for another match, only to find the box empty.

"Crap," she muttered.

Tossing the empty box away, she sat down on the cold wooden floor and swallowed, her throat tight, the knot of frustration in her chest a big, hard stone.

She was cold, hungry, covered in ash and she hadn't thought of food, and she couldn't light the fire. And it had only been through Noah being here that she'd even managed to get into the house.

So much for being successful.

Something ran down her cheek and she wiped it away with a dirty hand, blinking hard, hating herself for her weakness.

It had been a tough week, sure, but sitting on the floor crying because she couldn't get the fire lit? She should be thanking her lucky stars she wasn't in the homeless shelter or sleeping on the streets.

She had a roof over her head and electricity, so the oven would work and maybe there was hot water. Perhaps having a hot shower and going to bed was a good idea.

Ignoring the heavy stone in her chest, Bella pushed herself up from the floor and went to check out the oven. That seemed easy to operate.

A memory floated through her head of her grandmother standing at the stove and stirring a pot full of melted chocolate and cream and all sorts of other good things. Real hot chocolate...

Bella took a breath and went to the pantry, pulling open the cupboards hopefully. There were jars of staples, flour, pasta, sugar and different sorts of preserves. Spices, too. But no chocolate. And no bread. Nothing that could be made quickly into food that she could eat.

Disappointment sat heavy in her gut.

She shut the pantry and looked at the old fridge that stood next to it. There wouldn't be anything in it, but she checked it, anyway, and wasn't surprised to find only a couple of bottles of lemonade.

So no food and definitely no hot chocolate.

The shower, though. There had to be a shower.

She went over to the sink to check the hot water, but no water came out of the tap when she turned it on.

Bella stared at it, the stone in her chest getting heavier and heavier.

The pipes must be frozen. There wouldn't be a hot shower after all.

At least there was a shower at the homeless shelter.

She looked out through the window into the darkness, the cold settling down into her bones.

No fire. No food. No heat. Story of her life.

So much for this being a success.

Another something slid down her cheek.

Yay, crying again. Her mother cried at the drop of a hat. Whenever she needed help, or wanted money, or when things got hard, she turned on the tears. And someone helped her. It was magic.

Except when someone else was crying. Then Avery would get even more upset to make sure the attention remained with her. Bella had learned that the hard way.

She sniffed and wiped her face.

This was stupid. What she needed to do now was go to bed, and hopefully everything would be better in the morning.

Something moved in the darkness outside the window.

Shock arrowed through her and for a second she couldn't breathe.

Footsteps sounded on the porch, then someone knocked on the front door. Hard.

Bella's heart tried to beat its way out of her chest.

The knock came again and fear wrapped long fingers around her throat, choking her.

Another knock, this time accompanied by a deep, male voice. "Bella?" Noah Faraday called from the porch. "Are you in there? It's me. Noah. Open the damn door!"

NOAH STOOD IN front of Grandma June's door for the second time that night, cursing at his own inability to leave well enough alone.

But he hadn't been able to get pretty little Bella Jacobson out of his head.

All he could think about was her in soaking sneakers and a damp leather jacket, looking up at him with big blue eyes.

The place was old, that finicky woodstove hard to light, and if the pipes had frozen from the cold snap the night before and she couldn't get water for a hot shower, then she'd have a cold night.

He didn't involve himself with the people of Jasper Creek. To them he was the son of that drunk Hank. They hadn't liked his father, and by association, they didn't like him, either. Whatever, the feeling was mutual and so he kept out of their way.

But just because he didn't much like Bella Jacobson didn't mean he could leave her to fend for herself in the depths of a cold snap.

It wasn't neighborly and Grandma June was big on being neighborly. She'd been the only person in town who didn't make comments about the trouble Hank caused—his father had always been a mean drunk—and he appreciated that.

So, cursing under his breath, he'd turned around and gone back the way he'd come, once more standing before June's front door.

Except Bella wasn't opening it.

He'd knocked a couple of times, then shouted, and he was wondering if the damn door had got stuck again, and whether he needed to kick it in, when it was tugged violently open and there was Bella.

She still wore her beanie, but now her delicate features were smeared with ash, with more ash down the front of her jacket and staining her jeans.

She looked like an extra from a zombie movie.

"You didn't have to scare me like that," she snapped before he could speak. "Why are you here, anyway? I told you I didn't need your help."

Noah ignored the sharp edge in her voice, studying her face instead. Because running through the middle of the ashy smears on her cheeks were two white tear tracks.

The tight thing in his chest tightened even further. Dammit. He couldn't walk away now, could he?

"Did you get the fire lit?" he asked instead, knowing already what the answer would be since the air in the house was still chilly.

"Yes." She stared stubbornly back at him. "I'm fine."

"Uh-huh." Noah stepped into the hallway and, without a word, headed into the kitchen.

"Hey! I didn't say you could come in!"

He ignored her, going over to the woodstove and surveying the mess. Ash was everywhere, not to mention a shovel full of it sitting next to the stove. Also bits of twig and, most pathetic of all, an empty matchbox.

"It was going," Bella said from behind him, sounding defensive. "You knocking on the door distracted me and now it's gone out. So thanks."

Noah ignored that, too, turning from the stove and going over to the sink. He twisted the cold tap and was again unsurprised when no water came out.

He turned around.

Bella stood by the table, her arms folded, her chin at a stubborn angle.

Too bad, though. Those white tear tracks were evidence that this little city girl wasn't handling things the way she kept insisting she was.

"You'll come stay with me tonight," he said, in no mood for argument, because he wasn't feeling particularly warm himself. "Get your bag."

She stared at him as if he'd suggested she strip her clothes off and dance naked on Grandma June's kitchen table. "Excuse me?"

"You heard what I said. You can't stay here, not tonight."

"Of course I can. I've got everything I need—"

"You don't have heat and you don't have water. Do you have any food?"

"Yes. I'm not stupid." But her gaze flickered as she said it.

Noah fixed her with a look. "Do I need to check the fridge?"

"I have candy bars in my bag."

"Don't be an idiot," he said, losing patience. "My

place has a fire, a hot shower and I've even got a spare room. You can stay there, get warm, have something to eat, get a good sleep and come and deal with this in the morning."

She shifted on her feet, glancing away from him. There was a nervous energy to her that he hadn't noticed before. It was distracting. "I'm good, thanks."

"So you're fine with freezing to death here?"

"I'm not going to freeze to death here. There are blankets upstairs."

Noah frowned. Why was she was being so stubborn? Her mother wouldn't have argued. Avery Jacobson would have grabbed her bag and been over at his house, living it up like she owned the place.

Perhaps he should leave her. Maybe she wouldn't freeze, but she'd have a very uncomfortable night. And if she was going to be so stubborn, perhaps she might even learn something from it.

He took in her ash-stained face and damp clothing once again.

Nope. He couldn't do it. He didn't like the thought of her being cold and hungry, and him right next door in his warm house, doing nothing to help her.

He wasn't good with people so he wasn't sure what to say to convince her to come with him, so he simply moved over to the chair where her bag sat and picked it up, masking his surprise at how light it was, given she was supposed to be staying here for an entire season.

Her eyes widened. "Hey, what are you doing? Put that down."

"No." He threw the bag over his shoulder and headed back to the front door. "Come on. We can have this discussion at my place. I'm getting cold."

He could feel her astonished gaze following him, but he ignored it, stepping straight through the open front door and onto the porch.

Then he turned around to find her standing in the doorway, staring at him in outrage. "Are you coming or what?"

"No. Are you insane?"

"If you don't want to walk, I could carry you." He meant it, too, though why that thought sent a shot of heat through him, he didn't know.

"Oh, my God, no," she muttered, her gaze flickering to his shoulders, then away.

She'd done that in the hallway just before, too. Was she checking him out?

The tight thing in his chest shifted, moving lower, becoming a different sort of feeling altogether.

Noah shoved it away. It had been a while since he'd allowed himself female company, and when he did, he preferred women who were passing through town, who weren't staying and didn't want anything more from him, because he wasn't in a position to give anyone anything.

He was done with seeing to another person's needs. He'd been doing it all his life and he was done. And he had a feeling, looking at Bella Jacobson standing in front of him now, that she was a woman who might turn out to be an endless dark well of need.

Just like her mother.

Irritated for no good reason, Noah turned around. "If you want your bag, you're going to have to come and get it," he said over his shoulder.

And headed down the porch steps to the gate.

CHAPTER THREE

BELLA WATCHED NOAH Faraday's tall, broad figure retreat down the path, carrying her bag, with the sense that her handle on this situation was slipping slowly but surely from her numb grasp.

Who the hell did he think he was? Coming in and scaring her, then pushing his way inside to check out the woodstove and the sink. Not to mention picking up her bag and carrying it away with him.

Dammit, and all sorts of other curse words Grandma June would probably dislike.

Perhaps it was that her feet were numb in her wet sneakers. Or maybe it was the icy cling of her damp jeans and the emptiness in her stomach.

Whatever, the thought of a hot shower and food was too tempting to ignore. Yes, she had her pride, but there was proud and then there was stupid, and she was edging into stupid.

Not that he'd really given her a choice. Not now that he'd taken her bag.

Cursing under her breath, Bella pulled the front door shut, the hinges shrieking in protest, and locked it. Then she hurried down the steps after Noah.

The walk to his place wasn't pleasant. He had long strides and she had to trot to keep up. The air was bitter and her feet kept slipping in the snow, and she wanted to tell him to slow down because she couldn't keep up, but then she'd have to walk beside him, and since she had no idea what to say, she didn't want to do that. So she hurried along behind, shivering.

Night had fully settled in by the time they'd walked up Noah's long driveway to the large farmhouse at the end.

Momentarily forgetting her physical discomfort, Bella stared as she trudged closer, the lights shining welcomingly in the cold darkness.

She'd almost forgotten the Faraday ranch. Maybe she'd blocked it out since it hadn't been the best of times, not when her mother had spent much of the one year they'd lived there in tears—not real tears, fake tears—because Hank wouldn't do whichever thing she wanted him to do at the time. And Noah was there, silent and disapproving, watching her mother with obvious dislike.

There had been stairs. And she'd sat at the top of them, ostentatiously reading a book, but in actual fact waiting to catch a glimpse of him. Half of her had been desperate for him to look at her, while the other half had been desperate for him not to.

Just like she'd never gotten that smile from him, she'd never gotten that look, either. Not once.

It was a pretty house, though—she remembered that. Painted red with white windows and doors. It had looked more worn and neglected back then, but in the light coming from the porch, she could see the satiny shine of new paint.

Obviously Noah had done up the place. Or maybe that was Hank? She didn't relish seeing Hank again, not after how her mother had treated him. He'd been kind to her, which was more than she could say for a lot of her mother's boyfriends.

Noah went up the porch stairs, then dug into his pocket, extracting the key. He unlocked the white front door and pushed it open. "Go on in."

He still had his cowboy hat on, the top dusted with snow, and the brim shadowed his face from the light. His eyes were dark beneath it, gazing at her expressionlessly, the same way he had all those years ago.

Had he really not liked her then? Or was this his usual expression?

Strange feelings shifted in her chest, a sense of trepidation stealing through her.

"You haven't turned into an ax murderer, have you?" she asked, only half-joking. "Thought I'd better ask before coming inside."

"No." His face could have been carved from granite. "I'm pretty sure Grandma June wouldn't have given you my number if I was."

Good point.

Taking a silent breath, Bella brushed past his tall, silent figure and stepped inside.

A blast of warm air hit her and her whole body shivered violently as the warmth of the house enveloped her.

Then something heavy and warm draped around her shoulders; Noah had put his coat around her again.

She shivered again, though this time it wasn't from the cold, not with the way his scent hit her. Turning, she began, "Thanks, but—"

"Keep it on." Noah's tone was clipped as he gestured toward the doorway on the left. "There's a fire in the living room. Go sit down and I'll fix you something to eat."

Bella opened her mouth to tell him that she wasn't hungry, but he'd already dumped her bag in the hall, then headed off toward the back of the house, where the kitchen was.

Left with nothing else but to do what she was told, she gritted her teeth and went through the doorway into the living area.

Like the rest of the place it was vaguely familiar, with a heavy beamed ceiling and a big stone fireplace along one wall. A worn but comfortable-looking couch covered in dark blue fabric stood in front of the fire, with a couple of armchairs to either side and a soft-looking red rug on the floor.

She remembered those armchairs. Hank used to sit in one. It was empty now, as was the little side table that sat next to it and the coffee table in front of the couch. In fact, there was no clutter anywhere—the room was almost stark, which she was sure it hadn't been years ago. It felt oddly bleak.

Moving over to the fire, she stretched out her numb fingers to the flames, belatedly realizing they were filthy with ash. Oh, God, and she'd wiped those hands over her face, too.

No wonder Noah was helping her. She probably looked a complete mess.

You are *a complete mess.*

Embarrassment heated her cheeks, along with a healthy dose of anger at herself. And—unfairly—at him for coming along only to see her fall flat on her face.

To save you from a night of freezing your ass off, you mean.

"I got you a drink." Noah's voice came from behind

her, the gritty sound carrying its own static charge. "Come and sit down."

She should have protested. Told him she didn't want a drink and she didn't want to sit down, and could he please stop ordering her around like a drill sergeant. Yet she found herself turning and going over to the couch, sitting down on it without a word. As if she'd come to the end of whatever stubborn strength she had left.

He'd put a steaming mug on the coffee table and she caught the sweet, delicious scent of the liquid.

Dear lord. It couldn't be, could it?

She wrapped her ash-smeared fingers around the handle and lifted it. Noah stood on the other side of the coffee table, watching her. He'd taken his hat off, revealing black hair shorn close to his skull, and somehow she'd thought he might not look as imposing without the hat on, but if anything, he looked even more intimidating, the hard, masculine lines of his face standing out, his dark eyes watchful and guarded.

Disturbed, Bella avoided his gaze, taking a sip from the mug instead. And as soon as the liquid hit her taste buds she wanted to burst into tears.

Hot chocolate. Goddamned hot chocolate.

Not quite what Grandma June made, but still sweet and chocolaty and just what she'd been craving. How long had it been since she'd had simple hot chocolate? Years. And certainly no one had ever made it for her.

Conscious of Noah's intense gaze, she ignored the hot prickle behind her eyes and took another sip, relishing the taste and the heat, her fingers feeling less numb, a warm glow igniting in her stomach.

"That okay?" he asked eventually.

"Yes." She had to force the word out, hoping it didn't sound as graceless as she thought it did. "Thank you."

He gave a nod. "Drink that, then you can get yourself clean."

Oh, a hot shower...

Her throat tightened. Damn, why was she getting emotional? Must be the end of a long and trying day getting to her, plus the cold and maybe a bit of grief all mixed in.

Nothing to do with him and the heat of the fire or the drink he'd made for her.

A silence fell that wasn't entirely comfortable.

Noah didn't move, the pressure of his gaze making Bella want to fidget.

She resisted the urge, sipping at her hot chocolate, racking her brains for something to say and then feeling annoyed, because why should it be up to her to say something? It was his house and he was the host. Surely it was his job to be polite and say something, not her.

But he stayed silent, and eventually, Bella found herself looking around and asking, "So where's Hank?"

"He's dead," Noah said flatly.

A pulse of shock went through her and she lowered her mug. "Oh, I'm sorry."

He lifted one powerful shoulder, the fabric of his black thermal pulling tight over hard muscle. "It was five years ago."

His tone indicated that he did not want to talk about it, so she fell silent.

Did her mother know Hank had died? Bella wouldn't have put it past her to have known and yet not told Bella about it. Avery probably hadn't cared, anyway. Hank was just another man in a long line of men she'd discarded once they were of no more use to her.

"So...the ranch is yours now?" she asked.

"Yeah."

"It looks...nice." A lame thing to say and she didn't know why she was trying to make conversation, especially when he obviously didn't want to talk. Then again, he'd never been very chatty as a teenager. Not that she had been, either. She'd been far too shy and he'd been far too intimidating.

"Lila said you were staying for the winter," Noah said after another couple of excruciating minutes had passed. "That true?"

"Yes. I'm, uh, going to be fixing the house up to sell it."

"Sell it?"

It was clear from his expression that he did not like that idea one bit.

Too bad. It wasn't his house.

"That's the plan." She met his gaze head-on. "And before you say anything, it was Grandma June's idea."

His dark gaze ran over her in a clinical kind of way before settling on her feet. "You should take your sneakers off," he said. "They're wet through."

A strange urge to tuck her feet under the couch gripped her. Because, of course, her sneakers *were* wet through. The fabric was also a little worn and the rubber of one sole was starting to come loose, and there was a part of her that didn't want him to see just how worn they actually were.

He might ask questions such as why she wasn't wearing boots, or did she have another pair of shoes to put on? And then she'd have to figure out some lies to cover the fact that she was wearing these sneakers because they were her only pair of shoes, and since she'd been putting every penny she owned into her café fund, she didn't have any money to spare to buy any others.

Still, given that, it might be a good idea to take them off and dry them by the fire.

"Uh, yeah, okay." She put her mug down and bent to fiddle with the laces. But because they were wet she had problems undoing the knots.

She struggled for a moment or two and then Noah was coming silently around the coffee table, dropping down onto his knees in front of her. He took one of her feet in his big hands and propped the sole on one muscular thigh, then began to pull at the knots himself.

Shocked into immobility, Bella could only stare as he deftly undid the knot and pulled the laces free. Then his fingers were circling her ankle as he gripped the heel of her sneaker and pulled it off her foot.

She had no time to protest, no time to even jerk away. He'd already stripped her damp sock off, let the foot go and moved on to the other before she had the chance. But she could still feel the imprint of his fingers as they'd brushed her bare skin, burning like embers, making her heartbeat accelerate and her breath catch.

"You don't have to do that," she muttered.

He ignored her, tugging at the lace on her other foot, and for some weird reason, she felt something pull right down low inside her, a response she didn't want and wasn't ready for.

She almost jerked her foot away, but stopped herself at the last minute, too worried about what that might reveal. Except she could feel her cheeks heat yet again in a helpless blush.

Hell, what was wrong with her? She hadn't seen him in ten years and all she had to do apparently was lay eyes on him and she was back to being thirteen again and deep in the clutches of her first crush.

But these feelings didn't have the soft-focus romanticism of a young teenager. No, these feelings were a bit more...basic than that.

Bella swallowed and hoped to God he wouldn't hear the frantic beating of her heart. And despite the hot chocolate she'd been drinking, her mouth had gone dry. And even though her clothes were damp, she certainly wasn't feeling cold anymore.

Noah's shoulders were wide, his thermal outlining all the muscle beneath it, enough that she could see his biceps flex as he worked the laces. She could feel the heat of his thigh under her sole, too, seeping through the rubber, and when he finally got the shoe and sock off, she had the oddest urge to put her bare foot back on it, see what it would feel like when there wasn't rubber between them.

How weird. She'd avoided men for the most part, hadn't wanted a relationship and wasn't in any hurry to divest herself of her virginity. She hadn't met anyone she'd had any feelings for, anyway.

But this man... Whether she liked it or not, she did have feelings about.

As if he could feel her staring at him, Noah looked up, his dark gaze meeting hers, and what little breath remained in Bella's lungs vanished.

Something electric and hot passed between them. Something she'd never felt before, though it was familiar, as if she'd felt an echo of it at one time in the past.

She wanted to say something, but she didn't know what, because her voice wasn't working.

Before she could get a word out, Noah rose to his feet abruptly. "The shower's upstairs. You remember where." His voice was curt. "I'll go get you something to eat."

Then he stalked from the room without another word.

NOAH PULLED OPEN the fridge door sharply and stared unseeing at the contents.

He couldn't work out what the hell was wrong with him.

What on earth had made him kneel at her feet and take her shoes off for her like that? Because whatever instinct it had been, it had been a mistake.

When he'd held Bella's small foot and felt her watching him, and then he'd looked up, something in her blue gaze had hit him like a hammer.

There had been heat in her eyes and she'd been staring at him like she'd never seen him before in her entire life.

He didn't know why it had struck him so forcibly, but it had.

Yet that hadn't been the worst part.

The worst part had been when he'd felt something hungry stir inside him in response. Something he'd pushed down deep, that had been hibernating, and now was waking up.

Irritated, he grabbed the chicken casserole he'd made yesterday, slammed the fridge door shut and stalked over to the counter. Then he busied himself with heating up the food, trying to focus on that and not on Bella Jacobson's big blue eyes.

He didn't want to be attracted to Avery Jacobson's daughter. Avery had been a real piece of work, and though there was no guarantee that Bella would end up being the same, you could never tell. Hell, sometimes he was sure he felt the same hunger for oblivion or whatever it was that had propelled his father headfirst into a vodka bottle.

Not that he'd ever end up the same way. Not if he could help it. He had far more self-control than Hank ever did.

Yeah, you do. So just ignore whatever the hell is going on with Bella and be more of a gracious host, and less of a dick.

Noah growled under his breath. Yeah, he hadn't exactly been friendly, though again, he wasn't sure why.

Was it only because she was the daughter of the woman who'd ruined his father's life? Or did it have something to do with her mentioning that she was planning on selling Grandma June's house? June had loved that house and she wouldn't want it sold to some strangers, surely?

It's not about Grandma June's house and you know it.

He gritted his teeth. If all this irritation was simply the result of animal attraction, then he needed to handle himself and not let her get under his skin.

Getting some bread out, he put a couple of slices on the plate then grabbed some cutlery before taking it all into the living area.

Bella wasn't there, which presumably meant she was having a shower.

Automatically, Noah began straightening things.

He liked a tidy household and had done all the cooking and cleaning since his mother had left, driven away by the relentlessness of Hank's addiction. She'd given Noah the choice to come with her, but Noah hadn't felt able to leave Hank. Someone had to take care of him, and even though Noah had only been thirteen at the time, he'd made the decision to stay.

Things had been pretty bad after she'd gone.

He'd had one good year, when he'd thought his father had given up the bottle for good. That was the year he'd married Avery. But Noah had always known it wasn't going to last, because nothing ever did.

Sure enough, his father had hit the bottle hard as soon as Avery had left.

So much for the happily-ever-after.

And it wasn't that Avery and Hank's marriage hadn't lasted that had made him so bitter. It was that for a little while, he'd thought that it would.

The thoughts were uncomfortable so he shoved them away, picking up Bella's soaking sneakers and carrying them over to the fire so they could dry. They were worn and there were holes in them, the rubber starting to perish. She needed new shoes, not to mention socks. Those were full of holes, too.

Moving over to the coffee table where the empty mug sat, he picked it up to take it into the kitchen and then stared at it, slightly puzzled. The mug looked as if it had been licked clean.

She sure had seemed to like the hot chocolate. In fact, now that he thought about it, he'd had the strange impression that she'd been going to cry when she'd seen what was in that mug.

Probably due to her being cold and obviously hungry, because he'd never had a reaction like that to his hot chocolate before. Not that he'd ever made hot chocolate for anyone but himself. But still…

"Um, thanks for the shower."

Noah looked up to see Bella standing in the doorway, looking somewhat hesitant.

She'd taken her beanie off and her black hair lay damp and shining across her shoulders. The ash was gone from her face and her skin was flushed, the deep blue of her eyes almost luminous in the firelight.

No, she wasn't pretty. She was beautiful.

The hungry thing inside him shifted again, and for a second all he could think about was whether her cheek would feel as soft as it looked if he ran the backs of his fingers across it.

He'd lay money on the fact that it would.

Then he noticed something else: she was still wearing her dirty, ash-streaked clothing.

"Didn't you have anything else to change into?" he asked, his gaze flicking over her clothing again.

She flushed. "These are fine, just a bit damp. Hey, I couldn't find a spare towel so I—"

"They're not just a bit damp," he interrupted, frowning. "They're wet and they're dirty. Go change and I'll put them in the laundry."

Bella scowled. "What are you, my mother?"

His jaw tightened. "You shouldn't get clean just to put on dirty clothes again."

"Well, thanks for your concern, but I'm fine." She didn't look at him, coming into the room and making a beeline for the table where he'd put her food.

He reached out and gently wrapped his fingers around her upper arm, stopping her. "You *do* have other clothes, don't you?"

Her eyes went wide, staring first at where he gripped her arm before glancing up at him. "Of course I do. What's it to you, anyway?"

She was very close, the scent of his own soap rising from her skin, mixed with ash and the cold bite of snow. He liked it. Not so much the ash-and-snow part, but definitely the scent of him on her.

Damn, what was wrong with him? He didn't go around noticing the way a woman smelled normally, and he definitely didn't get territorial, either.

You're supposed to not let her get under your skin.

He let go and stood back, his heart beating faster than it should have been. To distract himself from his body's ridiculous reaction, he nodded toward the food on the coffee table. "Go eat."

She moved over to the couch without another word, sitting down and picking up the plate. There were no arguments now about how she wasn't hungry; she began eating like she hadn't seen food in months.

Maybe she hasn't?

The thought came out of nowhere and sat there in his head.

Goddamn.

"You don't have any supplies," he said into the quiet of the room. "And I know for a fact that JJ came over and cleaned the fridge about a week ago, so there's nothing in there. What exactly were you going to eat?"

Her fork clattered onto to her plate, her chin lifting, sudden anger gleaming in her eyes. "What's your problem? I know having me turn up here is probably the last thing on earth you wanted, but that doesn't mean you get to order me around, ask me rude questions and generally treat me like some dirt you got on your shoe."

"I'm not treating you like that," he growled, knowing he was and feeling pissed about it. "But if I'm going to be saving your ass from freezing to death, I want to know why you arrived with holes in your shoes, no food and clearly no clean clothes to change into."

She'd gone all stiff, as if he'd struck a nerve. "That's none of your damn business."

There was something familiar about this.

It reminded him of the arguments he'd had with his father, about whether Hank had eaten, had a shower, brushed his hair, changed his clothes. His father had always been a proud man and had been incensed at being asked. Usually because the answer was no, Hank hadn't done any of those things. He'd never admitted he had a problem with alcohol and he'd never admitted that he couldn't look after himself when he was in the middle of a drinking binge.

Bella wasn't a drunk old man, but she was looking at him with the same defensiveness and stubborn pride that his father used to. And Noah bet he knew why: she didn't want to admit that she had no money.

He considered asking her straight out about it, but confrontation had never worked with his father and he suspected it wouldn't work with Bella, either. Not that it was the time for confrontation. She'd only just arrived and he'd probably reached his being-a-dick limit.

Maybe he'd broach the topic in the morning, after she'd had a good night's sleep.

Why do you want to broach the topic, anyway? You weren't going to let her get under your skin, remember?

He was done trying to fix people, especially people who didn't want to be fixed, and most especially people with more pride than sense.

But he wasn't trying to fix Bella Jacobson. He only wanted to help her.

He normally wasn't that altruistic, but he couldn't leave one of Grandma June's granddaughters to fend for herself when he knew that she needed a hand. June had been the only person who'd visited him after his father had died, to make sure he was okay and to see if he needed anything, and he owed her for that if nothing else.

Noah met Bella's stubborn blue gaze and only nodded. "Fair enough," he said. "I'll go get the room ready for you."

CHAPTER FOUR

BELLA WOKE UP the next morning with no idea where she was.

A window near the bed gave a view out into a cloudless blue sky, a ray of sunshine coming through the glass.

Sitting by the door was a neatly folded stack of clothes.

She stared at it and gradually the memories of the night before began to filter through. Of Grandma June's cold farmhouse and the failed fire lighting. Then walking through the snow. Hot chocolate and food and a warmth...

Noah.

Bella let out a breath.

She'd gotten the distinct impression the night before that not only had he *not* wanted to help her, he was somehow angry with her, too. And she had no idea why.

Perhaps it was all history. Or perhaps he wasn't a very friendly person in general. Whatever, she didn't appreciate his attitude.

She definitely hadn't appreciated his questions about her clothing or her lack of supplies. It was perilously close to him finding out she had no money and she did *not* want that.

That didn't mean she was going to tell him about

how she'd lost everything, though. She didn't want *anyone* to know. It was her problem and she would fix it.

Deciding that she'd better get up, Bella slipped out of bed and hunted around for her clothing, only to find that the neatly folded stack by the door *was* her clothing. Somehow it had been magically cleaned and dried, and was all ready to wear.

She scowled at it.

Noah again, of course.

Why does it bother you so much? You've got clean clothes. Isn't that a good thing?

Sure it was. And getting annoyed was ridiculous.

She'd slept in her underwear the night before and since she did have a couple of spare pairs in her bag, she put on clean panties then dressed in her freshly laundered clothing.

Somehow another sweatshirt had made its way into the pile, which puzzled her since it wasn't hers. Had Noah put it in by mistake?

Unlikely.

He knows you don't have any other clothes.

A flush spread through her cheeks and she was tempted to leave the sweatshirt on the floor. But the fabric was thick and soft, and the faded blue color appealed to her, and she was at the point where she couldn't really afford to turn down offers of help, no matter how subtle they were.

Bella slipped it on. It was far too big but it was warm and that was the main thing.

She fussed around with the rest of her clothing, putting on her clean, dry socks, then she grabbed her bag and cautiously opened the bedroom door.

The long upstairs hallway was quiet so she padded

along it, then approached the stairs and went silently down them.

Her sneakers were sitting by the door, mostly dry, so she put them on, grimacing at the residual damp.

Once they were on, she put a hand to the front door.

She should say goodbye, but part of her didn't want to. It was easier simply to leave. That way he wouldn't feel he had to offer her anything else and she wouldn't have to feel embarrassed about taking his sweatshirt.

She'd text him a thank-you once she'd gotten back to the farmhouse. That should do it.

Bella pushed open the front door.

"You're leaving?" Noah's gritty voice sounded distinctly annoyed.

She muttered a curse and turned around.

He was standing at the top of the stairs looking down at her, dark eyes disapproving, mouth in a hard line.

He was in a pair of dark green Carhartts today, with another black thermal, and the way he was standing, all broad muscularity and strength, made him seem even more intimidating.

Bella forced herself to smile. "I was just coming to find you to say goodbye."

"No, you weren't." He came down the stairs, his movements slow and fluid. "You were leaving without saying goodbye. Or even thank you."

Heat tinged her cheeks.

Busted.

"I thought it would be easier," she said hardily.

Noah came to a stop at the bottom of the stairs, not that it made him any less tall. "Why?"

"Like I said last night, it's clear you weren't particularly happy about helping me, though I'm grateful you did. So I thought it would be easier if I just left."

"What makes you think I'm not happy to help you?"

"You really have to ask?"

His expression gave nothing away. "You weren't exactly happy to receive help yourself."

"I'm not." She lifted her chin. "I'm not like Mom, Noah. So don't worry. I'm not going to be begging you to do things for me every five minutes and then collapsing into tears when it doesn't happen."

He was silent for a moment. "Let me grab my coat," he said finally. "I'll come with you and help you get that fire lit."

"I said I don't need—"

"You won't be able to light it if I don't show you how," he interrupted, a certain amount of gentleness in his tone that hadn't been there the night before. "It requires a bit of a knack. Once I show you, you'll have no problems doing it yourself, okay?"

She didn't want to accept and yet she did need to know how to get that fire going. So maybe it wouldn't be a bad thing for him to show her. Be even more irritating if she had to keep calling him to light it for her. "Okay," she said, only slightly grudgingly. "Thanks."

He nodded, then his attention dropped to the sweatshirt she was wearing, and if she wasn't much mistaken, the hard cast of his features softened. "You can keep that, if you like."

"Oh, I was going to return it." She could feel herself going red. Again. "I mean, it was nice of you to lend it to me, but I don't need—"

"Like I said." His gaze returned to hers. "Keep it."

For a second she was held there, caught by those

compelling dark brown eyes, another of those electric moments shivering in the air between them.

Then he turned and grabbed his coat off the peg by the door. "Come on." He went past her, stepping through the front door and out into the cold.

Static was still sizzling over her skin, but she ignored it, following him out the door.

It was a perfect winter snow-globe day, with crisp new snow and a clear blue sky. The sun wasn't warm but it made the walk more pleasant. Bella didn't even get her shoes wet this time.

Noah went up the steps to the porch once they got to Grandma June's house, and waited for her to fiddle with the key. Again there was a problem with the lock that he had to help her with.

"I guess that's number one on the list of things to do," Bella said as he got the door open for her. "Call a locksmith."

Noah shrugged. "The mechanism might only need oiling. I can do that if you like. Save you a bit of money."

"I don't need to save money," she said before she could stop herself.

He straightened, his gaze far more penetrating than she would like it to be. "How many more things need fixing? And how much money do you have to fix 'em with?"

There was money. Hidden in a safe in the basement, according to the details sent along with Grandma June's letter. But the money was strictly for repairs only—not that Bella would ever have considered taking any of it, since she didn't want any free rides—and it wasn't a lot to start with. And who knew how much the repairs for the rest of the house were going to cost?

Maybe she shouldn't spend the money on a lock-smith.

"There's a list of things," she said guardedly. "And there's some money. But I guess I need to see how much everything is going to cost."

Noah lifted one muscular shoulder. "The offer's there." He stepped through the front door and headed toward the kitchen.

Bella trailed after him, discomforted and not sure why.

The kitchen was still freezing, ash dusting the floor from her abortive fire-lighting attempt, and she felt a renewed sense of embarrassment about her failure.

Then again, Noah had said there was a knack to it, so maybe it wasn't all about her being an idiot.

He was crouched down in front of the stove, and as she entered the kitchen, he beckoned her over. "Come on. I'll show you how it's done."

More kindling was needed and he spent a couple of minutes showing her where the wood was in the basement. There was a stack of it, plus kindling, and after producing a lighter from the depths of his coat, within five minutes he'd built a small, fledgling fire. He showed her the trick with the damper to adjust the air flow, and then where her grandmother disposed of the ashes.

"I think I can remember all that," she said when he'd finished, watching him as he fed a couple of big-ger logs into the fire.

"Yeah, you'll be fine now you know how it's done." He rose to his feet in another of those smooth, ath-letic movements. Then he frowned and reached into the pocket of his coat, bringing out his phone and glancing down at the screen.

"Lila. Wanting to know you're okay." He glanced at her. "She doesn't have your number?"

Bella pulled a face. "Uh, no. I didn't give it to her."

"Why not?"

How to explain the difficult feelings she had around Jasper Creek? Around her family? Or rather the strangers that comprised her family, because she didn't know any of them. Avery had made sure of that.

"I don't give out my number to just anyone," she muttered.

"She's your cousin."

"Yeah, but I don't know her. I don't know any of them." She pushed her cold hands into the pockets of her jacket. "When Mom and I went to Seattle, we kind of…lost contact with everyone."

Noah's gaze narrowed and Bella's shoulders tightened. She didn't want to answer any more questions about her cousins, about anyone, not right now.

"Right," he said. "Well, I'll text her to let her know you're okay."

The tension in her shoulders eased. Apparently he wasn't going to push her today, which made a rush of gratitude fill her. "Thanks," she said hesitantly. "I, uh, really appreciate it."

"No problem." He put the phone back in his coat. "Let's have a look at these pipes." He didn't give her the option to refuse, but simply moved over to the sink and began fiddling around with the tap.

Left with no choice, Bella hovered around the woodstove, alternately watching him and checking on her fire.

Noah went out of the kitchen and was gone for a considerable length of time.

Figuring she might be able to leave the fire for a while, she went cautiously out to the hallway and into the living room opposite the kitchen.

It was a comfortable room, with a big window that looked out over the front yard and a worn couch beneath it. The couch was covered with one of Grandma June's hand-sewn quilts, a couple of armchairs on either side, a coffee table in front of it.

In the wall opposite the couch was the fireplace and a mantelpiece crowded with photos and knickknacks above it.

Bella drifted over, staring at the collection of photos. They were in different silver frames and were of different young women. She recognized them from the one photo album her mother had. Keira. JJ. Lila. The strangers who were her cousins. There didn't seem to be a photo of her, though… No, wait, there was. In a small frame right on the end, of her as a child. It looked as though she'd been cut out of a larger picture, since she was standing close to someone else, her hand reaching up and out of the frame. She was gazing warily at whoever was taking the photo, not smiling like the others.

Bella picked the picture up, staring at it, a tight pain sitting behind her breastbone. Was this really the only photo her grandmother had of her?

Her throat closed, a strange longing tugging at her.

Avery had never gotten on with Grandma June. She remembered the tension in her mother's rare visits. It had felt so thick sometimes that she couldn't breathe. Her grandmother never said anything awful—it was

only Avery who did. Tight, vicious words and sometimes bitter tears.

Avery had never said what the problem had been,
only that she was done with Jasper Creek, and if Bella
knew what was good for her, then so would she.

So she had. But it was clear from the photo that
Grandma June was not done with her.

She only had one good memory. Of that summer at
June's with her cousins, the last summer she'd had before she'd left for Seattle. Of playing sardines and her
finding the best place, down in the basement behind the
stacks of wood. She'd sat there a long time by herself,
listening to the shouts and laughter of the other kids
and feeling lonely and isolated the way she always had.

Then, one by one, her cousins had found her hiding
place and they'd all piled in to hide with her, sitting
at her side with lots of whispers and giggles. Dreamy
Lila and serious JJ. Keira, seventeen already and a kid
no longer.

And Bella had imagined that they weren't cousins.
That they were her sisters. That she wasn't alone, the
way she always seemed to be...

Would that have been what her life would have been
like if Avery had gotten on with her mother? Would
Avery have stayed? Would Bella have grown up with
the lovely women in each of these photos? Would they
all have been sisters to one another the way they had
that summer long ago?

The pain in her chest tightened and she put the photo
down abruptly.

It didn't matter. She hadn't grown up here and she
didn't know those women. She was here for one thing

and that was to fix up the house, sell it and get some money for her café.

And then she'd never have to come back here again.

Bella turned and nearly ran into a broad male chest. Gasping, she put her hands up to steady herself, her palms connecting unexpectedly with hard muscle and heat.

Her head snapped up and she found herself staring straight into Noah's eyes. His irises were a deep, dense brown, almost black, and they were framed by thick, sooty lashes. Beautiful eyes. Enigmatic, fascinating.

She stared up at him, hypnotized by what she could see in that velvet darkness, a shift in his usual guarded expression. A swirling glitter of…heat.

Noah stepped back so sharply she almost stumbled again, whatever heat had been in his eyes vanishing. "Pipes are fixed." His gritty voice sounded even more gritty than usual. "I'm going into town this morning. I'll pick you up some groceries while I'm at it."

Bella's heartbeat was loud in her head. Her hands were raised as if her palms were still resting against his chest and they felt scorched, as if the remembered heat of his body had imprinted itself into her skin.

She lowered them, curling her fingers instinctively into fists, and tried to focus. Groceries. He'd offered to get her groceries. Or rather, he'd said that he was going to get her some and she had a feeling that meant he'd get them whether she wanted him to or not.

She opened her mouth to refuse, but he went on, "Pay me when I get back, okay?"

Damn. And now she didn't know what to say. Because even though it would solve her immediate dilemma, she was still left with the issue of how to pay him. Maybe a check that he could cash…never?

Then again, she was going to have to eat something while she was here. Perhaps she could solve the money issue later. Hey, maybe if she got him to fix the lock on the front door, she could use the money she would have spent on the locksmith to pay him for food instead? Which would mean technically she *was* paying for repairs.

"Uh, sure." She cleared her throat, disturbed by how husky it sounded. "That would be great."

"Good. Write me a list of what you want. Oh, and—" he reached into the yet another pocket of his coat, bringing out a candy bar and handing it to her "—since you like candy bars so much, here's breakfast. Keep you going until I get back."

She looked at the candy bar, the conversation from the night before unreeling in her head. He'd remembered it. He'd also remembered that she hadn't had breakfast.

A warm glow sat inside her, edging out the pain that had been there earlier, though she tried not to pay it any attention. "Thanks," she said, taking the candy bar from him.

"Sure." He gave her another of his dark, enigmatic looks that did nothing to slow the rush of blood in her veins.

Then, without another word, he turned and strode from the room, leaving her with nothing but the silence of the house around her.

TWO DAYS LATER, Noah stood on his porch and looked over the fence line of his property toward June's place.

He could see the farmhouse roof and the chimney, and smoke was coming out of it this morning the way smoke had been coming out of it every morning for the past few days.

He'd been checking, because he'd decided that if he could see smoke, that meant she'd managed to get the fire lit and that she was warm. And she didn't need his help.

He'd helped her with the fire, gotten her groceries from Jasper Creek's small market—which she'd paid him for in cash, he noted—and as far as he was concerned that was his responsibilities done.

Except apparently he wasn't done because for some reason he simply hadn't been able to get her out of his head.

He'd known he'd had to leave her alone the second she'd turned around and nearly walked into him that day in June's living room. Her palms had pressed against his chest and he'd realized in an instant that the woodstove in the kitchen wasn't the only fire she'd ignited.

There was one inside of him, too, and those little hands were lit matches, setting him ablaze.

He hadn't been able to get away fast enough.

It was either that or he did something stupid like grab a handful of silky black hair and pull her head back, kiss that little rosebud of a mouth.

Temptation was always there and he'd always managed to resist. He was the goddamn king of resisting. But not with her and he wasn't sure why.

She was small and vulnerable and he didn't want small and vulnerable. He didn't want anyone who needed him. He didn't want anyone who looked like they might need fixing, and Bella certainly looked like she needed fixing.

Even if he'd been inclined to indulge himself, she didn't strike him as the kind of woman he could have a couple of nights of easy pleasure with. She seemed complicated and he'd had enough of complicated to last a lifetime.

Yeah, it was easier all around if he stayed away.

That door was a worry, though. What if it had jammed and she wasn't able to get out of the house? She had his number, sure, and he'd told her to contact him if she needed anything, but she'd shown herself reluctant before. What if she was too damn stubborn? Maybe he should grab his tools and head down there, check on her and fix the lock. One less thing for her to have deal with and one less thing for him to worry about.

What about that temptation bullshit you keep telling yourself?

Noah scowled in the direction of the farmhouse.

Yeah, maybe it would be better to spend five minutes fixing that lock and then he wouldn't be standing out on his porch every goddamn morning watching for smoke and wondering whether she was okay.

Growling under his breath at his own ridiculousness, he went off to the barn to grab his tool belt, then made his way down toward the farmhouse.

Everything seemed normal as he strode up the steps to the front door and knocked.

There was a moment's silence.

He'd raised his hand to knock again when the door jerked open. Bella stood on the threshold, her hair an inky spill over her shoulders, her blue eyes dark and wide as they took him in. She was wearing the sweatshirt he'd given her again, the color making her eyes seem darker and bluer, and her skin smooth and pale as fresh cream.

He'd forgotten how pretty she was.

Then her mouth softened, like she was going to smile, and something hit him hard in the gut. Prettiness alone was nothing. But that almost smile…

No one smiled at him these days. His own fault, since he never smiled at anyone else, not when he didn't have much of anything to smile about. Yeah, he'd cut himself off pretty thoroughly from the rest of Jasper Creek. And he'd thought he was fine with it. Yet the way Bella was looking now, as if she was pleased to see him, made him want to see what she looked like when she really smiled. At him.

This is a mistake.

Maybe. But he couldn't turn around and walk away now. And besides, maybe it would be good for him to have a little temptation. A test. Self-control, after all, was a muscle that needed to be exercised.

"Hey," he said.

"Hey back." Faint color tinged her cheekbones. "What are you doing here?"

"Come to fix the door." He paused. "Unless you got a locksmith in?"

"No." She shifted on her feet, like she was nervous, though what she had to be nervous about, he didn't know. "I called one, but he was booked up. I'd forgotten about Christmas."

So she *had* called one. He didn't like that. Odd since getting a locksmith meant he wouldn't have to come down here and fix it for her. Which would have made him happy. But, no. He felt irritated instead.

"If you've got things you want done around here, it might be best to wait until after Christmas," he said brusquely. "Unless you want me to do them, or you."

"I didn't really want to—"

"Ask for help? Yeah, I got it. Loud and clear."

The color in her cheeks deepened, but a familiar blue spark glowed in her eyes. "It isn't that I'm not grateful, Noah. I'm just not some damsel in distress who needs a man to come and rescue her all the time."

Why are you so irritated? Shouldn't you be glad she doesn't want help?

He should be, yet he wasn't. It was that damn need he had to fix things, the way he'd tried to fix his father. Throwing out the old man's booze and hiding his car keys. Once he'd even gone to Jasper Creek's lone bar to tell them not to serve his dad anymore, and that had worked for maybe a week. But Hank had always gone back to the bottle.

His father hadn't wanted to be fixed, so why Noah was standing around expending energy trying to help yet another stubborn mule, he had no idea.

But he didn't move. "It's only a door, Bella. Nothing more. Nothing less. Me fixing it doesn't mean you're a damsel in distress."

Restless energy swirled around her. "I guess so. Why do you want to help me, anyway? Because Lila told you to?"

"Some. But mostly because your grandma was a nice woman."

"Oh." Her jaw went tight.

Why? Had she not liked his answer?

"You want it to be because of you?" He shouldn't

ask. He should be fixing her door, not getting interested and talking to her.

The blush in her cheeks—already red—became scarlet. "No, of course not." She turned away. "I'll leave you to it."

Afterward, he didn't know why he'd reached out, gripping her upper arm so she didn't turn away. So he could look at her face. Because touching her was stupid.

Yet he did, his fingers curling around her upper arm, stopping her.

She turned back, her eyes wide and full of surprise. And he realized he was standing a lot closer to her than he'd thought, and that a fresh, faintly sweet scent was rising from her hair and skin. She blinked and for a second her gaze dipped to his mouth.

He felt the impact as if she'd touched him.

Cold air swirled around him, but he wasn't cold. And when her gaze lifted to his, he knew she wasn't, either. Something very blue and very hot glowed in her eyes, the electricity he'd felt from the get-go shimmering between them.

You know this is a mistake.

Was it? Getting close might be a good thing. Because if he could resist her, he could resist anything.

"You want it to be for you, don't you?" His voice had gotten rough.

"No. I don't care why you're doing it."

"Then why did you ask?"

She looked pointedly down at where his fingers circled her upper arm. "You can let me go now."

But he didn't. He lifted his other hand instead and put one finger beneath her chin, tilting her head back. "Why did you ask?" he repeated, softer, quieter.

Her long, thick lashes fluttered. "You don't like me, Noah. So why do you want to know?"

"Who said I didn't like you?"

"Oh, come on. It's obvious. You didn't like me back then and you don't like me now."

Her skin was very soft against his fingertip, all satiny and warm, and the urge to stroke it gripped him tight. "I didn't not like you, Bella. Either then or now."

She stared up into his face, challenging. "You certainly acted like it."

Had he? The year Avery and Bella had come to live with him and Hank had been strange. For the first time since his mother had left, Noah hadn't had to clean up after his father, or cook or do any of the other things he usually had to do. He'd stalked around, discomforted by the sudden influx of femininity in what had previously been a male-dominated house, not knowing what to do with himself. Watching Avery and her subtle manipulations with a growing sense of unease.

Bella, with her curtain of black hair and big blue eyes and her silence, he'd barely noticed.

"It wasn't you I didn't like. It was your mother." He should really take his finger away, let her go. Yet he didn't.

"So you had no feeling about me either way?"

He frowned, not understanding. She'd been so quiet back then, not saying a word to him, her nose either buried in a book or stuck in her bedroom. "Did you want me to?"

She said nothing, but the sharp glitter in her eyes betrayed her; yes, she had wanted him to.

His chest tightened. "You never said a word."

"No, because you basically ignored me the entire year."

You did. Asshole.

Noah gritted his teeth. "You always looked like you'd rather be anywhere but at the ranch with me and Dad. So, yeah, I decided to leave you to it."

Her gaze was direct, challenging. And he was conscious of her scent and the warmth of her body. The soft curve of her bottom lip. The fine grain of her pale skin.

Then she looked away. "Are you going to fix my door or what?"

Oh, no, she wasn't doing that. She'd introduced the subject, made it clear that she was pissed off he'd ignored her all those years ago, and now she didn't want to talk?

He hadn't mattered to anyone in a very long time, yet it seemed like he'd mattered to her.

Well. He needed her to be clear about that.

Noah didn't question why he needed her to be clear, he simply took her chin in his fingers and turned her back to face him. "I don't give a shit about the damn door," he said roughly. "Be straight with me, Bella. Did you want me to notice you?"

"Does it matter?"

"Yeah." He stepped even closer. "It does."

"Why?" she demanded.

She was so warm and she had no idea what kind of fire she was playing with. Or maybe she did know. Maybe driving him mad was what she'd been hoping to do this whole time.

If so, it had to stop. He'd had enough.

He'd never allowed himself to have anything he wanted, so he tried not to want anything. Because that hunger inside him sometimes felt too big to contain. It was easier to deny himself everything than it was to allow himself something.

But one sip wouldn't make him an alcoholic.

One kiss wouldn't make him an addict. He was stronger than that.

He firmed his grip on her chin and looked down into her luminous blue eyes. "This is why," he said.

Then he bent his head and covered her mouth with his.

CHAPTER FIVE

BELLA HAD KNOWN he was going to kiss her. There had been intention in his dark eyes before he'd bent his head, as well as a fierce heat, and she found herself trembling with anticipation.

She hadn't realized that could happen. That a person could shake with longing and not with fear.

But then she couldn't think anymore because his lips covered hers and it was like she'd been plugged into an electrical socket, and someone had flipped the switch.

She was electrified, frozen in place by the most intense heat racing through her veins.

Bella trembled harder and she couldn't stop.

Noah was kissing her. *Noah* was kissing her.

Back when she'd been thirteen she'd imagined it. She hadn't been able to conceive of what it would feel like, so her imaginings were confined to watching herself be swept up in his arms and his head bent over her. A TV kind of kiss.

But the reality was nothing like that.

She hadn't thought that his fingertips would burn where they pressed against her skin, or that his big body would feel like she was standing before a roaring fire. She hadn't thought she'd feel as if she was going up in flames or that she'd be desperate to burn.

His mouth was firm, coaxing hers to open for him,

so she opened it, the kiss deepening, the flames licking up her spine. He tasted of coffee, dark and delicious, or like the hot chocolate her grandmother had made her, and she leaned into him, wanting more.

She'd never kissed a man before and if she'd known how good it would be, perhaps she'd have gotten over her scruples about men earlier. But then maybe not. She couldn't imagine kissing anyone other than Noah.

He touched his tongue to hers, exploring her, and electricity burned and fizzed in her blood, making her lift her hands and press her palms to the hard plane of his chest, desperate to feel his heat and all the firm muscle that lay beneath his thermal. He felt like he was carved out of warm, living rock, and she wanted to explore him, trace the dips and hollows of him, see what a man was shaped like.

A need opened up inside her and her fingers curled, grabbing his thermal and pulling as she rose on her tiptoes, kissing him back hungrily, wanting to fill the emptiness inside her with more of his taste, more of his heat.

He made a guttural masculine sound and suddenly the door frame was against her back, Noah at her front, holding her against it as the kiss changed, became hotter. Deeper. Feverish.

His body surrounded her, the width of his shoulders and broad plane of his chest right in front of her. So strong. She could push at him with all her strength and he wouldn't move. He'd stay right there, like a mountain.

She didn't know why that made her frantic. Suddenly and completely desperate. He smelled like snow and a warm, musky scent that made her shiver all over.

Made her want to burrow her face into his neck, lick the salt of his skin.

Her fists tightened, pulling hard on his thermal, arching her body against his. God, she'd never really understood how cold she'd been until now, until he was pressed against her.

He made another sound, one hand in her hair, the other gripping her jaw, tilting her head back so he could he could kiss her deeper, and she groaned.

That need welled up inside her, too big to contain so she didn't try. She let it pour out of her, a desperation she didn't know what to do with except clutch him closer, kiss him back as desperately as he was kissing her.

He gripped her hips, propelling her back into the house. The door slammed behind them as he kicked it shut, then he pushed her back until the staircase was against the backs of her calves.

She gasped, stumbling, off balance and afraid to fall, but his big, warm hands were holding her, lowering her gently, sitting her on one of the steps while he knelt on the one below, his thighs spread on either side of hers, his mouth ravaging her.

Then one hand was at the small of her back, his big body pressing down on hers, pressing her back against the hard edge of the stair above her.

She didn't care. The only thing that mattered was Noah's mouth, the heat of his powerful, muscular body, the scent of him, and the deep, regular pulse that throbbed between her legs like a giant heartbeat.

There was a void inside her and she needed him to fill it.

"Bella." His voice was so rough and gritty she could

barely understand him. "Bella, honey. I can't… I don't think…"

No, he couldn't stop and leave her here like this.

She panted, clawing up his thermal so she could get to the hot skin beneath it, sliding her hands over his bare chest. Oiled silk over hard muscle, with the slight prickle of hair.

This wasn't enough. She needed more.

"No," she whispered against his mouth. "Don't leave me. I need you."

He made another of those delicious, harsh masculine sounds and his mouth was on hers again, the kiss ruthless this time, with an edge of the same desperation that was tearing her apart.

His hands deftly opened her jeans before jerking them down her legs, taking her panties with them.

Bella sighed. The wood was cold beneath her bare butt, but she didn't care. She was burning up. And when he slid one hand between her thighs to touch her, she groaned into his mouth as pleasure licked over her. No one had ever touched her like this, his fingers gentle, sliding over her slick flesh, making her want to push against him, do something to make the feelings stronger, harder.

"Noah." His name was a prayer whispered against his mouth. "Oh, Noah…please…"

His breathing was ragged and uneven, yet he paused to reach into his back pocket. His features looked harsh in the light and shadows of the stairwell, the skin drawn tight over the bones of his face, his eyes glittering and hot as he looked at her.

And she had the sense that though he might be bigger and stronger than she would ever be, she was the one with the power. That she was the one who'd reduced him to this, turned him into this creature made of nothing but desire.

He pulled a silver packet from his back pocket. After tearing it open, he flung away the foil and ripped open his jeans. She itched to touch the long, hard length of him, but he shook his head, deftly rolling the latex down himself.

Then she was pushed back against the stairs, his hands sliding beneath her butt, the heat of his palms searing, the blunt head of his cock pressing against her slick entrance.

She tilted her hips, arching up, desperate as he thrust into her.

Bella gasped, riveted by the darkness of his eyes and the unfamiliar feeling of him filling her. Of herself stretched around him, gripping him. Holding him tight.

There was no pain. Just Noah. Inside her, over her. Surrounding her in heat and strength and the most intense pleasure.

An intimacy she couldn't have imagined.

She'd never been so close to another human being. Never felt so connected. And now she was. To him.

Noah. Whom she'd always wanted.

She was lost in the velvet darkness of his gaze, his hands gripping her tight. Then he flexed his hips and thrust, making her gasp again, reaching for his powerful shoulders and holding on tight as he drew back and thrust again.

"Noah." Her voice cracked with the ecstasy of it all. "Oh, God."

He didn't kiss her. His gaze was on hers as he moved, a rhythm that made her pant and claw at him, not knowing how to meet it. But then he showed her how and it was so good. Unimaginably so.

He filled the empty spaces inside her, the void that had been in her heart for so long, with heat and pleasure and all the good things she'd been missing out on and never knew. She didn't want it ever to end.

She closed her thighs around his lean hips, wound her arms around his neck, holding him close, and he began to move faster, his fingers digging into her hips. But it wasn't painful. It only added to the intensity of the experience.

"Bella." Her name sounded rough and guttural, thrilling her. *"Bella..."*

She couldn't tear her gaze from the raw pleasure on his face, the hot darkness of his eyes, her own hunger reflected back at her. As if he, too, felt the intensity between them.

Then everything got more desperate. Noah moved harder, driving her back into the hardwood of the stairs, and she cried out, the pleasure an indescribable tension. A pleasure that was going to end and she didn't want it to.

His hand reached between her thighs to where they were joined, stroking her until the tension pulled so tight she wanted to scream. Then it broke, ecstasy flooding through her, filling her eyes with tears, a sob catching in her throat.

Noah's mouth covered hers, hot and desperate, swallowing her sob and cry of release as his thrusts got wilder and out of rhythm, the release coming for him, too.

He buried his face in her neck, a groan escaping him as his big body shuddered, then went still.

For a second there was silence, broken only by the sound of their frantic breathing.

Then Noah lifted his head and stared at her and the reality of her situation descended on her like a ton of bricks.

She'd just lost her virginity to her ex-stepbrother, two days after meeting him, on the stairs of Grandma June's house.

And it wasn't as simple as losing her virginity—that she maybe could have coped with if the experience had been anything less than transcendent.

But it hadn't been less. It had been everything she'd ever thought it would be and more. It had changed her.

It had made her aware of everything missing from her life, of the emptiness inside her. The void she'd told herself wasn't there.

But it was and now she knew it.

Noah stared at her like he'd never seen her before in his life. He was going to push himself away from her and leave, wasn't he? He was going to tell her this was a mistake, that it should never have happened.

He was right, though.

Now she knew what she wanted and it wasn't something she could have. That void at the heart of her, that need, was the same as her mother's. Noah had given her a taste of what she could have, and she'd been so needy. Clawing at him and arching against him. Begging him not to leave.

She'd given up too much, revealed herself when she shouldn't have.

You're just like your mother in so many ways.

Suddenly she couldn't breathe. She pushed at the

hard wall of his chest, and instantly he moved, with-drawing from her.

"Bella." His voice was husky. "Wait."

But she didn't want to wait. She didn't want to talk. She didn't even want to look at him.

She felt like a snail without a shell, soft and exposed, with nowhere to hide. All her defenses stripped away.

Her jeans had gone and so had her panties, and all she could do was pull her sweatshirt down over her bare butt and scramble up the stairs.

"Bella," Noah called after her. "Wait just a damn minute!"

But she felt awash with shame and regret, and couldn't face him. She didn't even turn as she got to the top of the stairs and raced into the bedroom that she'd chosen for herself a couple of days earlier. The small room at the back, with the single bed and the view of the sky.

Bella slammed the door, then turned around and leaned against it, her heart thumping hard behind her breastbone, her thighs shaking. Everything shaking.

Every sense was attuned to the man she'd left on the stairs, half of her desperate for him to come after her. Half of her desperate for him not to.

But there was only silence in the hallway outside.

She slid down the door until she was sitting on the floor, the wooden floorboards freezing against her bare skin, but she ignored it. Instead, she drew her knees up and covered them with the sweatshirt; it was so big it didn't even stretch the fabric. Then she wrapped her arms around her knees and put her head on them.

She didn't know how long she remained like that, but eventually it got too cold to keep sitting, so she pushed herself up, dressed in her one fresh pair of underwear and jeans. Then she went back over to the door and pulled it open.

Silence reigned, so she cautiously went to the stairs and peeked down them.

They were empty.

Heart still thumping, Bella made her way down the stairs. As she got to the bottom, she paused and took another look around, holding her breath.

Again, silence.

Noah had gone.

A rush of emotion filled her and she blinked back tears again. Ridiculous. Seemed liked she'd done nothing but cry since she'd come back to Jasper Creek and she was sick of it.

She swallowed past the lump in her throat and the sudden flood of loneliness and regret, the emptiness inside her echoing.

Damn Noah for showing her what she was missing.

Damn him for making her want more.

Forcing the feelings away, Bella went to the front door and pulled it open to check that he wasn't lurking on the porch.

But the porch was empty.

The door had swung open without a sound or any resistance, and when she shut it again, she didn't have to jerk it closed.

Apparently, not only had Noah Faraday taken her virginity, he'd also fixed her door.

WHEN NOAH GOT back to his house, he threw himself headfirst into the various tasks he had to do around the ranch.

Anything so he didn't have to think about Bella Jacobson. Or about what had happened back at June's house on the stairs.

About how she'd taken great handfuls of his shirt in her fists and pulled him to her. How her mouth had opened under his, flooding his senses with heat and a sweetness that reminded him of summer days and the strawberries he used to steal from Grandma June's strawberry patch.

He definitely didn't think about the hunger that had escaped its shackles, making him propel her down onto the stairs. A burst of intense need to get her under him, bury himself in her heat and softness.

She should never have kissed him back. Should never have made that sweet little noise and arched against him. Never whispered not to leave when he'd tried to handle himself, the husky sound of her voice shattering his tenuous control.

No one had clung tightly to him and told him not to go before. No one had ever told him that they needed him.

He'd made a mistake when he'd looked down into her lovely face and seen the flush to her skin and her glowing blue eyes. Seen the pleasure that he was giving her...

He'd never managed to fix his father. Never managed to make things better and not for want of trying. But he could give her pleasure. He could make a difference to her.

And he hadn't been able to stop himself.

It had been the most intense, incredible sexual experience of his life.

Women didn't hold him close. Didn't kiss him like they were starving and only he could feed them.

And they certainly didn't look up at him as if he was the most incredible thing they'd ever seen in their lives.

Or run from you when it was all over like the hounds of hell were on their tail.

The wrench slipped and Noah cursed as he banged his fingers on the tractor engine he was fixing.

Stupid. He shouldn't be thinking of *any* of this.

June would turn in her grave if she knew what he'd done to her sweet little granddaughter, while his father would be laughing his ass off in his.

Temptation sure does taste sweet, doesn't it, son?

The wrench slipped a second time, so he turned from the engine and flung the offending tool onto the floor of the barn.

This was straight-out crazy. It was just sex. Nothing more.

He was pissed that Bella had run, that he hadn't had a chance to make sure she was okay, but she'd been clear that she hadn't wanted to talk and so he'd decided that it would be better if he left.

He'd repaired the door first, because he'd promised, but if she didn't want to talk, then fine.

So you just left her alone. Nice.

Noah growled and turned from the tractor, stalking to the entrance to the barn. He could see June's farmhouse from here, too.

There was no smoke coming out of the chimney.

Aw, hell.

What if she hadn't wanted what they'd done? She'd clutched him to her like she was drowning and told him not to leave, but still. He hadn't been gentle. He'd been too desperate. And she'd been so warm and soft. Small and fragile, yet with a surprising strength in her legs wrapped tightly around his waist and in her hands as she'd gripped him. A fascinating contrast...

"Damn you," he said to the snowy, empty hillside.

He couldn't *not* check on her.

It didn't have to mean anything, though. Okay, he'd had sex with her when all he'd meant to do was kiss her. Drunk the whole bottle when he'd only intended to take a sip. But he knew the danger now and would make sure it didn't happen again.

It was one mistake. He could resist temptation. He was stronger than his father ever had been.

Noah didn't go down to June's immediately. First he went into the kitchen to gather some supplies, because he didn't want to go down there without a peace offering, and put them all in an insulated bag. Then he grabbed his coat and his hat, took the bag and strode down the hill for the second time that day.

Bella didn't answer his knock and he decided that going away meekly like a good little boy wasn't his thing, so he opened the door and walked inside.

Bella wasn't in the kitchen or the living room, which meant she was probably upstairs. But since a chill was starting to settle over the house, he decided to tackle the fire issue first.

It didn't take long to get the fire going and then he put some of the supplies he'd brought in the old oven to heat, before quickly setting to making the other peace offering he'd brought: Grandma June's special hot chocolate.

The scent of melted chocolate filled the air as he poured the thick, dark brown liquid into a mug. Setting a couple of marshmallows floating on top, he then picked up the mug and started for the stairs.

He made a mental note of which steps creaked as he went up them, because obviously that was going to need to be fixed, whether she liked it or not.

There was only one door on the second floor that was closed; the small bedroom at the back of the house. Obviously Bella's room.

He went over to it and knocked. "Hey. It's me. It's Noah."

Silence.

"I have something for you. Something you might like."

More silence.

He scowled. "Hell, the least you could do is let me know you're okay."

The thump of small feet came from behind the door and then it was yanked open.

Bella glared up at him, her hair hanging loose down her shoulders in an inky wave, a very real anger burning in the depths of her eyes. "Yeah, well, I'm okay. As you can see."

Physically, maybe. But no hiding that anger.

Who was that aimed at? Him? He was the most likely target and he had to admit that a primitive part of him liked that, because he'd affected her.

Except anger wasn't what he wanted from her.

You want her naked and under you again.

He shoved the thought away. That wasn't happening again. But maybe having a chat wouldn't go amiss. They were going to have to clear the air sometime.

"We need to talk," he said flatly, making sure it wasn't a request.

"Uh, no, we don't."

"Yes, we do. Especially if I'm going to help fix up this house."

She looked incensed. "You're not going to be helping with anything. I don't need your—"

"I'm not stupid, Bella. I know you're not your mother. And accepting my help doesn't turn you into her, either."

Her expression twisted and she glanced away.

"Also," he added, "you're not running out on me again."

"Hey, I'm not the only one who ran out."

"I know," he said, willing to own it. "But now I'm back. And we need to clear the air."

"You don't get to—"

"Here." He lifted the mug. This was going to go his way for once. "I made this for you. If you want it, be downstairs in the kitchen in five minutes. If you don't... Well, I'll come up here and get you myself."

Blue sparks of anger glittered in her eyes. "Go away, Noah. I don't want you here."

He ignored her. "Five minutes."

Then he turned and went back downstairs.

He might have completely pissed her off. But he was hoping the hot chocolate might swing it.

Just sex, huh?

It *was* just sex, but they did need to talk about it. Especially since he'd be helping around here. If she wanted this placed fixed and ready for sale, she was going to have to use him since she sure as hell wouldn't be able to get anyone else, not this close to the holidays.

He put the hot chocolate down on the table and then leaned back against the kitchen counter, folding his arms and glancing down at his watch.

She left it till the last second, but exactly five minutes later she appeared in the doorway, looking reluctant and belligerent. Yet also somehow luminous and unbelievably sexy.

Her gaze flickered over him, lingering on his mouth, his shoulders and his chest. As if she couldn't help herself.

It made him catch his breath.

She met his gaze at last and there was a second's silence, the memory of what happened burning like a torch between them.

"You shouldn't have run away," he said, which was not at all how he'd meant to open the conversation.

She lifted a shoulder and went over to the table, pulling out the chair forcefully and sitting down.

So she was going to push him, was she?

He noted her tight shoulders and the tight look on her face. The way she picked up the mug and wrapped her fingers around it, her lips parting slightly, as if she'd just picked up the scent of it and was amazed.

Guarded and wary. So angry. Mistrustful. Why? What had her life been like since she'd left Jasper Creek?

Had anyone been kind to her? Not her mother, that was for sure.

His chest constricted. Perhaps being angry with her was the wrong way to go about this. Perhaps he needed to be gentler. Firm, but patient. Like with a spooked horse.

Her attention was on her hot chocolate, thick lashes veiling her gaze.

"That good?" he asked.

"Yeah." She took another sip. "Thanks."

"No problem."

A silence fell and he let it sit awhile.

Then he said quietly, "What happened, honey?"

She blinked hard, but didn't speak.

"I didn't mean to scare you," he went on. "And if I did, I'm sorry. I hope I didn't hurt you, either, because that's definitely not what I intended."

Again, she didn't speak, staring fixedly at her mug. Then, just when he thought she wouldn't, she said, "You didn't scare me. And you didn't hurt me. I just…"

The tight thing inside him relaxed slightly. "You just…?"

She looked at him all of a sudden. "Why did you come back?"

He could lie but she deserved more from him than that.

"Because I couldn't see smoke. And I wondered 'why not?'"

"You couldn't see smoke? What do you mean?"

"From the chimney." He paused. "I've been check-ing for the past couple of days. Just to make sure you got your fire going okay."

Surprise flickered over her features. "You have? But…why?"

"I don't want you getting cold."

"Because Lila asked you to check on me?"

"No." He stared into her eyes. "It's got nothing to do with Lila, or Grandma June for that matter. I don't want you to get cold because I don't want to see you hurting. Because it looks to me like you've been hurt-ing too much for too long. And I don't like it."

She looked shocked. "But…you don't even know me."

"I know you have holes in your shoes. I know your

bag was way too light for a whole season's vacation. I know you haven't got any money for food. And I know that you're probably going to deny it and tell me that everything is fine." He watched the shift of color over her face. "But it's not fine, is it?"

She glanced down at the mug in her hands. "I...had a few difficulties before I got here, yes."

"Want to tell me about them?"

"Not really."

"Why not?"

She sipped at her drink, then sighed. "It's no big deal. I had some money I'd been saving for something, then someone stole my debit card and cleared me out. I thought the bank would pay it back, but they refused. Said I was negligent. So, yeah. I have no money." She flashed him a glance, a stubborn light glowing in her eyes. "Then Grandma's letter turned up, telling me that if I fixed up the house I could sell it. And that's what I'm going to do. So you don't need to be concerned about it."

She was such a stubborn, proud little thing. He respected that even if it was infuriating.

"What do the others think about selling this place?"

"I assume they don't know. It's not their business, anyway." Her shoulders hunched higher. "I feel bad about it. I don't want to be happy that Grandma died and I'm going to get all this money from the sale of her house. But I...need it."

"Everyone needs money," he acknowledged. "You were saving for something in particular?"

"I wanted to buy a café." It sounded reluctant; clearly she didn't want to tell him. "I wanted a place for people to...connect with each other. Drink coffee and chat and relax. Feel at home. Stuff like that."

"So? Get a job and start again?"

She shook her head. "It took me years to save what I had and that wasn't much. Living in the city is expensive."

Well, she wasn't wrong about that.

"I get it," he said. "But losing your money wasn't your fault. And accepting my help doesn't make you a lesser person."

Bella put the mug back down on the table. "You didn't like my mother and I thought you didn't like me, either. So accepting your help... Well, it's problematic."

"Why? I didn't think you cared what I thought one way or the other."

A flush crept into her pale cheeks, as if she was embarrassed, though what she had to be embarrassed about he had no idea. "Actually," she said, "I did care. I had a giant crush on you, Noah. Didn't you know?"

CHAPTER SIX

BELLA HAD NO idea why she'd confessed her most embarrassing secret to him. Maybe it was the way he stood there, his dark eyes watchful, as if he was genuinely interested in what she was telling him.

Or maybe it was how he'd cared that she was cold.

Or maybe it was simply that he'd called her "honey" and she'd never been anyone's honey before. She'd only ever been Bella.

Perhaps the hot chocolate had helped, too, but suddenly it felt like she could give him a few answers about herself.

Admitting about the money had been easier because he'd guessed already and that wasn't something she could hide. But she'd never told anyone about her café plans. She didn't particularly want to tell him, either. However, he'd asked her straight out and she hadn't wanted to lie. And it hadn't been until she'd told him that she realized, with a twisting sensation in her gut, that she felt weird about how the money was connected with Grandma June's death and that if June hadn't died, she wouldn't be getting anything at all.

She couldn't feel right about that and she couldn't feel happy.

The whole situation was messed up and now she'd

messed it up even more by having sex with Noah, then telling him about her crush.

He stared at her now, a tall, dark silent figure in the kitchen. He still had his coat on, his cowboy hat on the counter beside him, his expression impenetrable. A hard man to read.

Yet she could see the glitter of heat in his dark eyes. And it all came rushing back to her again, the way he'd kissed her. The way he'd growled as he'd pushed her against the door frame. The catch in his voice as he'd murmured her name...

He hadn't been hard to read or impenetrable then. She'd known exactly what he was thinking and what he wanted.

Her.

Her heart beat faster at the thought, because that same look was back in his eyes, yet also what looked like anger. Which was strange. Why would he be angry about a dumb teenage crush?

"No," he said. "I didn't know."

"Right." She took a breath. "And why would you? I didn't tell anyone."

"Is that why you never spoke to me? Why you hid in your bedroom all the time?"

"I didn't think you noticed that."

"I did notice. And, yeah, I wondered why."

Her face got hot. He'd never paid her any attention that she could remember, but apparently she'd made an impression all the same. "You never said anything."

"Neither did you."

"You were nineteen. And I—I was thirteen. Nothing could have happened."

"No, it couldn't." His arms dropped to his sides. "But I could have been your friend, Bella."

She hadn't thought of that. But then, he couldn't have been a friend to her, not with the way she'd felt about him.

"It wasn't a friend I wanted," she said.

"And yet you needed one, I think."

You did. You were so lonely.

Her jaw felt tight and she wanted to look away. He seemed to know things about her that she didn't even know herself, and she hated how vulnerable that made her feel.

"Why would you say that?" The defensiveness in her voice made her want to cringe.

"Why?" His dark eyes were full of an expression she couldn't read. "Because I felt the same way."

Shock rippled through her. She'd never considered that, certainly not back then. He'd always seemed so strong and self-contained, never needing anyone or anything. Lonely was the last thing she'd thought he'd be.

"I had no idea," she said huskily. "You didn't seem to need anything, let alone a friend."

"I didn't think I did, either. Not at the time." His gaze sharpened. "But I could be your friend now, Bella. If you wanted me to be."

She caught her breath, an ache settling in her chest at the intensity in his expression, a ghost of the need that had turned her inside out on the stairs rising inside her.

You don't want him to be a friend. You want more.

That was crazy. She didn't want more. She'd had sex with him and now her curiosity was satisfied. She didn't need to do it again.

"Okay," she allowed, shoving away any doubts. "I think I'd like that."

There was a single moment of tension, where Noah stared hard at her and she thought he might say something else. But then he gave one of his sharp nods, dismissing the subject. "Are you hungry? Because I brought dinner over. And, no, you can't refuse. We're friends now, understand?"

She ignored the ache in her chest, because that didn't matter. She could do friends. Friends was good. "You're incredibly bossy, you know that?"

His hard mouth relaxed and she held her breath, wondering if she was going to get a smile. "And you're incredibly stubborn, so I guess that makes us even."

"Unstoppable force meets immovable object. This should be fun."

Then there it was, the beginnings of a slightly crooked grin. "Fun, huh? Is that what you call it?"

Her heart seized, the faint quirk of his mouth stealing all the air from her lungs. Lord, getting a smile out of this guarded man could easily become an obsession.

"Yeah." She couldn't help smiling back. "I do."

His grin deepened, then he turned toward the stove. "Get us out some plates, honey. I'll get this out of the oven."

Honey. He'd called her honey. And he'd smiled at her. He'd full-on smiled.

You can never be friends with him. It'll never be enough.

But Bella ignored the voice in her head and got out the plates instead.

They ate at the table, a simple meal of chili and rice that was one of the most delicious meals she'd ever eaten.

"This is really good," she said as she took another bite. "Do you have a housekeeper or what?"

"No. I made it myself."

She put her fork down. "You did?"

"Don't look so surprised. Men can cook, you know."

"Yeah, I know, but I didn't think you did. You work on the ranch all day."

He lifted one powerful shoulder. "I have to eat, and who else is going to do it? And, no, I don't have a housekeeper. I used to do all the cooking and stuff for Dad so it made sense to keep on doing it."

"Was Hank not much of a cook?"

"Hank wasn't much of anything." His voice had a bitter edge. "Dad was a drunk. You knew that, right?"

Bella had heard the rumors about Hank. But she'd been a kid and what kid would understand what an alcoholic was? Her mother had never said anything and she'd never seen Hank get drunk while they were married.

"Maybe," she said carefully. "But I was really young. And then we left town so…" She stopped. "Was he? An alcoholic, I mean?"

Noah's gaze was opaque, but she sensed currents moving below the surface. Deep, treacherous currents. "Yeah. He'd been drinking all my life. Mom got sick of it and left when I was thirteen."

Horrified, Bella didn't know quite what to say. "I'm sorry. That must have been awful."

He shrugged again. "It was what it was."

"But… I didn't see him drink."

"He didn't while he was married to Avery."

She was almost afraid to ask him what had happened after Avery had left, because she had a feeling she knew already. He would have gone back to the bottle, wouldn't he?

"Yes," Noah said, obviously reading her mind. "He did."

Bella's chest tightened. Hank had died not long after, which must have meant he'd hit that bottle again pretty hard. "I'm sorry," she repeated, not able to think of anything else to say. "I'm sorry about Mom. I'm sorry she left him. I don't know why she's like that. She wanted something that no one was ever able to give her, I think."

"It doesn't matter why she was like that." Noah looked down at his plate. "I thought Dad had given it up, but he hadn't. And he died, anyway."

There was pain in his voice. Anger, too.

Instinctively, Bella reached out and laid her hand over his where it rested on the table. "That's awful, Noah. It really sucks."

Slowly, he looked up, the darkness in his eyes catching her, holding her. His hand was very warm beneath hers.

And abruptly the static charge that leaped between them shimmered in the air.

"You shouldn't do that, honey," he said quietly.

"What? Touch you?"

"Yeah."

Something quivered inside her. He was probably right, yet she didn't take her hand away. "Why not?"

"You know why not."

Her skin prickled, the quiver becoming a throb, an ache.

She should take her hand away, but his skin felt good against hers and those currents in his eyes fascinated

her. She wanted to know what had made him so angry—
was it her mother? Or was it directed at his father? What
had his life really been like living up at that ranch house
all alone except for an alcoholic dad?

Lonely. Just like yours.

Her heart squeezed. He'd done a lot of stuff for her
since she'd arrived here. But what had she done for him?

Nothing. Because if she never did anything for anyone, then she'd never have to accept anything from
them.

That had always seemed easier, safer.

Except now it didn't. Now it felt selfish and mean.

She took a silent breath. "Perhaps you better tell me,
so I know for sure."

The static in the air became denser, electric, the way
it did before a thunderstorm.

He wanted her, she could see it in his gaze.

The need she thought she'd put away pushed at her,
and she wanted to give him something to sand away the
edges of the pain she'd seen in his eyes.

But the only thing she had to give was sex.

And why not? He wanted her and she wanted him,
and now she knew what he did to her, she'd be better
prepared to control it. She wouldn't let herself get so
carried away. After all, she wasn't a virgin any longer.

Bella stayed where she was and kept her hand on his,
and eventually he gave a rough curse, pulling his hand
away and shoving his chair back, getting to his feet.

She didn't move, watching him as he headed around
the table, hauling back her chair, reaching down to slide
an arm around her waist and drawing her up.

She pressed her palms to his chest, feeling the heat
of him again.

"You shouldn't have done that." His voice was rough, his hand hot as he cupped her jaw. "You shouldn't have touched me."

She barely heard him over the thunder of her heart. "I wanted to. I like touching you."

"Honey." He stroked his thumb across her cheekbone. "We shouldn't do this again. Friends, remember?"

"So let me go." She spread her fingers out, the heat of his body warming her right through. "Walk away."

It was a gamble, but he didn't call her bluff and release her.

If anything, his hold on her tightened, his eyes shadowed and hungry, burning as hot as the fire in the woodstove.

"I can't give you anything more than this." The brush of his thumb on her skin tantalized her. "Understand? Just sex, nothing else."

Her heart gave a little kick, but she ignored it. "I don't want anything more, either. Once I've sold the house, I'll be going back to Seattle."

The lines of his face were sharp with the same hunger she recognized from before, and she could feel how tense he was. Suddenly all she could think about was how to release that tension. And what it would feel like if he did.

No, she knew. It would feel like it had when he'd taken her on the stairs.

Need abruptly spilled out of her and she rose up on her toes, making the decision for them both by capturing his hard mouth with hers.

There was a moment of silence and stillness.

Then Noah gave a husky growl against her lips, and both arms came around her, fitting her tightly to him.

She sighed, opening her mouth to his kiss, sliding her palms up his chest and around his neck, pressing against him.

Too much, yet not enough.

A low moan of hunger escaped her, turning her frantic for more.

He tangled his hands in her hair, drawing her head back. "Hush," he murmured, soothing her. "Hush, honey. I've got you."

Then he swept her up into his arms, gathering her against his chest.

"You don't have to carry me," she murmured, settling against the ferocious heat of his body. "I can walk." But it was a faint protest. She didn't want him to put her down. She wanted him to carry her.

And he did, holding her as if she weighed nothing at all, heading upstairs and not for the room she'd chosen for herself, but for the master bedroom instead.

June's room.

A big dormer window sat above the wrought-iron bedstead covered in chipped white paint, the mattress bare, all the bedding stripped from it.

"My bed's already made," she pointed out.

"I'm not having you in a single bed." Noah set her down by the door. "Wait there and don't move."

It was an order, so she did as she was told, unable to take her eyes off him as he moved to the big old wardrobe in the corner of the room, pulling out one of Grandma June's quilts and throwing it over the bed.

Then he turned to her and held out a preemptory hand.

The expression on his handsome face was fierce, his dark eyes challenging.

Waiting for her to take it.

Bella put her hand in his, his fingers closing around it, drawing her close. Then he gave her a little push, sitting her down on the bed, before dropping fluidly to his knees.

"Noah," she breathed, reaching for him.

He ignored her hands, nudging her legs apart so he could kneel between them before reaching to grab the hem of her sweatshirt. "Lift your arms."

Trembling, she did so, letting him undress her so at last she was sitting there, her top half clad in nothing but her worn black bra.

The chill in the air made goose bumps rise on her arms, though that may have been the way his gaze moved over her, heating every place that it rested. "No wonder you're cold," he murmured. "You were only wearing a T-shirt under that."

"I—I'm not cold now," she stuttered.

No one had seen her in only a bra. No one had seen her naked, not since she was a very young child. And perhaps she should have felt embarrassed about Noah seeing her like that. But she didn't.

She felt as if she'd been waiting for this moment all her life.

He leaned forward and reached behind her, unclipping her bra and slipping it off.

She didn't feel self-conscious. Not with him looking at her as if she was a feast he'd been starving for.

"Beautiful." He ran his palms up her bare arms, scorching every inch of skin he touched. "You're so lovely."

She shook when he leaned forward and pressed his mouth to her throat, and again when his hands moved to her breasts, his fingertips brushing over her skin as if she was precious and he didn't want to break her.

His care made her throat tighten, his touch making her moan as his thumbs teased her nipples into hard little points.

Bella shut her eyes, somehow both eased by his touch and inflamed by it. She reached for him, but he caught her hands in his and held them down, kissing his way down her body, his hot mouth finding one nipple and sucking gently. The sensation was so exquisite she cried out, pleasure heating her up from the inside out, chasing away the relentless cold.

Then Noah pushed her back on the bed and took off the rest of her clothes.

She wasn't embarrassed then, either, because he gave her no time to be, his hands on her thighs, pushing them wide, placing his mouth where she was hot and wet and aching.

A groan escaped her as his hands firmed and he began to explore her with a relentless gentleness that made her shake and shudder, made the pleasure build even higher.

It felt like he was building her a house made of touches and licks, of kisses and caresses. A house constructed of pleasure, with many rooms and levels. With stairs that went higher and higher, reaching up into the sky.

Bella gasped at the sharpness of the sensations, every part of her gathering impossibly tight. And then she came apart, shattering between his hands, sobbing and overwhelmed.

He let her lie there for a couple of minutes, caressing and soothing her. Then he tucked her into the quilt before shrugging out of his clothes. And what little breath she had left escaped her lungs.

Because he was beautiful. A work of art carved by long hours of hard physical labor. Broad shoulders and powerful chest, his stomach flat and corrugated with cut muscle. His skin was tanned in the light of the room, and smooth, with the odd scar here and there, and her hands itched to touch him, explore every beautiful line of him.

Naked, and without any self-consciousness, he bent to retrieve something from his coat pocket, then stalked to the bed and got in beside her, hauling the quilt over them both.

Then she was enclosed in heat, his large, hard body settling over her, lean hips nudging her thighs apart, his hands coming down on the pillow on either side of her head. He was wonderfully hot. Warming her, scorching her.

She stroked him hungrily, loving the feel of firm muscle and the prickle of hair against her palms.

"You okay?" His voice had a gritty edge to it that thrilled her.

"Yes." The hard press of his erection burned against her stomach and she tilted her hips, enjoying the way the movement rubbed it against more sensitive parts of her anatomy, sending delicious chills through her. "More than."

A muscle in his jaw leaped, his gaze hot and fierce. He didn't smile or speak, his body rigid, hunger in every line of his face.

"I mean it." She stroked him the way he'd stroked her, soothing him. "I'm okay. Don't look so worried."

That muscle in his jaw jumped again, the raw expression on his face filling up all the empty spaces inside her. Warming the frozen parts of her.

She wanted to tell him that he could fill up those empty spaces with her, too, but she didn't want to ruin the moment. Instead, she ran her hands over him, using touch to communicate what she didn't want to say.

He remained very still, the glitter in his eyes becoming sharper. "This is just for the winter," he said harshly. "And then it's over."

Something shuddered in her chest, but that was what she'd told him downstairs, and so she nodded. "Yes. Just the winter. Then I'll be going back to Seattle."

He gave her one more long look, then shifted back on his knees, tearing open the foil packet he'd been holding, then sheathing himself. Easing between her thighs again, he lifted her, fitting her to him.

Then he pushed inside her, staring at her so fiercely she almost ignited on the spot. The intense pressure made her shudder, and then completeness she felt as he settled deep inside her made her shudder again.

And she sighed his name in relief, her nails digging into his skin, arching up into the heat and all that delicious, rock-hard muscle. Her legs wrapped around his waist, holding him to her, as he began to move.

He said nothing, the thrust of his hips lazy and slow. A complete contrast to the intensity of his gaze.

She tried to urge him to up his pace, but he only kissed her instead, filling her up yet making her hungry. So that she groaned, kissing him back, winding her arms around him, aching for more.

His movements slowed, pleasure drawing out until she was shuddering like a tree in a high wind, clutching at his back, gasping his name.

And just when she didn't think she could bear any more, he thrust deep, making the tight knot of sensation inside her suddenly burst apart.

She cried his name, pleasure rushing over her, lights bursting behind her eyes. And then he was slamming himself into her, over and over until his big body went rigid, a guttural groan echoing in the room.

She held on to him, stroking his muscular back, reveling in the shift and flex of his muscles beneath her palms. In the way his body curled around hers, surrounding her in heat and the warm, spicy scent of his skin.

Filling up those empty spaces inside her as perfectly as the last missing piece of a jigsaw puzzle.

But it can't feel perfect. Because you're leaving.

Bella shut her eyes, ignoring the lurch that particular thought gave her. She didn't want anything to disturb the perfection of lying in bed with Noah Faraday.

Because, of course, she was leaving.

But not yet.

NOAH COULDN'T SLEEP. He lay awake, staring at the ceiling, Bella warm and naked and curled in his arms, her hair a silken black storm over his chest.

He hadn't meant to sleep with her. When she'd put her hand over his on the table down in the kitchen, he'd thought he'd had the strength to stop himself. Certainly he wouldn't have offered to be friends with her if he thought he couldn't resist their undeniable chemistry.

But she hadn't taken her hand away when he'd told her to, only looked right at him, blue eyes glowing with heat. And he felt his resistance burn to ashes.

He'd told himself this was the equivalent of another

sip, another taste. And hell, he'd already had one taste so what harm would another do? He wouldn't get addicted.

She'd revealed things about herself that had made him realize how lonely she was, yet how strong, too. Her confessing to her crush had made him stare, but when she'd mentioned how she'd had all her money stolen, he'd wanted to find whoever was responsible and punch their lights out.

She hadn't given up her dream, though. She was still working toward it with all the grim determination in her soul.

He respected that. He respected her.

Then when he'd told her about his father, she'd put her hand on his and looked at him with such sympathy that his chest had felt like it was full of barbed wire. He couldn't remember the last time anyone had looked at him like that. As if he was someone who deserved better than what he'd got.

And there's nothing more tempting than being made to feel like you matter, either.

No one had ever laid their hands on him, tried to soothe him the way she had. Stroking him as if he was the one who needed gentling, not her.

You did nearly lose it.

She'd been under him, naked. Soft and warm, needing him. And he'd felt nothing but hungry. As if he wanted to cover himself with her heat and scent, with the taste of her. Like he'd die if he didn't have her.

He hadn't wanted to be like that with her again. He hadn't wanted to feel at the mercy of an appetite he couldn't control.

He wasn't going to be like his father.

Then again, she wouldn't be here forever. She'd

be leaving at the end of winter and knowing that had helped him hold on to his self-control. So he could take her the way she deserved, slow and hot and easy. Drawing out her pleasure.

Easier for you to stay in control, too.

She shifted in his arms and instantly he was hard again. He wanted to roll her on her back, slide inside her, but he didn't want to wake her. If they were going to have sex again he needed to go back up to his house for more condoms, anyway.

Are you going to have sex again?

The question sat uncomfortably in his head, chasing away any sleep he might have had.

At last he moved, sliding carefully from the bed, finding his clothes and dressing before going downstairs to make coffee.

As it brewed, he leaned against the kitchen counter, staring through the window and out into the darkness.

There was no denying it. The thought of her being right next door all winter was one hell of a temptation. Perhaps too much of one.

But was there any point in resisting? They'd already had sex twice, so maybe it was better to embrace temptation wholeheartedly rather than resisting and failing. It wouldn't be forever because she would be leaving and that would be the end of it.

Keep telling yourself that.

No, why couldn't he have something for himself for a change? He always denied himself, so why should he do that with Bella? She wanted him. And it had been a long time since he'd allowed himself something good. Something soft and warm and his.

A tension that he hadn't realized was there relaxed.

and he almost smiled as he turned to get the coffeepot off the stove.

Then he noticed the little notepad sitting next to his cowboy hat on the counter. A list of things that needed fixing was written on it, plus a few added extras such as "repaint hallway" and "polish woodstove" and "clean windows" and "new curtains?"

Bella hadn't spent the last two days doing nothing, clearly.

Noah picked up the notepad and tore off the page with the list on it.

Looked like he had some work to do.

CHAPTER SEVEN

BELLA DIDN'T KNOW what was happening with Noah, but whatever it was, she liked it.

Nothing was said between them, but he came over to the farmhouse every day. He'd found the list she'd made of what needed doing and while she worked on her business plan for the café, sketching designs in her notebook, or scouring various property websites looking for appropriate café venues, he got to work on whichever thing needed fixing or finishing next.

A part of her wanted to protest, but since he didn't ask if she needed help, often she didn't even know he'd fixed something until it was done. Which made refusing next to impossible.

She wanted to find such behavior infuriating, but the truth was, she didn't. It made her feel cared for instead.

And he didn't only work on the house. He'd also either make them both a meal or bring down some food from his house. He'd do the pitiful amount of laundry that she had as well, often making extra clothes appear in her pile.

They'd come to an agreement on the food—he'd buy groceries for her while she made sure he kept a running total so she could pay him back when she could.

Every night he stayed over. They didn't talk about that, either, but at the end of each meal he'd get to his feet, take her hand, and they'd go up to bed together, where he'd make love to her, slow and sweet.

Everything he did for her was like a small gift that she didn't want to either like or accept, yet she did both.

It made the ache inside her less intense, the void less empty.

It also made her want to reciprocate.

She'd always been a good waitress at her few waitressing jobs because she listened to people. She was observant, too, paying attention to their likes and dislikes, and enjoyed putting them at ease, mainly because being paid to do so took the pressure off the interaction.

Now she wanted to do that for Noah. Serve him and care for him the way he was serving and caring for her.

She started small, bringing him a beer or making him a cup of coffee. He always said thank you, his hard mouth relaxing in that tantalizing almost-smile that made her heart beat fast.

She wasn't much of a cook, but one morning she made him eggs and was rewarded with an honest-to-God actual smile when she'd brought them to him in bed.

And, yes, his smiles were as addicting as she'd thought they'd be.

She didn't want to think about selling the house. Or about what her cousins would say when they found out. Or how in a couple of months she would be leaving.

So she didn't.

Noah was up on the roof replacing a couple of the shingles a week or so later, and she'd gone outside to check on his progress, when she found something leaning against the wall beside the front door.

For a second she wondered why the hell there was

a pine tree on her porch. And then she realized that it wasn't simply a pine tree.

It was a Christmas tree.

She scanned the front yard and the street beyond to see where the tree had come from, because she hadn't heard anyone deliver it.

But both the yard and the street were empty.

A scraping sound came from overhead and Noah appeared, coming back down the ladder that was leaning against the porch roof. He jumped down onto the snowy ground and dusted off his hands.

"Damnedest thing," he said, coming up the porch steps. "When I went to get some replacement shingles today, I ran into Cade Mathewson. Apparently he fixed up a few things in the house this summer."

Cade Mathewson. A familiar name, but like so many of the people connected with Jasper Creek, she couldn't put a face to it.

"Did he? Doesn't seem like it."

"Yeah, I know. Swore he fixed them properly, too. No chance of them breaking over fall."

"Perhaps he only thought he fixed them?"

"No. Cade knows what he's doing. If he fixed them, he fixed them." Abruptly, Noah frowned. "That a tree?"

"What? Oh, yes. It just kind of turned up."

Noah didn't seem surprised. "It's probably from Remy. He brought June a tree every year."

"Remy?" Bella asked blankly.

"Remy West," Noah clarified.

Another familiar name. That last summer at Grandma June's, when they'd all played sardines, and a tall, handsome teenage boy had found them. He'd been Remy West. And he and Keira had had a thing, hadn't they?

"Oh," she said, not wanting to give away how little she knew about the town and the people in it. It made her feel ashamed, even though it hadn't been her fault her mother had taken her away. "I wonder why he left it here, then? He must know Grandma June isn't here anymore."

"He knows. It might be that your cousin put him up to it."

Keira. Tall, beautiful Keira. So much older than Bella and way cooler. A little awe-inspiring even. But Bella had lost touch with her the way she had with JJ and Lila, too.

What had their seasons been like in the farmhouse? Had they found it difficult? Or had they found a little scrap of happiness here the way she had?

You should contact them.

But she wasn't ready for that. She wanted to exist in this fragile little bubble she'd created with Noah. Where it was just her and him, and the outside world meant nothing.

Bella moved over to the tree, brushing her fingertips through the prickly green needles. "I've never had a Christmas tree. Mom didn't like Christmas so we never got one."

"We used to." Noah's voice was a gentle rumble at her back. "At least until Mom left and then Dad just… forgot."

Her throat felt thick. She didn't want to turn and look at him, because by unspoken agreement, they'd avoided talking about emotional stuff. She'd even forgotten it was Christmastime.

"When is Christmas again?" she asked.

"Couple of days."

"Oh, right. So…what should we do with the tree?" It seemed a stupid question, but she seriously didn't know. "I didn't ask for it. I mean, we could put it around behind the back of the house or something."

Warmth behind her, the familiar scent of snow and Noah mingling with the spicy smell of the pine needles. He wasn't a man given to casual contact and he didn't touch her now, even though a part of her very much wanted him to.

But she didn't say anything, settling for enjoying the delicious heat of his nearness in contrast with the chill in the air.

"There are some decorations up in the attic." He sounded very close. "I used to help June decorate the tree after Mom left, and she made me go up there and get the box."

Bella stared at the tree, conscious of Noah at her back, thinking about her grandmother and all the Christmases Bella herself had missed out on. Of the Christmases Noah had missed out on, too. Christmases June had clearly tried to make him part of, because Bella was sure giving one lonely boy some Christmas cheer had been intentional on her grandmother's part.

Lonely. Yes, that was what they'd both been. But they weren't so lonely now. And this Christmas could be different. This Christmas they had each other.

Temporary, remember?

Sure, but wanting one Christmas with Noah wasn't going to change anything. She'd still leave at the end of the season. But before she did, how could having one traditional Christmas hurt? With a tree and decorations. Snow and a fire and hot chocolate. Maybe even presents. Not that she could afford presents, but she could make something. It would be nice to give Noah something in return for everything he'd done for her.

Longing unfurled inside her, a sweet ache for something she never even knew she wanted until now.

"Shall we…?" She stopped, swallowed, and tried again. "Shall we have Christmas, Noah?"

He didn't speak.

She turned to look at him. His face had that impenetrable look that he got sometimes at night when he held her, or when she caught him looking at her sometimes. She wished she knew what it meant, what was going on behind those enigmatic dark eyes.

"Do you want Christmas?" His voice was expressionless.

Well, he might be expressionless, but Bella realized she wasn't. "Yes. I think this year, I do. Actually, I think *we* do."

Fierce emotion flickered briefly over his features, like a door opening on a raging fire before abruptly shutting. "Yeah, okay. Why not?" He glanced at the tree. "Where do you want this, then? The living room?"

Noah found something to put the tree in, and while he was doing that, Bella ventured up the rickety pull-down stairs that led up into the dusty attic. She didn't linger, scanning the piled up boxes and old bits of furniture. Eventually she discovered a box that had *Christmas* written in thick black marker on the side.

The box was large, but not heavy, and she managed to maneuver it downstairs.

Noah had finished erecting the tree and now the living room was full of the scent of pine needles, and the sweet ache in Bella's chest began to spread out, making it almost hurt to breathe.

She'd never had that scent filling her house, yet, somehow, it was familiar, anyway.

Clasping the box tightly, she brought it into the room, setting it down next to Noah, who was crouched beside the tree, adjusting the bucket the tree stood in.

"It looks great," she said. "Thank you."

"No problem." He glanced at the box. "You found it."

"Yeah." She pulled the box open, revealing glittering tinsel, baubles, lights and other Christmas paraphernalia, then looked at him. "You want to help me with this?"

The currents in his eyes shifted. "Did you just ask me for help, honey?"

She blushed for no good reason, but didn't look away. "So? What are you going to do about it?"

The corner of his fascinating mouth quirked. "Apparently I'm going to help you."

"Excellent." She pulled out a length of red tinsel and held it out to him. "Make yourself useful, then."

Noah wasn't much for artistic draping, so she made the most of showing him how to do it properly, loving the way amusement lit his gaze as she did so. He wasn't above being teased or given directions to hang things in spots she couldn't reach, and after a little while, the amusement in his eyes began to take on a familiar heat.

"You're good at that." His deep voice was full of approval.

"What?" Her cheeks felt hot. "Hanging decorations?"

"I mean making things look good. June's tree always looked like someone had emptied the decoration box over it. But the way you've done it… It's like something out of a magazine."

His praise made her feel warm inside—had anyone ever told her that she was good at something?

"Thanks." Her cheeks got even hotter. "I like doing that stuff. You know, creating an atmosphere."

"I bet you could use that for your café."

She shifted nervously on her feet, hesitant. No one else had seen her design notebook. "I have. I've got some sketches of what I want the interior to look like already."

Instantly, his gaze lit. "Show me."

A little quiver went through her, the warmth inside her glowing hot. He made her breathless and giddy, a part of her wanting to jump him right there under the Christmas tree, sketches be damned. But she hadn't finished decorating and she wanted to do that before they got looking at her café design or...other things.

"Later." She gave him a naughty grin. "The tree's not finished yet."

Bending over the nearly empty box, she pushed aside the last bit of tinsel to see if she could see a tree topper. And there, right at the bottom, was a small battered cardboard star painted silver.

Bella lost her breath. Because she recognized that star. She'd made it at school when she'd been a kid and had given it to June.

She hadn't realized her grandmother had kept it.

"Oh, good," Noah said from behind her. "You found the star."

Her star.

Sensing her sudden distress, Noah turned her gently around to face him. "Hey. What's up?"

She swallowed, gazing down at the dog-eared star in her hands. "This is my star. I made it when I was a kid. I didn't realize Grandma kept it."

Noah was silent a moment. Then he took the star from her hand and turned to the tree. "June always let me put the star up. She said it wasn't Christmas until the star was on the tree." He reached up and deftly fixed the star right at the top, then turned, his dark gaze focusing on her. "I guess it's Christmas now."

Bella's throat closed, tears in her eyes. So many things she'd missed out on. Things she hadn't even realized she wanted. But it seemed a little piece of her had remained here all along.

Her grandmother had made sure of it.

Noah's gaze turned searching. "You okay, honey?"

Oh, God, when his voice got tender... It undid her.

"I didn't realize she'd kept it," Bella said. "Mom didn't go to any of the family stuff that Grandma organized so I never did, either. And then we left and I lost contact with everyone. I just... I thought they'd forgotten about me."

Noah pulled her gently against him. "You weren't forgotten, Bella."

She put her hands to his chest. "You forgot me."

"I never knew you to start with."

Bella tilted her head back, looking into the swirling darkness of his eyes. He was such a closed book. As isolated as she had been, though, she had the sense that his isolation had been self-imposed. That he'd cut himself off purposefully.

"Did you ever know anyone, Noah?" she asked. "And did you let anyone really know you?"

BELLA LOOKED UP at him, and Noah had to bite down on his instinctive, defensive response. Because there was no sarcasm in her tone; it was a genuine question.

Yet he still didn't want to answer it.

Not when you know what the answer's going to be.

He hadn't *let* people know him. A few had tried, but they'd been put off by Hank's behavior and his reputation. And Noah had been touchy about their sympathy. He didn't want anyone's pity, either.

That's an excuse. You never made any effort to get past that.

And why should he? They'd all kept their distance and he'd been fine with it. He didn't want anyone to know him, anyway.

"What kind of question is that?" He released her, finding her closeness painful for reasons he couldn't articulate.

A crease appeared between her eyebrows. "You seem kind of…isolated. And I wondered why."

He pushed his hands into his pockets, fighting the urge to walk out the room, because he didn't want to stay and have this discussion.

He'd known helping her with the tree would be a mistake, but she'd looked so wistfully at it when it had appeared and the faint husk in her voice when she'd told him she'd never had a Christmas had made his chest constrict.

This whole week he'd been doing little things for her and she'd let him, and the enjoyment he'd gotten from her simple pleasure had been balm to a wound he hadn't known was festering.

He'd never made such a difference to a person before and he liked it. He'd liked the cups of coffee, the odd cans of beer and the meals she'd made for him, too. All things he preferred done in a particular way and she'd done them exactly the way he'd preferred. She'd paid attention to him and that made him feel good. He hadn't been taken care of like that since his mother had left.

So helping her with Christmas seemed like another of those small things.

Except the way she'd looked at that star and the gleam of tears in her eyes hadn't been a small thing. Neither was the way she looked at him now, as if she wanted to know things about him.

He'd assumed that controlled exposure to his drug of choice would help him control it better, and it was true to a certain extent. It meant his brain wasn't constantly occupied by thoughts of her.

It was only at night in that bed that the hunger felt too much. As if what she gave him wasn't enough. As if he wanted more, though what he wanted more of he didn't know.

What he did know was that he didn't want to talk about himself.

"I'm not isolated." He tried to sound casual. "I get plenty of company."

"With who?"

"You want a list of my friends or something?"

"Noah…"

"I don't need company, anyway. I like being on my own." He stared belligerently at her. The look in her eyes was suspiciously like sympathy, or understanding, and it made him feel as brittle as one of those fragile blown-glass baubles she'd put on the tree.

Bella put her hands in her pockets, too, mirroring him. "I thought I liked being on my own, too. But turns out…" Her lovely mouth curved in a shy smile. "I prefer being with you."

There was no reason for those words to make him feel as if she'd peeled apart his chest and reached for his heart. Yet they did.

Why the hell would she like that? No one else ever had.

A dull anger simmered inside him that he'd successfully ignored for years. Until now.

Until she'd uncovered it, dousing it with gas, making it burn a hell of a lot hotter.

"Why? Because you like having dinner made for you and the house fixed?" He'd meant it to sound dry yet the words came out sharp.

She frowned. "No, of course not. Those are nice things that you do, but that's not why I like being with you."

"You don't know me." He sounded like an asshole, but he couldn't seem to adjust his tone. "That's just the orgasms talking."

The sparkle in her eyes and the blush in her cheeks that had been there while they'd been decorating the tree slowly drained away. Great. Now he not only sounded like an asshole, he felt like one, too.

"It's not the orgasms," she said.

"How do you know?" He should really shut up. "You don't know me from a goddamn bar of soap."

"And whose fault is that? You never talk about yourself. You never talk about anything. As soon as I ask a question about you or the conversation moves to a topic you don't like, you don't speak. Or you change the subject." Her chin lifted. "Or you get all stone-faced."

He wanted to tell her that he didn't do any of those things. But she was right. He did.

"You're not exactly chatty yourself," he said, aware he sounded defensive as hell.

"Okay. What do you want to know?"

So now she was going to be open with him? Yeah, that wasn't happening. Not when he couldn't give her the same openness in return.

Couldn't? Wouldn't, you mean.

"I don't need to know anything," he said flatly. "What I need to do is go buy some paint for the hallway."

"Didn't you want to look at those sketches?"

Yeah, he'd said that. And he did want to look at them, because he had a feeling they'd be good. But right now, doing that made him feel as if he'd be getting deeper into something that would overwhelm him if he wasn't careful.

"Bella…"

She just looked at him. "Okay, here's something else you might want to know, then. I haven't been with a guy before. You're my first."

He felt like she'd punched him in the gut. "What?"

"You heard me." Her gaze was very level. "I was a virgin."

Shock rippled through him. On the stairs, where he'd pushed her down. The hard stairs. And he'd thrust inside her with no care. He hadn't even considered the possibility that she was a virgin, not when she'd clawed at him in her desperation…

Heat washed through him, possessive and territorial…

Shit, he couldn't be *pleased* about that surely?

He ignored it, reaching for anger instead. "You should have told me."

"Why? What difference would it have made?"

"I might have been gentler. I would at least have taken you to a goddam bed."

"It didn't even occur to me." Challenge glowed in her eyes. "I wanted you. And besides, if I told you, you might have stopped.

Would he?

No. You wouldn't.

The possessiveness tightened at the same time as a sense of shame gripped him. At himself and what he'd done. At the need inside him that he'd lost of control of that day on the stairs.

He should have gotten a handle on it and he hadn't.

Yet another reason why being here with her had been a bad idea from the start.

Tension crawled through him, his fingers curling into fists in his pockets. "Anything else you want to tell me? Before I get that paint?"

"There's plenty I could tell you." She lifted a shoulder. "You only have to ask."

He didn't understand why that made him angrier. "I'm not going to be asking," he said harshly. "I don't want to know."

The way she looked at him felt like she was cutting him to pieces, discovering all his secrets, seeing inside his head.

"It's all right." Her voice was soft. "You don't have to give me anything back. You've done a lot for me this week so you get to ask for whatever you want."

Her. You want her.

The thought was instant and crystal clear, but he

couldn't say it. He had to resist the temptation. He had to prove himself stronger than his father.

"I don't want anything." He tried to sound convincing.

"Don't you?" Bella's gaze felt like delicate fingers closing around his heart. "Not a single thing?"

"No." Maybe if he told himself enough times, he'd believe it. "I told you, I don't want anything. Not from anyone."

A flicker of distress rippled over her face, then vanished. "Not even…from me?"

The hesitancy in her voice and the spark of hope in her gaze broke him. He had to shut her down. Had to give her the same honesty she'd given him. And maybe once he had, she'd understand.

"Not even from you." He kept the words flat. "I'm done with wanting things from people, Bella. I almost failed school because I had to look after Dad and I missed out entirely on going to college. I couldn't date, couldn't travel. Couldn't spend time with my friends, all the usual stuff guys my age did. And that's not even going into the years I didn't get of him actually being a goddamn father to me. It was like pouring myself into a black hole, and I'm done." He held her gaze. "I'll help you fix this house, because I said I would, but that's it."

Hurt bloomed in her eyes, but she masked it quickly, black lashes coming down, veiling her gaze. "Okay," she said. "I understand."

But she didn't.

So tell her?

No. He'd told her the truth. He was done with giving

pieces of himself to people who didn't want them. People who took and took and didn't give anything back.

He'd given away too much. There wasn't anything left for her.

"I'll go get that paint," he said brusquely and brushed past her.

CHAPTER EIGHT

BELLA LEANED IN and lit one of the candles on the mantelpiece in the living room, then stepped back, surveying her handiwork.

The fire was burning and the candles she'd put on the mantel gave the room a warm glow, illuminating Grandma June's collection of photos.

Everything was in place.

Pleased, she hurried across the hall to the kitchen, where her pot of mulled wine was cooking gently on the stove.

She'd unearthed a bottle of red wine from the cellar earlier that day and after a quick consult in one of Grandma June's cookbooks, she'd found a recipe for mulled wine. The pantry had all the spices she needed so she'd gone ahead and started making a batch.

Now the kitchen was full of the rich, spicy scent and it made her feel good every time she inhaled.

It was Christmas Eve and she'd wanted it to be special for Noah. Because she hadn't been able to get what he'd told her the day before out of her head.

He'd basically given up years of his life to look after his father, had missed out on things he should have had and clearly gotten no thanks and no appreciation for it.

That he'd been trying to help Hank, fix him even, was clear. And that he felt he'd failed was also clear.

No wonder he didn't want to talk about it.

No wonder he was so angry; she'd seen it burning in his dark eyes.

Whatever, if he didn't want to talk about it, she wasn't going to force him. But she *did* want to do something for him, especially since he'd done so much for her. But she hadn't known what to offer. She had no advice for him, no words of wisdom, and no money with which to buy him anything.

And then she'd had a brain wave. The gift idea wasn't that great, but she thought he might appreciate the thought at least.

So when he'd gone back to his place earlier that day, she'd thrown herself into action, tidying up the farmhouse and making everything nice and welcoming. She put a chicken in the oven with some veggies, then texted him not to bring anything when he came back down.

Then she stood at the stove stirring the pot of mulled wine gently, her heart full and painful as she thought about why doing something for him was so important to her.

And it wasn't because of everything he'd done around the house, or the interest he'd shown in her café project, although she appreciated that more than she could say.

It was important to her, because Noah was important. Because he'd had a crappy life and he deserved more than that.

Because he was a good man. A caring man. A protective man.

His father hadn't appreciated him, but dammit, she did.

And she wanted to show him exactly how much.

Not long before six, she heard the front door open and she rushed into the hallway to greet him.

Sure enough, over six feet of hard, muscular cowboy stepped into the hall in a swirl of cold air. He was in jeans and his coat, one of his thermals underneath, and his arms were full of firewood, snow dusting the brim of his cowboy hat. "Brought some more wood for the living room," he said as he went past her.

"Oh, thanks." She followed him, watching as he dumped the wood in the log basket by the fire.

He straightened, dusting off his hands, and she went straight to him, putting her hands on his chest, rising to kiss him.

His lips were cold from the outside, but they warmed almost instantly, his muscles gathering tight the way they sometimes did when she touched him and they weren't in bed.

She didn't understand his tension. Maybe she'd ask later. After he'd opened his present.

She stepped back, smiling. "Give me your hat and coat and I'll hang them up for you."

His eyes glittered strangely and he didn't return her smile. But slowly, he reached up and took off his hat, then shrugged out of his coat.

"I need to talk to you," he said, handing them to her.

A note in his voice made a shiver of foreboding go through her.

Turning away so he wouldn't see her sudden disquiet, Bella took his things into the hallway to hang them on the peg beside the door. "Oh? Can it wait? I have dinner in the oven and some mulled wine on the stove. Do you like mulled wine? I got it out of Grandma June's cookbook."

"Bella—"

"At least let me give you your present." She plastered a smile on her face and turned, trying to ignore the frantic beat of her heart, because she had a feeling she knew already what he was going to say, but she didn't want to hear it.

He stood in the living room doorway silently, the granite expression on his face making her heart shrivel up like a flower covered in frost.

"Let's have Christmas." She hoped the desperate note in her voice wasn't too obvious. "Please, Noah. Let's have it just once."

A muscle flicked in the side of his jaw, then he glanced away without speaking.

She would take that as a yes.

Ignoring the cold shreds of doubt drifting through her, prickling like snowflakes landing on hot skin, Bella went into the kitchen. She poured some mulled wine into a couple of mugs and then carried them back into the living room.

Noah had gone to stand beside the fire, staring down at it. He glanced up as she came in, the combination of firelight and candlelight enhancing the handsome lines of his face. His hard jaw, strong nose and high forehead. His eyes were shadowed, a dense, compelling darkness that drew her in.

She caught her breath. "Wait. I've got something for you."

"What?"

"A Christmas present." She went out, dashing upstairs to grab one of Grandma June's quilts. It was very Christmassy, all red and green. The perfect wrapping paper for the present she wanted to give Noah.

Her hands shook as she slipped out of her clothes and wrapped the blanket around herself. Then she went back downstairs and into the living room, shutting the door behind her to keep in the warmth.

Noah's eyes narrowed. "What's this?"

Bella's heart thumped hard, trepidation curling in her stomach. "It's your present."

"What do you mean?"

She took an uncertain step toward him. She'd hoped to do this after a leisurely meal and a couple of glasses of mulled wine, not now, at the beginning of the evening. Maybe it had been a mistake. Maybe this was stupid.

Maybe he won't want you.

But he did want her. He'd made that very clear.

"I mean, I'm your present." She smiled tentatively "I wanted to give you something, but I didn't know what and I don't have any money. The only thing I have is me so…anything you want, Noah. It's yours for the night." She lifted her arms and dropped the blanket. "Including me."

The air shimmered with tension, his black eyes boring into hers with sudden, fierce intensity. And her own hunger rose to meet it, her breath catching and her heart along with it.

But he didn't move.

Her mouth was dry and her pulse was thundering, goose bumps rising on her skin as chill air whispered under the closed door.

He looked like a starving man with a feast before him that he couldn't let himself eat.

"Noah?" Uncertainty made her voice shake. "It's okay. You can—"

"It's not okay." His eyes were so dark they looked like black holes. "It's a lovely gift, Bella. But I can't take it."

Her face got hot and she wanted to cover herself, but she ignored the feeling. "Why not? Do you not want me anymore?"

He murmured something vicious, his gaze wandering down her body, and this time there was no hiding the hunger in his expression. "It's not that I don't want you. I do. I want you too much." It looked as if he might go on, but then he shut his mouth tight.

Tension gathered in the air around him, an electrical charge of energy.

"I don't understand," she said.

"No, and you won't." His gaze flickered away. "You should put some clothes on."

But Bella didn't move. "I know I'm not much, but I did mean it. I'm yours for the evening. You said that you were sick of giving to other people so I thought I'd give you something instead."

"Bella." He bit her name out tightly. "I can't do this with you."

"Can't do what with me?"

"This." He made a sharp gesture. "Coming here. Talking to you. Seeing you. Sleeping with you." His posture was so rigid it looked like he might snap. "I can't do it."

She blinked, not expecting the bright burst of pain in her chest. "What do you mean you can't do it?"

"It's too much. You're too much." He looked away, a seething mass of energy gathering around him. "Dad was an alcoholic. And nothing I did made any difference to him. Nothing made him give up the bottle. He was a slave to it. He wouldn't even admit he had a problem." Noah glanced back at her, the darkness of his eyes pulling her in, sucking her under. "I can feel it sometimes, the same thing that made him pick up that damn bottle. It's in me, too. A kind of…pull. And I feel it whenever I look at you."

Shock rippled through her. "Me?"

"Yes." Another bitten-out word. "I won't turn into him, Bella. I won't be a slave to any damn addiction— it doesn't matter what the drug is."

She stared at him, bewildered. "But… I'm not a drug."

He laughed harshly. "You don't think so? I'm here every day. I'm in your bed every night. I can't stay damn well away."

She was his drug? Homeless Bella Jacobson, whom everyone forgot about and whom nobody really wanted, not even her own mother? *Her?*

"But…why?"

Noah didn't say anything at first. Then in an explosion of movement, he crossed the distance between them, his warm palms cupping her face. "Why do you think?" he said in a dark, gritty voice. "You're beautiful and you're kind. You're generous. And you're vulnerable, yet not afraid to show it. At least you're not afraid to show it to me." His thumbs stroked her cheekbones very gently. "You trust me, Bella, and I don't know why. Because what you want, I'll never be able to give to you."

"I don't want anything." But as soon as she'd said it, she realized it wasn't true. She did want something and she had a feeling that something was him.

You've always wanted him.

Noah shook his head. "You do. And what's more, you deserve it. You deserve to have everything you want."

"And you don't? You've done nothing but look after me and help me since the moment I got here. Even when I was awful and rude to you. You've been patient and kind and amazing. So why don't you let me do something for you?"

His jaw flexed, the intensity in his eyes almost too bright to look at. "But I can't have it. I can never have it. I can't let myself, Bella. Even a sip is dangerous, don't you understand?"

She did. Perhaps in a way that no one else did because her mother had been an addict of a kind. Addicted to the attention men gave her, dropping one when she'd sucked another dry before taking up with yet another.

Bella felt that same need. The hunger that made her too like her mother for comfort.

It destroyed you, if you weren't careful. And it destroyed others around you, too.

Yet right now, a little destruction didn't seem like a bad thing. Keeping all that need inside her was exhausting and she didn't want to have to do it. Not tonight.

"I do." She gripped his wrists. "I do understand, believe me. But what would happen if we let ourselves have this? Just for now? Just for a night?" She stared into his dark gaze, letting her own need show. "A night where we don't hold back and let ourselves have what we really want. It's not going to hurt, Noah. I promise."

His hold was gentle, but the look in his eyes was not. The door inside him had opened and she could see the fire burning at the core of him. A blaze of raw feeling so intense it took her breath away.

Maybe the Bella of a week ago would have found it

too scary and would have run back into the cold. But
the Bella standing naked in the living room in front of
the man she'd wanted since forever didn't run away.

She ran headlong into the fire instead.

"Noah," she said softly.

He made a sound, half a groan, half a growl, then
his mouth was on hers.

HE SHOULD HAVE RESISTED. But Bella was naked and vulnerable, and offering him something he was desperate
to have and he couldn't resist it.

He didn't want to resist it.

One night, she'd said. What could it hurt?

Nothing. It would hurt nothing. And they'd *both* get
what they wanted. She wanted to give herself to him and
he wanted to take her without holding anything back.
Wanted it so badly he could barely speak.

Without another thought, he lowered his head and
captured her warm, hungry mouth with his. She tasted
of spices and wine, hot and sweet, and he drank his fill,
then some more again.

She shook, her small, naked body arching into his,
and he couldn't hold back the hunger that was flooding out of him.

So he didn't.

He laid her down on the soft red rug in front of the
fire, bathing her in candlelight and firelight, and the
light from the Christmas tree.

And she watched him with luminous blue eyes as
he clawed his clothes off, taking the condom packet he
had in the back pocket of his jeans and ripping it open.
Sheathing himself.

Then he was stretching over her, shuddering at the

feel of her silky skin against his. She gripped tight to him as he positioned himself between her spread thighs, thrusting in deep.

"Oh, Noah," she whispered, her hips lifting to meet his, the wet heat of her body clamping around him, holding him tight.

He should have kissed her, should have stroked her, given her at least a couple of orgasms before he took what he wanted. But he didn't have the time. He didn't have the strength.

He wanted to be inside her and now he was.

Something in him relaxed at the same time as it grew more desperate, and he slid his hands beneath her, gathering her closer, holding her tighter. Her arms wrapped around him, too, her legs winding tightly around his waist, her mouth finding his, kissing him hungrily.

He lost himself in her heat. In the hunger that burned inside him more fiercely than the fire in the grate. Than the woodstove in the kitchen. Than the stars in the winter sky above the house.

He moved faster, harder, gripping her tighter. Immersing himself in the pleasure that burned with the same ferocity as his hunger.

She stroked him, and he let himself have that, too. Let himself have her care and the way she gentled him. Let himself have this closeness. Because he wouldn't have it again.

She was wrong.

It was going to hurt.

This night would break him in so many ways, but he would survive. He'd built his life around resistance and denial, subsuming himself in the ranch and using all the tasks required to keep it running as a focus, so he wouldn't be tempted by anything else. It had helped him stay strong.

She was strong, too, but her heart was fragile.

This night might hurt him, but it would hurt her more. Yet he'd taken her, anyway. Because he was selfish. Because he couldn't help himself. Because he was just as bad as his father, taking and taking and giving nothing back.

Noah thrust harder, looking down at the beautiful woman beneath him. Her gaze was dark, shining. Giving him everything. But then she always had.

Out there on the stairs, she'd given him her virginity and her hunger. Her need. She'd given him everything she was and if he wasn't careful he would take it all, suck her dry and leave her with nothing.

He knew how it went. What it was like to live with someone like that. Someone who'd never give him what he wanted, no matter what he did.

But Bella would give him everything and she'd wreck herself doing so, because she wasn't like her mother. She was generous and warm and giving. She was loving.

She was everything he'd ever wanted.

Everything he couldn't let himself have.

He moved harder, deeper. He wanted her to remember this, to never to forget. She was his and even though she might find herself another man, he'd make sure she'd remember him always. Remember this night forever.

He drove her over the brink twice, holding her tight as she sobbed against his chest, then he pushed his hand between them and pushed her over a third time. And this time he went with her, turning his face into her neck, growling as the orgasm broke him into pieces.

He should have left it there, but he didn't.

He indulged himself shamelessly, because if he was going to overdose he was going to do it properly.

Beneath the Christmas tree, he put her hands on his body and let her explore him, lavish her touch on him. He watched her ride him, the Christmas tree lights bathing her lovely face.

Showering them both in color as pleasure exploded yet again, brilliant as fireworks in a night sky.

Afterward, he snuggled her up in the quilt and they sat together beneath the tree, sipping mulled wine as she showed him the sketches she'd done of her café.

She was talented, with an eye for design, and when he made his admiration known, she blushed.

"I had a friend who thought it was too mainstream," she said, looking down at the sketches of rustic tables and dressers full of old china. There was even an old woodstove. "He said I needed to be edgier. But I wanted it to feel homey and welcoming." She flushed deeper. "Like Grandma June's kitchen, actually."

"I thought it looked familiar." Because her drawings did and he hadn't been able to put his finger on why until now. "And your friend is wrong. These are perfect. More people want homey and welcoming than they do hard and edgy."

Her forehead creased. "You think?"

"I don't think, I know." He had to kiss her then, because she was smart and creative and beautiful. "If your café feels anything like the Christmas you've created for us both tonight, then you're going to have people lining up in the streets to get a table."

She blushed even harder at that, which made him do more than kiss her. Her sketches showed him the depth of her need for a connection, and since it was in his power to give her that connection, he did so, leaving their mulled wine to cool on the coffee table.

Much later, he finally let her sleep, wrapping her up in the quilt and putting her on the couch, before putting another log on the fire.

He got dressed, because he wouldn't sleep and, anyway, it was Christmas morning and he had a present to give her when she woke up.

It wasn't much, but it was all he had.

He had to let her go, but she wouldn't leave empty-handed.

CHAPTER NINE

BELLA WOKE UP to find herself wrapped in a blanket on the couch in the living room, naked but not cold. A fire burned in the grate, the smell of hot chocolate in the air, along with the scent of pine.

Christmas morning.

Her heart tightened and then, when she sat up, it tightened even further.

Noah sat in one of the armchairs by the fire, watching her, his dark eyes impenetrable.

She shivered, remembering the night before.

He hadn't held back, taking her fiercely and with a passion she couldn't help but meet. Raw and demanding, unapologetic.

He'd taken everything she had to give and then some, and it had been everything she'd wanted.

And now it's over.

Cold licked beneath the warmth of the quilt.

She knew without him having to say a word. She'd told him one more night and now they'd had it.

If he'd wanted more he would have been curled up naked next to her.

But he was already dressed in jeans and a thermal, and that door to the passion inside him was firmly shut.

Bella's heart kicked painfully against her ribs.

"Merry Christmas," she said and tried her best to smile.

He didn't return it. "I made you some hot chocolate."

On the table, a mug of hot chocolate waited for her— the good kind, with real chocolate.

"Oh, thank you." She reached for the mug and her hands only shook a little. "You're not having any?"

"No. I've got a few things to do up at the ranch."

Her heart kicked again and it hurt. Really hurt. But she'd always known this was going to happen so getting upset was ridiculous.

"I got you a present." Noah reached into his back pocket and pulled a small slip of paper from it. "I didn't wrap it, sorry."

She stared at it. A present? No one got her presents. Slowly, she took it, unfolding the paper.

It was a check. And the sum written on it made her stare.

She looked at him. "What's this?"

His black eyes were like stone. "I don't want you to sell June's house. You lost your money and that's not your fault, and I don't want you to leave here empty-handed. You should have what you want, Bella." He nodded at the check. "That's for your café when you get back to Seattle."

She felt like he'd put his hand inside her chest, wrapped his fingers around her heart and twisted hard.

He'd given her money.

Her throat felt like it had a boulder sitting in it.

A couple of weeks ago this would have meant everything. But now...

He hadn't just twisted her heart. He'd ripped it clean out of her chest.

"Oh." She should say more than that, sound more grateful. "This is…" She tried to smile and not feel like a drowning woman handed a rock rather than a life preserver. "A lot of money."

"Don't worry about that. I can afford it."

She wanted to tell him that wasn't what she was worried about, but the words wouldn't come.

She felt like a little girl who'd expected presents only to get coal in her stocking instead.

You don't want the money. You want him.

Tears pricked her eyes. Of course she did. And it wasn't until now, with that check in her hand, that she realized it.

She wanted him. She'd *always* wanted him.

She loved him.

But he'd made his position very clear the night before. He couldn't give her anything more and she wouldn't be like her mother, desperately grasping for love from anyone.

Desperately grasping for love from him. A love she'd never get back. And that would end up destroying both of them.

Her fingers trembling, Bella folded up the check and put it on the coffee table. "Thanks," she said, not knowing what else to say.

An awful silence fell.

"You should have your café." Noah voice sounded hoarse. "I know how important it is to you."

Bella blinked hard to stop the tears and reached for her hot chocolate. She suddenly had no appetite, but the mug was hot and her fingers were cold.

"And now I will." Her voice sounded just as hoarse as his. "Thank you."

Another silence, thick with something terrible and desperate.

"Okay," Noah said. "I should go."

She couldn't look at him. Didn't want to see that granite look on his face.

She wanted to remember him from last night, burning fiercely above her, making her feel wanted, pouring all his need into her.

She heard him move and when he paused beside her, she didn't look up. "Don't say it." The words were scraped raw. "Whatever you were going to say, don't."

"I'm sorry." His voice held the same raw note.

She didn't look at him.

She just sat there until she heard the door shut behind him.

Then she let herself cry.

She didn't know how long she sat there, crying into her hot chocolate, her heart bruised and battered, shattered into pieces.

Stupid to indulge herself. Stupid to sit here weeping when their affair had always been temporary. She'd never meant to stay. So why she should feel wrecked, she had no idea.

It was only love. People got their hearts broken on Christmas day all the time.

Eventually, Bella got herself dressed. Then sat morosely on the couch in the living room, her hot chocolate slowly cooling on the coffee table.

At some point, a knock came on the door and she flew off the couch, her heart thundering, because there was only one person who'd be knocking on her door.

She dashed into the hall and flung open the door.

But it wasn't Noah.

Three women stood on the porch, studying her with wariness and hope.

Her cousins.

Elegant Keira, blond hair in a loose knot, a soft blue shawl draped around her shoulders. Serious JJ, straight dark hair in a band and a steady look in her eyes. Red-headed Lila, full of boundless optimism.

It was Lila who stepped forward, holding up a basket, giving her a tentative smile. "Hi, Bella. I hope you don't mind but we thought we'd come and wish you a merry Christmas."

Bella stared, disappointment like ash in her mouth.

Then she burst into tears for the second time that day.

Instantly, she was surrounded in a cloud of feminine concern. Keira took her into the living room and got her to sit on the couch, while Lila covered her with a blanket. JJ bustled off into the kitchen, coming back with a steaming mug that smelled of spices.

"You need something stronger than hot chocolate." JJ put the mug on the table. "And there was mulled wine all ready to go."

Bella gripped the mug gratefully and took a long swallow, letting the alcohol bloom warmly in her stomach, though it didn't touch the block of ice where her heart should be.

"It's a man, isn't it?" Keira gave Bella's shoulders a comforting squeeze.

"Of course, it's a man." JJ pulled a crumpled tissue from her jeans pocket and handed it to Bella. "Who else would make you cry on Christmas Day?"

Lila sat down on the couch. "Come on, out with it. Who do we need to kill?"

"I can get Cade's shotgun," JJ agreed. "It won't take a moment."

Bella wanted to laugh, but it was too painful. They looked at her with sympathy and concern, and she felt ashamed.

She didn't know them and they didn't know her, yet here they were, offering her comfort, despite the years of silence she'd given them.

"This is lovely," she said hoarsely. "And thank you. But...why are you here?"

"To wish you merry Christmas," Lila said. "We didn't want to disturb you, but we thought we'd come say hi. Let you know we're around."

Bella blew her nose. "Why? I don't even know you guys."

"You're our cousin." Keira arched an eyebrow. "What else needs to be said?"

She didn't know. She'd never had family or this easy acceptance she didn't need to do anything for but exist. "I'm not sure I deserve it. I haven't exactly kept in touch."

Lila made an airy gesture. "Oh, don't worry about that now. What's important is who made you cry and what we can do to make sure he dies."

JJ nodded. "Seriously. I'll shoot him for you if you want."

Bella gave a watery laugh. "It's okay. I'll be fine. I'm just..."

"Heartbroken?" Keira finished.

She let out a sigh. "It wasn't supposed to be permanent. I was always going to leave once winter was over."

The three women shared glances that Bella couldn't interpret.

"Sounds familiar," Kiera murmured.

"Horribly so," Lila agreed.

"Bastard," JJ added.

"Oh, no," Bella said, feeling defensive of Noah. "It wasn't his fault. We agreed. I thought it would go on a little longer and—"

"It's Noah, isn't it?" Lila asked quietly.

There was no point in hiding it. "Yes." She cleared her throat. Might as well tell them. "Hey, it's not all bad. He gave me a present. Which is great since now I don't need to sell the house."

"Wait, what?" Keira frowned. "Sell the house?"

"Grandma June left me a letter. She told me that I had to fix the house up to sell, if I wanted to." She wiped uselessly with the soaking tissue at the tears on her cheeks. "And I was going to. I needed the money, but... Noah gave me a check." She gestured at the small square of paper on the coffee table.

JJ's eyes widened. "He bought you off?"

"No," Bella protested, not knowing why she was defending him. "It wasn't like that."

"Oh, yes," Keira said with distaste. "It most certainly was."

"Right, I *am* going to shoot him," JJ said with certainty.

"It's fine," Bella sniffed. "Please don't. He didn't do anything wrong."

"So why are you crying?" Lila asked.

Tears filled her eyes again. "I don't know."

"I do." Keira's voice was quiet. "I think we all do."

Of course she knew.

"I didn't want the money. I wanted him," Bella said raggedly.

"Did you tell him that?" Lila asked.

"No." Tears ran down her nose. "He didn't want a relationship. He was very clear and he had good reasons."

A small silence fell, then Keira asked, "Do you want a relationship, though?"

She'd been so certain that she was going back to Seattle and get her café. Resume her life. Except the thought of that life...

Loneliness she'd always been able to handle.

But not now. Not after Noah.

"I thought I didn't." She made another swipe at the tears. "But I think I changed my mind."

"So? Tell him." Lila this time.

Bella blinked, her eyes sore. "He already told me he can't give me what I want. And I don't want to ask him for it."

"Why not?" Lila said gently. "If you never ask you never get."

What you'll have to do is ask for help.

The words in Grandma June's letter were in Bella's head all of a sudden. Pushing at her. Going against everything she thought she'd believed in.

But it wasn't his help she wanted.

It was his heart.

"He'll say no," she croaked.

Lila gave her a look. "Do you love him?"

It sat inside her chest, so painful, an ache that would never go away. "Yes," Bella said thickly. "Yes, I do."

"Then you need to let him know how you feel." Lila's expression was so full of understanding it made Bella's chest hurt. "Love changes a lot of things."

But would it be enough to change Noah's mind? And who was she to demand more, anyway? That was her mother's tactic, taking and taking, sucking people dry, then moving on.

You're not your mother, though. And you're not taking anything.

Realization broke over her, like snow dumped down the back of her neck.

Because this morning, she'd kept back the one thing she had left to give. She wasn't her mother. And she didn't want to take anything from him. What she wanted was to give. And not just her body this time and not for a night.

She wanted to give him her heart, and forever.

Bella pushed herself off the couch before she knew what she was doing.

"You look like you've decided something," JJ said.

"Yeah." She gave them all a quick look, her heart beating frantically. "I'm sorry, I have to go."

She didn't wait for them to reply, launching herself toward the front door.

"Bring Noah back for Christmas dinner," Lila shouted after her. "Everett and I are having everyone over."

But Bella had already rushed through the door, hurling herself down the steps, heading toward the Faraday ranch.

It was freezing, but she barely noticed the cold. Only one thing was important.

Noah. Who'd sacrificed so much for so long. And who didn't have to sacrifice anything more except his loneliness.

Bella hurtled up the front steps of his house and came to a stop, her quickened breathing in white clouds around her.

Fear gripped her as she raised her hand, but she wasn't going to listen to that, not now.

She knocked hard.

He didn't answer.

So she kept on knocking until finally the door was pulled violently open. Noah stood on the threshold, filling the doorway, staring at her with a face like stone. "What the hell are you doing here?"

Bella took a shuddering breath. "I forgot to give you my present."

"Present? What present?"

She looked into his intense black eyes. "I gave you myself last night," she said. "But what I really wanted to give you was my heart."

NOAH COULDN'T BELIEVE IT. Bella stood on his doorstep in his oversize blue sweatshirt, jeans and nothing else. Her eyes were red and so was the tip of her nose, and she looked at him like he was the only thing in her entire universe.

He'd never thought he'd see her again.

He never wanted to.

He'd thought the money would be enough because he couldn't give her anything more, and he'd told himself he was content with the decision.

Except as soon as he'd gotten home he'd headed straight for the liquor cabinet. He'd never wanted a drink as badly as it he had right then. Yet he'd held off, pacing around in his living room, trying to ignore the agony clawing at him.

If he ignored it, it would go away. He just had to ride it out.

But now she was right here, he knew that pain would stay forever.

"What do you mean, your heart?" Cruel of her to come back. To tempt him like this.

Bella stepped into his hall, kicking the door shut behind her. "I mean, you're all I've ever wanted. From the moment I first saw you at thirteen. It's always been you and it'll only ever be you." She didn't hesitate, closing the distance between them, her blue eyes burning like a gas flame. "And you're wrong. I'm not asking you for anything and I won't. You don't have to give me a single thing. But you should know that I love you, Noah Faraday. And I'll keep on loving you whether you want me to or not."

He felt as fragile as he had the day before. Like blown glass. Ready to shatter at the slightest touch.

She loved him. What the hell did he do with that?

"You can't." He didn't want to move. Just in case. "I told you I can't give you what you want."

Bella's expression softened and she cupped his face with one small hand. "Then don't. But you have my heart all the same."

In that moment, with the heat of her palm burning against his skin, he knew that all the things he'd said about addiction and self-control were lies.

Convenient excuses so he didn't have to face the terrible fear that he wasn't enough. Not for his father to give up the bottle, not for his mother to stay. Not for anyone.

"You can't love me." His voice sounded as rusty as the hinges on an old gate. "I'm shut-off and mean. I'm selfish and self-centered. I'm—"

"Caring and protective and kind," she finished

gently. "You gave me help when I was awful. You let me know that I wasn't alone."

He should tell her to leave. Take her precious heart and break it so thoroughly she'd never darken his door again.

Like your old man broke your heart?

The thought was dark and raw, and he knew he couldn't do it. He couldn't break her the way his father had broken him. He couldn't be that selfish.

So where does that leave you?

Almost of its own accord, his hand rose to cover hers, holding it there. "I'm a bad bet, honey," he said roughly. "Dad didn't give a shit about me and neither did Mom. And I wonder sometimes if they were right not to. I'm not a good guy."

"No, they weren't right," Bella said fiercely. "And I give a shit. Because whether you like it or not, you're a good man."

Her words vibrated through him, the ache in his chest crushing him.

It would be so easy to give in. To take what he wanted. But...

She loves you. Are you really going to throw that back in her face?

He couldn't breathe. He couldn't do that to her. Destroy her like his father had destroyed him every time he picked up another bottle.

She was beautiful and generous and warm, with a stubborn, determined spirit. And he couldn't bear the thought of hurting her.

Which left him with only one option.

Loving her instead.

Noah curled his fingers around her hand and pulled

it away from his face. Then he turned it up and kissed her palm.

She shuddered, tears gleaming in her eyes. "Does that mean what I think it means?"

He was a man of few words. But he could say these words. Because they meant more than anything else he could have said. "I love you, Bella Jacobson. And I don't know how long you mean to stay, but I'll spend every minute of it showing you how much."

Tears slid down her cheeks. "How does forever sound?"

"Perfect," he said, pulling her into his arms and holding her tight. "That sounds perfect."

And it was.

CHAPTER TEN

BELLA WALKED INTO the living room of Grandma June's house and took a last look around. The scent of pine needles lingered in the air, though the tree was gone and the snow outside was melting.

She smiled, remembering, then moved to the mantelpiece, where the photos sat. She touched them, reflecting on the last few weeks, and the sisters she'd found. The people who'd welcomed her despite the years of no contact.

She and Keira had gotten together and had a chat about Keira's coffee-cart business. It was such a success that Keira needed help, so Bella had worked with her on the cart in between helping Noah out on the ranch. Now she and Keira wanted to expand, and the perfect place had just become vacant in Jasper Creek itself.

June's was about to expand into a café called June's Kitchen.

It was good. It was right.

It was so much better than Seattle that she could hardly believe it was real.

Bella glanced around just in case someone was watching, then scooped the photos up and put them in the pocket of her new winter coat.

No one would know. And they'd look great on the mantel above the fire at Noah's. Correction, Noah's and *hers*.

Still smiling, Bella walked out of the house, pausing

to lock it carefully behind her and put her key under the mat.

A tall, broad figure waited for her at the bottom of the porch stairs.

"All done?" Noah's dark eyes glittered from underneath the brim of his cowboy hat.

"Yep. The house is looking great." She ran down the stairs to him and slid her hand into his.

His fingers closed around hers, warm and secure.

You'll find that hand to hold, like you used to hold mine when you didn't think anyone was paying attention.

Bella's heart swelled, the sweetest pain. Grandma June had been right all along. She'd found that hand and, most important, it was holding hers right back.

They walked down the front path toward the gate, then Noah paused beside the gnarled shape of the dogwood tree.

"Look," he said. "Can you see it? Right at the top."

Bella lifted her gaze and saw what he was pointing at. A fresh green leaf unfurling.

New life after the long winter.

Seemed like the old tree wasn't as dead as she'd thought.

Like your heart.

She smiled, feeling that new life inside her unfurling along with that leaf. "Oh, good. I'm so ready for spring." She touched her stomach unconsciously and when she looked at him, he was watching her, everything she'd ever wanted in his eyes.

Noah Faraday smiled that smile, the one he kept only for her, slow burning and sweet as the promise of spring. "So am I," he said.

* * * * *

Rachel Henderson's family is falling apart. Becoming a widow—especially at this age—is heartbreaking. And now with her teenage daughter, Emma, leaving soon for college, her life has completely changed shape. Rachel's never felt more lost—her friendship with local diner-owner Adam is the only thing that's keeping her grounded.

As secrets bubble up, and Rachel's old life unravels, she'll need all her courage as she discovers that sometimes, an ending is just the beginning...

Turn the page for a sneak peek of Secrets From A Happy Marriage, *the powerfully emotional new novel by* New York Times *bestselling author Maisey Yates!*

When Rachel pulled up in front of the diner, she could see that there was still a light on. She parked by the curb and walked up to the door. It was locked. But she could see Adam, standing there behind the counter. She knocked, and he looked up, his blue eyes clashing with hers. His beard was a little longer than normal, and it made him look just a little bit dangerous.

Which was weird. More than weird.

Because Adam was her safe space. He wasn't dangerous at all. But she couldn't quite shake that thought, even as he came over to unlock the door.

"Is everything all right?"

She didn't have an answer to that. "Can I come in?"

He looked her up and down. "Of course."

He backed away from the door, and she slipped inside, the smell of his aftershave catching her for a moment. Then she just walked over to her regular stool.

"I hope you're not after food, because I just got everything cleaned up."

"No."

"You want some of Anna's pie?"

Of course, he offered food, even when he'd just said she couldn't have it. "I didn't come for food. I don't really ever come for food. I just need to talk."

He nodded slowly. "Did you want me to turn the lights on?"

She looked around. It was pleasantly dim, the only light coming from back behind the counter. She felt like it offered her just a little bit of privacy. Almost like a confessional.

"Off is fine," she said.

"Whatever you want."

"What do you know about Emma's boyfriend?" Of all the new information she had to process tonight, this was the safest place to start.

"Um, I don't know her boyfriend."

"The boy who works at the mechanic place over there," she said, gesturing broadly toward the windows.

"Right. Well... I don't know that I consider him a boy."

"What? How old is he?"

"I'm not sure," he said. "But...older. Not like... I mean, he's still a kid to me."

She narrowed her eyes. "Is he a good kid? Should I be worried?"

"Probably," he said. "Just because as a parent it's your job to be, right?"

She laughed hollowly. "Right. Sure." She sighed. "She... She's going away to Boston. And she has a boyfriend. And I didn't know any of it. Because I thought I was there. And I thought that I was part of her life. But I'm not." She felt like there was no ground under her feet.

She didn't know her daughter. She didn't know her mother.

"That's normal. You do know that, right?" he asked.

"Is it normal to not have any idea where your daughter has decided to go to college?"

"Well, maybe not *that*. But it's pretty normal for your teenager to not tell you every detail about her life."

"She had a plan to go across the country. Before Jacob died. She and her friend Catherine both want to do the marine biology program at that school, and she spent a lot of time talking to this woman who runs an aquarium that has a connection with the college, and she was sure she was going to get a position there. But she told me she didn't get accepted to the school. And I... I was glad. Because I wanted her here. With me. But she wanted to go. And I didn't realize that."

"You still don't want her to go," Adam said.

Those words cut through her chest.

"Of course I don't. I didn't particularly want her to go before I was living by myself. And that's...awful. It's so selfish. I hate that I even have that...feeling inside of me. I want to be the kind of mom who just wants the best for her kids and doesn't take her own happiness into consideration at all."

"I think they call parents like that liars."

She huffed a laugh. "No. Surely there are truly selfless mothers in the world." That comment just brought her back to her own mother, but she didn't want to get into that with Adam.

"Maybe Emma won't like it," he said. "Maybe she'll get over there and she'll want to leave."

"That would be terrible. She would be across the country from me and upset..."

"But at least it would be her decision. Or maybe she'll love it. And she'll come back and visit at the holidays, and it will be hard for years. But God knows you've been through worse."

Silence stretched between them. She hadn't come for advice, but for that neutral listening ear he'd provided all this time. But she had broken their unspoken rule, and she had mentioned Jacob. She had talked about the problems in her real life.

And she hadn't realized it until it was too late.

She splayed her hands over the counter and looked down at them. Her wedding ring was still on her left hand. She should probably take it off before she went out with Mark. Which was such a weird, stupid thought to have right now.

"Yes. I *have* been through worse. You're right. I don't exactly want to go through more."

Adam leaned forward slightly, and his hands went with him, sliding over the countertop, and she watched them. The tips of his fingers were so close to hers.

It wouldn't take much. A slight shift, and their hands would touch.

"How are you?" His voice was low, and it skimmed over her skin in a way that made her feel edgy and uncomfortable.

She should move, because being close to him was making her uncomfortable, too.

But she didn't.

"Ugh. Don't ask me that," she looked up at his face. "I'm here asking you advice at nine p.m. How do you *think* I am?"

"In general," he said.

"We don't talk about that stuff."

He shrugged. "We do now, I guess."

"I don't know. I don't know what to call how I am.

Sad, and tired of being sad, because I feel like half of my life has been sadness for years. And it's all kind of bittersweet, because the end that I knew was coming, came, and I don't know what to do with myself. Except... I have a date."

Adam's hands moved back a fraction. "Really?"

"Yes."

"With who?" Another fraction away.

"That is not your business." Her own hands slid back slightly.

"Why not? Do I know him?"

"Probably. Mark."

"Mark from the plumbing store?" They moved an inch.

"Yes. I went in to buy a pipe and he asked me on a date."

"Really?" His hands slid back with that repeated question.

"Yes. You asked me that already." She curled her hands into fists, still resting on the counter. "I mean, we're going out as friends. It's just...practice for being a human in the world. It's not *a thing*."

"Well, I guess that's the thing," he said. "You go out, you find yourself a guy. You go on dates. That's what you do while your daughter's at college. Because...you can. Isn't that kind of the point of empty nests?"

"I don't want one," she insisted. "Not really."

"Life doesn't tend to ask what you want. It's not a diner. Things aren't made to order."

"Neither is your food."

Their eyes caught. And then he quit moving away.

He leaned in just slightly, and she caught that scent again. His aftershave. His skin. Her stomach fluttered, just a little bit. And she was absolutely and totally taken aback by the sensation.

By her need to stay where she was, right in his orbit.

She had always felt drawn to him. From the moment they met. But it was different right now.

She swallowed and leaned back. For some reason, that motion triggered a response in him, and he straightened, taking two large steps backward.

"Am I a bad mother?" she asked.

"I'm not going to comment on anyone else's parenting."

She frowned. "Anyone else's?"

"Never mind. Just…love her, Rachel. Like you do already. You're going to make mistakes. But…don't drive her away."

"I—I don't want to. But I worry about her."

"She's eighteen. You have to trust that the parenting you already did will keep her from doing too many things you don't want her to do. And then you have to remember all the things that you did that your mom wouldn't have wanted you to do."

She laughed. Hollow and bitter. "Except I barely did anything my mom wouldn't have wanted me to do. My reasons were…silly. Because apparently my mom was a bigger rebel than Anna and I combined. Well, Anna up until a couple of months ago."

"Was that the source of the tension from earlier?"

"Yeah. Oh…my dad, Adam. I just… I just thought that I would have to survive going through this huge milestone of my daughter being a legal adult without my husband, I didn't think I'd also have to deal with family secrets, my daughter's secrets and…" She met his gaze and the words died on her lips. "I'll tell you. About my mom sometime."

"Well, if you ever need to talk. You know where to find me."

She did know where to find him. She always had.

Hannah's words echoed in her head and lodged a wedge of discomfort in her chest.

"Yeah," she said, "apparently you never leave."

"It's true. I don't actually have a life. I exist right here in this spot for whenever you show up."

He was joking, but there was something in his blue eyes that didn't feel like a joke, and she had to turn away from him.

"Good night, Adam," she said, sliding off the stool.

"Good night, Rachel." His voice was low and husky, strange. "Have a good date."

She turned, and it took a lot longer than it should have for her to find some words. "I will."

"You deserve good things to happen to you," Adam said, his voice soft now. "I mean it."

"Thank you." She hoped more than anything that what he said was true. That maybe she deserved good things. And if he thought so…maybe they would happen.

She had no other reason to hope.

SPECIAL EXCERPT FROM

⊕ HARLEQUIN

DESIRE

*When billionaire bad boy Mercury Steele discovers his
car is stolen, he's even more shocked to find out who's
in the driver's seat—the mysterious beauty
Sloan Donahue. As desire and secrets build between
them, has this Steele man finally met his match?*

Read on for a sneak peek at
Seduced by a Steele
by New York Times *bestselling author Brenda Jackson.*

"So, as you can see, my father will stop at nothing to get what he
wants. He doesn't care who he hurts or maligns in the process. I
refuse to let your family become involved."

A frown settled on his face. "That's not your decision to make."

"What do you mean it's not my decision to make?"

"The Steeles can take care of ourselves."

"But you don't know my father."

"Wrong. Your father doesn't know us."

Mercury wondered if anyone had ever told Sloan how cute
she looked when she became angry. How her brows slashed
together over her forehead and how the pupils of her eyes became
a turbulent dark gray. Then there was the way her chin lifted and
her lips formed into a decadent pout. Observing her lips made him
remember their taste and how the memory had kept him up most
of the night.

"I don't need you to take care of me."

Her words were snapped out in a vicious tone. He drew in a
deep breath. He didn't need this. Especially from her and definitely
not this morning. He'd forgotten to cancel his date last night with

Raquel and she had called first thing this morning letting him know she hadn't appreciated it. It had put him in a bad mood, but, unfortunately, Raquel was the least of his worries.

"You don't?" he asked, trying to maintain a calm voice when more than anything he wanted to snap back. "Was it not my stolen car you were driving?"

"Yes, but—"

"Were you not with me when you discovered you were being evicted?" he quickly asked, determined not to let her get a word in, other than the one he wanted to hear.

"Yes, but—"

"Did I not take you to my parents' home? Did you not spend the night there?"

Her frown deepened. "Has anyone ever told you how rude you are? You're cutting me off deliberately, Mercury."

"Just answer, please."

She didn't say anything and then she lifted her chin a little higher, letting him know just how upset she was when she said, "Yes, but that doesn't give you the right to think you can control me."

Control her? Was that what she thought? Was that what her rotten attitude was about? Well, she could certainly wipe that notion from her mind. He bedded women, not controlled them.

"Let me assure you, Sloan Donahue, controlling you is the last thing I want to do to you." There was no need to tell her that what he wouldn't mind doing was kissing some sense into her again.

Don't miss what happens next in
Seduced by a Steele
by Brenda Jackson, part of her Forged of Steele series!

Available April 2020 wherever
Harlequin Desire books and ebooks are sold.

Harlequin.com

Welcome to Gold Valley, Oregon, where the cowboys are tough to tame, until they meet the women who can lasso their hearts, from *New York Times* bestselling author

MAISEY YATES

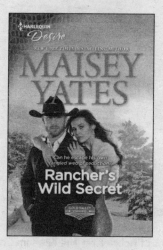